THE LADY OF THE LOCH

ELENA COLLINS

Boldwood

First published in Great Britain in 2023 by Boldwood Books Ltd.

Copyright © Judy Leigh, 2023

Cover Design by Alice Moore Design

Cover Photography: Shutterstock

A CIP catalogue record for this book is available from the British Library.

Paperback ISBN 978-1-80280-026-5

Large Print ISBN 978-1-80280-027-2

Hardback ISBN 978-1-80280-025-8

Ebook ISBN 978-1-80280-029-6

Kindle ISBN 978-1-80280-028-9

Audio CD ISBN 978-1-80280-020-3

MP3 CD ISBN 978-1-80280-021-0

Digital audio download ISBN 978-1-80280-022-7

Boldwood Books Ltd
23 Bowerdean Street
London SW6 3TN
www.boldwoodbooks.com

For G, Liam, Maddie, Cait, (remembering our trip to the Highlands.)

KING ROBERT DE BRUS' FAMILY TREE

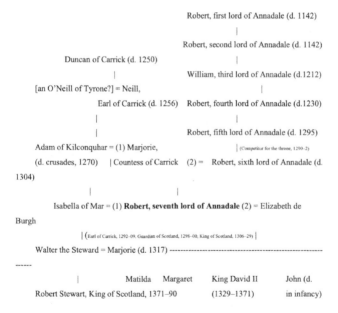

Robert, first lord of Annadale (d. 1142)

|

Robert, second lord of Annadale (d. 1142)

Duncan of Carrick (d. 1250) |

| William, third lord of Annadale (d.1212)

[an O'Neill of Tyrone?] = Neill, |

Earl of Carrick (d. 1256)   Robert, fourth lord of Annadale (d.1230)

| |

| Robert, fifth lord of Annadale (d. 1295)

Adam of Kilconquhar = (1) Marjorie, | (Competitor for the throne, 1290–2)

(d. crusades, 1270) | Countess of Carrick   (2) =   Robert, sixth lord of Annadale (d. 1304)

| |

Isabella of Mar = (1) **Robert, seventh lord of Annadale** (2) = Elizabeth de Burgh

| (Earl of Carrick, 1292–09, Guardian of Scotland, 1298–00, King of Scotland, 1306–29) |

Walter the Steward = Marjorie (d. 1317) ---

| Matilda   Margaret   King David II   John (d.

Robert Stewart, King of Scotland, 1371–90   (1329–1371)   in infancy)

Ravenscraig Castle

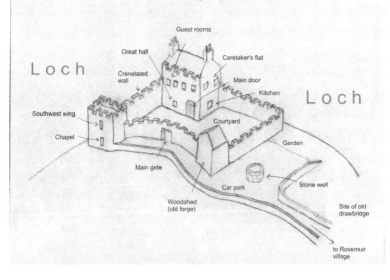

Pronouncing Scottish Gaelic:

Sealgair, Cam's horse, meaning 'hunter', is roughly pronounced
Shall-eh-garr.
Eaun, Hendrie and Maidlin's son, is roughly pronounced Yoo-ihn.
Allaidh, 'wild one', is roughly pronounced All-i.
Réidh ri Dia, 'Rest in Peace', is roughly pronounced Ray-eh ree
Jee-ah.

Glossary

Scotia. Scotland north of the Forth, from the eleventh century.
Queynte. A coarse obsolete English word meaning vagina.
Gie it laldy. Give it your best shot.

PROLOGUE

RAVENSCRAIG CASTLE, SCOTLAND. 1307

My Scotland is untamed, wild, a warrior who knows no fear. The rugged landscape of mountains and mists, climbing firs and clambering heather, shows no mercy to the unready stranger who ventures too far across the border. The endless lochs run deep with secrets. My Scotland is heroic and stout-hearted, sharp as the kiss of a Highland champion with strong ale on his breath, wild as the flash of a lassie's eyes when she spurns the advance of an enemy soldier. Aye, and I'd know all about that.

Scotland is the blood in my veins, the dense forests and snow-clad mountains. The home of the proud stag, his antlers held high, and the wild boar running free. Starved of my homeland, I fade away. If ye deny a flower water, it will shrivel and perish, even a thistle, such as I.

Aye, I am not your conventional flower: there is more to me than a blossom that pleases the eye. My prickle-sharp tongue has oft brought me a beating and oft saved me from danger. I had no father to tame my spirit and my mother repeatedly warned me as a child, *Agnes, ye will never learn.* And she was right.

But now I ache for the sustenance of the rivers and the mountains, and without it, I grow weak. From a high window up here in the tower, there is a view of the loch. I can feel the wind against my face. I can see the edge of the water, the smooth grey light of the morning as a new dawn comes, the shifting mists that glide across the surface. I glimpse the rise of the hills, and I cry to be there again among the heather.

If the window was lower and the gap wider, I would hurl myself out, feeling the freedom of the fall before I plummet to the depths of the loch. I'd catch my breath with the cold of the bitter water until it filled my lungs, then I'd sink like a stone to the bottom. I could lay my head on the depths and dream forever of the Scotland that fills my heart. I am not afraid of that.

But I am kept within these walls. I hear people come and go, talking in low voices, but I see no one. It is bitter cold here and the hours are so long, they stretch for an eternity. All I have is the narrow window, the stars each night, and I watch the wandering moon until dawn creeps in with a grey shroud across the loch. I watch and wait and hope.

I cannae barely breathe for the fear of it all. I have witnessed much in my twenty-three years: love, betrayal, bloodshed. But now, I fear the walls that hold me, the intense cold that makes my body shiver, even as my heart stays strong.

Because my heart is not my own. I gave it away the first time we met. I remember him in each moment that passes. He is my soul and I am his: we swore that we would be together for eternity. Although I believe I will die here in this castle, my spirit will never be silent.

I wither away because I want for the warrior who is beyond my arms, until we are together in that place where we have promised to meet. I will keep searching and waiting and crying out loud to him if it takes forever. I willnae find peace until then.

1

BIRMINGHAM, ENGLAND. THE PRESENT DAY

Zoe's feet pounded rhythmically against the canal path, her breath leaving a speech bubble of vapour in the autumn air. She ran past the Gas Street Basin crammed with narrowboats, a few pubs and cafés on either side, before jogging along Broad Street, Brindley Place, past the aquarium. She'd already covered three kilometres – she'd intended to do her normal four-kilometre run, but the cold air was clearing her head and the path was quiet, so she decided to keep going. It was after three o'clock: the light would be good for at least another hour. She'd go on to St Vincent Street and head up the Birmingham and Fazeley Canal. She was warm enough in Lycra, a beanie covering her dark curls, loping steadily along the towpath past the pretty moored boats flanked by grass and bushes, her feet crunching gold and russet leaves.

Another jogger was going in the other direction, a man probably her own age, thirty, perhaps younger. He paid her no attention; she noticed that he was handsome and then immediately forgot about him. Her thoughts moved to plans for the evening; she'd go back to the flat, shower and head into town to meet friends in a wine bar as she usually did on Saturdays. She'd go through the regular pretence of asking Leah to come with her and Leah would avoid her eyes and make sounds of disinterest, then she'd say she'd be happier by the fire with a book and a takeaway. Their friends always said the same thing – they were twins, but they were so very different.

Zoe increased her pace; she felt good, heart and lungs and legs thrumming in harmony. She'd jog the two kilometres towards the university and then head home, another kilometre. She felt the familiar feeling of belonging as she passed the landscape she knew so well. She'd been a student there, completed a degree in philosophy and remained in the city, where her career had gone from strength to strength. She loved Birmingham, the lively bars and clubs, the warmth of the people, the bustle of buildings in the daytime and the vibrant pulse of the nightlife.

Leah had been there at her elbow and Zoe had always given support. But recently things had become more difficult. She wondered when things had started to deteriorate. It would be easy to put it down to the disastrous relationship Leah had had with Aaron, which ended a year ago. But, before that, Leah had been clingy, unsure of herself. Perhaps it was Zoe's fault; she'd been popular, the more sociable one, and Leah had hovered nearby. She'd gone to uni in Birmingham because her twin was there; her heart was never in it; she was just treading water. Perhaps Leah's last job had been the catalyst for the downward plummet: it had been wrong for her and she had left last July feeling a failure. Since then, things had certainly become more strained.

Zoe increased her pace as she settled on the old familiar solution; she, Zoe, was the problem. Born first by an hour, she seemed to have been dealt all the lucky cards: Zoe did better at school, she had more boyfriends, she was successful. Leah had so much potential – more than Zoe in some ways: she could be determined, single-minded – but she simply stood watching from the sidelines. Zoe felt responsible and, as ever, she racked her brains, not knowing how to help. She wondered if Leah should go home to their parents in Winchester, but at thirty years old she was past returning to the fold. Besides, when their parents weren't working, they were busy with their own lives and, at almost sixty years of age, they deserved it.

Zoe was ten minutes from their first-floor flat in a smart terraced street close to shops and cafés, a cosy two-bedroom with all mod cons that she had found. She paid for the mortgage, the car, holidays, nights out; Leah simply went along with it all. The muscles in her legs tingled as she increased her pace and her body moved rhythmically towards home.

Zoe pushed keys in the front door, headed up the small flight of stairs and paused at the door to her flat. No sound came from inside. A twist of a key and she was in, through the narrow hall, standing in the living room. She tugged off the beanie, shook her curls free and called out 'Leah?' She waited, then tried again. 'Leah?'

There was no reply.

* * *

Leah Drummond wore a coat and boots over her pyjamas: no one would notice what she was wearing in the supermarket. She wandered aimlessly up the aisles, pausing at the frozen section. The wire basket containing two bottles of cut-price Prosecco banged against her hip.

She glanced around, wondering if she'd see Aaron, if he'd be there with a new girlfriend. It wouldn't bother her if she did. He'd told her she was holding him back and he needed to move on, but, in truth, it was only after they were apart that she realised that she'd been walking around with constant tension between her shoulder blades. His relentless criticism had done that to her; even now, some of his caustic comments came back to her when she least expected it.

But she didn't care enough about Aaron now to mind if she saw him. That was the trouble: she didn't care very much about anything. She wondered why she'd even thought about Aaron as she selected a family-sized pizza with double cheese. The cardboard box lodged against the sides of the basket, squashed against the bottles of Prosecco. She put a hand to her hair – it needed washing or tying back.

She shuffled towards the vegetable section, snatching a bag of salad leaves to ease her conscience about all the carbs. She'd watch television tonight. Saturday night TV always involved programmes with smiling people in glittery clothes. It would pass the time until Zoe arrived back from seeing their friends, and then they'd have a quick chat and disappear to their separate bedrooms.

It was a good job she'd saved so much money while she'd been working and that Zoe paid the mortgage and the bills, but her bank balance was running precariously low. At thirty years old, she should be contributing. Leah knew she relied on Zoe too much and it made her feel useless.

She wandered back to the frozen section and picked up a tub of cookie dough ice cream, ambling along, pausing in the biscuit aisle, selecting a red tartan packet of shortbread biscuits. She recalled Uncle Duncan, her father's brother; the last time she'd eaten shortbread was during a holiday to Gairloch when she and Zoe were teenagers.

Leah sighed – *she and Zoe*, never just *Leah*. She needed to get a life.

She paused in the section that sold make-up, eyeing the dazzling display. She chose a red lipstick carefully, holding it up. It was called Chilli Chic. She imagined wearing it with sunglasses, walking on a red carpet, her lips the same colour, as she slipped it into the basket.

Leah headed towards the exit, dragging her feet tiredly. As she turned a corner, she almost bumped into a woman pushing a trolley, who exclaimed, 'Leah. Great to see you.'

Leah forced a smile: she didn't really want to see anyone. She recognised the woman by the dangly earrings the children in her class always used to comment on. Leah forced a half-smile. 'Avril.'

Avril leaned over the handle of her trolley: Leah realised to her dismay that she intended to have a conversation. 'Oh, we all miss you at St Joseph's.' She lowered her voice confidentially. 'To be honest, the new TA isn't half as much fun as you were.'

Leah frowned. Her time as a teacher's assistant wasn't fun at all. It had been a disaster. She had been responsible for two children with special learning needs, both of whom had been bright and a real handful.

Avril was talking again; Leah watched her mouth move.

'So, what are you doing now?'

'I'm in between jobs.' Leah said, noticing Avril's eyes flick over the contents of her basket.

'The children in my class still ask, "Where's Ms Drummond?" and they always talk about the Roman day you organised.'

Leah recalled the Roman day; that had been a disaster, too, spiralling out of control. She'd struggled to keep the toga on securely, a sheet fastened across her shoulders that kept unclipping and showing her bra. Too many children had brought in wooden swords and wanted to use them in brutal combat. Leah had tried her best to calm the conflicts, playing for time by explaining to the class that the word *decimate* meant killing one in every ten soldiers. Ranveer had declared that he was emperor, Faiza insisting that she was queen and therefore in charge of everyone, persuading the other children to decimate Anakin, the smallest, most nervous boy in the class. Leah's memory of the Roman day was that she had been fortunate to survive it: it wasn't an experience she was proud of.

She indicated her shopping basket with a wave of her hands. 'I'm getting supper...' Her eyes fell on the two bottles of Prosecco and she felt her cheeks warming.

'I always thought you'd go on to be a teacher,' Avril persisted. 'You had a really nice way with those kids.'

Leah thought about how she'd sit in the living room each evening surrounded by paper and pens, how she'd find herself crying, not sure how she was going to face another day of Tyler and Jack pulling each other's hair, trying to wipe Tyler's runny nose and help Jack line up the contents of his sandwich box in colour order. Before the TA job, she'd considered teaching as a possible career – it was something she might do with her lower second-class degree in history – but now she'd never enter a classroom again. People like Avril made it look so easy, with their calm voices and organised approach. Leah's time at St Joseph's had lurched from one crisis to another, until, worn out and lacking any self-belief, she'd handed in her resignation and left at the end of the summer term.

Avril eased herself from resting on the trolley handle. 'Well, I must go. Mike and I are off to a concert tonight. What do you have planned?' She glanced at the wire basket again, at the pyjama top visible beneath her coat, then back to Leah with a smile. 'Off out with your sister? You two have such a life. Mine revolves around organising childcare for Florence.'

Leah shrugged. 'Well, I hope you enjoy the concert, anyway.' She began to walk away. 'Nice to see you, Avril.'

Leah joined a queue of people waiting to pay, tears welling in her eyes. Avril had always been so nice to her during her time at St Joseph's. But being a TA had knocked her confidence and all the jobs she'd had since graduating had ended similarly – Leah couldn't work out where she fitted in the world. Meanwhile, Zoe was a high-flyer, a fundraising analytics officer for a charity, what-ever that meant. Leah knew she spent each day researching and analysing, sending reports. She enjoyed the flexibility of being able to work remotely and she was paid well for a job she loved.

Leah sighed again. She was level with the cashier, whose name badge said he was called Colin, a man with a friendly smile. Leah plonked her basket down and reached for her purse.

2

As soon as Zoe left, Leah switched the oven on full, shoved the pizza in on a tray and settled down to watch television. She poured Prosecco into a mug, slicked her lips with Chilli Chic lipstick and stared at the screen. A man wearing tight-fitting trousers was dancing with a woman clad in metallic gold. They flicked their hips and the woman's skirt whirled out like a mushroom. They were both slim and confident, flashing smiles towards the camera as they jigged to a Latin American beat. Leah swigged from the mug, not really tasting anything.

As she finished the first Prosecco, another couple in matching pink costumes were dancing closely, the women's dress all froth and lace, the man's face solemn with concentration. Leah wasn't really watching; thoughts of failure and loneliness leaked into her mind as if sliding through a sieve. Then the couple stopped waltzing and began to breathe deeply, their arms around each other. The camera focused on one of the judges as he said, 'You have improved. I thought you were awful at first, darling, but now you are just only bad.' The audience booed and Leah smelled the waft of burning dough.

The pizza was charred around the edges, the cheese blotched and dark. Leah slid it onto a plate and returned to the television, pulling the pizza apart with greasy fingers, pushing the sticky mess into her mouth, chewing something that tasted like hot plastic. She poured more Prosecco, realising that she had forgotten the salad leaves. Then, wiping her fingers on her dressing gown, she reached for the remote. She'd had enough of beautiful people in gorgeous gowns and smart-quipping judges.

There was a celebrity quiz show on another channel, a chirpy compère. Leah leaned forward, listening to the first question. 'Which country was previously known as the Dutch East Indies?'

The first contestant, a once successful cricket player, shook his head and Leah called out, 'Indonesia.' The compère agreed with her, and Leah rewarded herself with a swig from the bottle to wash the charred pizza from her mouth.

A second question: 'In 1539, which English king granted Hemel Hempstead a town charter?'

'I've no idea,' the cricket player answered, his face vacant.

Leah whooped. 'Henry the eighth.'

'Henry the eighth,' the quiz show host replied with a grin. He tried again. 'Right, next question. Although never taking her seat, who was the first woman to be elected to the Houses of Parliament?'

The suave cricket star had no idea, so Leah told him loudly: 'Constance Markievicz.'

'Constance Markievicz,' repeated the quiz host. 'And, next up, the United Nations was formed in 1945, which organisation did it replace?'

The cricket player grimaced. 'The World Peace Organisation?'

'No, don't be silly – The League of Nations,' Leah yelled at the screen.

'The League of Nations.' The host nodded. 'Zero points scored this round, I'm afraid.'

'And full marks to me.' Leah lifted the bottle. 'Cheers.'

She plodded to the kitchen for a reward, delving into the freezer, returning back to the cushioned depths of the sofa with a carton of cookie dough ice cream, a huge spoon and the shortbread biscuits.

'What did the Romans call Scotland?' the quizmaster asked.

The cricketer grinned. 'Did they call it... Scotland?'

'Caledonia,' Leah muttered between mouthfuls of melting ice cream. She dunked a shortbread biscuit and thought of Uncle Duncan again, the fun family holidays they'd had in Gairloch years ago. She and Zoe had always been inseparable; in those days, Leah had felt happy, equal. She began to work her way mentally through the following years: their schooldays, sixth form, Zoe achieving top marks while Leah was kept behind by Miss Carter, her form tutor, who picked on her constantly. Miss Carter was well-known for the way she intimidated students. Her sharp criticism found its way to Leah's softest place and lodged there.

She recalled all the fruitless crushes she'd had as a teenager that had always made Zoe laugh. Even now, she felt awkward remembering how her twin had mentioned to her parents during breakfast one morning that she'd seen Leah trying to talk to Kevin Freer during history. Leah had felt so ashamed that muesli stuck in her throat and made her cough until tears came.

At university, it had been easier not to try too hard at anything, to let the world pass her by while scraping through with acceptable grades. It was easier to hide behind Zoe.

Afterwards came a string of unsuitable jobs, no meaningful romantic relationships, then a turbulent year with Aaron that seemed to stop and start, along with more unfulfilling jobs.

Leah stared at the empty ice cream pot, the few shortbread biscuits left in the curling packet, and felt miserable. Zoe was out having fun with their friends – Leah liked Bex, Mariusz and Jordan – but she was here by herself in front of the TV, feeling sad. She put her hand to her cheeks – they were damp. A sob rose in her throat, then another.

A moment's defiance surged through her: Leah had to do something to take her life by the scruff, try again. The desperate feeling was swiftly followed by its companion, apathy. Why bother? It wouldn't work: it never did.

Leah swigged Prosecco, foam dripping down her chin, then a sudden pain clutched her stomach and twisted. She felt sick, dizzy. She lurched forward, moaning as everything began rising: unhappiness, discontent, the charred pizza, the warm ice cream, fizzing alcohol. She groaned and rushed to the bathroom, falling to her knees against the basin, her head spinning as she stared at white porcelain, retching and heaving for all she was worth.

Zoe played with the stem of her martini glass, swirling the liquid. Her two companions were deep in discussion as she stared around the bustling wine bar, now vibrant with chattering people and jangling music.

'I don't think people should fall in love until they're at least thirty,' Bex almost yelled, already on her second martini. 'People aren't really mature enough to handle complex relationships until then.'

Mariusz rubbed a hand over his tidy beard, disagreeing. 'It's a timing thing. It depends when you meet *the* one.'

'There must be more than just one for each of us, surely?' Bex spluttered, shaking her shiny hair. 'I think we should have three partners in life: one before we're thirty for fun and sex, then one to have children with, and one as a proper companion when we are in our fifties – you know, a soulmate.'

'I used to think Jordan was my soulmate,' Mariusz said sadly, reaching for his cocktail glass.

'Tell me you haven't fallen out...' Bex was shocked.

'We haven't been getting on. Since he started his new business, we argue all the time.' Mariusz sighed.

'Why didn't he come out with us tonight? It's strange being out without him.'

'He's too engrossed making pretty upholstery, Bex. Chair-works, he calls himself. Upcycling is everything to him. I'm feeling a bit neglected. He's too busy to find time for me nowadays.'

'That's awful. I'm still looking for Mr Right,' Bex added. 'Perhaps we'll all be single again soon. Oh, I'm sorry, Mariusz, I didn't mean—'

'No, don't worry. It'll break my heart in pieces, but I suppose I'll cope if it all comes to a big crashing end. I can imagine us together in our sixties, still out for a drink on a Saturday night, discussing whether we'll ever settle down.' Mariusz turned to Zoe. 'What do you think, Zo?'

Zoe glanced up from the martini glass. 'Uh?'

Bex's glass was almost empty. 'Love. Will it ever come our way, do you think, or are we doomed to the sexless life of nuns and monks?'

'It comes when it comes,' Zoe replied philosophically. 'Probably when we stop looking for it. That's always been my experience – things often leap out when you least expect them.'

'I hope so.' Mariusz pressed his fingers against her arm. 'You're a bit quiet tonight. Has it been a busy week?'

'Not particularly.' Zoe shrugged, forcing a grin.

'I envy you both, working from home, going into meetings whenever you like.' Bex smiled. 'I'm stuck in a boring stuffy office with boring stuffy men all day.'

Mariusz clapped his hands. 'Oh no, that sounds perfect. It's just me and a laptop, designing bits of submarine, the same routine, the same four walls. What I'd do for an enigmatic colleague or two to meet for a coffee break.'

Zoe sighed. 'I just wish Leah would find a job. She's just really... ground to a halt since the summer.'

'The teaching assistant job finished her off, I think. I spoke to her about it when she left – it sounded awful.' Bex peered into her empty glass. 'I don't think you'd ever find Mr Right in a school, though.'

'Oh, no, I wouldn't want to live with a teacher,' Mariusz agreed. 'All those long hours every evening, preparing lessons and writing reports. But I suppose you could get away somewhere really cool for the summer. I always liked Justin Timberlake in *Bad Teacher*. I'd probably give him the benefit of the doubt...'

'Or Antonio Banderas as the dance instructor in *Take the Lead*?' Bex rolled her eyes, making a ridiculous guttural growl.

'Definitely.' Mariusz turned his attention back to Zoe. 'Sorry, Zo – how can we help Leah? You should have brought her with you.'

'I tried. She wanted a night in watching TV. She's finding it hard to be sociable now. She's crawled into a shell and it doesn't matter what I do, I can't get her to come out of it...'

Mariusz shook his head. 'It's hard to support someone when they feel like that.' He shrugged sadly. 'If she doesn't want to be helped, what can we do?'

'Leah's too nice,' Bex offered. 'Really pretty and sweet, but she undervalues herself. That relationship with Aaron – she was content to play second fiddle while he just whinged at her and... what was his hobby again?'

'Gaming,' Zoe said.

'She's not at all like you, Zoe – no one would guess you were twins. I mean, you're dark, she's fair; you're slim and she's curvy.'

'You're both darlings, though.' Mariusz grinned. 'We should all plan something to cheer her up – take Leah to the cinema where she wouldn't feel that she had to worry that she had to be sociable, then we could call in here for one drink on the way home.'

'Or we could plan a weekend away?' Bex was enthusiastic.

'Maybe the four of us could go somewhere themed, a murder mystery or something.'

'The Orient Express.' Mariusz rubbed his hands together. 'I've always fancied it since I saw the film.'

'Or a weekend in Paris,' Bex offered.

'She couldn't afford that and she'd hate it if I paid. Maybe we could start small, the cinema, like you suggested...' Zoe hadn't touched her martini. 'Perhaps I should suggest she tries a counsellor or does meditation. But how can I even broach that?'

'Let's plan something that she'll enjoy that will take her out of herself,' Mariusz said, his eyes sparkling.

'What about going on an online date?' Bex suggested. 'Maybe we could all use one? I certainly could...'

'I have to sort out my life with Jordan first,' Mariusz grimaced sadly. 'I worry that it's run its course. My stomach is tight all the time with anxiety. He's in love with his new business.'

'Poor Jordan. Poor you.' Zoe squeezed his hand. 'Talk to him, Mariusz. Tell him how you feel. Whatever you decide, we'll support you.'

'Of course,' Bex agreed. 'And we're here for Leah too. At least when she was working, she'd come out with us from time to time.'

'And in the old days, she'd bring Aaron and I'd bring Jordan, and we'd all meet up here on a Saturday night for drinks, and you two would bring...' Mariusz's face shone with mischief. 'Some random or another.'

Zoe raised an eyebrow. 'That's been my best shot at romance – some random or another.'

'Me too, sadly.' Bex raised her glass. 'To the future, then... and to many more randoms for all of us.'

'I can't help thinking that a good job, one she'd really enjoy, would give Leah some confidence, something to focus on.' Zoe's eyes looked for her phone. There were no messages; it was almost eleven o'clock. 'I suppose I should be getting home...'

* * *

Leah washed her face, guzzled another mug of Prosecco, watched an episode of a new serial on Netflix and was about to go for a shower when she heard the door open.

Zoe hurried in, throwing her jacket and bag on the sofa. 'Hi, how was your evening?'

'So-so,' Leah said, non-committal. 'Yours?'

Zoe nodded. 'Good. I went to The Red Cellar. It was packed out. We drank dirty martinis. I think Mariusz might split up with Jordan. And Bex is still looking for Mr Perfect, but he doesn't exist.'

'Oh, right.' Leah stretched her arms above her head, unsure what to say in reply. Chilli Chic lipstick coated her teeth. 'I was about to have a shower and go to bed. I thought that sloshing myself in warm water might help me sleep.' She avoided Zoe's eyes. 'Did you want a cuppa?'

'I'd love one,' Zoe said.

Leah didn't move, and Zoe took a breath.

'I was wondering – how I can make things a bit better for you? You seem really down lately. In fact...' Zoe thought about her words carefully. 'Since you left St Joseph's, you haven't been... quite yourself.'

Leah brightened, feigning far too much enthusiasm. 'Not at all. I had a great evening.' She offered a wide lipstick-smeared smile. 'Pizza was nice, TV was fantastic. I chilled out.'

'Oh...' Zoe paused, thinking. 'Cup of tea, then? Shall I make it?'

'No... I'm fine, honestly,' Leah said loudly. She'd forgotten that she'd offered to make one just moments ago.

Zoe noted the signs that she'd been drinking heavily: her eyes sparkled, her words were slurred.

'No, I'll just go to bed, I... I'll see you tomorrow. Okay, night, Zo.'

Leah dragged herself to her feet, staggering towards the door. Zoe watched her sadly.

She stood for a while, before heading towards the kitchen. The remnants of charred pizza were left on a greasy plate, together with a discarded ice cream carton and a few shortbread biscuits. A bottle of Prosecco was empty on the worktop, a second had been opened, an almost-full mug by its side. Zoe gazed around anxiously and noticed the oven had been left on. She turned it off quickly, shaking her head, feeling troubled - Leah was becoming a danger to herself. Zoe would tackle the clearing up first and attempt to sort out her twin sister's life tomorrow. Now she needed to do some thinking.

3

Agnes Fitzgerald leaned over the trestle table, humming happily as she pummelled dough with her fists. Flour covered her apron and simple brown dress, a dusting of white settling on the end of her nose as she shaped the loaf into a round. 'This one's ready for the fire,' she called with a grin. 'That's eight bannock breads. Now I'll start on the wheat loaves.'

A voice called from the other side of the bakehouse: 'Right ye are, Agnes. We'll need enough bread to feed at least twenty guests tonight.'

'And some left over for ourselves,' Agnes said with a wink to the slender girl next to her, who was watching her every move. 'So, Effie, these loaves I'm making now are special. They are made from wheat flour and not oats, so there must be an important party arriving tonight.'

'Wheat, not oats, aye,' Effie Gale repeated slowly, her eyes wide. She gazed at the taller girl in admiration, noticing how she mixed the flour, working quickly with deft, skilled hands, pushing a stray curl behind her ear, her eyes twinkling.

Agnes smiled affectionately. 'We're expecting the best of the best to dine here with the master tonight. He's told us to spare no expense. Let's hope there will be scraps left over for us after the feast. Did ye see the wild boar we are going to roast? They've not enough space in the kitchen for it, so we must do it here in the bakehouse over the fire.'

'I've never eaten boar or venison,' Effie muttered. 'I've had beef in a stew, but never anything else. Do ye think it's nice to eat, deer?'

'They say it tastes like a sweet, deep kiss from a handsome gentleman's lips,' Agnes said, wrapping an arm around Effie. She noticed Effie's serious expression and gave a warm, spirited laugh. 'Och, who knows, Effie? Neither ye nor I will ever taste venison, or the kiss of a handsome gentleman. And I'm sure it's overblown – most gentlemen seem too wide in the girth and too big in the head.'

A gaunt woman came to stand next to them. 'Effie, ye can make the wheat bread by yourself for a while now you've been shown. I'll need Agnes. We are busier than ever.'

'I'll try,' Effie said hopefully. 'How many loaves must I do, Morag?'

'Make seven more, just as you've been instructed. And take care, do ye heed me, because it's the most expensive flour. Agnes, she needs to learn to do more than help the kitchen maids wash vegetables. So, will ye come and help me here now? I need a hand to put this boar on the spit over the fire.'

'I'll be back in a moment to help ye, Effie.' Agnes wiped her hands on her apron and rushed over to Morag, who was busying herself with the boar, pushing a long wooden skewer through the meat. The two women faced each other, Agnes, just twenty-two years old, energetic and bright-eyed, and Morag, twice her age, bent from work, her face worn.

Morag put her hands on her hips. 'Very well, Agnes. We must heave this big bruiser onto the spit and turn it well. The fire over here is ready for cooking the meat, making the skin crisp, just how the master likes.'

'It's a pleasure to help ye, Morag.' Agnes noticed her tired eyes and offered a conspiratorial wink. 'The work will soon be done and we can rest our bones by the fire.'

'Aye, God willing.'

Agnes and Morag lifted the boar, moving to the middle one of three open fires. The first and third fires were being used for bread and pastries; today, the second was designated for meat. The flames leaped as the two women struggled to heave the boar in position, and the skin began to crackle immediately. Agnes felt her palms scorch, her face warm in the orange glow of the blaze. She was a baker, rarely asked to turn the spit, but she watched Morag lean forward into the heat without complaint and copied the cook's movements, rotating the meat in the flames as it spat hissing juices into the hearth.

Morag's voice was confidential. 'Do ye think wee Effie will be all right with the bread? She's younger than her years and there's no' much going on in her head...'

'She'll do fine, Morag,' Agnes said loyally, changing hands, waving the free one to cool it. 'She's learning quickly.'

'I have to say, when they moved her from serving at the tables to the bakehouse, I wasnae keen. Ye ken her maw died birthing her feet first. It's not natural. And they say the lassie has been backwards ever since.'

Agnes panted in the heat. 'I'll keep an eye on her. She's a good lassie, Effie, a hard worker, you'll see.'

'I cannae recall how old she is. Twelve? Fourteen?'

'Sixteen, she might be seventeen by now – I'm not sure of the month of her birth.' Agnes leaned closer. 'She's a grown woman, but I take care of her. I cannae let people tease her.'

Morag looked up from her work, meeting Agnes's gaze. 'Ye ken what they say about her here?'

Agnes shook her head. She'd heard rumours, but she was no gossip.

Morag continued. 'Well, we all know she's a bastard child.' Her face glowed in the firelight. 'They say our master the Earl was fond of her mother.'

Agnes's brow creased. 'The Earl was fond of most women, my own maw included, God rest her soul, but he didnae help her when she was sick and dying. He let her go to her maker without a kind word or a prayer. And that was some ten years ago.'

'Effie's mother was a sly one, though. She made sure she was the master's favourite with all the benefits.'

Agnes frowned. 'Effie's not sly. She's sweet and good-hearted.'

'Then let's hope she doesn't fall prey to a mean man as many foolish lassies do. The master always liked servant girls. Ye should watch out for him, Agnes. You're of an age now.'

'Oh, I don't pay any mind to the master.' Agnes made a face. 'He's old and hoary and has agues in his legs. I doubt he has anything left in him for the lassies now. There are plenty of other young men in the castle who have a twinkle in their eye, mind.'

'And who might ye be thinking of, Agnes?'

Agnes tossed the curls that were escaping from her cap. 'Not a one of them will come near me. I'm my own mistress and I always will be.' Agnes sniffed once. 'And I can smell the bannocks are baked to a turn. Can ye hang on here, Morag, while I heave them out?'

'Aye, I'll manage. It vexes me that the kitchens cannae cook their own meat and we must be brought in to do the hardest work. Check on Effie while you're about it too – those wheat loaves have to be perfect.'

Agnes rushed over to the oven, lifted out the bannock bread and hurried to where Effie was busy, surrounded by a cloud of flour, her small arms struggling with large mounds of dough. Agnes winked. 'Here, hennie, I'll finish these. They'll be done in a moment.' Agnes began to pull and shape the bread for proving, while Effie watched, open-mouthed.

Morag was struggling with the boar on the spit as she called over, 'Effie, can ye wash more kale? And the cooks in the kitchen need more peas.'

'I suppose they have too much work on their hands today and not enough kitchen maids?' Agnes asked.

'I'll do it,' Effie said reluctantly, turning large eyes towards Agnes.

'Go on with ye,' Agnes smiled. 'Kale is easy.'

Effie looked at her hands. 'But they make my nails dirty and my skin gets chapped.'

Morag laughed, a throaty sound. 'She's clearly from aristocratic blood, that one.'

'Aye, that she is.' Agnes rushed over and placed a kiss on Effie's forehead. 'She's our wee princess.'

'She can come over here and help me a while.' A thick, toneless voice came from over by the brewing vat. 'I'll make an alewife of her yet.'

Agnes stood upright, straightening her spine, looking at Effie who had frozen. Agnes raised her voice. 'She's busy here with me, Biddy.'

'Tell her to come here.' A bent woman with matted grey hair beneath a cap emerged from the shadows of the brewing vat, waving a long finger. 'I've need of a small one.'

'She scares me,' Effie whispered. 'And she reeks...'

'It's just the barley fermenting that makes the beer reek,' Agnes soothed.

'Och, but she'll curse me.'

'She'll do no such thing – she has a big heart.' Agnes lowered her voice. 'She's just old, Effie, at least a hundred years, I've heard. And there is worse work here than being an alewife.' She finished shaping the dough to prove, then she turned, gazing through the gloomy bakehouse lit by three huge fires and the glow of the torches that burned low in their sconces. She inhaled slowly and smiled happily. 'There's nothing like a bakehouse, is there? Roasting barley, the baking of crusty bread, and today we have the spitting boar. Aye, Effie, there are worse places to be in this reeking castle in June, believe me. I'd hate to be the poor wee scullion who cleans out the master's garderobe in his chamber every morning after he's filled his belly the night before...'

Effie whispered, 'I like it here with ye best. It must be horrible to be a scullion – the young laddie who comes in here to clean the big pots always looks half starved. I feel sorry for him.'

'Ye are sweet and soft-hearted, Effie.' Agnes smiled. 'Go and prepare the vegetables and I'll help Biddy awhile.'

'I'm on my own with this hot roasting boar,' Morag bellowed.

'She should be so lucky.' Agnes grinned and propelled Effie gently, with a warm hug, towards the bucket filled with kale. Then she presented herself to Biddy over by the brewing vat, offering a curtsy. 'And what can I do to help ye while my bread is proving, Mistress Biddy?'

Biddy raised her long wooden spoon in the air, the one she used to stir the sugar into the hot liquid. 'I wish you'd hold your tongue, Agnes Fitzgerald. You'll be the death of us all one day with all your foolish daffin'. Now come here and mix my ale.'

'My pleasure.' Agnes greeted the small woman in a cap, a spray of wiry grey hair fizzing beneath, her bony body encased in black. 'Why don't ye stop and rest awhile? Help yourself to a wee cup of ale.'

'Oh, I couldnae do that. I only make the stuff,' Biddy protested, gazing down at the half-filled cup by her feet. She shrugged. 'Except to taste that it's fit for the master.'

'Aye, ye should taste it more often,' Agnes said affectionately. 'For ye deserve it.' Agnes took the long spoon from Biddy's curved fingers and leaned over the vat. 'Ye sit for a minute. I'll stir this for ye while my bread's proving.'

Biddy made a huffing noise and picked up her cup, swallowing a gulp of ale thirstily.

There was the sound of hurried feet on the dirt floor; a young man came into the bakehouse, gazing around.

Morag grumbled. 'What do ye want, Colban? Ye smell of horse dung.'

The young man was tall, slim, his face lean and his fair hair tousled. 'I was wondering if there might be any scraps going spare. Some porridge maybe, a wee bit of bannock bread, or even a bit of salted beef.'

'Go away with ye. Ye can give me a hand with this boar while you're here, help me lift it to the table. I'm fair puckled with all this heat and spit-turning.'

'With pleasure.' Colban grinned easily. 'And I hope you'll reward me with something tae fill my belly.'

He lifted the roast boar easily, still gazing around.

Morag snorted, 'If you're looking for Agnes, she's over there in the shadows by the ale vat, helping Biddy.'

'Hello to ye, Colban,' Agnes called cheerily. 'Just give me a moment and I'll come over and pilfer some scraps for ye.'

'I'd like that, Agnes, thanking ye kindly.' Colban pushed a hand through his hair and flopped down in front of one of the ovens, warming his palms.

Agnes brought him a cup of ale. She smiled. 'Here y'are – get this down ye. I'll find ye something to eat.'

Colban drank greedily. 'Och, this is good. I thought there would be some fine food here today, especially since we're expecting visitors'

Morag leaned forward. 'What earls and their ladies are visiting us tonight? I heard the master say we had to prepare a banquet fit for royalty.'

'Aye, and there's a good reason for it. The men are saying in the

stables that we've been told to make ready.' Colban took the bread
and cheese that Agnes gave him with a wide smile, noticing the slices
of salted beef she had hidden beneath the bannock out of Morag's
keen sight. 'It may be Elizabeth de Burgh herself, and her party...'

'No!' Morag gasped. 'The new wife of King Robert, he who was
crowned at Scone three months since by the Countess of Buchan?'

'Robert de Brus?' Biddy asked from the shadows.

'Good King Robert himself.' Agnes grinned. 'And his wife the
queen is coming here. But not the king?'

'So I ken...' Colban pushed the meat into his mouth. 'In the
stables, they say there will be many extra horses to tend tonight.
Queen Elizabeth and her party are on their way north tomorrow
morning. They are friends of the Earl de Mar and he invited them
to stay overnight here at Kildrummy. It's safer for them here – they
want to keep as far away from the English soldiers as possible.'

'Don't we all?' Biddy spat. 'I heard they rape women, then slice
them in half. Ye know what they did to that poor man William
Wallace last year, God rest his soul.'

Effie stared up from the bucket of kale and shuddered. 'Will
they come and do that to us, here in Kildrummy?'

'Och no, we're safe here.' Agnes glanced towards Effie before
she took Colban's empty cup. 'The visitors are most likely to stay for
the feasting tonight and be on their way tomorrow morning with
the lark.'

'I've never seen a queen before...' Effie breathed.

'I dare say she's the same as us, skin and bone and sinew, but
with better clothes on her back,' Morag grumbled.

'No, no, they are blessed by God, the royal family, and may He
preserve them from all harm,' Biddy shrieked.

'Amen,' Effie whispered.

Colban stood up and Agnes met his eyes, her gaze bold. 'Well,
don't let us keep ye here, Master Colban. I know ye are a busy man.

You've eaten your fill, drunk our ale, what else might ye be wanting afore ye go?'

Colban was suddenly bashful. He clutched his hands in front of him. 'Well, thanking ye kindly for the food, Mistress Agnes. I'll be on my way...'

'And be hasty about it, too,' Agnes called as he rushed from the bakehouse. She raised her voice. 'There will be a beating or someone to lug your ears hard if ye are missed.' Then she burst out laughing.

Effie commented, 'He's always coming here for food and ale.'

'Naw, he comes to see Agnes,' Morag observed. 'He's sweet on her. Everyone loves Agnes – the work is hard, but she brings in fresh air to this place.'

'Aye, but she's too spirited for the likes of a stable boy,' Biddy scoffed, still sucking the rim of her cup.

Agnes hugged Biddy spontaneously, then she sighed. 'He's a good laddie. Many a lassie could do worse than marry a kind soul like Colban. But...'

'But?' Effie wandered towards Agnes, her hands cold, smeared in damp soil.

Agnes placed the wheat loaves in the bread oven behind the fire, then wrapped an arm affectionately around the small girl's shoulders.

'But I'm just twenty-two, in the prime of life, and I don't intend to be a kitchen maid forever.' Her eyes gleamed. 'There's much more waiting for me outside in the big wide, world. I know it, Effie, I'm sure of it.'

4

The way forward was crystal clear to Zoe as she finished her morning run and headed towards home. She'd support Leah towards a new start. Mariusz and Bex had suggested taking her on a trip, somewhere exciting and different to take her mind away from her problems. But Zoe had been concerned last night as she'd tidied the debris of Leah's takeaway from the kitchen. Then she'd visited the bathroom: Leah had made a poor job of cleaning the basin after being sick. Zoe had peered into her bedroom after she'd finished scrubbing both rooms. The curtains were open, light from the street lamp flooding in, and her clothes were strewn on the floor. Leah was curled beneath the duvet like a child, her hair over her face, snuffling. Zoe had noticed the indentation between her sister's brow: even in her sleep, Leah was anxious.

Zoe rushed into the flat, breathless, to find Leah hunched on the sofa in a fluffy dressing gown, sipping coffee.

'How are you feeling?' Zoe asked, pulling off the beanie, shaking her hair. One look at Leah's clammy face gave her the answer.

'Fine,' Leah lied, her voice defensive as she returned her attention to the bottom of the coffee mug.

Zoe sat down, throwing an arm across the sofa behind her sister's head. 'I thought we'd go out.'

Leah shrugged, disinterested. 'No, I—'

'I could treat you to breakfast?'

'It's Sunday – nowhere's open.'

'Tatiana's is open all day – she does milkshakes and pancakes.'

Leah pulled a face. 'I'm not hungry…'

'What about a walk? It's beautiful outside.'

Leah met her eyes, her own gaze sad. 'You love it out there, don't you, Zo? Beautiful Birmingham, the autumn leaves, the bustle, the culture, the life…' Zoe nodded and Leah replied, 'I'll just feel cold.'

'Then we'll go for a coffee to warm up.' Zoe tugged her arm as she'd always done since they were toddlers. 'Come on, Leah. Let's go get some air.'

'Cold air,' Leah protested. 'And I'd have to get dressed…'

Zoe sensed that her twin was weakening. 'Come on, pull a jumper and jeans on, some boots. Let's leave the stuffy flat behind.'

'You always say you love the flat.'

'I do.' Zoe grinned. 'Come on.'

'All right.' Leah clambered reluctantly to her feet with an expression of discomfort.

Zoe secretly clenched her fist in triumph. 'I'll just grab a shower…'

* * *

It was past eleven as they walked along the pavements, back towards the park. Zoe was convinced that the sharpness in the air and the crunch of fallen leaves underfoot, handspans of russet and gold, would lift Leah's mood. She clutched her sister's arm as they trod on grass and looked up at overhanging foliage.

'So, are you glad to be outside?'

Leah shrugged. 'It's overrated.'

'The sun's shining.' Zoe's face was bright with optimism. 'The sky's a beautiful deep blue. The weather is gorgeous for October.'

'You can't see much sky for all the buildings,' Leah grunted.

'So where would you like to live?' Zoe asked. 'I mean, if you could live anywhere in the world?'

Leah didn't answer, so Zoe tried again.

'Somewhere warm? Barbados?'

Leah's nose was red with cold. 'I liked it when we went to Uncle Duncan's when we were kids, by the sea in the Highlands. It was nice there, calm.'

'It was cold some of the time.'

Leah smiled and her face shone. 'Even the cold was nice there. Exhilarating, fresh, all those pine trees.'

'I remember going with Dad and Mum to Gairloch.' Zoe smiled. 'We always had fun, didn't we? I loved Uncle Duncan.'

'I was really sad that we couldn't go to his funeral.'

'Only Dad went. I suppose he didn't want us to be there grieving – we were only fifteen.'

'Uncle Duncan was never very strong, all the time we were growing up. You'd see him smiling, teasing us, trying to play chase, leaning on his stick, thin and coughing.' Leah sighed. 'I really liked him, though – he was so sweet. He'd give me twenty pounds every time we visited, and he'd wink and say, "Och, don't tell your dad, or he'll want half."'

'He'd say the same to me too... bless him.' Zoe was thoughtful for a moment, then she brightened. 'So, shall we book a trip to Gairloch, just the two of us? We could go and look at the old places, the harbour, the beach?'

'What would we do when we came back?' Leah mumbled. 'We'd stay for a week, reminisce, then we'd be here again. I'd still have no job and no life.'

Zoe was about to tell Leah that she was being negative, but she stopped herself. Leah had a point. A quick fix would only be temporary. They needed a more effective solution to Leah's loneliness, her depression.

Zoe took a breath. 'Right, we'll go to Tatiana's. I'll get us drinks and we'll have a proper chat. We'll work out what would make you most happy, and then we'll do it.'

Leah shook her head. 'Nothing makes me happy.'

'Then we'll find something that does.' Zoe smiled. 'How about we start with a protein shake and a piece of apple cake?'

Leah raised her eyebrows, acquiescing. 'If that's a chocolate milkshake and a piroshki doughnut, you're on...'

* * *

They sat across a wooden table in Tatiana's, heavy red drapes at the windows, gold-sprayed lights, cushions embroidered with flowers. Balalaikas and folky voices rumbled through speakers. Zoe was staring at her phone; she'd hardly touched her protein shake. 'There's a job in a hotel in Gairloch, waiting on tables. What about that?'

'I'd drop the trays everywhere – I'd fall over someone's feet and everyone would laugh.'

'What about this one? It's a receptionist's job...'

Leah frowned. 'Frumpy me, on reception? I'd frighten the guests away.'

Zoe grabbed her hand. 'No, you wouldn't. Leah, you're lovely.'

Leah swallowed: she was already failing before she'd started. 'Where would I live? I'd never afford the rent?'

Zoe fiddled with the buttons on her phone. 'Right, let's think positive. How do you feel when you look at this picture?' She turned the screen to face Leah, holding up a photo of Gairloch. It was an expanse of sea, the sweep of a sandy beach behind, snow-topped mountains pressing against an azure sky.

Leah made a sound of happiness – the view was stunning.

Zoe found another photo: a bending road cut through the curve of a valley of purple heather and pale grasses, a vast sprawl of lakes, mountains and sky. Zoe tried again. 'How does this make you feel?'

'It lifts my spirits.' Leah rested her chin on her hands. 'I think of the clean air and the bite of the wind and I feel sort of free...'

Zoe smiled. 'You have Dad's Scottish blood in your veins. I'm more like Mum, English through and through, happy living in a city. But I think we're getting somewhere.'

'I'm not so sure.' Leah frowned. 'I know I need a holiday, but what I really need is a life.'

'Yes.' Zoe almost hugged her twin: at last, Leah had admitted that there was a problem and they could both agree on a starting place. She was unsure how to ask the next question. She took a deep breath. 'Do you think... I mean, might it be better for you if you were living away from Birmingham for a while...?'

Leah closed her eyes. 'We've never been apart.'

'Do you think it might be good for *you*, though?'

'I don't know.' Leah looked sad. 'It might make me stand on my own feet. It might, you know, make me take some responsibility.'

Zoe felt tears welling in her eyes: they'd always been a pair. She was surprised by the strength of her own reaction as she reached for her sister's hand again. 'Oh, Leah, I don't know what's for the best...'

'Right.' Leah clenched her teeth determinedly. 'Go on, look up jobs in the Scottish Highlands with accommodation.' She scraped back her chair. 'I'm going to order us another milkshake each.'

'I haven't finished this one...'

'I need the protein,' Leah replied.

Zoe watched Leah approach the counter, leaning forward in her baggy coat, shyly talking to Tatiana, who was resplendent in fur-lined boots, her hair in coils. Tatiana's voice resonated in contrast to Leah's quiet mutter. Zoe thought Leah looked vulnerable: she wondered how she would manage if she was by herself. Then another thought followed quickly; perhaps she, Zoe, was the dependent one, who needed Leah by her side in order to feel fulfilled. Leah had such potential, she was sure of it, but she couldn't fail again. The thought troubled Zoe as she watched her sister plod wearily back to the table.

Leah flopped down and put her head in her hands, remembering how she felt last night, her knuckles white as she clutched the basin, retching. She had reached a low point and the acutely desperate feelings she had felt frightened her. She couldn't allow herself to sink further. She had to try harder, although something in her cried to give up. She took a deep breath and offered a deliberately optimistic smile. 'Tatiana's bringing the drinks over. Have you found my dream job?' Leah's expression was hopeful. 'Live-in secretary to some gorgeous, retired actor writing his memoirs?'

Zoe fiddled with her phone for a moment, offering her most positive smile. 'Right, let's see what's here.'

'You look, Zo – read them out to me,' Leah said as Zoe scanned the screen.

'Okay.' Zoe flourished the phone. 'Room attendant, Kilbridge Hotel, Aviemore... that's seasonal, until January.'

'I can't ski.' Leah folded her arms.

'You could learn.'

'No way. I'd break a leg. Anything else?'

Zoe scrolled down. 'Security guard, no, that's no good. Food and Beverage manager... hotel in the Cairngorms...'

'I've no experience.' Leah wriggled in her seat.

'Live-in carer...'

Leah grunted. 'Not me, is it?'

'Wanted urgently. Bartenders. Live-in available.'

Leah shook her head. 'We should give up.'

'Dog walker?'

'No.'

'There's a job as a TA in a primary school—'

'Definitely no.'

'Oh, what about this?' Zoe held up her phone. '"Our client is looking for an outstanding live-in caretaker to manage a modest estate in the Scottish Highlands. They are ideally hoping to recruit someone who is happy to oversee a small amount of renovation work. For further information please get in touch..."'

'Where's that?'

'North of Inverness.'

Leah leaned forward. 'Any photos?'

'No, just a phone number.' Zoe brightened. 'It wouldn't hurt to ring.'

'Mmm.' Leah didn't look convinced.

Zoe pressed a button. 'It's ringing. Shall I pretend to be you?'

'No... Zoe, no...' Leah's expression showed real terror.

'It's only an inquiry. It doesn't commit... Oh.'

'What?'

'Oh, hello, this is Leah Drummond,' Zoe began, then she pushed the phone into Leah's hand.

Leah was momentarily stunned, her eyes wide. She faltered, 'Oh, hello, er... I was thinking about applying for the job, the live-in caretaker... Oh, I see.' Leah listened, chewing her lip. 'No, no, I'm not working at the moment... yes, I'd be available... Oh, right.' She pushed the phone against her ear. 'North of Inverness, yes, that would be okay... yes, I'll fill a form in... What? I mean, pardon...? Yes, I've got it, no problem... Oh, thanks, yes, thanks very much.' She ended the call and handed the phone back to Zoe, her lips tightly pressed together. 'Well, that was totally embarrassing.'

Zoe played with the straw of her milkshake. 'What happened?'

'I spoke to this woman, Abigail Laing. She said the deadline for the job had passed, but they hadn't found anyone suitable. She's asked me to fill in a form.'

'Then let's get home and fill it in.'

Leah was thoughtful for a moment. She nodded slowly. 'Would you come and visit me if I was living on an estate in the Highlands?'

'Every other weekend,' Zoe replied eagerly.

'Do you think I could do it, Zo? Take a job like that? Organise things?'

'Of course. You'd love it. Surrounded by mountains and deer and pine trees and lochs? All that peace and calm?'

'What did you say before about me taking after Dad? It might soothe the Scottish part of my soul,' Leah said. 'Do you think I'd be all right?'

'I think you should apply and see where it takes you.'

Leah was thoughtful for a moment. 'You're right... After all, I can say no at any stage. And they might not like me.'

'Or they might love you to bits. Go for it, Leah – even if it's just to practise applying...'

Tatiana arrived at the table carrying a tray; she placed a chocolate milkshake in front of Leah and another glass next to Zoe's half-finished protein shake.

'*Priyatnava appetita*.' Tatiana met Zoe's eyes. 'If you want to stay on for lunch, I have some nice hot borsch and good bread.'

'Oh, we were just thinking about going home – we have things to do...' Zoe began.

'No, let's stay and have lunch together,' Leah interrupted. 'Can I borrow a pen please, Tatiana, and I'll write down Abigail's email address before I forget it? Then we'll have two bowls of borsch and we can plan what I'm going to write in this application.' She caught her sister's delighted expression and smiled. 'I don't suppose I have any chance of getting it, but at least it's good practice. I'm going to spend this afternoon applying for a job.'

5

Agnes and Effie sat in the glow from the large fire, warming their chapped hands, nibbling a crust of bannock bread. Behind them, Morag and another woman were busy farcing fowl, grinding up the meat, mixing it with spices. Two other cooks were bustling around the bakehouse, making pastries. In the kitchen near the great hall, other cooks would be preparing soup. Morag had already collected the juices that had dribbled down from the roasted boar in a pan to take to them.

Biddy shuffled in the corner, muttering to herself. 'The Earl and his royal guests will be drinking wine tonight, and the ladies are too delicate for ale. They have no need of my labours, so I'll rest my poor aching bones.'

Agnes heard the glug of liquid: Biddy was pouring herself another cup. She wondered how long it would take Morag to notice that they were idle and clip their ears with her flat hand.

Agnes leaned towards Effie. 'Come, we have vegetables to prepare. There will be strife if we're found filling our bellies.'

'Do ye think we may see the Queen Elizabeth de Burgh when she arrives?' Effie whispered. 'We can see the courtyard from here. I so want to catch a glimpse of the queen and the wee princess. Do ye think she'll wear a silk gown and a cloak of furs?'

'Aye, I'll make sure ye get a peek,' Agnes promised. 'I want to see the royal party myself, the grand horses and the puffed-up attendants in all their finery. It will be a pretty sight, no doubt. But we have more peas to prepare first, and beans to cook. The crocks will need to come out of the fire so the pottery doesn't crack, and then the lamb will be tender.'

'Agnes.' Morag's voice was shrill. 'Have ye checked the stone pots? The stew will be ready, and there are oats to soak for the royal breakfast and fruit to prepare. I hope you're not slacking.'

'Not I,' Agnes piped cheerfully, grabbing Effie's hand and scuttling towards a long trestle table where vegetables were piled. They bent over a bowl of peas and began splitting shells.

Effie gazed around at the commotion of the bakehouse, meat sizzling, pots clanking, voices calling urgently to each other, then she leaned towards Agnes and hissed, 'And will the royal party stay here in the castle tonight?'

'Aye, they'll dine with the master and rest here, their horses will need water and tending, then they'll be away early tomorrow, after breakfast. The English soldiers will not be far behind them, I fear.' She leaned closer. 'They are being chased down by Prince Edward of England, auld Longshanks' son.'

Effie put a small hand to her mouth. 'How do ye know this?'

'Colban tells me – the talk of it goes on in the stables. The blacksmith is the worst of them. Colban says the smith prattles all the time – he's oft heard laughing and swearing with the castle soldiers, with anyone who'll listen, and he kens all the comings and goings around these parts.'

'I wouldn't like to hear the smith swearing with the other big men. It makes me fret.' Effie shook her head and Agnes was reminded that, despite her years, she was still very much a child.

Agnes turned her attention to the peas that filled the bowl. She popped one in her mouth, enjoying the sweetness.

Effie was keen to chatter. 'Morag often talks about my maw, who died giving me birth. Did ye ever see her?'

'Aye, when I was very young. She was very like ye to look at. She and my mother were close companions. I remember her being big with child, and I heard of your birth and of her passing.'

'And do ye believe what they say, that I was born backwards and therefore I am daft in the head?' Effie asked sadly, her lips drooping in a sulk.

'You're no dafter than anyone else in the bakehouse, Effie. Pay them no mind.'

'Was she beautiful, my maw?'

Agnes smiled. 'She was – she was small and bonnie, with the same blue eyes as ye have.'

Effie leaned closer. 'And who was the man that fathered me? Was it the master, do ye ken? The Earl himself?'

'I cannae say for sure.' Agnes looked at the peas tumbling from her fingers. 'They say he had an eye for the women and he was younger then, with an appetite on him, if ye take my meaning. If he had his mind set on a lassie, she had no choice but to say aye. My own maw was one of his favourites before she grew ill.'

'So do ye think...' Effie screwed up her small face. 'Do ye think we could be sisters?'

'How would I ken, hennie?' Agnes wrapped an affectionate arm around Effie. 'Half-sisters we may be. Why not?'

Effie turned shining eyes on Agnes. 'I'd like that – I need ye to look after me.' There was the sound of a horse neighing, and a commotion in the courtyard. Effie gasped. 'Is it Her Majesty? Are they here?'

Agnes took her hand and they rushed to the arched doorway. Several riders mounted on broad stallions were being greeted in the cobbled courtyard, grooms taking the reins, waiting to lead the animals away. 'It must be. Look, Effie – such fine horses.'

Colban was standing in the courtyard, dithering nervously as several women dismounted, their hair braided, clothed in silk and velvet, fine surcoats, kirtles, capes and bonnets. They were talking quietly to each other while two men barked orders and servants hauled baggage from the saddles.

Colban moved to Agnes's side as she and Effie stepped out to peer at the royal visitors. He pointed to a tall man with a tidy beard who wore a long sword at his hip. 'That's the Earl of Atholl. He's escorting the ladies, along with Sir Niall de Brus, the king's younger brother. Can ye see him, there, the broad-shouldered man taking a draught from the cup?'

'I can...' Agnes held her breath, listening to the king's brother, who was telling someone loudly that he was intending to travel to Tain, in Easter Ross, in the hope of finding a boat to take them onwards.

Agnes's eyes fell on five women who were now standing together. They were exquisitely dressed and their faces were composed as if they knew they were entitled to immediate obedience. The woman in the middle must be Queen Elizabeth, Agnes decided; the others stood closely to her as she looked around serenely, her expression one of a woman who commanded authority. The other four women were equally beautifully dressed in fur-edged capes clasped with pretty brooches. Three of them tended the queen, speaking quietly to her, but the fourth was aloof, more inquisitive, a young girl not much older than Effie. Agnes thought she looked like a perfectly dressed little doll.

Colban pressed her arm. 'The queen herself, Agnes. Can ye see the cabochon ruby ring on her finger? And two of the three ladies next to her dressed in mantles are the king's sisters. I don't know which is which, but they are called Mary and Christine, and the other woman is the Countess of Buchan.'

'Who is the younger lassie?' Effie hissed, wide-eyed. 'She is so beautiful.'

Colban nodded. 'She's the king's daughter, Princess Marjorie.'

'Aye, the bairn of Good King Robert's first wife, Isabella,' Agnes replied. 'I heard she died after the birth and it broke the king's heart. He didnae want another woman for six years after that, then he met the Queen Elizabeth and fell for her.'

The master, the Earl de Mar, was speaking to the group in a throaty bark, welcoming them, his chest puffed out and his manner extremely chivalrous: he bowed low, extended a hand, and he and the regal women began to make their way into the castle.

Agnes sighed. 'She'll be wanting a son and heir soon for the king, but she'll not make one while she's here, running away from the English. She should have stayed and fought Longshanks and his son alongside the king. I certainly would.'

Colban glanced at her with admiration. 'Ye are a bold one, Agnes Fitzgerald.'

Then the doll-like princess was striding towards them purposefully, as if she intended to talk to them. She wore a beautiful fur-lined cloak and mantle. Agnes had never seen anything so sumptuous: she marvelled at how the corner of the neck edge on one side was pulled through a ring sewn to the opposite corner and then knotted to keep in position.

The princess pressed a hand to her coiled hair and spoke directly to Effie in a high-pitched voice. 'Are you a servant girl?'

Effie's eyes bulged. She made a low curtsy and muttered something, her voice muffled.

Princess Marjorie's smooth brow creased. 'Do you have a lavender woman here in the castle?'

Effie's mouth opened but she could not reply.

Agnes curtsied. 'A washerwoman, aye, your Highness, we have one who works just beyond the castle walls.'

'Very well.' Marjorie's shrill pipe hung on the air. She pointed to

Effie. 'You will come with me to my room instantly, and I will give you some garments that have become soiled during the journey. It has been a long ride and I am weary. I want my dress and cloak cleaned and returned to me first thing tomorrow morning. They are my favourites and I want them made perfect. Do you hear me?'

'Aye, Madam...' Effie began, but the princess had swept after her royal aunts.

Agnes pushed Effie gently. 'Away with ye and follow her – ye will need to take her clothes to the washerwoman to be cleaned.'

'I can't...' Effie stammered.

'Go, hennie, be quick and come back here,' Agnes said more persuasively, and Effie scuttled after the princess.

Colban shook his head. 'Such finery they wear, and look at the costly livery of their horses. I've never seen the like.'

'Aye.' Agnes shook her head. 'They are a sight, to be sure, the royal party, and the queen is a fine woman. But the wee princess is just a slip of a lassie: her bones are tiny, just as Effie's maw was. Pray God Princess Marjorie won't go the same way as her mother when it comes her turn to bear an heir.'

Colban looked perplexed, then he met Agnes's eyes. 'Can ye come to the stables tonight? Ye could bring me some leftovers and... I'd be happy to spend time in your company.'

Agnes nodded. 'I'd like to see the queen's horses. They are such proud beasts. I'd love to ride one, although I've never done more than stroke a horse's mane.'

'I've seen ye do that many times.' Colban was still watching her, his eyes shining. 'Ye have a way with the animals, Agnes. People too, I ken. I believe anyone who knows ye must love ye.'

'Thank ye kindly, Colban.' Agnes smiled. 'I'd better away to the bakehouse before I'm missed. Morag won't spare me a beating.'

Colban's face was momentarily sad. 'Aye, there are horses to tend and water. I'll see ye later, I hope.'

Agnes rushed away and was soon back at work, preparing

purple carrots. For the next few hours, Agnes was busier than she'd ever been, heaving dishes of hot meat and steaming vegetables, piling peas and beans high on platters, while the serving men took them to the trestle tables in the great hall for the royal guests, returning with empty dishes to be refilled again.

Effie was by her side, silent in her chores, as if meeting the queen and waiting upon Princess Marjorie had left her in a trance. There was a smile on her face when she turned to Agnes, her arms filled with a broad platter of fruit, as she whispered, 'She was so fine, the princess. I've never met anyone quite so bonnie. She spoke to me and her voice was clear as a church bell. And her clothes, Agnes, soft as swan's down...'

'Did ye take them out to the lavender woman to be washed?'

'Aye, I did that.' Effie turned away, the dish in her arms, hiding a secretive expression Agnes had never noticed before. 'I must be about my business now. I have more fruit to prepare.'

Several busy hours later, the meal was over. The young scullions were washing the charred, greasy pots and Effie was sitting by the fireside, gazing into the hearth, an uneaten crust of bread clutched in her hands.

Agnes looked around quickly: Morag was stuffing handfuls of meat into her mouth and Biddy had fallen into a snooze. No one else was watching; she shovelled scraps of leftover boar's meat and vegetables into a hollowed trencher, a piece of bread holding morsels of food, and headed for the stables. Colban would be hungry and Agnes wanted to stroke the mane of a royal stallion and rest her face against its warm neck. If no one was looking, she might climb astride its back. She wanted to imagine how it would feel to ride a horse, its sinews moving in a gallop beneath her. She visualised herself thundering through the heather up a steep hill, past sharp-smelling pines and calm lochs in the twilight, the moon rising as she galloped on, a night sky crammed with stars. She would feel truly alive.

6

By nine o'clock on Monday morning, Zoe was sitting at her laptop ready for a video meeting with her boss. Her notes were in front of her and earbuds in place: she was in the process of writing a research document about how generational differences influence philanthropic donation and was going to update her boss Sharon on her progress. She sipped coffee, staring through the window at the pavement outside. A woman her own age was pushing a pram containing two wriggling babies and, for a moment, Zoe imagined herself in the woman's place, with small children, a family around her every day, always busy, always needed. Something about it felt warm and comforting; at the same time, she was aware of a faint sense of panic. She was used to being independent, and besides, she had Leah to consider. She'd have to want the alternative a great deal in order to give up the routine that kept her days ticking over so comfortably.

A message pinged on her phone: Mariusz asked if he could call round later and she replied quickly.

Come for lunch around twelve.

She heard Leah pad into the living room. Her sister was huddled in pyjamas, a dressing gown and fluffy socks, on her way to the kitchen, presumably to make coffee: Leah was usually unapproachable until she'd had a large dose of morning caffeine. She was up early: she rarely emerged from her bedroom before eleven nowadays. Then the laptop screen was filled with the face of a smiling woman with dangling earrings offering a warm greeting and Zoe forgot about Leah as she launched into a conversation about how 45 per cent of Boomers believed their financial contribution was important, while only 36 per cent of Gen Xers and 25 per cent of Gen Ys thought that money made a difference.

Leah exhaled: Zoe's work made no sense to her. She couldn't imagine working on a laptop writing articles and tweets and being involved in think-tanks. She boiled the kettle, clanked a spoon inside a mug and pushed bread in the toaster. Ten minutes later, she flopped on the sofa, munching a slice of peanut buttered toast, sipping sweet black coffee. She picked up her tablet and typed *Highlands of Scotland* into the search bar. She was instantly greeted with photos that took her breath away: stone castles rising between glistening lochs and low skies; snow-clad mountain peaks, purple sunsets. She concentrated on the taste of coffee in her mouth; the bitter taste gave her a buzz of immediate energy. Her mind floated to the Highlands, visualising herself in a warm coat and hat, solid boots, walking by the loch. She was not alone: in her reverie, a man was by her side. He had light curly hair, his arm was wrapped affectionately around her shoulder: he was smiling, wearing a kilt. Leah laughed: of course, he would be – in a daydream, she could evoke the perfect partner for the perfect landscape. She glanced over towards Zoe, but her sister's earbuds were in and she was chattering away.

Leah wondered again about the job she'd applied for on the estate in the Highlands: she'd sent her CV and application form off yesterday and Abigail had arranged a video interview just moments afterwards, which had gone well. Leah hoped she'd done enough. The idea of a new beginning in Scotland filled her with a shaky optimism. She was stirred by the romance of it all, imagining that a life in the Highlands would somehow transform her into someone independent, beautiful and a little bit wild. She would fall in love with the man in the kilt, who would be called Hector or Blair. They'd buy a country lodge, have four children and their lives would be bliss. Leah wanted to live somewhere very like Gairloch, where she'd been happiest as a child. She'd breathe the sharp air, walk on the vast beaches listening to the rush of the sea. It would make her happy. If the job she'd applied for wasn't successful, perhaps there would be others. She'd help run a hotel on Skye, or become a crime writer's personal assistant in the Hebrides.

She returned to her tablet to search for inspiration when her phone rang. Leah grabbed it with some trepidation. 'Hello?'

'Hello, Leah. This is Abigail Laing.'

It took Leah a moment to recall who she was, then her heart leaped, excitement and fright. 'Oh, nice to talk to you again.'

'Indeed,' Abigail replied. 'I enjoyed our video chat yesterday. In many ways, you're ideal for the post. You're a professional: you have a history degree. You've cared for children, which tells me you're organised. You're of an age where you're likely to settle into the job for a while – all that makes you perfect. We don't take youngsters who'll only stay for a month and, sadly, we've had a number of care-takers less level-headed than yourself who haven't lasted. The owner of the castle is looking for someone more permanent.'

'It's a castle?' Leah gasped.

'I'm afraid there is one stumbling block though – you said you were single.'

'Yes, I am...'

'That's a pity. The owner, whom I represent, will only take on someone in a partnership. I'm afraid it's one thing we insist on. The castle is remote, at the edge of a village, and we don't want the caretaker to feel – isolated.'

'Oh.' Leah was immediately jolted by disappointment. Her mind raced. She glanced across towards Zoe, who was still engrossed in her meeting, and she blurted, 'Would my twin sister do?'

'Pardon?'

Leah's hand shook. 'I have a twin sister. She'd come with me. We'd be a couple then, wouldn't we, of sorts?'

There was a pause, then Abigail Laing said, 'Yes, I don't see that as a problem. Right, let's think about this...' She waited again for a moment as if she was considering, then she added, 'I'll speak to the owner and see what he says. I'm sure he'd be agreeable. Meanwhile, I'll send you some photos of the castle and the village, showing its location. We're ten miles north of Inverness on the edge of a small village called Rosemuir. The castle is called Ravenscraig. It's very old, dating back to the thirteenth century, possibly earlier, and it has the sort of atmosphere you'd expect with an old building. There's an incredible view of the loch.'

Leah closed her eyes. It could be paradise. 'It sounds... very nice.'

'Well, I'll send over the photos, you discuss it with your sister, and I'll phone you in an hour or so with the owner's answer. I'd like to get this wrapped up as soon as possible. Does that sound feasible?'

'That's wonderful, thank you.' Leah nodded.

'Then we'll talk soon.' Abigail's crisp voice was followed by silence.

Leah leaned back into the softness of the sofa, catching her breath. She had a job, almost. After all, Zoe could easily come with her; her work was transferable; she only needed a laptop. It was the perfect solution. She gazed across at her sister, who was finishing the video call, and wondered how Zoe would take the news. Leah wasn't sure at all how to break it to her.

Zoe finished her call with a flourish: Sharon had been delighted with her article. She swivelled round on the chair, all smiles. 'Leah, you're up early? Fancy another coffee? I deserve a break.'

'Um,' Leah said and proffered her mug.

'Mariusz is coming over for lunch.' Zoe was already up, in the kitchen, filling the kettle.

'Oh?' Leah wondered when she'd have the chance to talk to Zoe about Scotland: she'd intended to work up to it before Abigail called back, but time was running out.

'I think he wants to talk about Jordan... I have a horrible feeling they are going to split up.'

'Some people do,' Leah began and put a hand to her mouth. She was thinking of herself and Aaron: she could do better than that, she could show more empathy. 'I hope not, I like Mariusz – and Jordan.' She listened to the kettle humming. 'What do we have for lunch?'

Zoe shrugged. 'Not much, a salad bag, some fruit. I'll just do us all a sandwich.'

'Oh, what if I go and get something?' Leah suggested, offering an encouraging grin. 'I can pop to the supermarket, buy some falafel, hummus, breadsticks, tomatoes – some of the elderflower pressé you like.'

'That would be awesome, thank you,' Zoe enthused, handing over a steaming mug. 'Leah, you're a star.' She was delighted. Leah was being helpful, interested; hopefully her depression was lifting. 'Thanks so much.'

'No problem.' Leah felt a mixture of pleasure and guilt. She'd made her twin happy, and that was always gratifying, but she had ulterior motives: this was about brownie points before she dropped the Scotland bombshell. She shuffled forward. 'I'll finish the coffee, go and change, leave you to your work and be back in no time.'

'Thanks, Leah.' Zoe's eyes shone. 'Seriously, thanks...'

* * *

Half an hour later, Leah was standing in a supermarket aisle, dressed in a heavy coat, staring at her phone. Abigail Laing had sent her some photographs and they'd taken her breath away. Her eyes were welded to the small screen as she flicked through a sequence of images: a turreted castle photographed from a distance, surrounded by water on three sides against a backdrop of blue sky. There were dramatic close-ups of the castle, small windows, tall towers. A separate wing loomed below the sky, across a courtyard. The castle was accessed by a narrow driveway, mounds of grass on two sides, a few trees, a garden area, crumbling fallen stones.

Leah gazed at the photos, already visualising herself there. She continued to browse and another photo pulled her into a grand hall, where she imagined feeling small amid high ceilings, tapestried walls, a long table and flagstone floors and a vast kitchen with an open fireplace, furnished with antique pots. Leah pictured a four-poster bed; her bedroom would be enormous, the walls painted deep burgundy. She'd look out onto the loch that would reflect the moon at night, and each morning it would be shrouded in fine mist. She'd lean out from the arched window, breathing the invigorating scent of fresh pine needles, the bite of winter air on her skin. The idea of living in such a beautiful building, full of history, thrilled her.

Leah tugged herself from her daydream, remembering the shopping, then the phone rang and she held it to her ear.

'Hello?'

'Leah, this is Abigail Laing.'

'Oh...' Leah gripped the phone in anticipation.

Abigail's voice was efficient. 'I've spoken to the owner. He is absolutely fine with you taking the post as long as you have some sort of partner. A sister would be acceptable.'

Leah swallowed. Her heart was beating too fast.

'So, can we discuss start dates?' Abigail continued. 'As you know from the application form, we run a trial period of three months as standard.' She paused and Leah felt herself nodding in agreement.

'Yes, of course, that's fine.'

'So, today's the tenth. Could you start on Monday the twenty-fourth? I wondered whether it would be convenient to arrive at the weekend, say, Saturday the twenty-second of October. Your initial three months would last until the week ending January the twentieth. Of course, I hope all parties will be happy for you to continue at that point.'

'Yes, I hope so too.' Leah was excited. 'That sounds wonderful, yes, yes thank you.'

'Excellent.' Abigail might have been smiling. 'It will give me time to rearrange the accommodation so that you and your sister have a room each. Does that sound all right?'

'Oh yes,' Leah breathed.

'You know the job entails general caretaking and supervision of the property, basically making sure everything ticks over, and you'd liaise directly with me, especially if any visitors need to be shown around or there are issues to discuss. You have my number if there are any questions. I'll email some paperwork to you, and then the job is yours.' She paused momentarily and added, 'Congratulations.'

'Thanks. Oh, I'm so pleased.' Leah was hopping up and down in the supermarket, oblivious of stares from passing shoppers.

'Excellent. Then we'll be in touch. Welcome to Ravenscraig.'

'Thank you – oh...' Leah heard Abigail end the call and realised she was smiling. She was filled with new energy and excitement:

she had a job, she was in charge of a castle, living in a beautiful place overlooking a loch in the Highlands of Scotland. She held her chin high and rushed towards the delicatessen counter. She hadn't felt this good in a long time. She just hoped Zoe would agree to come with her.

7

There was frenzied bustling in the stables as Agnes approached quietly, clutching a trencher hidden beneath a linen cloth. Inside the forge to one side of the stables, a huge furnace raged, illuminating the courtyard with leaping orange shadows. The heavy smell of straw, sweating horses and heated iron met her nostrils and Agnes thought of hell and the inferno she'd heard about in chapel on Sundays. She had always imagined the smith as a broad-shouldered Satan, all narrowed eyes, coarse hair and bristly beard. Now he stood over the anvil, his face lit crimson as he muttered to himself and brought his hammer down, a sharp rhythmic sound of clanking metal. A small boy stood beside him, heaving the bellows.

Agnes shifted furtively to the stables, watching as stable boys brushed the steeds vigorously and others tended to the carisons, the embroidered saddle cloths with bold insignia that adorned all royal horses. The smaller rounceys and the sumpter horses that carried the side bags and panniers were quietly munching hay, but Agnes's eyes were drawn to the taller, majestic destriers, the men's imposing battle horses.

The smith was inspecting the shoes of a noble-looking grey

palfrey. Colban stood at a distance, his eyes on Agnes. Then a tall man in a dark tunic, one of the castle soldiers, a sword in his girdle, moved closer to the smith, who tethered the horse to one side as the men began to talk quietly. Agnes moved nearer and heard the soldier mutter the words 'as much gold as ye can carry'.

The mention of gold made Agnes's ears keen, and she slipped through shadows to a position just behind the smith, where she could hear better. She leaned as far forward as she dared.

The smith grunted, 'Aye, but ye ken it's a big risk to me...'

The castle soldier lowered his voice. 'See to it straight away, and you'll be well recompensed. I'm told to tell ye that Prince Edward has given his word. Once the castle is ablaze, the English soldiers will attack. It's the women he's after... they'll be ransomed and The Bruce will pay.'

Agnes understood what was happening and froze. Her stomach lurched with fear, but she propelled herself forward, her heart hammering. She scurried towards Colban, pressing the trencher into his hands and placing a finger on his lips. 'Follow me. And make no sound...'

They hurried from the stables towards the bakehouse. Colban was already pushing food into his mouth. 'What is it, Agnes?'

'I heard the smith talking to one of our soldiers...' Agnes whispered. 'He's going to be paid gold to set the castle on fire – so the Earl will have to surrender and the English can come here and grab the queen.'

Colban shook his head. 'But that would make the smith a traitor...'

'We've no time to waste.' Agnes pulled him forward.

'Where are we going?'

'Where else? To tell the queen.'

'But how can we do that?'

Agnes tugged his hand. 'They are finished supping in the great hall. Come on with ye.'

They rushed through the gate, across the cobbled courtyard, past the bakehouse and the kitchen. In the great hall, the servants were clearing away platters, basins and linen towels for handwashing, removing trestle tables. Most of the royal party had gone. Niall de Brus was speaking to the Earl de Mar, who was calling him by the familiar name Nigel and clapping him on the shoulder as they both roared with laughter. Queen Elizabeth had risen from her seat and was talking to one of her sisters-in-law; she was holding a goblet, sipping slowly. Agnes marvelled at her silk robe, the rings on her fingers, an ornamental brooch on her fur-lined cloak, the clasp of gold and silver. Then she recovered her wits, grabbed a platter of fruit that a servant was taking away and rushed towards the queen.

'Will ye be wanting cherries, Your Majesty?'

Queen Elizabeth glanced at Agnes briefly and then looked away.

Agnes edged closer, her voice low. 'Your Majesty, listen to me – the smith is planning to set fire to the castle and then the English will come for ye. I just heard it whispered in the stables.'

The queen turned to her, wide-eyed. 'What did you say?'

'Madam, there's no time to waste.'

Elizabeth de Burgh leaned forward. 'Go back to the stables now, girl. Tell them to prepare the horses.'

'Aye, Madam, I will.' Agnes was on her way, running to the courtyard.

She heard the queen call out, 'Niall. Can you come here, please – I believe there is a whisper of treachery...'

Then Agnes cannoned into Colban, grabbing his tunic. 'I can smell fire already.'

Colban nodded, the muscles in his face tense. Smoke was curling from behind the walls of the southwest tower and beyond the gatehouse.

Agnes tugged at his tunic again. 'Go, saddle the royal horses, for the queen will need to escape as soon as she can.'

'But where are ye away to, Agnes?'

'I'll fetch wee Effie. We'll come to meet ye straight.'

She watched Colban make a dash for the stables, then she turned towards the bakehouse and ran as fast as she could.

She found Effie by the fireside, hugging a bundle of cloth. Agnes recognised the beautiful fur-lined cloak immediately; it was Princess Marjorie's. She frowned. 'I thought you'd taken the garments to be cleaned?'

Effie's face crumpled. 'I couldnae let them go. The cloak's so soft. And the dress is real silk. I'll take them to the lavender woman now...'

'Effie, no.' Agnes grasped her wrist and pulled her to her feet. 'The blacksmith has betrayed the queen. We must go.'

Effie was confused as Agnes propelled her from the bakehouse into the courtyard. They were greeted by noise and bustle. Servants were rushing, shouting frantically as smoke billowed from beyond the walls and flames leaped towards the darkening sky. Bonfires had been started on three sides.

Agnes hurried towards the stables, dragging Effie after her. She hesitated by the door, turning once to glance at the small girl clutching her oversized bundle, her round eyes staring up in disbelief. Inside, the cacophony was thunderous, horses neighing, turning and twisting, nostrils flared, as they were saddled; men shouting.

The queen and her party were there already; Elizabeth de Burgh was being helped onto a grey palfrey while saddle bags were strapped to the sumpter horses. The Earl of Atholl touched the long sword at his hip as he gazed around anxiously. Niall de Brus was at his side and the earl said, 'We'll go north, find refuge in a friendly castle. There's one I know of in Rosemuir, north of Inverness. I ken the owner there, Ross McNair, and he'll help us. We'll ride there directly. It's called Ravenscraig.'

Colban brought the black destrier to the earl, saddled and ready, speaking quietly into the horse's ear as the earl swung himself astride. Agnes felt Effie's grip on her arm tighten.

Many more men rushed in, wearing armour, swords held high. The earl cried out, he dug his heels into the side of his horse and urged it forward. The queen followed, her face tight as her mount sprang into action and galloped furiously from the stables. Agnes watched in admiration: she was clearly a skilled horsewoman. Others followed, the three women in surcoats, cloaks and mantles, gloves on their hands. A man in armour lunged for the Princess Marjorie who was being helped to her mount; the groom next to her threw himself at the soldier and was immediately hacked down, but the princess, warmly wrapped in another fur-lined cloak, encouraged her horse forward and followed her party. In that moment, Agnes wished her Godspeed with all her heart. Several men leaped on horses and galloped in pursuit, although Agnes was not sure in the darkness and the chaos if they were Scotsmen or English soldiers.

The fire had taken hold of the castle now: the straw was burning in the stables, flames leaping. The stench of scorching and the thick black smoke made the panicking horses neigh and rear in fear. Soldiers in chainmail coifs and hauberks heaved their swords into the air, clanking in brutal combat as bodies were felled to the ground.

Colban waved frantically to Agnes and she rushed across to him, pulling Effie behind her, who clung desperately to her bundle. Then Niall de Brus mounted his destrier and was about to ride away when he was surrounded by more English soldiers. His horse bucked and he was dragged to the ground, held roughly by four men. A voice barked orders – he should be taken into the courtyard, hung up for all to see – then he was manhandled roughly and marched away.

Colban seized the horse and hissed, 'Agnes. Take the mount and go.'

Agnes was already heaving Effie onto the horse's back. 'Come with us, Colban. It's not safe here.'

'I will.' He pushed Agnes's foot deftly and she was seated behind Effie.

'We must flee.'

A soldier in chainmail pitched towards the horse and Colban fought to push him away. A dagger glinted in the man's fist and Agnes watched in horror as Colban's throat was opened wide, a red waterfall, and he fell from the man's grasp. Then the soldier lunged towards her and Agnes remembered how the queen and her attendants had dug their heels into the horse's side to propel it on. She repeated the movement, clinging to the horse, pressing her body against Effie's as the horse hurtled out of the stables and into the cobbled courtyard. A group of soldiers were standing around Niall de Brus, now hanging by the neck. His tunic had been torn and blood dripped from his stomach. The English soldiers were shouting insults towards him – they had no eyes for her.

Agnes dragged at the reins and hoped the destrier would know where to go. Smoke filled her throat. The castle walls were engulfed in roaring flames, orange against the velvet night sky. Soldiers swarmed, weapons aloft, and everywhere there was shouting and the heavy clanking of combat. The bakehouse was alight now; a woman ran into the courtyard screaming and Agnes thought of Morag and Biddy, hoping they would be safe. Then she thought again of the image of Colban falling from the soldier's hands, his throat cut, and she was racked with sadness. Tears blurred her eyes, but she had no time to think of it, not now. The huge horse shied, then, as Agnes clung on, galloped away from the rising flames, through the arch of the gatehouse, the raised portcullis and into the darkness.

Agnes gripped the reins, one arm tightly around Effie, who had her head down against the wind, as the horse blundered forward over hills, past forests. For a long time, her eyes were almost closed as she clung on, hoping that she wasn't being chased by soldiers or that she wouldn't somehow cross a border into England and be greeted by more men with swords. It occurred to her that she had no idea how far away England was or where the soldiers might be camped. The violence of the night stayed with her, chilling her to the bone more than the cold night air. The noise was echoing in her ears, shouting, the clash of metal swords, and the images terrified her: wild angry eyes, spittle on beards, the smell of burning and the oily stench of blood. She couldn't shake away the memory of Colban, falling like a dropped rag, more blood on his neck than she'd ever seen. And the king's brother hanging, his body sliced open: the horror of it was scorched on her mind.

Agnes had always believed herself to be strong; she'd wanted to ride a stallion and now here she was, clutching Effie, shaken to the bones by the bouncing motion of the galloping horse. She'd once believed she could fight as well as any man, but that belief had changed now. She was trembling inside her own skin. She had no idea where she would go or what she might do. She couldn't go back to Kildrummy Castle. She would look after Effie; she would use her wits to keep them both safe.

The horse's skin was frothy with sweat as it slowed and came to a stop beneath a yew tree. As it bent its neck to graze, Agnes helped Effie down. Her face was dirty with smoke and streaked with tears. Agnes managed to tie the horse to a thick branch, then she wrapped the fur-lined cloak around them both and they huddled down against the tree trunk, clinging together for warmth.

Effie's voice was small. 'What happened to Colban...?'

'Don't pay mind to it now...' Agnes sighed; she wasn't sure how much Effie had seen. Her mind was full of the way the men had surrounded the king's brother, pinned him down. They had shamed him, then taken him into the courtyard and strung him up. Agnes shuddered at the soldiers' brutality. She had heard of how William Wallace, the brave Scots knight captured the previous year in Glasgow, had been put to death by the wicked English. The word was that they had crowned him with a garland of oak, mocking him as an outlaw before they tortured him, naked and humiliated. Morag had told her that Wallace's bold last words were 'I could not be a traitor to Edward, for I was never his subject'. Then the English had shown no mercy. Agnes knew that a swift death would have been a kinder end.

'But what will we do, Agnes? What will become of us?'

Agnes kept her voice steady. 'We'll find a sheltered place to sleep the night, then tomorrow we'll ride to Inverness. We'll find someone and ask the way. Then we'll head north. I heard the earl mention the place where the queen's party are heading – a village called Rosemuir, north of Inverness. They might help us, give us work. There's a castle there – it's called Ravenscraig.'

8

Leah couldn't stop thinking about the photos of Ravenscraig Castle, the stone turrets reflecting gold sunlight, as she pushed the key in the door of her flat. In the sitting room, Zoe was on the sofa, sharing a cup of tea with Mariusz, who smiled warmly.

'Hi, it's great to see you, Leah.'

'Hi, Mariusz.'

Zoe rushed over to hug her sister, taking the shopping bag from her fingers. 'And you've brought lunch. Perfect. I'll get plates.'

'Let's eat,' Mariusz said. 'I'm starving. And there's so much I want to tell you.'

They sat around the small table as Leah poured sparkling elder-flower into glasses. Zoe observed her sister carefully: her skin had taken on a healthy sheen, she seemed purposeful and much more positive. She turned her attention back to Mariusz.

'So, what's your news?' Zoe recalled their last conversation in the wine bar, and she touched his arm sympathetically. 'How's Jordan?'

Leah leaned forward nervously. 'I hope everything's all right.'

Mariusz grinned broadly. 'It's never been better. We had a long talk. I was totally honest about how I felt about his business being the new love of his life.'

'Chairworks...' Zoe remembered. 'What did you say?'

Mariusz sighed. 'I just came out with it, that he's so engrossed in making the business work that he doesn't seem to notice me. And I admitted that I'm annoyed our flat is full of all his junk, bits and pieces of wood and material. And do you know what? He told me he loves me, that the business is about making a future for us both, and he's committed to that.' His face shone as he clapped his hands, eager to share his news. 'He wants us to get married.'

'That must have been a surprise.' Leah reached out a hand to squeeze his. 'But it's great news.'

'I almost fell over with shock,' Mariusz agreed. 'It wasn't what I expected. I was feeling second best. But I'm bowled over.'

'So, it's all resolved – and a wedding is on the cards?' Zoe smiled.

'It is.' Mariusz beamed. 'Tell me you'll be there.'

'Definitely,' Zoe enthused.

'I can buy a ridiculous hat.' Leah clapped her hands. 'When will it be?'

'We're thinking of Valentine's Day next year. I mean, that's so romantic, isn't it? A February wedding.'

'Perfect,' Zoe chimed. 'We should have had champagne for lunch.'

'We'll be celebrating properly on Saturday. We haven't even told Bex yet.' He turned to Leah. 'You will come to The Red Cellar with us on Saturday?'

'Definitely.' Leah glanced at Zoe and seized the moment. 'I hope we'll be able to come to the wedding too, but I may be in Scotland in February.'

'Really?' Zoe was perplexed. 'Why Scotland?'

'I have a job.' Leah flourished her phone and held up a photo of Ravenscraig Castle. 'I'm the newly appointed caretaker.' She smiled at Mariusz. 'Oh, I've had an idea. Perhaps you can hold your wedding reception there? Maybe I'll get a discount...'

Two faces were staring at her, then at the picture.

Mariusz spoke first. 'A reception in a Scottish castle. How gorgeous! I didn't know you had a new job, Leah.'

'Nor did I.' Zoe's grin broadened. 'Congratulations! When did you find out?'

'While I was in the supermarket... Abigail Laing rang me.'

'I have to say,' Mariusz's face shone, 'the idea of a wedding reception in that beautiful old stone castle... oh, wow. We'd love that.'

'Well, I'll ask about it.' Leah was pleased with herself. 'I start work in Ravenscraig on the twenty-fourth of this month, so we'll be travelling up on Saturday the twenty-second of October.'

'We?' Zoe smiled. 'Am I invited for the weekend?'

'No, I... I hoped you'd come with me,' Leah blurted. 'It's a job for a couple, and I'm not a couple, so I asked if you could come instead, and they said yes. That's how I got the job.'

'Ah.' Mariusz looked from Leah to Zoe.

Zoe frowned, resting her chin in her palm. 'I wasn't intending to move to the other end of the country, Leah. I like it here.'

'But you *can* move, Zo. You work remotely. And I really want the job. It's only for three months. That's the trial period. And I thought, well, if they like me, I could stay on after January, and we won't tell them you've come back here to Birmingham. There must be a way round it.' She met her sister's eyes, her own pleading. 'Please say yes.' Leah increased the intensity of her gaze, the desperation. 'Please?'

Zoe recognised the expression, the persuasive tone. It had been the same way since they were children. She shook her head. 'I love my life here.'

'It's only for three months. Please.' Leah pressed her hands together as if in prayer. 'I so want this job. If there was any other way Zoe, I wouldn't ask you, honestly... and it'll be fun.'

Zoe rubbed her eyes, recalling her childhood, her teenage years, their father's cajoling voice urging her to give way, just for Leah, just this once. It had always been the same and she'd always acquiesced: it was her responsibility to support her sister who had been born second and Leah had spent her life reminding Zoe of the fact. She said weakly, 'I don't really want to leave the flat.'

'You could come back here at weekends?' Leah offered hopefully.

Mariusz was suddenly excited. 'Or – what about this for a solution? – Jordan could rent the flat from you, just for three months while he looks for premises, and he could run his business from here?'

'Oh, that's perfect,' Leah enthused, holding up the photo of the stone castle. 'What do you think, Zoe? What do you say?'

Zoe sighed, feeling her resolve softening further; she was capitulating, as she often did. In fairness, Leah had a point: she could work remotely, and it would only be for three months. It could be like an extended holiday. Zoe noticed how bright Leah's eyes were, how eagerly she smiled. The new job was already doing her good, and Zoe might enjoy the change of scenery. She imagined jogging along high hilltop paths, the loch glistening below in winter sunshine, snow reflecting the blinding gleam. They had a bond, she and Leah. They'd been everywhere together through good and bad times. This would be an adventure that might take them both forward and enrich their lives and if Leah became independent, then Zoe, in her way, could be independent too; she'd move back to Birmingham and continue her own life.

She nodded. 'All right. It's a yes from me, Leah. Why not? I suppose it works all round.'

Mariusz smiled and Leah's grin widened as Zoe reached over to squeeze her sister's hand.

'We'll drive up in the Mini; we'll take turns, split the journey. It's decided. That's wonderful. So, when did you say we were going?'

* * *

The twenty-second arrived quickly, and the journey to Scotland started early. They were both quiet in the car, Zoe concentrating on the busy roads as she negotiated the motorway. The windscreen was spattered with rain, the wipers swishing hypnotically, and she was humming along to the radio to keep alert. They had been driving for three hours already as they passed the junction for Carlisle. Leah had taken the first stint from Birmingham to Manchester, and now she was gazing out of the window watching the scenery change from urban to countryside. They'd driven on through the undulating hills around Kendal, then north. Despite the slanting rain, the landscape was beautiful and Leah was lost in thought, excited about her new job, but at the same time anxious about the responsibility of running the castle. She had spoken to Abigail Laing the night before about housekeeping arrangements, where she would find the key on arrival, and she'd been fascinated as Abigail had told her about how the castle was reaching the end of the lengthy process of renovation. A photo shoot had taken place in the late summer, a glamorous session lasting two days featuring an expensive car pictured in gleaming sunshine by the castle and the last couple who had lived in the castle had liaised with the camera crew and thoroughly enjoyed the experience. Leah imagined herself doing the same thing, working on a film set, meeting celebrities before retiring to the calm of her beautiful bedroom overlooking the loch. Leah hoped the job would be easy enough – supervising workmen, giving guided tours, emailing interested visitors. She recalled Abigail's tight tone when she'd asked why the previous couple had left: 'I think they found it a little remote.'

Leah smiled. The last caretakers were obviously people who

weren't looking for solitude and calm. She glanced at Zoe, who was leaning forward staring into traffic as she overtook a lorry. Leah noticed her sister's taut neck muscles and she said, 'Shall we stop somewhere soon?'

'What time is it?' Zoe muttered, her eyes on the road.

'Just past eleven.' Leah pointed to the bag at her feet hopefully. 'We could have a break for coffee? I made a flask.'

'If we stop for half an hour now and have another half an hour break later, what time will we get there?'

Leah thought for a moment. 'Five o'clock. But we can stop for lunch and still be there for six.'

Zoe nodded. 'I'll just want to fall into bed once we get to the castle. We must be mad to take on this journey in one go.'

'Are you okay?' Leah was momentarily alarmed. 'We could stay somewhere overnight in Glasgow. I could ring Abigail and say we'll arrive tomorrow...'

'No, let's stop for a rest at the next services. Can you take over then?'

'Of course – it's my turn,' Leah beamed.

It was raining hard as Zoe drove the Mini into the motorway services at Gretna Green.

Leah dived into the bag between her feet and produced a flask of coffee, pouring a cup for Zoe and one for herself. Zoe sipped eagerly, leaning back in the driver's seat, stretching stiff muscles. 'Well, we've done a good chunk of the journey. We're at least a third of the way there. Leaving before eight o'clock was a great idea.'

'I'll treat you to lunch,' Leah announced suddenly. 'Where-abouts do you think we will be at one o'clock?'

'This side of Glasgow.'

'You find somewhere nice on the internet while I drive.' Leah clutched her phone. 'What do you fancy? Café, restaurant?'

Zoe shrugged. 'Something light. I thought we had sandwiches.'

'Mmm, but...' Leah met her eyes. 'I want to get lunch to say thanks. I'm really grateful for everything – I couldn't have taken this job without your help.'

'It's an adventure. And Sharon's absolutely fine about me working from Scotland for a while,' Zoe said. 'You must be really excited.'

'I want to make it work. I'm determined this will be the start of something special for me – for both of us.' Leah pushed her hair from her eyes and grinned apologetically. 'Let's face it, it's about time. I can't get this wrong, Zo. You have a great job, a great life. I want to step up. You know what Mum and Dad said when I rang them, to tell them about it?'

'They were delighted, I bet.'

'They were. Dad said he thought living in Scotland would be perfect for me. But when I told them you were coming, Mum said it was about time I relied on you a little less.'

Zoe frowned. 'Oh, I'm sure she didn't mean—'

'She means exactly that, and she's right. Do you know, working as a TA did nothing to build my confidence. Being with Aaron was exactly the same – it was all about him, what he wanted to do, and I just went along with it like a spare part. I lost my sense of worth...'

'Don't be too harsh on yourself.' Zoe shook her head. 'We're always learning – that's life.'

'My biggest realisation came when I was puking my brains out after that lonely binge on pizza and Prosecco.' Leah stared into the murky depths of coffee. 'I hit a new low that night and something just clicked in my head. I knew I had to turn things round or I'd spiral even lower. I couldn't let that happen. And you were there for me, Zo.'

'You're more resilient than you know.' Zoe wrapped an arm round her sister.

Leah rested her head on Zoe's shoulder. 'I promise you, after the next three months, I'll be standing on my own feet. You'll be back in your flat in Birmingham and I'll be in my castle...' A smile spread across her face. '*My* castle – how great does that sound?'

'I'll miss you.' Zoe was surprised how small her voice sounded.

'And I'll miss you too. But...' Leah grinned. 'We're thirty years old. We need to move forward, get a life. Our own lives.'

Zoe snorted. 'You're not saying we should both be married off by now, are you?'

'Not at all.' Leah wrinkled her nose. 'One day, maybe, who knows? It doesn't matter, not yet.' She gave a sudden laugh. 'I'd have to find someone who really cared about me. I'd have to be on equal footing, not like with Aaron. Anyway, I need to learn to be the best person I can be for myself first.' Her grin grew broader. 'I'm not going to settle for an Aaron again. It would need to be someone special. You know, rich, handsome... Next time it might be a Hector or a Blair. Or no one at all. What about you?'

'I'm hopeless, Leah – you know me. I jump into relationships with both feet and then I leap out again.' Zoe shook her head. 'I've just never found anyone who holds my attention long enough...'

'You've had loads of boyfriends,' Leah protested.

'Yes, but I've never really been in love with any of them.'

'Ah, well, that's the problem.' Leah finished her coffee. 'I think it would take a very special man to really keep you interested, Zo. Most of your boyfriends haven't cut the mustard.'

'What would it take then?' Zoe asked, suddenly serious. 'I mean, what would he be, the perfect man who'd make me fall in love with him?'

'Certainly no one like the last ones you picked...' Leah counted on her fingers. 'James was obsessed with his appearance, Martin was obsessed with his job, Oliver was obsessed with you, and I've no idea what you saw in Casper, or Harry... or Tom.'

Zoe shrugged. 'I can't pick a good one, can I?'

Leah brightened as an idea came to her. 'You need someone unusual, intelligent, empathic, with a great personality, who loves

you passionately and will whisk you off your feet and elope with
you to somewhere exotic and romantic.'

'Ha! You mean like Gretna Green?' Zoe stared at the rain
pounding harder against the windscreen and grinned. The service
station was shrouded in grey fog, awash with puddles beneath
heavy clouds.

'Why not? The wild windy borderlands. It's perfect weather out
there for romance.' Leah smiled and the sisters hugged each other,
amusement in their eyes.

Then Zoe sat up straight and stretched her legs. 'Right, Leah, we
should get going. We're on the borders of Bonnie Scotland. Let the
fun begin.'

'Indeed.' Leah leaped out of the Mini as Zoe did the same,
rushing around the front to exchange seats.

Leah started the car and Zoe listened to the comforting rumble
of the engine as the Mini pulled away from the parking space. She
hoped Leah was right, that this job and the fresh start would be
perfect. They both had so much to gain.

9

Agnes and Effie were tired, hungry and shivering with cold. They had travelled for five days, changing direction, begging for scraps of food and water where they could, haplessly asking strangers for directions to Inverness. A farmer with a cart had taken pity on them and handed Agnes handfuls of apples, which they'd shared with the horse. They'd paused, exhausted, in a small village of thatched timber and wattle houses which smelled of smoke, where a widow woman fed them thin broth. They'd slept under trees, in fields or cowsheds, grateful for the high moon that illuminated crowded shadows and for the cool, windless summer nights. The horse was battle-fit and newly shod, able to carry them both steadily on its back, and Effie snuggled happily in Agnes's arms each night, wrapped in Princess Marjorie's fur cloak, sleeping soundly beneath the stars. Agnes had dozed fitfully, her keen ears alert for any sound that might belong to English soldiers in pursuit of the queen. The murder of Colban and Niall de Brus returned to her each night in the darkness, and she shivered at the thought of how the English might treat her and Agnes, particularly if they were discovered with the princess's cloak riding on the king's brother's destrier.

A kindly farmer's wife had pointed towards the road to Inverness and given them bread to eat and water to quench their thirst. Agnes had been terrified as the horse strolled through the streets of the town: she had never seen so many people together. The townspeople had turned curious faces in her direction, asking far too many questions about the horse, the royal emblem emblazoned on its saddle cloth. One woman had grasped the hem of Effie's cloak in her fist and swore harshly, trying to tear it from her shoulders. Agnes had hissed an insult and kicked out, then urged the horse onwards. She knew she had to keep her wits about her. She had ridden on until she came to a friary, where a gently spoken monk gave her and Effie soup and bread, then showed them the road that would take them on to Rosemuir.

They travelled north through a terrain of pine trees and rivers, mountains rising high on one side. It was late afternoon as the horse stumbled into a village of smoky huts, flies buzzing in the warm air. Effie was asleep, slumped against the destrier's neck as Agnes caught sight of the castle by the loch and felt her heartbeat quicken. It was smaller than Kildrummy, but the stones took on a golden sheen in the sunlight and the loch shimmered on three sides. Agnes thought she had never seen anything so beautiful. She wondered if the owners were loyal Scottish people who would keep the English at bay, and if they needed the services of a good baker or a kitchen maid who could turn her hand to most things. It crossed her mind that Queen Elizabeth might still be at Ravenscraig Castle. If so, Agnes would claim to have taken the destrier belonging to King Robert's brother to return Princess Marjorie's cloak and dress safely to her and to tell the queen about her misfortunate brother-in-law. Agnes would beg a favour to stay in the castle and work there; in her wildest imagination, she hoped that the queen would take her on as a servant and allow her and Effie to accompany their party north.

As she rode through the village towards the castle, Agnes was plotting her stories: she would say that Effie was her sister and they were inseparable: it was almost the truth. She would explain that she, Agnes, was the one who had rushed into the great hall and warned the queen that the castle was under siege and saved her from the English: perhaps the queen would recognise her. Agnes doubted it: she'd hardly given her a glance.

Her thoughts slipped again to Colban, to the moment she saw him slaughtered. A life could slip away in an instant, and she wished she'd brought a dagger to protect herself.

Then she heard a gruff voice call from nearby: one of the villagers approached, a bucket of water in his hand. 'That horse needs looking at, lassie, or he'll go lame on ye. He's exhausted, and the wee one too, by the looks of her. When was the last time this fine beast was properly tended and watered?'

'Is this place Rosemuir, and the castle Ravenscraig?' Agnes glanced towards the castle. The portcullis was raised and there was bustling beyond the gatehouse. She stared at the giant of a man, his brawny arms bursting through the rough material of his tunic, his belly protruding over his girdle above flat feet. She didn't hesitate. 'Can ye not see this is a royal horse, man? He will only have the best care. I need to speak to the lady of the castle immediately.'

'Forgive me, wee mistress.' The man laughed scornfully, shaking a shaggy red-brown mane. 'Then ye are in the right place. I am the castle smith around here. I can take your mount for ye. He's too big for the pair of ye – he's a soldier's horse. He could do with some food and water.' He glanced from Agnes to Effie, who was still asleep against the destrier's neck. 'The wee lassie's ready for her bed too. Have ye travelled far?'

Agnes held her head high. In her limited experience, smiths weren't to be trusted and she had no intention of handing over the horse. Words formed in her mouth. 'We were with the royal party. We've come from Kildrummy Castle, where we were entertained by the Earl de Mar. This horse belongs to Niall de Brus himself,' she blurted by way of explanation. 'He gave it to us... Isn't he here?'

'No one's arrived in days...' The giant frowned beneath thick brows. His eyes moved from the royal insignia on the saddle cloth to Effie's fine fur-trimmed cloak. Agnes watched the mocking smile slip from his face and he bowed low. 'I beg forgiveness – I ken now who ye have there.' He lowered his voice conspiratorially. 'It's the princess herself, King Robert's daughter, the bairn whose mother died birthing her.'

'Aye, it is, the Princess Marjorie, tired from her travels,' Agnes replied quickly, attempting a haughty face. If the smith thought Effie was a royal princess, it would ensure a safe introduction. She had no idea what she'd do when Princess Marjorie arrived, but, for now, they had shelter. 'So, will ye take me to the castle so that I might receive some hospitality for my weary young mistress?'

'Indeed, please, follow me. I was fetching water from the well when ye arrived. I am busy at my work.' The giant bowed again. 'I am An-Mòr Logan, at your service. I will take ye and the princess to the master and the mistress. Then, if ye wish it, I'll take your horse to the stables and tend him there. And I'll ask my wife to minister to ye too, lassie – my Rhona is the alewife here. Ye must be hungry after your travels.'

'Indeed...' Agnes was aware that her stomach had been growling all day, but she lifted her chin. 'A little refreshment for me and for the princess would be quite welcome, thanking ye.'

Agnes was trembling as An-Mòr Logan led the destrier across the drawbridge, through the raised portcullis towards the castle, a solid grey-stone building. They passed through the arched main gate into a courtyard, where several soldiers in chainmail coifs and hauberks stood alert, on guard. Agnes breathed deeply; the master was well prepared for a visit from the English armies. She gazed beyond the castle to the loch and held her breath at the beauty of its stillness.

Despite the peaceful setting, her mind was racing, thinking about the reception she might face: the smith had believed Effie to be Princess Marjorie by the cloak she wore and the horse they rode, and in a moment's madness Agnes had deceived him. But the master of the castle might be already acquainted with the royal family and realise that she was lying, or, worse still, Queen Elizabeth and her party might arrive at any moment. Princess Marjorie herself could be seated at a high trestle table in the great hall in a few hours' time, supping with the mistress.

Agnes took a breath; whatever happened, she would find a way to keep herself and Effie safe. And, if the worst came to the worst, she had strong legs – she could run fast.

An-Mòr was speaking to her through his rough beard, and Agnes dragged herself away from her troubled thoughts to listen. He held up a hand that was half the size of a shield, his face gleaming with pride. 'Look at these working hands. They say that my father was a bear and my mother a she-wolf. I can beat any man in a trial of the strong arm. I'm tougher than most, and bigger, but my good wife says I have the heart of a lamb.' He spoke as he walked beside her. 'I live in the village – I make weapons and armour that are needed in the castle, fine daggers too. Many a time I've taken a burn from the scorch of the fire, but I'm the best blacksmith north of Inverness, ask any man. Blacksmiths are called black because they work with metals like iron, did ye know that, lassie?'

Agnes shook her head. 'No, I didn't.' A question formed in her mouth. 'Can ye tell me about the master of the castle? And are there any other visitors expected soon? I mean, the princess is weary and needs to sleep...'

An-Mòr shook his head. 'We've had no visitors for months and we don't want any.'

'No visitors?' Agnes had expected a messenger to have ridden ahead and told of the royal party's imminent arrival.

An-Mòr continued, 'The English aren't welcome, and our

soldiers are ready for them if they do try to attack. The master and his wife are good people – they are kind to the villagers and loyal to King Robert. I hope The Bruce will stay far away from here.'

'Oh?'

'His presence would only bring trouble. There are rumours, lassie, in these parts. We live in terrifying times and there's bloodshed waiting around every corner.'

'What rumours?'

'I heard The Bruce sent his family to safety after the English attacked, and he was forced to hide himself as they gave chase.' An-Mòr frowned. 'And now the wee princess has come here. Ye say that Kildrummy Castle was surprised by the English attack? Did the queen escape? The others?'

'All but one...' Agnes nodded.

The giant's brows lowered over glimmering eyes. 'Aye, and if the English might follow ye here... we don't want that. They'll be searching for The Bruce and his family. The master of Ravenscraig is a peaceful man, although he's ready to fight the English if needs must. But we don't want an attack on our village. We lead a quiet life and it's best kept that way.' He raised a huge palm and Agnes flinched, thinking he might slap the horse and send her onwards, away from the castle.

Her mind raced; she had to play for time.

'Perhaps the master will let us stay for the night. The princess is exhausted – she needs a soft bed and some food. Then tomorrow...' Agnes blurted desperately. 'Perhaps her father the king will be looking for her.'

'King Robert has fled for his life.' An-Mòr led the horse across the castle courtyard, its hooves clacking on cobbles. 'They say he has only a few men around him – no more than fifty. If the English find him, he's done for. And there are always traitors who will sell him for a handful of gold. Old Longshanks believes all Scots men are traitors and that The Bruce is the worst of them all.' His voice lowered confidentially, 'If King Robert came here, the English might follow him. I know The Bruce would rather burn a castle to the ground than let the English have use of it. Every home in the village would become rubble in the name of peace.' He nodded towards Effie, who was still slumbering, the face of an angel crumpled against the horse's neck. 'Aye, the wee princess looks innocent enough, but she may cost us all our lives.'

Agnes met his eyes, her own flashing angrily. 'Are ye afraid to fight for Scotland?'

'Never.' An-Mòr held the horse's reins and extended his free hand, offering to help Agnes dismount. She did so shakily. An-Mòr towered above her and she met his gentle gaze. He gave a sigh that shuddered from his whole body. 'I'd tear the English soldiers limb from limb to the last man with my bare hands if I had to. But...' He brought his face closer to hers. 'Bloodshed is a terrible thing. The stench of spilled blood is foul. Men, women, children, old or bairns, the hard blade of a sword doesn't care where it finds its rest. And the English are savages – they butcher our men as if they were chickens slaughtered for the table, and I ken what they do to our women. I don't suppose you've seen such things in your short life? Aye, death is a shadowy visitor we don't want to greet here at Ravenscraig.'

Agnes stood tall; An-Mòr's shoulder hovered above her head. She was suddenly overcome with anger. 'I'm not afraid.' Her voice was thick with emotion. 'I saw men crushed at Kildrummy. It was the worst thing I've ever beheld and I'm not sure I shall ever recover from the terror of it. But I'm no coward, even if others are. I'm ready to thrust a dagger in the heart of any English soldier to save Scotland, ye can be sure of that.'

'Brave words, lassie. But let's hope they are away and lost in the cold air now they've been spoken. We don't want any bad luck.' The giant shook his head as he lifted Effie gently from the horse, cradling her in his arms asleep like a baby. 'Come along with ye.

We'd better take the wee princess into the castle. I'll find someone to take your horse to the stables and then I'll send word to the mistress that a royal guest has arrived.'

He gave a low whistle and a small boy came running, leading the horse away gently as he made clucking noises. Then An-Mòr strode forward through an arched doorway into shadows, Effie wrapped in the fur cloak in his arms. Agnes looked around at the castle, the busy courtyard, the narrow windows in high turrets, the unmoving soldiers on guard anonymous in chainmail coifs surveying all who passed by, and she took a deep breath, trying to fill her lungs and heart with courage. She had no idea what would happen, but she was ready. She would go into Ravenscraig Castle, tell the best version of her story and, somehow, she'd find a way to keep herself and Effie safe.

10

As Leah drove along the motorway, the rain slowed to a drizzle, then stopped. She felt her mood begin to lift. She stared through the window, watching the scenery change, filled with the thrill of new beginnings. Undulating peaks rose on both sides, steep stretches of green forest.

After lunch in a café on the outskirts of Glasgow, Zoe took over the driving and Leah announced that she was in the mood to channel her 'inner Scot'. She searched on her phone for all the Scottish songs she knew and began to play them one after another, singing along with passion. By the time they reached Perth, the sisters had worked their way through everything they knew by Paolo Nutini, Wet Wet Wet, the Bay City Rollers, Simple Minds and Lulu. Zoe and Leah gazed at snow-covered Aviemore, bawling Franz Ferdinand's 'Take Me Out' at the top of their voices, complete with guitar riff. As they passed through Inverness, they glimpsed the sea, although the sun was setting and the sky had become dim.

An hour later, they approached Rosemuir in darkness; the winding road narrowed through a small village of glimmering houses on both sides. Leah was filled with excitement as she burst into The Proclaimers' 'I'm Gonna Be (500 Miles)' with a dubious Scots accent, drumming lightly on the dashboard with her fingers. Then they saw Ravenscraig Castle.

At first, it was just a silhouette at the edge of the loch, the outline grainy and grey against the night sky. The battlements were illuminated by a few glimmering outdoor lights, giving the courtyard an eerie glow. Zoe shuddered unintentionally as she drove the Mini across a hump in the track where a drawbridge might once have been, towards the main gate, stopping a distance away by the stone well. She gazed towards the loch: the water was inky black, the moon casting a silver reflection on the surface.

Leah was already out of the car, calling excitedly, 'Abigail Laing said she'd put the key under a stone near the main entrance. She said it wouldn't be too hard to find if – oh, here...' She heaved a rock to one side and held up several large cast-iron keys on a ring. 'How about these? Oh, isn't this fantastic?'

Zoe grinned as she rubbed her eyes and stretched tired limbs. 'I can't wait to get in there. We can finish the sandwiches and the drinks we bought, then it's an early night for me.'

'Yes, then tomorrow we'll get our bearings, find a supermarket, buy some food, settle in. Abigail will pop over later in the afternoon. We can explore the castle. Oh, Zoe...' Leah's eyes gleamed. 'This is home for the next three months. I'm so excited. Thank you so much.'

Zoe wrapped an arm around her sister. 'Let's get our cases from the car and go in, shall we?'

A case in each hand, Leah passed beneath the broad stone archway of the walled main gate and led the way across the cobbled courtyard. The fortified loch wall rose high and next to it was a separate wing, a high building which was mostly intact behind a heavy door, although there was rubble from crumbling stones on the far wall.

Zoe walked behind, feeling the uneven ground beneath her

feet, glad that the yellow lights illuminated the corners of the courtyard.

The main building of the castle stood before them, solid and silent. Leah fumbled with the keys, then she pushed open the heavy door that creaked as she stepped into the hall.

Inside, the darkness seemed to move. Leah searched for a light switch and couldn't find one. Zoe paused in the open doorway while Leah edged forward, her footsteps echoing on flagstones as her fingers touched a switch and a dim light came from a heavy chandelier overhead. They found themselves standing in a vast stone hall with a high ceiling, rooms off the corridor to both sides and a narrow spiral stone staircase beyond. The door slammed behind Zoe and she lurched forward, startled.

Leah whispered, 'Well, this is... old. I don't know what I expected, but this place is the real deal. So authentic, even though it's been renovated, it's kept its character, straight from the thirteen hundreds. I'm going to love it here.'

Zoe was less sure. Her voice was nervous. 'Why are we whispering?'

'I don't know,' Leah said. 'Shall we go up the stairs and find our rooms? Abigail told me they'd be at the top, to the right.'

'Right,' Zoe replied. The handles of the cases were digging into the flesh of her hand.

They trudged slowly up the stone steps that twisted round a corner into shadows. Then Zoe became aware of the cold. It wasn't merely the icy cold of October, or the moving draught of the stone interior of a castle. It was beyond cold, Zoe thought: a chill that numbed bones and made them brittle, a cold that hung in every shadowy corner as if holding its breath. And the smell was thick dust and something else, something rotten – leaves or soil. It slipped into her mind that it was the smell of death. She had no idea why the thought had entered her head. It stayed with her, and she shivered.

They reached the top of the stairs and Leah found another switch. An ornate light gleamed high overhead. They were standing in a long corridor of wooden floors, several rooms on either side. Leah led the way into the first bedroom, a sign on the door reading *Private – staff only*. She switched on a lamp by the bed. They stared at wooden panelled walls with a shuttered window and heavy velvet drapes. There was a dark tapestry on the wall depicting a woman in a fitted dress, a bird perched on her finger. The bed was an ornate wooden four-poster, covered with a cream silk eiderdown.

Leah caught her breath. 'Oh, this is just what I hoped it would be. It's glorious.' Her eyes shone as she dropped her cases to the floor and turned to Zoe. 'I'm going to love it here. Isn't this fabulous?'

'It is,' Zoe replied, but her voice was toneless. The air in the castle was all ice and dust. There were none of the home comforts of her warm little flat in Birmingham. She wondered if she had made a wrong choice, coming all the way to the Highlands for three months. She took a breath: she was tired from driving. She would feel differently in the morning.

Leah grabbed one of Zoe's cases. 'Let's find your room now, Zo. It's bound to be just as nice.'

She bounded back to the corridor and rushed into the next room, again switching on a bedroom lamp that cast dim light around. The room was narrower, but there was another four-poster bed with carved wooden posts, a tapestry on the wall of a crowned man in a tunic standing in a circle next to a friar who was writing with a quill. Zoe looked at the bare stone walls, a wooden chair, the high ceiling. She placed her case on the floor and sighed.

Leah was delighted. 'This room is so pretty. Just think who might have slept in here years ago, Zo – princesses or royal visitors. Or perhaps a handsome young man, the son of the lord and lady.'

'Weren't they called lairds?' Zoe asked, tired, half interested.

'Lairds were Scottish landowners in the fifteenth and sixteenth century,' Leah explained. 'This place was built much earlier – late twelve hundreds, Abigail says. I'm going to research it properly for when I do tours.' She tugged her sister's sleeve. 'Shall we go back to my room and have the last sandwiches? It will be just like having a midnight feast when we were kids. We could go exploring afterwards if you like. Abigail said we have a kitchenette and a living room on this floor, a newly fitted bathroom with a shower, and that's our little flat. But I want to see downstairs, the main castle, that is – the crumbly southwest wing is accessible by another key apparently. We could look for the kitchens, the banqueting hall.'

Zoe nodded. 'I'll just have a sandwich and share the last of what's in the flask, then we'll find the bathroom. I was thinking of having an early night. I might get up first thing tomorrow and go for a run. Then we can explore. Or... perhaps we can drive into Rosemuir and see if they have a local pub? We could get brunch there?' She shivered. 'At least it would be warm...'

* * *

Leah slept soundly. She had been cold at first, her feet like ice, her shoulders hunched beneath the coverlet. But as she'd drifted into sleep, she was enveloped in a warmth that carried her into a dreamless slumber, where she stayed until the early morning.

She opened her eyes, blinking into the absolute darkness of the room, reached for her phone and saw that it was approaching eight o'clock. She lay on her back for a while: this was her new life. The thought filled her with a sense of satisfaction: more, anticipation and excitement. Weeks ago, she had found herself sinking into a place where there had been little hope. But now here she was in Scotland. The joy of it propelled her out of bed, her feet quickly numb against the cold flagstone floor. She felt a moving draught ice her skin through thin pyjamas. Her dressing gown was in a case –

she'd unpack later, but excitement launched her into Zoe's room with a pillow in her hand, intending to wake her twin with a gentle thump to the head. The bed was rumpled, but Zoe wasn't there. Leah wondered if she'd gone out running.

Leah headed back to her room; a new thought had come to her. Outside, the sun had risen and there would be a stunning view over the loch. She tugged back the heavy velvet drapes and pressed her nose against the glass. She could see the loch to the left; below was a patch of garden, a clump of trees. The water was pale, mist hanging on the surface like a hovering ghost, and Leah couldn't help the sigh that escaped from her. The view belonged to her now, it was hers every morning.

She gazed around the grounds towards the trees. The garden was damp and strings of mist drifted in clumps. The picture through the window was hazy, in soft focus. Leah leaned forward: there was a figure hiding behind one of the trees. Her eyes narrowed as she tried to see better and a woman emerged from the shadows. She wore a long dark coat, her hair a pale shade of grey to her shoulders. She was hunched, as if looking for something or waiting. Leah wondered why she was in the castle grounds; Abigail had not said there were any other residents, although the woman seemed to be in no hurry to leave. She moved slowly, her face the colour of the whitewashed sky overhead. Then she looked up.

Leah was startled. The woman's eyes were dark against the pallor of her face; she had an almost insolent stare, as if the castle belonged to her. Leah stood back, puzzled, and pulled the drapes across. She'd ask Abigail later who the woman was.

She rushed over to one of her cases, heaved it onto the bed and whisked clothes in all directions until she found a fluffy dressing gown. She shrugged it on and set off down the cold spiral staircase. She'd have a brief look around the castle, then she'd come back to the private rooms and visit the kitchenette to make coffee.

The air was chilly as she turned a corner into the vast great hall.

The ceilings were high, the walls covered in tapestries, primitive pictures of horses with bright carisons, colourful saddle cloths, knights astride holding lances high. A chandelier hung low over a long wooden table, reflecting a circle of golden light on the wooden surface. Leah glanced around in awe: this was home now, and it was incredible.

She moved to the table, sitting down on one of the high-backed chairs, wondering how much of the furniture was original. There was a sense of time having stood still and she closed her eyes for a moment and imagined how it might have been centuries ago, back in the thirteen hundreds. Images flooded into her mind, pictures she had probably seen in history books or on screen. But the scene was certainly vivid; men in dark tunics were sprawled, some on benches, crowding around the table, the master and mistress perched on tall chairs, their heads together, drinking. The master had a thick beard and was leaning across, whispering something; the mistress, her hair plaited and coiled, met his eyes and smiled. In the shadows, guards stood, clad in silver chainmail. There were many guests at the long table, laughing, talking loudly, the noise buzzing and echoing towards the high ceiling. Leah imagined dishes of food crammed on the table: wild boar, venison, rabbit, grouse, fish, even swans and peacocks. There were colourful fruits in bowls, bread, oatcakes, fritters. The gathering was merry as a slender servant girl, her curls pushed beneath a cap, brought more dishes, filling goblets from a jug.

Leah opened her eyes and the noise had gone. She gazed around the vast hall from the vantage point of her tall chair and shuddered.

11

A serving woman led them up a stone spiral staircase, pointing to the second room on a long corridor, promising in a quiet voice that the mistress would be up to greet them 'by and by'.

An-Mòr placed Effie carefully beneath soft covers in the four-poster bed of a narrow room with a high ceiling before bowing and disappearing quickly. Effie slumbered as Agnes shivered, pushing her curls beneath the dirty cap as she sat at the foot of the bed, the silk dress and fur-lined cloak that Effie had taken from Princess Marjorie rumpled on her lap. She wondered what to do as she tugged the cloak around her knees, thinking hard. An-Mòr had said that the master and mistress were kind people; he had told her that there were no other visitors, that the royal party wasn't here. Agnes was concerned for their safety: perhaps they'd changed direction and gone elsewhere. She hoped they hadn't been apprehended. An-Mòr had assumed that Effie was the king's daughter and Agnes should have told the truth there and then. But there was much to be gained by everyone believing that Effie was Princess Marjorie: they would be given food and shelter, treated kindly. But what if they were discovered, especially if one of the king's loyal soldiers found out and told The Bruce that his daughter was at Ravenscraig. If he arrived and Effie was exposed, there would be trouble. Which was worse, that they had stolen the cloak and Niall de Brus's horse, or lied about Effie's identity?

Agnes was still shaken from the events at Kildrummy, her mind slipping back to Morag and Biddy in the bakehouse, and she wondered what had become of them at the hands of the English soldiers. She had not quite made up her mind what to do when there was a knock on the door.

Agnes looked into the strong gentle gaze of a woman in fine clothes, her plaited hair coiled, dropped a curtsy instinctively and said, 'Madam.'

The woman stepped into the room and spoke with a calm voice. 'The princess is asleep?'

Agnes nodded and curtsied again.

'And ye are her maid?'

Agnes shook her head vigorously. 'No, Madam. I worked in the bakehouse at Kildrummy. I helped... the young lady escape. I took the destrier because the owner was killed and we were afraid for our lives. The English soldiers were there—'

The woman held up her hand. 'And the Queen Elizabeth? What of her and the rest of her party?'

'The rest of the royal party escaped before us, Madam, apart from the king's brother. I saw what the English did to him. They hung him up and...' She stopped as she noticed the mistress's brow crease. 'I'm so sorry for it, Madam.'

'Yet they haven't arrived here before ye. I fear the worst for them, but we've heard nothing.' The mistress nodded. 'Poor child, what ye must have seen. And I suppose ye haven't eaten in days?'

'Wee scraps, not much more...' Agnes gazed down at her muddy hands and dirty nails.

The woman smiled. 'I am Muriel McNair. My husband Ross owns this castle. We are no friends of the English here.'

Agnes nodded. 'I'm glad to hear it.'

'I will speak with Princess Marjorie when she wakes. But we'll let her sleep the while. She's exhausted, poor bairn. I'll have a maid come up to wait on her and bring her something to nourish her.'

'I can look after her,' Agnes spoke quickly. 'She trusts me...'

Muriel smiled. 'Go to the kitchens and tell them to feed ye. Then I'll ask some of my girls to get ye some clean clothes.' Her face took on a softness. 'Ye must have been through a hard time. We heard here that an English army had descended on Kildrummy. We've no news of the Earl de Mar and his family. I'm sure we'll hear it from our loyal men soon. Meanwhile...' she gazed towards the bed, 'let the young one sleep. Go and get yourself some food.'

'Madam, I will.' Agnes curtsied as she watched Muriel walk away. She frowned, unsure whether to wake Effie. Her stomach growled; there was food in the kitchens and the thought of it reminded her how hungry she was. She rushed to the head of the bed and shook Effie's shoulder gently.

Effie moaned and rolled over.

'Effie...' Agnes hissed. 'Open your eyes the while. I need to tell ye something...'

Effie's eyes flickered. 'Where am I?'

'You're in a bed – we're in a castle in Ravenscraig, and the mistress is very nice, but ye—'

Effie sat up. 'How did I get here? I was on horseback and I felt so cold...'

'Effie, listen.' Agnes grasped her hand. 'They think you're Princess Marjorie, because ye have her cloak and we were riding the king's brother's horse...'

'I dinnae understand...'

'Listen to me, hennie.' Agnes urged. 'When they come up here, pretend to be asleep. Don't wake. And if ye do, don't speak. Your voice will give ye away. Say nothing...'

Effie was smiling. 'So I'm the princess now?' She looked pleased with herself. 'I'm Princess Marjorie? Then I can keep the dress and cloak.'

'Say nothing until I'm back, ye hear?' Agnes insisted. 'I have to work out what to do. If they find out the truth, we're done for.'

'Where are ye going?' Effie was alarmed.

'To the kitchen to fill my belly. You'll have a maid bring food to ye here…'

'I'm half starved,' Effie began.

Agnes put a finger to her lips. 'Just stay silent,' she whispered. 'Give me time to work out what to do. Do ye understand?'

'I do,' Effie said quickly, dropping her head onto the pillow and squeezing her eyes closed. 'I'm asleep now, can ye not see?'

Agnes almost smiled. Then she made her voice stern. 'Not a word, Effie. Not a single word.'

'I cannae even speak,' Effie muttered into the pillow and laughed. 'Aye, but it's fun being a princess and being given a bed to sleep in. I could get used to it. And are my servants bringing me food? Can ye tell them all to make haste?'

'Hush awhile.' Agnes gave Effie a severe look. 'Feign sleep. And I'll make plans for us when I'm back.'

'Very well,' Effie whispered. Agnes moved to the door and Effie called, 'Aye, but can I keep the cloak?'

'Say nothing – sleep,' Agnes whispered, and was gone.

* * *

Agnes smelled the kitchen before she found it. The aroma of baking meat in her nostrils led her to a vast room where several cooks were roasting a pig over a huge fire. Rushes covered the dirt floor. A young woman was seated, her face creased in concentration as she plucked a grouse, feathers flying around her head, and two small girls were preparing beans. Two men were bringing in water in buckets, baskets of fish, fruit and vegetables.

Agnes stood quietly, taking in her surroundings, remembering the bakehouse at Kildrummy. To her surprise, her legs were shaking. Then someone was by her side, a small bony woman wearing a cap. Agnes inhaled the scent of roasted barley and said, 'Ye must be the alewife.' Then she remembered. 'You're Rhona, An-Mòr's good wife. I'm pleased to make your acquaintance...'

The grip on her arm tightened. 'And you're hardly able to stand up, lassie. Sit ye down before ye fall down. I'll bring ye ale and bread and some pottage.'

'Thank ye.' Agnes was glad to be led to a stool, where a cup was pushed into her hand, a hunk of bread and a trencher of food laid in her lap.

Rhona's eyes glinted. 'You're filthy dirty and half starved. My husband told me he'd found ye in the village on a battle horse, with the wee princess.' The alewife's face came closer. 'Aye, what ye must've seen at Kildrummy is frightful.' She whispered, 'Did the English come over the wall with swords and daggers? Tell what happened there to the queen and the royal party? And how did ye come to escape with the princess?'

Agnes sipped her drink eagerly. Behind Rhona's shoulder, several other people had gathered, the cooks and the maids standing in a huddle, all staring at her. The fire in the hearth threw orange light around the kitchen and Agnes saw a figure move in the shadows, then stand still, listening. Agnes thought of the smith at Kildrummy, of his eager treason, and she met Rhona's gaze. 'There's no princess.' She raised her voice. 'There's no one else arrived here today but me.'

Rhona narrowed her eyes: she understood Agnes's fear of being overheard immediately. She nodded slowly and hissed, 'I hear Kildrummy was razed to the ground?'

'I saw the fire.' Agnes bit into the bread hungrily. 'I saw what happened to the king's brother. Then I left.'

'Did ye see English soldiers?' Rhona asked.

'Aye, many of them. I saw them murder good Scots people...'
Agnes's eyes moved to where the shadow had been standing, just
beyond the firelight. 'We were betrayed by the castle smith.'

'What did he do?' Rhona pressed thin lips together.

'They paid him as much gold as he could carry to start a fire so
the English army could surprise the castle,' Agnes said. She saw
another movement in the shadows.

'He'll be made to suffer, the traitor,' Rhona spat, then she turned
to the crowd of listeners. 'Away with ye all – the lassie's exhausted.
Let her eat in peace.' She watched the servants move back to their
work, then she whispered, 'Ye are wise to say nothing about the
princess. Aye, ye never know who's listening, friend or foe. An-Mòr
will keep a secret too. And our son, Hendrie. He's loyal to the king –
he's with The Bruce at the moment, keeping close, biding his time.
There will be a battle against the English armies when they have
amassed enough loyal men, you'll see.'

'Your son is a warrior of the king?'

'Aye, I'm proud of him.' Rhona took the empty cup from Agnes's
hand. 'My laddie Hendrie is ready to fight for *Scotia*. Will ye take
another spoonful of pottage?'

'I will – it's good.' Agnes closed her eyes for a moment; her
strength was returning. 'And I like it here in the kitchen. It's warm
and the company is friendly.'

'Not all here are to be trusted, lassie...' Rhona took Agnes's cup
in her bony hand. 'Walls have ears in Ravenscraig. But the master
and mistress are good people and most here are loyal to The Bruce.
For every traitor, there are fifty, a hundred, loyal Scots men and
women. And we are not afraid to stand up for what we love most –
our country, our king.'

Agnes watched Rhona move across to the fire, ladling pottage
into the empty bowl. She returned on silent feet. 'Here. Fill your
belly.'

'Thanking ye,' Agnes said. 'You've been very kind.'

'Then you'll be off upstairs, back to the princess?' Rhona asked gently. 'How fares the wee lassie? What that poor bairn must have suffered, losing her mother at birth. But they say the Queen Elizabeth is a strong woman and as kind as any true mother would be. Did ye see the queen at Kildrummy?'

'I did,' Agnes whispered. She trusted Rhona, who was honest and spoke from the heart. 'It was I who told her that the English had surprised the castle, and she rode away on a palfrey along with the other women and the earl. She was very calm the whole time. I managed to get away on the destrier, but not before I saw them cut the king's brother open. They hung him in the courtyard. And I saw them kill my friend, Colban. He was trying to help me escape and...' Agnes was surprised that tears choked her words.

Rhona grasped her hand. 'You've been brave, lassie. And you'll be safe here awhile, God willing. A young one your age should not see such things. How old are ye?'

Agnes sat up straight, wiping her eyes. 'I'm no child – I'm twenty-two years old.'

'I was wed at your age,' Rhona said softly.

'I've no need for a husband.' Agnes's eyes flashed. 'I can live well enough by my own wits.'

'You've never had someone special, a handsome laddie?'

'None at all.' Agnes thought about Colban. He had been sweet on her and she'd liked him, but there had been nothing more than friendship on her side. She wished she could have felt more but, she told herself secretly, she'd never meet a man with enough courage and wit to match her own. The thought of such a person made her smile. 'Aye, I've no doubt I'll be a spinster all my days. Being a good wife, waiting on a man's every wish or dying in my bed while birthing isnae how I intend my life to be.'

'Do ye intend to stay in kitchens working your fingers to the bone?'

'For now, aye,' Agnes retorted. 'But I know there's something else for me. I ken not what it is yet, but I have fire in my heart.' She frowned. 'When I saw the English kill my friend at Kildrummy, my first thought was to escape and to look after... after the princess... But my second thought was to grab a dagger and fight back.'

'There are more ways to fight than with a dagger in your hand,' Rhona said quietly. 'My advice to ye is to find yourself a good man. Someone whose spirit matches your own and settle down, raise a family.'

Agnes laughed. 'I don't believe there's such a man.'

'There's someone for every one of us,' Rhona said sagely. 'Ye met my husband. He's a good man.'

'He is,' Agnes agreed.

'He has a big heart.' Rhona chuckled. 'A big man in all departments, that's the truth of it, and I love him dearly. Now...' She glanced towards the door. 'You'd better get back upstairs, or you'll be missed. But we'll meet again...' Rhona's face was set determinedly. 'Oh, aye, we'll see each other soon and talk some more. Now take care, lassie.'

'Thank ye for your kindness.' Agnes grasped Rhona's hand. 'I'm grateful, truly...'

'Get on with ye,' Rhona said, then she was on her way back to the wide barrel where she was soaking barley.

Agnes gazed around and saw the young woman who had plucked a grouse was now skinning a rabbit. Agnes glanced towards the shadows where she had seen movement, but all was still. She'd make her way back to Effie.

Agnes rushed up the narrow stone staircase. It had been warm in the kitchen, but a draught spiralled from the upper corridor and made her shiver. The light from the wall sconces led the way to the bedroom where she had left Effie. Agnes pushed the door open and stood still, suddenly afraid, her heart pounding. Effie was sitting upright in bed, clutching the fur-lined cloak, tears on her cheeks. The mistress, Muriel McNair, was standing at the bottom of the bed, her arms folded, her face creased in displeasure. Agnes was unsure what to say, then Effie burst out, 'I'm sorry, Agnes. It wasnae my fault. I didnae mean to speak. Ye told me to keep my mouth shut... but the mistress asked me things and I couldnae help myself.'

12

Zoe and Leah drove back from Rosemuir, their car full of groceries. Zoe was keen to stay for longer in the village to visit the local inn, but Leah was anxious to return to the castle as Abigail Laing had texted that she'd arrive at two o'clock. Zoe drove the Mini across the hump in the track, into the castle grounds, stopping by the old stone well, parking next to a silver Porsche Boxster. It was one fifteen.

Leah scrabbled out towards an elegant woman in a woollen coat, who extended her hand and said, 'Hello, Leah. I'm so pleased to meet you. I'm Abigail Laing.'

'Hi, Abigail – you have a lovely car,' Leah said nervously.

'It's one of my many indulgences.' Abigail put a hand to her smooth light hair. 'I'm amused by the way it makes male drivers react – some are aggressive, others fawning. It makes me smile every day.' She turned to Zoe. 'And this must be your sister.'

'Zoe Drummond.' Zoe stretched out a hand and shook Abigail's. 'Pleased to meet you.'

'It's kind of you to come out to see us on a Sunday,' Leah said breathlessly.

'Not at all,' Abigail replied. 'I wanted to make sure you were settled into your rooms and that you had some time with me by way of an induction. Shall we go in?'

'Let's,' Leah shivered as she produced the huge metal keyring from her handbag.

Abigail led the way up the stone spiral stairs, her heels echoing on each step. She paused outside one of the doors marked *Private* and said, 'Shall we go into the living room?'

'I'll make us all tea,' Zoe said tactfully, dashing to the kitchenette, leaving Leah and Abigail standing in a dark sitting room. The walls had been painted deep red, the sofa was brown leather and the carpet a plush burgundy. Overhead, a cluster of gilt-edged lamps hung low. The rest of the furniture was heavy polished oak, a dresser, a small dining table and a television in the corner.

Abigail smiled. 'We keep these rooms for our caretaker, so it's less about historical accuracy and more about comfort, somewhere you can relax. The fourth room was used as an office, but I had it converted to the second bedroom for your sister. I hope you'll be warm enough. The castle itself can be quite cold in wintertime. I suggest you keep the fire on all year round.'

'Thank you.' Leah sat on the sofa.

Abigail walked over to the window, tugging open heavy drapes, and gazed out. 'I love the view of the loch from here.'

'It's beautiful,' Leah agreed. 'I can see it from my bedroom window too, but there's also a good view of the garden.' She remembered that she had a question. 'I wanted to ask – I looked out this morning at about eight, and there was a woman in the garden, grey-haired, slim. Does she work here?'

Abigail still had her back to Leah as she said, 'That will be Mirren Logan. She's paid to come in from time to time to look after the southwest wing – the building that's across the courtyard. It's the last one we need to renovate. I'll let you have the timeline for that later. I'd give Mirren a wide berth – she can be a little eccentric, but she does a good job, so I keep her on. We keep the southwest wing separate, it's not to be included on tours or photo shoots.'

'Oh?' Leah was interested.

'It's all dust and cobwebs – the stonework needs repairing. The owner's aim is to restore the entire castle to its former glory. He's had it built up from a semi-ruin.'

'That must have been expensive,' Leah said.

'It's a passion of his.' Abigail moved to the sofa and sat down, crossing her legs. She was still wearing the woollen coat. 'The castle was not much more than rubble for centuries. He bought it as a project seven years ago and he's spent a small fortune doing it up. He plans to open it up eventually for tourists, film crews, visitors, but at the moment it's just used for small projects. That's why you're here.' She looked up as Zoe came in with a tray of tea and biscuits. 'Just a dash of milk.'

'So, who is the owner?' Leah asked. 'Does he live locally?'

'Oh no.' Abigail reached for her cup and took a small sip. 'I do all his accounts from here, but he travels extensively. He's based in Guangzhou, in China, at the moment.'

'Really?' Leah was impressed. 'He must be incredibly rich.'

Abigail put her cup down. 'I doubt you'll meet him.' She changed the subject. 'Have you had a chance to have a look around the castle properly?'

Zoe shook her head and Leah said, 'I went into the great hall this morning and sat at the long table. It's a very beautiful room.'

'You should familiarise yourself with the whole castle.' Abigail pointed to a shelf behind the television. 'There are books and some files of information about the history and background. You'll no doubt be contacted by interested parties over the next few weeks: we get more inquiries than bookings, though. People love a castle and a loch or a good medieval interior as part of their photo shoot, so you'll be expected to have all the information to hand.' She smiled. 'I was delighted that you have a history degree, Leah.

You're ideal for this post in so many ways. And you seem level-headed.'

'Oh, she is.' Zoe offered biscuits. 'We both are.'

Abigail lifted a hand, declining bourbons. 'That's good. An old castle by a loch will come with baggage, visitors expecting spooks and skeletons in cupboards, that sort of thing.' She almost smiled. 'This is a modern business, and I'm not keen to encourage superstition, although some of the locals are steeped in tradition.'

'Of course,' Leah agreed. 'I'm going to love it here.'

Abigail turned to Zoe. 'I've made sure these rooms have good internet reception for remote working, so I'm sure you'll soon settle. It's peaceful here, but Inverness is only a short drive away and all the modern amenities are there.'

'I like peace best,' Leah said as Abigail stood slowly.

'Well, is there anything you want to ask? Would you like a quick tour of the place before I go?'

Leah shook her head. 'I'm sure you're busy...'

'Then I'll leave you to get acquainted with Ravenscraig. I won't call in unless you need something – I have plenty to keep me occupied, but...' She met Leah's grin, her own face serious. 'We'll update each other each week by email. Do keep me in the loop of what's going on here, let me have details of any tours or visits you arrange, and don't hesitate to contact me if there's anything else.'

'Oh, of course, yes.' Leah stood up and stretched out a hand. 'Thanks, Abigail.'

'It's a pleasure to have you here,' Abigail smiled professionally. 'I'll see myself out.' She glanced towards Zoe. 'Good to meet you.'

Leah reached for a biscuit, listening to Abigail's heels ring down the stone staircase. She raised her eyebrows. 'Well, I get the feeling I'll be left to my own devices most of the time. That's good. She seems like the perfect boss.'

'She knows she can trust you to do the job well,' Zoe agreed. 'And she'll be there if we need anything, so that's ideal.'

'I can't believe how easy it was to get the job. I just seemed to breeze in. Perhaps it's because there were no other applicants?'

'She loved your application.' Zoe frowned. 'She didn't say much about the last residents... except that they didn't stay long.'

'They didn't like the place. I love it. I'm disappointed we can't meet the castle owner, though.'

'Me too,' Zoe agreed. 'But he's in China. He probably has a luxury high-rise penthouse there.' She grinned. 'Shall we unload the shopping and make some lunch? Let's have some soup. I'm starving.'

'Okay. Then I'm desperate to look round the castle.' Leah's eyes shone. 'Zoe, it's going to be such good fun living in Ravenscraig.'

* * *

An hour later, Leah was leading the way down the spiral staircase, a notepad in her hand. Zoe followed behind her, wearing a thick jumper and gloves. Leah didn't seem to notice the cold as she strode into the great hall, marvelling at the high ceilings. The floor was made of grey flagstones, the walls stone, and there were two enormous windows, each with a view of the loch. The long table filled much of the space, chairs and benches all around.

Zoe indicated a huge hearth, filled with logs. 'That must have thrown out some heat in its time.' She shivered. 'The people who lived here probably needed a fire that size to stay warm.'

'This was quite a humble castle compared to many,' Leah said. 'But it would have supported a great number of people living and working nearby. I think the woodshed in the courtyard used to be a forge and stables. The walls are thick and high for defence, so I imagine it was built that way to hold back the loch or to keep invaders out.' She smiled. 'The English, probably.'

Conscious of their echoing voices, Leah and Zoe left the banqueting hall and walked along a stone passageway into the kitchen. The light inside from the window was dim; hooks with iron cooking pans of various size hung from the ceiling. Leah and Zoe gazed at shelves stacked with plates, trestle tables with huge pots, ladles, knives, even a primitive grater. Zoe was fascinated by the open hearth with adjustable hooks for hanging cauldrons.

Leah said, 'They'd have been able to roast a whole ox on that fire. Or delicate things like quails. Bread too, and stews. And they'd have made their own ale in barrels.' She was thoughtful. 'Imagine all the bustle and noise in here, Zo. Servants rushing about, the whole place full of smoke.'

Zoe breathed in deeply. 'I'm sure I can still smell it, the smoke of the fire, the roasting pigs and venison.'

'It's your imagination.' Leah shook her head. 'But it's easy to visualise how life would have been in the thirteen hundreds. I'm so looking forward to showing people around Ravenscraig.'

'Do you think any of this stuff is original, the pots and plates?' Zoe frowned. 'Or do you think the rich owner bought it all in as props for visitors?'

'Who knows? The floor in here isn't authentic – kitchen floors were covered in straw and dirt,' Leah replied. 'But you can imagine a servant's life here. It would have been hard work being a kitchen maid.'

'Where's the sink?' Zoe asked.

'Water would come from the well outside, or the loch,' Leah explained. 'There was no running water, so even simple washing tasks meant bringing in bucketfuls from outside.'

'What about baths and toilets?' Zoe pulled a face.

'People didn't have the luxury of baths.' Leah grinned. 'Rich people like the ones who owned this castle might have had toilets, called garderobes, that stuck out the side of the castle, with a hole in the bottom so that everything dropped into a pit or the loch.'

'Yuk!' Zoe grimaced, but then she clapped her hands. 'Leah,

you're amazing – you're going to be so good at taking people around the castle.'

'Oh, I hope so.' Leah grinned, then she adopted a clear, authoritative voice. 'Right, ladies and gentlemen, we continue our tour of Ravenscraig castle to...' She rushed to the kitchen door. 'There's a corridor along here and another spiral staircase.' She had already disappeared and her voice flowed back as an echo. 'Come on, Zo – we're going upstairs to look at the guest bedrooms.'

Zoe was about to follow her sister when a metal goblet on the table caught her eye. She picked it up and studied it carefully. It was mottled and dented now, but it had the remains of an ornate decoration, the face of a bearded man next to a woman with curls. Zoe smiled as she turned it over in her hands. A serving girl might have filled it full of ale and taken it to the master in the great hall before she dropped a low curtsy.

Then she shuddered. The air had become stone cold, the harsh chill of it made her bones rigid and she couldn't move. Zoe caught her breath, her senses tingling. Someone was behind her, inches away, she was sure. A cold breath touched her neck. Zoe believed that if she turned, someone would be standing right in front of her, facing her eye to eye. She was tense with fear, but she steeled herself and whirled around. There was no one there.

Zoe blinked hard, scanning the kitchen for the final time, then she placed the goblet on the table and rushed through the doorway, running towards the spiral staircase as fast as she could.

13

'Come inside and close the door behind ye.' Muriel McNair narrowed her eyes as she spoke to Agnes. 'Now, I want the truth, and all of it.'

'I'm sorry, Madam...' Effie began to sob. 'I didnae mean—'

'Hush your mouth.' The mistress lifted a finger, her face flushed with anger. She stared at Agnes. 'Well? Why are ye both here? Where is Princess Marjorie and how did ye come by her cloak and dress, and Niall's horse?'

Agnes examined Effie's face for a clue about what had happened, but Effie was sobbing, her eyes swollen, her expression desperate.

'We didn't mean to deceive ye, Madam,' Agnes began slowly. 'The smith who works here saw the cloak and the horse and he thought...' Agnes took a deep breath: it wasn't fair to blame An-Mòr. 'I am deeply sorry. We had the cloak because we were going to take it to the lavender woman so that she could clean it for the princess. The truth is, we escaped from the castle on the king's brother's horse. There was so much fighting and I heard mention of

Ravenscraig Castle, so we came here to seek help.' She tried again. 'To seek work, if we can...'

'There's no sign of the queen and her party here yet.' Muriel sighed. 'How many people believe the wee girl is Princess Marjorie? Who knows she's here?'

'Only the smith and yourself, Madam. In the kitchens, everyone was asking if there was a royal guest, and I told them nay, it was just me.'

'I see.' Muriel was thoughtful. 'It may yet be well if the English don't suspect Marjorie's here. Or perhaps the king has discovered where his wife and child are already. Perhaps they've reached a safe place – Skye, one of the islands. I've heard no word...'

Agnes said nothing. Effie was snivelling, her eyes wide with fear.

Then Muriel's expression hardened. 'I ought to throw ye both out into the wilds, leave ye for the wolves to feed on. There are bears out there too...'

'Madam, I beg ye...' Effie was crying again.

Agnes found her tongue. 'We can work hard, Madam. We are both good workers, my... my sister and I. We'll work for scraps and sleep on the floor the nights. We can both bake good bread, and I can cook wild boar on the spit and skin rabbits—'

'Enough.' Muriel held up a hand. 'If you're both seen working in the kitchens, it will be clear to all that there's no princess here, which is just what I want people to think. It matters not to me if they ken ye are no more than a brace of lying lasses. Mind, I have no time for liars here in Ravenscraig, so be warned...'

'I'd rather my tongue be cut out, Madam—' Effie began.

Agnes interrupted her. 'We beg forgiveness. Our lies came only from fear for our lives. We are no friends to the English, ye can rest assured of that.'

'I'll speak to An-Mòr and Rhona Logan, explain to them how ye escaped from Kildrummy. God knows what has happened to all those poor people there. The English army will have hold of the place now.' Muriel sighed again. 'Well, ye will both go to the kitchens and earn your food. I'll expect ye to work hard. And ye will answer to Rhona – she'll be told to give ye both a beating if ye slack. And if ye lie to me again, or if I hear of ye talking to strangers, I'll throw ye both to the wolves myself. Ye ken?'

'Aye, Madam,' Effie said quickly and Agnes nodded once.

Muriel picked up the cloak from the bed. 'It is to be hoped Marjorie and Elizabeth are safe. Who can imagine what will become of them if they are caught?' She stroked the soft material thoughtfully, collecting it in her arms. 'I'll show this cloak to my husband. We have much to talk about.' She pulled herself upright suddenly. 'Well, what are ye waiting for? Tell Rhona Logan I sent ye. And be quick about it.'

Effie was already scuttling away towards the door.

Agnes curtsied low. 'Aye, and ye won't regret this, Madam. I swear it on my life.'

* * *

Rhona made sure Agnes and Effie worked hard into the night. There was much scrubbing of fire-blackened pots and washing recently unearthed beets. Agnes was sent to prepare oats for the breakfast porridge and Effie was shown how to skin a rabbit by a thin-lipped young woman called Una, who Agnes had seen earlier, plucking a grouse. Una appeared to take a delight in tweaking Effie's ear until she cried.

Rhona watched Agnes constantly, sending her to make bannock bread, standing behind her shoulder to observe her deft hands at work.

Then she said quietly, 'The mistress is angry with ye, Agnes. She's not a woman to be crossed.'

'Aye, I ken.'

Rhona didn't move. 'Tomorrow morning you'll wake before

dawn and go to the well, outside the keep. You'll bring in some water so that we can heat it on the fire. Ye hear me?'

'Aye.' Agnes shaped the bread for proving.

Rhona was quiet for a moment, then she said, 'I believe ye and Effie came here from Kildrummy with no malice in your hearts. I believe ye should have a chance in the kitchen.'

Agnes murmured thanks without turning round.

Rhona put a hand on her shoulder. 'I'm a good judge of people, Agnes, and I know a traitor when I see one.'

'I'm no traitor,' Agnes replied firmly.

'I ken. You're a strong lassie, ye have your wits about ye and ye can speak up for yourself. That's well. But your sister, she's softer somehow. How old is she?'

'Sixteen, I think, but she has some growing to do yet.' Agnes placed loaves in trays for baking. 'She's not had it easy since her mother died.'

'Her mother? I thought ye were sisters?'

'We share the same father,' Agnes replied quickly. 'She's as good as any sister to me.'

'Agnes, there are people in this castle who are not to be trusted, who would sell us to the English for a pocketful of gold. Be careful who ye talk to.'

'I will.'

'My son Hendrie is living out there in the wild, fighting for the king. He has a wife, a bairn I've not seen yet. I'm proud of him. My husband is a good man and a strong one, but he likes a quiet life. Whereas I—'

Agnes picked up the tray laden with bread. 'Aye, you'd not be afraid to stand up to the English soldiers. Nor I, Rhona. I saw what they did to my friend Colban. I can promise ye, I have no love for them.'

'We will talk more of this later,' Rhona said. She glanced around the kitchen. 'Get that bread baked, then get yourself some pottage.

When the bannock bread is done, find a place to settle for the night. You've both had a long day of it.'

'Thank ye,' Agnes muttered, looking round for Effie. She saw her sitting by the fire, her arms wrapped around herself, staring into the flames half-asleep.

Zoe could not sleep. She lay in the four-poster bed staring into the darkness. It was so different to the night-time she was used to in Birmingham. Whenever she woke in her own bedroom, she was snug and warm; she could always see the room clearly when she opened her eyes by the glowing lights outside in the streets. This Scottish darkness was like treacle, impenetrable, and the silence was oppressive. Zoe was used to the reassuring swish of car tyres against tarmac, the occasional rhythm of a police car's siren or the shuffling of a bus starting and stopping. But here in Ravenscraig the silence was unsettling. The castle was cold; even beneath the coverlet, Zoe's feet and the skin of her face were chilled. She curled up, hugging herself for comfort and promised herself she'd order a high-tog duvet and some knitted bed socks on the internet the following morning.

Her mind was racing; sleep wouldn't come. Zoe's thoughts moved back to the incident in the kitchen, the profoundly real sense of someone standing close behind her. She offered herself all the rational responses: she was alone in a kitchen of an ancient castle; her imagination was at its strongest. It hadn't been real; there was no one there. She hadn't mentioned it to Leah; they'd visited the guest bedrooms upstairs, gazed at rich velvet drapes, ornate tapestries, carved bedposts, glorious views of the loch, the castle courtyard and the southwest wing opposite. But the cold feeling in her bones, the prickling sense of someone watching not far away, had lingered. It was with her now.

Zoe thought about the desolate wing; Leah had said that it was going to be rebuilt and that there was a woman who came in to clean it sometimes. Zoe wondered why it wasn't part of Leah's duties. Leah was so happy; the role of caretaker at Ravenscraig had already transformed her, filled her with a sense of purpose and importance. Zoe was not going to spoil that by telling her that she'd felt a strange presence earlier today. Leah would only tell her she was imagining things.

Zoe glanced at her phone on the bedside table: it was past four. She'd get up early, go for a run in first light before she started work: she had a meeting with Sharon at ten to discuss the progress of a charity project. She recalled a path she had found that ran parallel with the loch. It was beautiful, pine trees to her right, a forest that concealed deer, perhaps wild boar. She might find a detour into the woods, explore a little before autumn became winter and the bad weather arrived.

Zoe imagined herself warmly clothed, her cheeks glowing as she ran along a snow-encrusted path, the sunshine dazzling against the white drifts. She was looking forward to the rest of her stay in Scotland. She wasn't going to let the incident in the kitchen spoil her fun or Leah's. It was Leah's first working day and she was already full of enthusiasm, talking non-stop through dinner of the tours, the photo shoots, how Ravenscraig would be a perfect wedding venue and how wonderful it would be if Mariusz and Jordan were the first couple to enjoy a wedding reception in the great banqueting hall on Valentine's Day.

Zoe stretched aching limbs. She'd get herself a cup of calming chamomile tea and go back to bed. She flicked on the bedside lamp and eased herself out, reaching for a dressing gown. Her bare feet were cold against the wooden floors as she crossed the hall to the kitchenette, switched on a light and filled the kettle. Her hands moved automatically, finding a cup, a teabag, pouring hot water, then she sat at the small table and cupped her hands around the mug, breathing in the aroma of crushed flowers. Zoe pushed a hand through her curls and smiled; a week ago, her life had been routine and Leah's had been a car crash. Now they were living in a beautiful castle in Scotland and, despite the numbing cold that now encased her feet, they would enjoy the adventure.

Zoe finished the tea, her fingers warmer now. She took the mug to the sink, washing it beneath running water, upturning it to drain. The clock on the stone wall showed that it was twenty minutes to five and Zoe was ready to go back to bed. She was about to turn off the light, then she realised she hadn't yet seen the view from the arched window that overlooked the courtyard. She walked over, gazing down at the yellow lights that illuminated the cobbles, the main gate of the keep, the crenelated loch wall to the right and the dark water beyond. In the corner stood the southwest wing, a column of grey stone in shadow. Zoe wondered what the southwest wing had been used for in medieval times, a place of worship or if someone important had resided there.

She was about to move away when something caught her eye: there was a faint light in the ground-floor window. She looked again: she must have been wrong. The southwest wing was in darkness. Then she saw it behind the window, a small moving light. Zoe wondered if it was a torch, but the light disappeared again.

Zoe shook her head. It was probably the reflection of a car's headlights. She'd think no more about it. She flicked off the light and walked back to her room, her limbs felt heavy. She was tired now: sleep would come soon.

14

Leah was thoroughly enjoying herself: she'd set up her laptop at the desk by the living-room window, enabling her to look out over the loch and the courtyard. There was a leaping fire in the hearth; Zoe was sitting at the table opposite, earbuds in, ready for her video meeting with Sharon.

Leah checked the emails of her new account linked to the caretaking role at Ravenscraig. Abigail Laing had sent her a welcome message an hour ago and Leah had replied immediately, asking if she could update the Ravenscraig Castle website. She'd explained carefully that some photos were dark, making the rooms appear a little unwelcoming, and she'd like to replace them. She also asked if she could add some historical detail to the website, making the venue an ideal location not just for the scenery but also for its medieval background.

Leah imagined herself with a clipboard in hand taking academics on tours, discussing Robert the Bruce and his battles with Edward I. Although Bannockburn, the site of the first war of Scottish independence where King Robert had beaten Edward II in 1314, was two hours south, he had fought the Battle of Barra in 1307 or

1308, not far from Inverness. And hadn't his wife and child escaped to a castle not far away, the English army in pursuit? She reminded herself to look up the historical details of Elizabeth de Burgh and her stepdaughter.

Leah was sure that Ravenscraig Castle held some fascinating history too, and she was desperate to research it. She imagined the new website, rich in information, showing a gorgeous Scottish castle that could be enjoyed by all. She decided not to mention that it would make a wonderful wedding venue; she'd keep that idea up her sleeve until she knew Abigail better.

An email sat in her inbox: Abigail had replied with measured enthusiasm. Leah was welcome to upgrade the website, which hadn't been worked on for several years, but could she run any changes past Abigail first. Leah was delighted, replying eagerly that she'd start immediately.

She listened to Zoe behind her, discussing how to increase funding for charity. Leah smiled. This was exactly what she'd wanted for so long, sisters working together, valued professionals doing things they loved.

Leah gazed through the window; autumn sunlight played across the loch, golden as syrup, and the courtyard below basked in a hazy warmth. Leah wondered if she shouldn't take some photos for the website while the weather was bright. She could make the castle gleam. She'd take some photos inside the castle first, a few in the courtyard, then later she'd go outside and take some shots of the loch in moonlight. The thought thrilled her as she pulled on a warm coat and hat, gesturing to Zoe that she was heading off with her digital camera. Zoe nodded, and Leah was on her way.

Leah started in the great hall, photographing the long dining table with the hanging tapestry in the background, making the room appear majestic. Then she took several views through the window towards the loch, framing the pictures with a border of the grey stones of the wall. She took a few more shots before moving to the kitchen. She felt the familiar draught blowing from the spiral staircase and she was glad she'd dressed warmly. She photographed the old metal pots hanging from hooks and chains, rows of shelves stacked with plates, the vast hearth that would have been used for cooking and baking. Click after click, then she had pictures from all angles.

She paused for a moment: Zoe had been right, there was a faint smell of something in the air, the fire, roasting flesh from a spit. It amused her that an aroma could linger for centuries. It was improbable, her imagination – she wouldn't mention it in her guided tours.

She photographed the spiral staircase, hoping the winding stone steps appeared intriguing rather than cold and eerie. She took a few photos of the guest rooms, and decided to go outside.

Leah strolled through the main gate, beyond the stone well, to take photos from a distance to include the whole castle. She was pleased with the view through the lens, the loch appeared almost golden in the sunlight. She walked through the garden to have a better view of the loch and wondered if she'd bump into Mirren Logan. Leah decided she'd like to meet her, invite her into the castle for a coffee and chat, and pick her brains for local knowledge.

Her boots were damp from the grass as she made her way round the back of the castle. She took more photographs, adjusting the lens for the perfect photo, before turning back towards the main gate and on into the courtyard. Her face was cold; there was an icy breeze funnelling from distant mountains. She was excited by the thought that there would be snow soon; she'd photograph the castle again, white icing sugar peaks in the distance.

She gripped the camera, her knuckles stiffening in the wind's chill, and photographed the courtyard, the fortified wall in front of the loch, and she thought about how the castle would have been constructed to defend against attackers. She recalled her university course; she had enjoyed English history and they had studied the conflict with Scotland briefly. Leah sighed: if she could do it all again, she'd spend less time being anxious about fitting in and she'd revel in the fascinating research instead.

Then she turned to the southwest tower with one crumbling wall, wondering briefly if she should go inside and take a look around. It might be better, she decided, to wait until she met Mirren Logan. She could ask for a tour by way of introduction. She photographed the stone exterior of the southwest wing from various angles, including the crumbling rubble, which she thought made for an atmospheric shot with the loch in the background, then she decided it was time to go in for lunch. It was past one, and she could edit the photos this afternoon and work on the website.

Zoe was making soup in the kitchenette. Leah joined her and they sat at the small table overlooking the courtyard, talking about their busy mornings.

Zoe listened carefully as Leah gushed about how thrilled she was to be working on the castle website.

'I really want to make this job work for me, Zo. It's such an opportunity.' Leah's eyes gleamed.

Leah's enthusiasm was contagious. Zoe clapped her hands in excitement. 'We'll embrace everything the Highlands has to offer. We should go into Inverness at the weekend and spend some time in Rosemuir too. We need to meet people.'

'Do we?' Leah hadn't thought about making friends. 'Yes, I suppose we do.'

'I had a few moments free this morning and I ordered us a duvet each, the highest tog. We'll need it as the winter comes.' Zoe grinned. 'I need it now. And furry slippers.'

Leah raised the spoon. 'I love that biting cold of the Scottish air, though, it's so fresh and exhilarating. Besides, we can have hot chocolate and sit in front of the fire.'

'We can,' Zoe agreed. 'I was looking online and there's a place we can ski not far from here. The pub in Rosemuir might do themed evenings, whisky tastings. I thought we could join in. Maybe they have a quiz night. You're great at quizzes.'

'We could.' Leah was interested, although secretly she knew she was less interested than Zoe was to make new friends. Then she remembered Mirren Logan. 'It would be good to find out more about the area from some local people, and maybe discover about this castle.'

'Do you know what else I researched while I had a spare moment?' Zoe's eyes twinkled. 'I tried to find out a few facts about the owner. All sorts of other things came up. There were some fascinating photographs of Ravenscraig as a ruin in the twentieth century, how it was used as a defence against the English attack, really useful information for your website. Do you know, your name came up too? "For further information, contact leahdrum-mond@..." There was something about Abigail Laing, too, that she's looked after the interests of Ravenscraig Castle since 2016. She's an accountant who studied at the University of Stirling in 1995. There was a great photo of her skiing on the slopes at Aviemore, but there was nothing about the person who owns this castle.'

Leah was surprised. 'Nothing at all?'

'Zilch.' Zoe had forgotten about her soup. 'Doesn't that seem odd? I tried everything. I even looked at Scottish businesses in Guangzhou, China, to see if I could find a trace of him there.'

'That is very mysterious,' Leah admitted.

'Do you think he even exists?' Zoe asked. 'Perhaps Abigail's the real owner and she doesn't want us to know.'

'Or perhaps he prefers to be anonymous,' Leah said. 'Maybe he's an elderly man with a love of history and he wants to be left alone? He's a recluse in his twilight years.'

'In China?' Zoe burst out laughing. 'I bet he's young and handsome and extremely rich. It would be nice to meet him. Maybe he'll come over for Christmas to take his loyal staff out to lunch.'

Leah rolled her eyes. 'He's probably an oligarch with a flat in London and another in Rome.'

'And five ex-wives to support, and twelve children.'

Leah smiled. 'What if he's a local lad who made good, spent all his money on the castle to do it up, out of love and passion?'

'Maybe he won the lottery?' Zoe was enjoying the conversation. 'Or perhaps he's just a spoiled rich kid who didn't know what to spend his money on, so he bought the castle as a way of paying less tax?'

'Can you do that, Zo?'

'Abigail Laing would know – maybe she's his accountant because he's stinking rich.'

'We could ask her...'

'Or...' Zoe grinned. 'We could find out in secret, you know, make it an assignment to discover who he is?'

'Why would we do that?'

Zoe's eyes sparkled. 'I'm fascinated to know. Your employer is nowhere to be found on the internet. He must be quite something.'

'I suppose.' Leah began to collect their bowls. 'Okay, let's see what we can find out.' She glanced at the clock on the stone wall. 'I'd better be getting back to work.'

'Me too,' Zoe agreed. 'I'll just make us a cuppa and we can take it through.'

Twenty minutes later, Zoe was busy typing frantically on her laptop and Leah was drinking tea while her photos were transferring. She spent a few minutes googling *who owns Ravenscraig Castle?* and discovered the same looping trail that Zoe had, finding her own name, that of Abigail Laing, but little else. She researched some of the history, mostly stuff she knew already: that it was founded in the thirteenth century on a site visited by an Irish monk in the time of the Picts, that it probably played a role in the Wars of Scottish Independence in the fourteenth century. She continued to probe and found a reference to the castle in a page devoted to local primary-school learning. Apparently, Ravenscraig Castle had a connection with the burning of Kildrummy Castle from where the royal party escaped in 1306 and Niall de Brus had been hung, drawn and quartered in the courtyard. It seemed that the blacksmith who took the bribe to burn Kildrummy came to a sticky end. Leah jotted down some notes and references; she'd return to the story later. Her photos were transferred and she was impatient to see them.

One by one, she brought them up on the screen, delighted by crisp, clear pictures of the great hall, the expansive view through the window and some magnificent views of the glimmering loch in sunlight. But as she examined the ones she'd taken in the kitchen and in the courtyard and the shots of the spiral staircase, she was puzzled by a strange blurring on several photographs. She frowned and called, 'Zo, can you come over here a second?'

Zoe was at her shoulder as Leah flicked back through the pictures, most of which were clear and perfect. The kitchen had come out well, apart from the one of the blackened hearth where a misty circle of light floated. The same thing had happened in a photo of the spiral staircase: a hazy orb was hovering over one of the stairs. Leah continued to show her sister a sequence of sharply focused pictures of the loch and the garden. Then again, in the courtyard, just above the southwest wing, there was the same blurred shape.

Leah frowned. 'What's happened?'

Zoe took a breath. 'It's called backscatter. It's where the flash reflects on dust or water. It's perfectly normal.'

'Do you think so? I mean, if you look at this one in the kitchen...' Leah pressed the mouse. 'I can see why it might be dusty there, but, look... it has a sort of trail, as if it's moving. It's the same with the one on the spiral staircase.' She clicked the mouse again, stopping at the picture of the southwest wing in the courtyard. 'This one is exactly the same shape too, and there was no flash – I was outside. Look at the circle of light – it's identical.'

'You have enough clear photos – I shouldn't worry about the few that have come out a bit weird.' Zoe shook her head, dispelling thoughts of the strange light she had seen inside the southwest wing.

'But why are they there?'

'It's just a trick of the light,' Zoe shrugged.

'Oh, all right,' Leah said matter-of-factly and her fingers twitched to move the mouse. Then the screen of her laptop flickered once and switched itself off. The screen was suddenly black. 'Oh no,' Leah gasped. 'Is the internet down? The electricity?'

Zoe glanced over her shoulder: her own laptop was as she'd left it, the screensaver bright. She shook her head. 'Maybe you should switch it back on again.'

Leah sat down and pressed a button: the screen immediately burst to life. She smiled. 'There we are... just a glitch.'

'Nothing more, just a glitch,' Zoe agreed hopefully.

15

Life in Ravenscraig was hard, much more so than in Kildrummy where there had been many more servants to share the work and Agnes had been given more liberty and respect. Now she had to prove her worth: under Rhona's careful watch, she was constantly rushing to fetch water, bake bread, clean pots, prepare vegetables. She could no longer rely on the reputation that she'd enjoyed at Kildrummy as a reliable worker; here, she was a recent arrival, and there was much talk of her lies to the mistress. Few of the kitchen servants would speak to her, other than to hiss orders.

Effie found life even harder; she was under the instruction of Una, just a few years her senior, who took great delight in constantly scolding her and giving her the hardest jobs, sometimes beating her because she was not quick enough. Before they fell asleep by the hearth each night, Effie would whisper to Agnes about how much she hated her work, and she'd show the marks on her hands where she'd cut herself with a knife or scorched her flesh holding a spit. Agnes offered words of encouragement; things would not always be so difficult, then Effie would mutter, 'Life was so much better when I was a princess,' before they fell asleep on each other's shoulders in front of the dying flames.

Two weeks passed and Agnes kept herself busy. Rhona was kind to her, making sure she had enough food for herself and Effie, handing her warm beer and pottage to fill her belly twice a day. She was keenly aware that there was sometimes an awkward atmosphere among the servants: occasionally, men or women would whisper in corners, eying each other suspiciously; from time to time, a stranger would arrive and stand in the shadows, then disappear as quickly as he had come. The soldiers who guarded the castle often hovered in the kitchen, watching through narrowed eyes. She had asked Rhona about it, who told her bluntly to keep her nose out of things that didn't concern her and mind her own business: there were deeds afoot it was best not to know about. Agnes agreed: she was far too busy, she shunned gossip and intended to do her best to avoid trouble.

One early morning in mid-July, she woke before the sun rose, as was her usual practice nowadays, stacking logs in the fire to feed the blaze. Effie was enjoying the last moments of sleep, her small face puckered as she curled in a tight ball on the floor.

Agnes collected two empty buckets, making her way quietly through the courtyard to the well outside the main gate. She drew water to wash her face and hands, then she filled the pails, listening to the chickens wake in the garden beyond, clucking and screeching. A rooster crowed once, and Agnes gazed into the distance. The loch was an inky shadow, outlines of mountains rising beyond. She noticed the sun's rays glimmer in a dip between the hills, tingeing the sky orange, the water purple. The beauty of the landscape made her recall an old song and she began to sing, her voice mellow.

> *O, where are ye gone, my Scottish warrior?*
> *'Twixt the thistle and the mist o' the morn*
> *O, where are ye gone, my Scottish love?*

Will ye come back to me at dawn?

Agnes smiled at the memory of her mother singing as she'd worked in the kitchens at Kildrummy making bannock bread, flour rising in a cloud from her hands. Agnes had stood beside her, never taking her eyes from the bread, watching her mother's deft movements, copying and learning. At moments like this, Agnes missed her mother intensely, although the ten years since she had died of a fever seemed like a lifetime. She recalled her mother's gentleness, her wisdom, and more than anything, she remembered the touch of her hands, hard but soothing as she'd taught her to make bread and pastry. Her mother had regularly chided her gently for not guarding her tongue, Agnes remembered: she'd been warned daily that her impudence would land her in trouble, but Agnes always caught the fondness in her mother's eyes.

She gazed towards the loch, where the mist spread across the surface like a shawl. The sight of the loch made something in her soul lift. Agnes breathed in pine-scented air: she'd stay a moment longer. No one would miss her for a few minutes.

There was a broad black horse grazing nearby and Agnes was tempted to go over and stroke its mane. She recalled riding the king's brother's destrier; it had been a difficult journey from Kildrummy, but, astride a horse with Effie in front of her and the landscape stretching beyond, she'd felt a new, exciting sense of freedom. Her gaze swerved back to the loch, still and soundless, like a painting. Then she noticed something move beneath the surface of the water and a shape emerged, round, sleek and black, perhaps a fish of some sort.

Agnes edged forward to watch it, the smooth glossy dome parting the calm water. It swam, dipping and rising as it neared the bank of the loch, then once it was in shallow water, it stood up tall, emerging from the water with a loud splash. It was a man, his hair slicked to his head. Agnes was amazed someone would swim in the loch; it was summertime, but the water would be cold.

The man strode forward, and Agnes saw that he was naked. He stopped to push back wet locks from his face, shaking the drops from his beard. Agnes stared: the dark hair continued to his chest, where it was thick, a line of it to his navel. He strolled forward casually, bending to pick up a tunic concealed behind a tree stump, and Agnes gaped at the tight muscles in his long legs. She found it difficult to pull her gaze away: she had never seen a naked man before, and this one was broad, muscular, with an expanse of tangled hair.

It was equally difficult to breathe; her heart was beating too quickly and her lungs had lost the ability to take in air as he turned, water gleaming on his arms and legs. He was about to pull on his tunic, then he paused: he'd noticed her.

Agnes took a step backwards in horror, looking for a tree to conceal herself behind, but it was too late. He was laughing; she could hear the rumble from his chest. Amusement filled his face as he saw her reaction.

Then he called, 'Good morning to ye, lassie,' his voice filled with light mockery as he dressed himself.

He moved towards the horse; in a leap, he was astride and galloping towards the collection of thatched timber-built houses in Rosemuir. Agnes watched him ride away, then she scuttled to the stone well, grasping the buckets and hurrying back.

There was already a bustle of activity in the castle kitchen, and Rhona was waiting for her, hands on hips. 'You're late with the water, Agnes.'

'I'm sorry for it.' Agnes wondered whether to mention the swimmer in the loch, but she decided against it.

She was momentarily lost in thought as Rhona said, 'Well, what are ye waiting for? Get on with the work – the bread won't bake itself.'

'Sorry,' Agnes said again and rushed over to the table.

Una had already started the daily torture, tweaking Effie's ear as she scrubbed a blackened pot that had not been properly cleaned the day before. Effie had tears in her eyes. Agnes winked in her direction, a complicit sign between them to be brave, and then she set to making the bread.

As she worked methodically, Agnes hummed the tune of the song she had been singing earlier. She thought about the dark-haired man again. He was strong and handsome, and he'd seemed so unconcerned as he swam naked in the cold loch, so casual as he'd dressed and leaped onto his horse. She thought he must be bold, unafraid of anyone. He'd ridden away in the direction of Rosemuir, so Agnes hoped he might be local; she might see him again. She would not be so bashful next time. She was annoyed with herself that she hadn't met his eyes and made an impudent remark in response to his greeting. Then she wondered what it was like to bathe in the loch. Agnes imagined the ice of the water against her skin, the tingle of the sudden cold. She had never learned to swim, but the man had made it look so easy, gliding through the water like an arrow. She imagined herself swimming with him, diving beneath the surface, emerging with a splash, laughing together. She wondered what his name was, and if she would see him again. She would make sure to be punctual as she collected water from the well tomorrow; she'd allow herself enough time to look towards the loch, in case he was there.

'Agnes.' Rhona's loud voice pulled her from her thoughts.

'Sorry...'

'What is wrong with ye today?'

'I was busy...'

'Busy dreaming the day away,' Rhona grumbled. 'We've to drop our work and gather ourselves together in the courtyard now. The master wants to talk to us all. It's important – word has just come that he has something he wants to tell us.'

'I've never met the master,' Agnes said, shaping the bread to prove.

'He's a goodly man. He's like the mistress, a kindly person and fair-minded, but he'll suffer no fools. Come along. We cannae keep him waiting.'

Soldiers stood around the courtyard, their chainmail coifs glinting in the sunlight. Effie pushed next to Agnes and gripped her hand as the servants assembled. There was much chatter and consternation, questions about why they had been called together to listen to the master.

Agnes caught sight of An-Mòr, and she smiled a greeting. He nodded in return, an anxious expression on his face, then he bent to talk to Rhona, who had seized his huge arm.

The bustle grew louder until the sound died away as Ross McNair strode from the castle, his wife a few paces behind. Agnes observed him carefully; he was immaculately dressed in a long tunic dyed a deep red and he wore a fur-lined cloak. His movements were slow and dignified: he stood quietly in front of the servants, commanding immediate respect. Agnes observed his silvered beard and grey hair and decided that she liked him immediately. He was the sort of man she'd have liked for a father. Muriel McNair stood at his side, her hair braided, wearing a blue dress pinned with an ornate brooch. He raised a hand and the crowd was silent as he spoke.

'I have gathered ye all here today to tell ye some news that I believe will sadden your hearts.'

There was a low murmur. Effie squeezed Agnes's hand.

'I hear from my sources that our beloved queen, Elizabeth de Burgh, has been captured.'

He paused, allowing the crowd to mutter, then he began again.

'The English have taken her to Yorkshire, where she is kept under severe conditions of house arrest.'

There were sounds of dissent, then someone called, 'What about the princess, Master? What of her?'

'I'm afraid she too is a prisoner.' Ross McNair's face was momentarily sad. 'The young princess has been separated from the rest of her party by the English. Their king has ordered that she be sent to a convent in Yorkshire.' He bent towards his wife and spoke quietly. The noise of the crowd rose: Agnes could hear the words 'treachery' and 'revenge'. Then Ross held up a hand. 'I can tell ye this. King Robert will stay strong until the time comes that the enemy are brought to account for their actions. And he will not pledge fealty to the English king. We will not bend to their armies, no matter how far north they travel, looking for our king.'

There was cheering from the crowd. In front of Agnes, a man clapped another on the back. Effie squeezed her hand hard and whispered, 'So the poor princess has been taken? Will she be killed?'

Agnes quietened her with a glare: Ross McNair was speaking again.

'Ye all know I am a peaceful man and Ravenscraig is a place where we do not seek conflict. But we are well guarded and we are loyal to our king. I hear rumours that there are some who would betray him to the English for their own gain. And our king is not far from us now. He is building a strong army as we speak and he will fight the English, he will defeat them in glorious battle and his queen and his family will be brought safely back to Scotland where they belong.'

There were loud cheers and applause again.

Ross raised his hand, his face now stern. 'And I will tell ye all this. No treason will be tolerated. I am no friend of the English and I am no friend of bloodshed, but if I discover anyone who talks to English soldiers or gives them any information that will help them against our king, I will not fail to do my duty.'

A silence fell over the crowd as each person pondered the master's words.

Effie gazed at Agnes, her eyes anxious. 'Will they come here, the English army? Will we have to escape again like we did before?'

'Shh,' Agnes whispered.

'Back to your work now,' Ross commanded, his voice clear. 'Except for one of ye. The kitchen maid who is called Agnes Fitzgerald, she is to come to the great hall immediately, where I would speak with her.'

Faces turned to stare: many knew who Agnes was, of her reputation as one who lied, who stole a horse, who escaped from Kildrummy castle.

Agnes felt her body tense with fear: it was impossible to move.

Then An-Mòr was at her shoulder, pressing her arm with his huge paw.

'I will come with ye, lassie. I've heard the talk in the village this morning. I think I know what this is all about. Have no fear.'

16

On Saturday evening, Leah and Zoe sat in the snug of The Canny Man in Rosemuir. Leah was celebrating her first week at work with a glass of whisky, chattering happily about the progress of the new website. Zoe was glad to be in a warm room, away from the draughty halls of the castle. She thought for a moment about the incident in the kitchen, the sense of someone standing so closely behind her as she held the goblet. She wondered about the castle, what might have happened over the years to create such a sense of oppression. The old kitchen made her feel uncomfortable – she had no desire to go back in there, although Leah seemed unaware of the chilling atmosphere. Zoe asked tentatively, 'Leah... tell me about the background of Ravenscraig.'

'I've been researching it all week.' Leah grinned enthusiastically as she put the glass of whisky down; it was strong, made by a local distillery, and she could only manage infrequent sips. She gazed around the snug; they were the only occupants at the moment and she wondered if the inn was always so quiet. A log fire blazed in a wood burner. The room was panelled with dark wood and the wall sconces shaped like candles shed yellow light. 'Apparently, the site was discovered by a priest travelling from Ireland in the fifth century – it might have been St Columba – he blessed a Pictish man who was dying in his hut. There's a documentary record that says the castle was built in the late twelve hundreds and there was some involvement with Edward I, Hammer of the Scots, at some point against Robert Bruce. Over the next hundred years, the area was raided frequently by the MacDonalds, who were Lords of the Isle, and the castle was uninhabited for a long time. There's not much information until the 1770s, when the castle was roofless and crumbling, and was regarded as a romantic ruin by nineteenth-century painters and visitors to the Highlands.'

Zoe sipped her Coke, still thinking about the incident in the kitchen. 'It's been abandoned for a long time then?'

'Until the new owner bought it and started to rebuild, I suppose. Abigail mentioned that, and we still have no information about him.' Leah attempted her drink again. 'My goodness, this local spirit is some strong stuff. Are you sure you won't have one?'

Zoe grinned. 'If you're going to ask the barman in the Highlands for his recommendation, he's always going to suggest a strong local whisky.'

'At least it'll keep me warm while we're walking back home. I'm determined to develop my Scottish side and get a taste for it.' Leah puffed out her cheeks. 'It's cosy in here. The fire belts out some heat.'

'It's warmer here than being in the castle.' Zoe raised an eyebrow. 'Have you noticed how cold it is there? At least we have nice warm duvets now.'

Leah shook her head. 'It's draughty, but I'm not cold. I just wear layers...'

'I'm cold all the time,' Zoe complained.

Leah gave her a sympathetic look. 'It'll probably get worse as winter comes, but at least we have our four rooms and they are well heated. We'll keep the radiators on all the time. We'll be fine.' She grinned. 'I'll just be cold when I'm showing people round the castle. Oh, I forgot to say – I have my first tour coming up. A man has contacted me – he wants to look round. He's after a Highland location to make an advert – I sent him a couple of the photos that I'm going to put on our website. Abigail is delighted.'

'Oh, I bet she is – you've only been in the post for a week. What's he advertising?'

Leah shrugged. 'He didn't say, we've just emailed. I'm speaking to him on the phone on Monday. He's called Aidan Irving, so I'm guessing he's a Scot.'

'Great.' Zoe noticed Leah's pained expression as she gulped the whisky. 'Are you still struggling with that?'

'I might just get a Diet Coke and pour it in. I expect that's sacrilege in Scotland,' Leah quipped.

'I'll get you one.' Zoe was on her feet and off towards the bar, leaving Leah toasting her fingers in front of the fire.

In the main part of the inn, there were people sitting at tables and standing at the bar; the room was larger and brighter than the snug. Zoe gazed around at groups of men and women playing darts and pool, five women on high stools talking together, a young couple holding hands, whispering. She watched the barman, a short burly man in jeans and a polo shirt, who was pouring beer from a bottle. He had long sideburns and slicked hair in the style of a rock and roller. He took money from his customer, an older man who wore a green and white scarf, then he strolled over to Zoe.

'Whisky again? And a Coke.'

'Just two Cokes with ice, please.' Zoe smiled. 'The whisky was lovely, but it's very strong.'

The barman raised an eyebrow. 'Whisky is meant to be strong. It's Scotch. The one you just tried, the smoky Glencharaid, is new on the market and very popular with the youngsters here. What did you think of it?'

'Very quaffable,' Zoe said politely. 'My sister and I are new to the area. I'm sure over time we'll develop a taste for local whiskies.'

The barman said, 'I expect we'll be seeing more of you in The Canny Man.'

'Oh definitely,' Zoe said with enthusiasm. 'It's our local now. Is there much going on here, quizzes and the like?'

'We've a good darts team, but we're always looking for new talent,' the man replied. 'I'm Kenny Wilson, by the way.'

'Zoe Drummond. And my sister is Leah, she's caretaker at Ravenscraig.'

'How are you finding it there?'

'It's wonderful.' Zoe decided that she was mostly telling the truth, then she added, 'It's a bit cold.'

'Aye, I can imagine.' Kenny proffered two glasses with ice and two bottles of Coke. 'It's very quiet up there by the loch.'

'Yes.' Zoe pulled her purse from her bag and swiped her card. 'We're trying to find out as much as we can about the place. We haven't even met the owner yet. In fact,' she met Kenny's eyes, 'we don't even know his name.'

'Oh, I've met him. He stayed here twice, last time maybe a year ago, less.' Kenny scratched his ear. 'Daniel Lennox, his name is. Nice man.'

Zoe leaned forward, interested. 'Is he local?'

'I believe so.' Kenny shrugged. 'He's a Scot, educated, but no airs and graces. He could have afforded to stay in the plushest hotels, but he stayed here for a week in Rosemuir. He picked this place because he wanted to support local people, he said. He had a nice hire car, wasn't short of a penny or two.'

'Oh? What does he do?'

'No idea.' Kenny gave a short laugh. 'He owns that castle you're staying in – that's all I know. He's put a lot of cash into doing it up. A couple of guys who come in here work for him – Jackie, who keeps the gardens nice, and Christie, who does the building work at

Ravenscraig – he knows Daniel Lennox well – they talk often about bringing the place back to the way it used to be.'

'Oh, I hope I can meet him.'

'I'm sure you will. Well, I hope you'll be happy in Rosemuir, Zoe. See you again.' Kenny nodded, then he moved to one of the women seated on a stool by the bar, who asked for a bottle of wine.

Zoe took her drinks and rushed excitedly back to the snug, where Leah was still toasting her fingers.

'Guess what.' Zoe deposited the glasses and bottles on the table. 'I've discovered some facts about the owner of Ravenscraig.'

'Oh?' Leah poured her Coke onto the ice in her glass. 'Do tell all.'

'He's called Daniel Lennox and he's stayed here. Kenny, that's the barman, said although he's rich, he's a really ordinary bloke.'

'How old is he?' Leah asked.

'I didn't ask. I should have.' Zoe lifted her glass to her lips. 'But there are some locals who know him well, the builder and the man who does the gardens.'

'I don't suppose we'll see much of either of them during the winter.' Leah seemed disappointed. 'Still, you've made a great start on our search for the mysterious owner. Well done, Zo. We'll drink up and head off home, shall we? I think I need an early night.'

'Me too,' Zoe agreed. 'Unless you fancy joining the darts team.'

Leah pulled a face. 'It's not for me...' Then an idea came to her. 'Unless Daniel Lennox plays in the team. He sounds interesting.'

'He does,' Zoe agreed, sipping her Coke. 'I don't think I've met a millionaire before. I can't wait to find out more...'

* * *

It was dark as they walked back to the castle, arm in arm. Leah glimpsed the dim outline of Ravenscraig in the distance, lit by the glimmering outdoor lights, and she felt a surge of warmth. Being caretaker there felt more than a job already; it was something she was proud of, somewhere that was beginning to feel like home. She hugged her sister's arm. 'Do you think we could go for a walk tomorrow? Round the loch, explore a bit?'

'I'd love that,' Zoe agreed. 'We could go into the forest and, if you like, we could take a drive towards the mountains, maybe do a bit of climbing.'

'That would be great, but you'll have to go easy on me, Zo – you're much fitter than I am.'

'You're fit enough – and being here will do wonders for both of us. We can go on loads of walks. And you can take some more photos for the website.'

Leah nodded, delighted.

Zoe's mind moved again to the photographs Leah had taken of the mysterious orbs of light. She thought about the strange glow she had seen coming from the southwest wing, the unsettling moment in the old kitchen as she held the goblet, and she was suddenly cold.

17

Agnes and An-Mòr stood side by side in the great hall, waiting in silence. Agnes's heart throbbed in her throat: she had no idea why she had been summoned.

An-Mòr's voice was hoarse as he whispered, 'What's about to happen here isnae good, but ye should have no fear, lassie. Just speak up and say the truth and all will be well, I give ye my word.'

They waited, Agnes staring at her feet, then Ross and Muriel McNair swept into the room, flanked by two soldiers in chainmail, carrying swords. An-Mòr inclined his head respectfully. Agnes didn't move.

Ross glanced towards his wife. 'My dear, is she the one?'

'She is.' Muriel's voice conveyed no warmth.

'Agnes,' Ross spoke quietly and she raised her chin to look at him. 'Ye came here from Kildrummy after it was laid siege by the English?'

'I did, Master...' Agnes wondered whether to apologise again for the deceit, but she remained quiet.

'Agnes, I want ye to tell my husband what happened at

Kildrummy before the English arrived,' Muriel said. 'Did ye over-hear anyone speaking about the attack?'

'Aye, Madam, I did.'

'Tell my husband what ye heard.'

'The smith was tending to one of the noble ladies' horses.' Agnes met Ross's eyes boldly. 'A man approached him, one of the castle soldiers – I didn't see his face, but I overheard him speaking to the smith.'

'What did he say?' Ross asked kindly.

'He offered him as much gold as he could carry.' Agnes spoke quietly. 'I heard the man say to the smith that the castle should be set ablaze and the English soldiers were after the king's women.'

'Are ye sure of that?' Ross glanced at his wife.

'I'm sure,' Agnes said.

Muriel nodded. 'Do ye ken this smith?'

'Aye, Madam, I ken him well – everyone at Kildrummy did. He used to swear a lot and most of us would pay him no mind as he had a temper on him.' Agnes stood tall. 'He set a fire and the English used it to mask the surprise attack on the castle.'

'What did ye see before ye took the horse and left with your sister?'

'I saw a soldier kill Colban, my friend – his throat was cut as if he was a lamb slaughtered. Then they took Niall de Brus and hung him in the courtyard for everyone to see...'

'I'm sorry ye witnessed such things, lassie,' Ross muttered.

Muriel put a hand on his arm. 'Agnes, would ye recognise this smith, if ye saw him again?'

'I would, Madam. His face is printed in my mind. He looked like the devil at his forge.'

Ross raised an eyebrow, glancing at An-Mòr, then he said, 'Come with me, both of ye.'

Agnes followed the master and mistress into a corridor where a stone staircase spiralled upwards into darkness. From the shadows, three men emerged, dragging a fourth who was bound with rope, struggling. Agnes recognised the captive smith at once; there was blood on his face, and he was swearing and protesting. Agnes froze.

An-Mòr put his mouth close to her ear. 'Tell the truth, lassie – is this the smith who took the gold as a bribe?'

Agnes took a step back; the smith was so close, she could see the spittle on his beard.

He hissed angrily, 'I've never seen the lassie before. Ye cannae believe a word she says – she's a whore...'

Agnes stared at the face she recognised so well and the feelings from the last moments at Kildrummy came flooding back, the stench of the fire, more blood spilt than she had ever seen. She glanced at the three men who were holding the smith, and one of them held her gaze. She had seen him before; he was imprinted on her memory and she recalled the way he had faced her naked and laughed so carelessly as he emerged from the loch. Her eyes met his and she caught the glint of recognition.

'Agnes?' Ross spoke her name gently. 'Is this the man?'

She was still staring at the dark-haired man, who raised an eyebrow, encouraging her to speak. Something in her soul trusted him instantly and she said, 'Aye, it is.'

The smith resisted, swearing, and the three men held him fast.

One of them, a tall slim man with broad shoulders held out a heavy pouch. 'We found this on him, and he has more. It's gold.'

'It isnae mine – I came across it... on a dead man,' the smith protested. 'I was on my way here to ask for work. I am no traitor.'

The slim man handed the gold to Ross as the other two men held their writhing prisoner fast.

Ross spoke directly to the smith. 'Tell the truth, man. Did ye take the bribe?'

'I did not...' The smith suddenly became very humble. 'I am a true Scot, Master. I love The Bruce...'

The slim man spoke again. 'He's the one. The lassie here knows him for what he is.'

Agnes stepped back again, glancing towards the dark-haired man whose eyes seemed to burn into hers as he gave an imperceptible nod.

Ross spoke directly to An-Mòr. 'Take this gold to the forge and melt it down. The smith wanted gold, so he shall have it all.' He nodded towards the slim man. 'Take him to the top of the tower in the southwest wing.'

The smith's face contorted with horror as he tried to wrench himself free. An-Mòr turned and strode away without a word, but Agnes saw the hunch of his shoulders and the sadness in his eyes. The three men followed, dragging the smith, who continued to swear and protest his innocence.

Agnes blinked as if coming from a dream.

Muriel put a gentle hand on her shoulder. 'Ye did well, Agnes. We knew his guilt, but we had to be fair and ye told us what we needed to know. The gold in his pockets proves that he is guilty of treason.'

'Aye,' Ross agreed. 'And we have to show that there is no mercy for those who betray our king and his family.'

Agnes was puzzled. 'What will they do to the smith?'

'His precious gold will be melted and the hot liquid poured down his throat.' Ross said gently. 'He was a traitor.'

Muriel's eyes were round with regret. 'Return to the kitchen, Agnes. Do not think more on what happened today.'

'Who were the men?' Agnes couldn't help her words. 'The three who held him?'

'Brave Scotsmen,' Ross replied. 'The tall man is Hendrie Logan, An-Mòr's son. The other two warriors are loyal to The Bruce. Pay them no further mind.'

'Go back to your work, Agnes. Ye have done well,' Muriel said, then she and Ross were gone.

Agnes put her hands to her face, not quite able to understand what had happened. She had sent a man to his death, a man who was a traitor, who caused the slaughter of so many people, who betrayed the queen and her party. Agnes trembled as she stood at the foot of the spiral staircase, horrified by the manner of his death: there was no compassion, no forgiveness and no second chances to be had. She resolved to keep her wits sharper than ever.

But what had shaken her to the core was the complicit gaze of the handsome dark-haired warrior. He'd recognised her: in that moment, she felt he knew her through and through. Agnes shivered, and the image of the dark man, his steady eyes, his nod of recognition imprinted themselves on her heart. She knew in a moment that she would never be the same again.

Agnes returned to the kitchen deep in thought and all eyes turned in her direction as she shuffled to the table.

Rhona was at her side; she seized her wrist. 'I need ye to work with me soaking barley, lassie. There's no time to slack.'

Agnes followed Rhona to the large vat, noticing Effie on her knees, her face streaked with tears as she scrubbed a large, blackened cauldron. Una stood beside her, piling up more pans to be cleaned.

Agnes took her place beside Rhona, who hissed in her ear, 'Keep your mind on your work, Agnes. Think of nothing else. Work here like it's just another day, because that's all it is. Ye and I will talk of what took place anon.'

Agnes nodded, concentrating all her energy on the piled grain. A sudden thought came to her and she said, 'Shall I go and draw more water from the stone well? We will need hot water to pour on all this barley...'

'Water is already heating on the fire.' Rhona lowered her voice. 'You'll not step outside here for a while now. There's some important work being done in the tower, I ken. Ye can fetch more water later.'

Agnes nodded, wondering how Rhona knew so much: she was An-Mòr's wife, but she seemed more interested in the furtive goings-on of the castle than her husband. Agnes continued to work, rhythmically crushing the hard grains of barley in the vat, and her mind wandered again to the dark warrior. She'd met him twice now: but neither occasion had revealed her at her best: she wondered what the warrior had thought of her. She shook her head: she knew already. The moment their eyes met, she had felt the connection. They would meet again, she was sure of it, and then she'd take her chance; she'd talk to him, she'd show him that she was strong and independent, that she had a wild spirit equal to his.

She accompanied Rhona to the fire to collect the hot water, carrying the steaming pan carefully across the kitchen, lifting the weight of it high to splash it into the vats. A rich aroma of warming grain filled her nostrils as she began to stir the mixture. Agnes whispered, 'Rhona, the other people view me strangely. Do they know what the master asked me to do?'

'They know nothing yet. They gossip among themselves. I knew from my son that the smith of Kildrummy had been taken and must answer for his treason. I remembered what ye told me, how he was a traitor to the English for gold. An-Mòr will tell me the end of it later, but I have no doubt the traitor will suffer for his betrayal of the queen. Ye were asked to tell the master what ye saw at Kildrummy. And did ye?'

'Aye, I did.'

'And what happened next?'

'An-Mòr was sent to heat the gold at the forge. The men will force it down his throat.' Agnes shuddered. 'It's a terrible end for any man.'

'It is,' Rhona agreed. 'He must pay for the terrible end that came to all who died at Kildrummy, and the killing of the king's brother. Because of his greed, our queen and the princess have been taken prisoner and our king is out there in the wild with fifty men to protect him from the English. Keep your sympathy for The Bruce and the brave men who fight with him. Do not think of the smith again.' Rhona sighed. 'Tonight, my husband will be like a bear with a sore paw. He hates the violence. But I tell him it is the only way. These are bloody times.'

Agnes nodded, continuing with her work.

Rhona said, 'Ye did well, Agnes. You're a strong lass and the master will remember your bravery and thank ye for it.'

Agnes saw her chance. 'The three men who held the smith – one of them was your son?'

'Aye, Hendrie fights for the king. I'm proud of what he does. He's loyal.'

'He looks very like ye...' Agnes began.

'He does. He's tall, but not as tall as his father.'

'And the other two men...' Agnes was staring into the vat to hide the interest in her eyes. 'Who were they?'

'Both brave warriors of the king,' Rhona's voice was low, '...who risk their lives every day against the English.'

Agnes's eyes gleamed. 'It must be a hard life for those men. It must be hard on their sweethearts too...'

'Hard for the mothers, no doubt...' Rhona glared, then her expression softened. 'Hendrie lives in hiding most of the time. He is thirty years old. The other two men are younger – they've no time for sweethearts.'

Agnes felt the blood rush to her face. 'They are brave men indeed.'

'They are. I see them both in Rosemuir sometimes. They visit with Hendrie and I always have a meal ready.' Rhona eyed Agnes suspiciously. 'Why do ye ask?'

Agnes stirred the hot grain vigorously. 'No reason.' She forced a smile. 'My stomach is growling – I havnae eaten since first light.'

Rhona rested a hand on her shoulder. 'Go, get yourself a trencher and sit by the fireside awhile.' She glanced across the kitchen. 'Take wee Effie with ye. She's elbow-deep in cleaning pots, then she'll need to prepare peas. I'll tell Una I bade her eat – it will save her a beating.'

'Thank ye.' Agnes was grateful for the chance to be alone with her thoughts. She hoped Effie would eat quietly and give her some time to think about the dark-haired young man. She wished she could have asked Rhona his name.

Fifteen minutes later, Effie wiped pottage from her lips, sucked her fingers and rested her head on Agnes's shoulder, her face flushed orange in the firelight. Her voice was quiet. 'I'm glad for a chance to fill my belly. Una hates me. I hate her too.'

Agnes had hardly eaten, despite her hunger. She was staring into the flames. 'Do not hate, Effie. It's not a good way to be.'

'I do hate her,' Effie protested. 'And there's hate all around us here in Ravenscraig. Word is everywhere that ye were called to speak to the master because a traitor had been discovered. Is that true?'

'I cannae speak of it...'

'Ye can speak of it to me.' Effie snuggled closer. 'I'm your sister, everyone believes that here now. I believe it. Ye are all I have in the world. And if I tell it to Una, that ye helped the king's men to punish a traitor, she might like me more and not beat me.'

Agnes turned to Effie, grasping her arm. 'Tell no one, Effie. Talk is dangerous. Let them all gossip, but tell them nothing of what we saw at Kildrummy.'

'But what shall I say?' Effie pouted.

'Say that the master and the mistress are good people and loyal to the king. Una needs to hear no more from ye than that.'

Effie frowned, puzzled, then Rhona called from the shadows, 'Agnes, we need more water. Can ye run to the stone well and fetch some?'

'Aye, I will.' Agnes was on her feet immediately, collecting two buckets.

The courtyard was strangely quiet as she crossed the cobbles; there were few people around. She glimpsed the leaping fire in the forge, gleaming orange in the shadows, and she shuddered. As she passed the fortified loch wall and southwest wing, she paused for a moment to stare up at the high slit of a window, wondering if the smith was chained inside. She visited the small chapel on the ground floor every Sunday, but she had never taken the stone steps to the top of the tower. She'd heard that there was a prison cell beyond the winding staircase. It was likely that the smith was still there, confined at the top where the high window overlooked the loch. She clutched the pails in her hand and scurried through the main gate towards the stone well.

As Agnes bent to draw water, something bright caught her eye. On the stone surround of the well, a single thistle had been placed. She picked it up, holding the thick green stem carefully, avoiding the thorns. The stalk divided itself into two blooms, a purple flower, the colour of heather, its petals long above the prickly base, and a tiny bud pushing from a thorny cap. Agnes held it gently: a thistle, strong but beautiful; a bud, the promise of the future. It had been placed by someone who knew she would come to the well to draw water. Agnes held the petals to her cheek. It was a token, and there was no doubt in her mind about who had left it for her. She closed her eyes and wondered where the handsome warrior was now and what would come after.

18

Zoe drove the Mini down the open road, the loch to her left, dense forests to the right, mountain peaks rising in the distance. Leah closed her eyes dreamily, then she gazed through the window taking in every detail, pointing excitedly, providing a running commentary.

'Look – the mountains will be covered in snow soon. I can't wait for Christmas in the castle. I wonder if Abigail would let me do a festive event, an open day? Do you think we'll see deer? The forests are supposed to be full of them. We can go for a walk and then find somewhere for Sunday lunch. Oh, stop, stop, Zo – I want to take a picture of the loch. That view would be perfect for the website.'

Zoe smiled indulgently and brought the car to a halt in a narrow layby. Leah clambered out clutching her camera, running to a place she'd already chosen for a photo. She framed a picture: the view of the loch was edged by a crop of thistles, fists of golden brown and green clutching a spray of floating seeds, stalks waving in the breeze.

Leah breathed out slowly. 'Isn't this heaven?'

'It is.' Zoe was at her shoulder, breathing the sharp clean air, her eyes scanning the view.

'I want to stay here forever.' Leah's cheeks were flushed with the cold. 'I was meant to live in Scotland. I never want to go back to Birmingham.' She saw something in her sister's eyes, a moment of sadness. 'Oh, Zoe, I'm sorry – I've dragged you here. Have I been selfish? Will you be all right for three months or are you desperate for the city?'

'I don't know.' Zoe thought for a moment. 'I love Birmingham, I miss my friends and the social side of things, the wine bars, live music, but... Scotland certainly pulls at your heart strings. I'm not sure any more. I think I might like to travel. Being here has made me question everything. Maybe I was becoming a bit too comfortable with the routine. Something is changing in me. I don't know... one part of me wants to settle, but another wants to try something else. Does that make sense?'

'It does – and it'll be fun finding out.' Leah wrapped an arm around her sister. 'I really hoped coming here would make me feel more confident. And it's working – already I feel like I've come home.'

'It's going to be an interesting three months, for sure,' Zoe agreed, smiling. 'I'm glad I came.'

Leah was delighted. 'I'll take a few more pictures, then we can drive somewhere and go for a long walk.' She squeezed Zoe's arm. 'And I want to see some deer.'

An hour later, they were exploring a forest, walking along a dirt path. The icy wind blew into their faces from the mountains, but they were swathed in warm coats and snug in woolly hats and gloves. Their feet crunched on leaves as they walked up the incline, dense foliage on either side, a lattice of branches above them. The sunlight dappled the ground, casting shadows. The occasional flash of rays dazzled them from above as they pushed on uphill.

Leah's breath was a warm mist. 'I'm loving this, Zo. I'm going to send some pics to Mum and Dad tonight. They'll be so pleased we're having such a great time.' Her eyes widened. 'When do you think they'll visit us?'

'After their December Northern Lights cruise and their trip to Spain next year. Maybe they'll come up in March. It will be great to see them.' Zoe wondered what her parents would make of Ravenscraig Castle, whether they'd find it as welcoming as Leah did, or whether they'd share her feelings that it had an eerie atmosphere, somehow still stuck in the past. Zoe pushed the idea away: of course, it would seem stuck in the past – it was a thirteenth-century castle. Leah's enthusiastic chatter tugged her from her thoughts.

'It's November the first on Tuesday. I'm going to leave it another week or two, then I'm going to suggest the idea of holding wedding receptions. I'll write a business plan, with costs, a timeline for the work. The castle would be ideal; there are enough guest bedrooms to accommodate over a dozen people, and I'm sure other people could stay in Inverness, or even in The Canny Man... And it's so romantic. Then I'll message Mariusz and suggest it as a venue for him and Jordan. I'll send pictures, and some to Bex – she's bound to be a bridesmaid. Mariusz could be the first to try it out.'

Zoe smiled. 'Don't get too far ahead of yourself...'

'I could ask Abigail to mention it to the owner – what's his name?'

'Daniel Lennox.' Zoe smiled.

'Perhaps he'll come back to Scotland after doing business in... wherever he is... and we could have a meeting. There's some small building work to do to bring the place up to perfection and then it would be a great venture.'

Zoe was impressed. 'You've really taken this new job to heart, Leah...'

They came to a clearing, the forest opening onto a wide expanse of moorland. Clumps of brown thistles bowed hoary manes, swaying on either side, the landscape rising towards distant hills.

Zoe said, 'Oh, this is lovely.'

'And look...' Leah pointed, then she was scrabbling in her coat pocket for her camera. Not far away, a lone deer stood on a rock, its head held high, staring back at them. Holding her breath, Leah took several pictures and the deer stayed still, as if posing. She turned wide-eyed to Zoe, and Zoe nodded in agreement: the scene was breathtaking. The deer offered one final stare, then loped away. Leah flicked through her photos. 'These will...'

'...Look great on the website.' Zoe finished the sentence with a smile. 'I know. Come on – let's get to the top of the rock. I bet the view from there will be absolutely stunning.'

'Brilliant,' Leah said, glowing. 'And maybe we'll see even more deer – a whole gang of them.'

'Herd,' Zoe suggested. 'But a whole gang of them will do fine.'

* * *

The sky was fading, a swirl of sweet melting orange and crayon blue, beyond the darkening loch as Zoe drove the Mini into the castle grounds and parked by the stone well. The outdoor lights in the courtyard glowed dimly and the air held a hint of ice.

'Let's get the fire going and watch TV this evening,' Zoe suggested. 'I just want to hunker down.'

'Definitely – but I want to transfer the photographs too. The website will be finished next week, and I'm talking to the client tomorrow, Aidan Irving, about his campaign.'

'I'm thrilled by how well it's going...' Then Zoe stopped, feeling her heart lurch as she grabbed Leah's arm. There was a figure in the courtyard, standing by the castle door, not moving. She wore a long coat and her grey hair covered most of her face, but her eyes were hollow.

'I've been waiting for you,' she said, her voice a dry whisper.

Leah marched forward, holding out a hand. 'You must be Mirren Logan? I'm so pleased to meet you.'

Mirren did not move. 'You're English.'

'Leah Drummond. I'm half Scottish...' Leah said with a smile, but Mirren continued to glare.

'I knew you were here,' Mirren said tonelessly. 'You're the new caretaker.'

'And you came to visit?' Leah asked encouragingly. 'That's great. Come in for a cup of tea. Or coffee?'

'No, I won't. I always come here on Sundays. I like to spend time in the chapel.'

Leah frowned. 'There isn't a chapel...'

'In the southwest wing. The bottom floor is an old chapel. I like to sit there and think about how the castle used to be so many years ago.'

'Would you like to show us round the chapel?' Leah was delighted. 'I'd love to see it. We haven't been in the southwest wing yet.'

'You should stay in the castle. I look after the wing.' Mirren frowned.

'I have a key to it, I think,' Leah pointed out.

'You don't need to go in there. I clean it, keep it special. It should remain untouched.'

'I thought it was going to be renovated, that the owner intended to make the whole castle a good business venture.'

'It can't ever be touched,' Mirren said simply. 'Don't go in the southwest wing.'

'We could go together. What's upstairs in the tower?'

'You can't ever go there.' Mirren's eyes flashed. 'Stay in the castle. That's what I wanted to tell you.'

'Won't you come in for coffee?' Leah asked again, but Mirren was walking past her, away into the darkness towards Rosemuir.

Zoe whispered, 'That was a bit strange.'

Leah gave a small laugh. 'I expect she wants to keep her territory to herself. We'll see if we can break the ice. I'm sure she's just a bit eccentric.' She hugged Leah's arm, dragging her towards the castle. 'I can't wait to take a look in there, though. Abigail said the owner was going to restore it. And if there's a chapel – well, that's perfect for a wedding venue.'

Zoe smiled. 'Let's get the fire on and warm up. It's freezing.' She followed her sister, who was striding towards the heavy door. Zoe looked back over her shoulder. The southwest wing was swathed in darkness, a dark outline against a grey starless sky. She wasn't sure she wanted to go in there at all.

They stepped inside and Leah rushed ahead up the stone staircase, soon out of sight. Zoe closed the door behind her and once again she was conscious of the iron cold that instantly inhabited her bones and made them feel brittle. She walked past the great hall in darkness, crammed with shadows that seemed to threaten to push forward and engulf her. She hurried up the steps to the wooden landing and into the lounge. Leah had already coaxed a fire in the grate. Zoe left her to it and dashed to the kitchenette to make hot chocolate. She needed to be warmer.

As she waited for milk to heat in the pan, Zoe gazed through the window towards the southwest wing, recalling the moving lights she had seen. They must have come from the chapel and Zoe tried to convince herself that it was torchlight, that Mirren must have been in there, moving around. She shook her head: the sliding orbs didn't seem like the beam of a torch.

Mugs in her hands, she scuttled back to Leah, quickly sitting down by the hearth.

Leah accepted the hot chocolate gratefully. 'I'm going to import my photos. Then how about we watch a film?'

'Okay.' Zoe was relieved to drag herself back to normality: warmth and a good chick flick or a comedy would be ideal. She slurped her drink, enjoying the comforting thickness of chocolate, licking the curve of moustache imprinted on her upper lip.

Leah's eyes were shining in the firelight. 'I can't stop thinking about what Mirren said about the chapel in the southwest tower. I mean, how perfect. The wedding idea could be such a money-spinner. Don't you think that Abigail will love it?'

'She might, yes...'

Leah grabbed Zoe's hand. 'Shall we go and explore?'

Zoe opened her eyes wide. 'Now?'

'I'm sure one of the keys fits that tower. We could go and take a look at the chapel... we could take torches...'

Zoe tried to think of an excuse. The idea of roaming round the southwest wing in semi-darkness made her feel extremely uncomfortable. 'What about tomorrow? When it's light?'

'I'm talking to Aidan Irving tomorrow and working on the website...'

'Please... let's just stay here in the warm,' Zoe pleaded.

Leah saw desperation in her sister's eyes. She reached out and felt Zoe's hand. It was still ice cold. 'All right. We'll go another day. Let's stay by the fire tonight.'

'Thanks.' Zoe sipped from her mug, staring into the flames.

Leah thought how nice the southwest wing might look filled with candlelight, perhaps with the addition of a cleverly designed stained-glass window to reflect the style of the thirteen hundreds. She hoped there was already an altar in there, perfect for a wedding. She could fill the space with flowers, flooding each corner with the scent of sweet petals.

She glanced towards Zoe, who seemed to be a bit tired, in a half-dream. The walk must have taken it out of her. Leah's heart lurched towards her sister. Zoe was the kindest and most generous of people. She'd come to Ravenscraig for Leah's sake, leaving her friends and her busy social life behind in Birmingham. Leah would find more ways to show her gratitude; they'd go out, visit the pub in Rosemuir, have an evening in Inverness. She'd talk to Zoe, ask her what she'd enjoy most. A spa day, perhaps, somewhere she'd feel pampered.

Then Leah's thoughts returned to the southwest wing. She wanted to go there so badly. She'd write a business plan to incorporate the whole castle: the grand hall for the reception, a wedding suite upstairs. It would be Scotland's newest and most sought-after wedding venue.

She glanced towards Zoe. The castle was a chilly place, and Zoe seemed to feel the cold. Maybe it would be best if Leah took the keys tomorrow or the next day and explored the southwest tower alone. Then she'd tell Zoe about it later, coax her to come along for a second visit.

Leah sipped hot chocolate and closed her eyes. She breathed out slowly. She'd wait her chance, then she'd go to the chapel by herself and take a look around.

19

On Sunday morning, Agnes stood silently in the small chapel between Una and Effie, listening to Friar John speak to the congregation about loyalty to the king and to the master, how the English presence in Scotland made its people hold their breath. He spoke about love and how hatred was its enemy. Several soldiers guarded the door, still as statues. A cold wind from the loch cut through her shift and tunic, making Agnes shiver despite the August sunshine. Friar John was a Franciscan monk who travelled across the parish and was a friend and frequent visitor of Ross McNair, now standing at the front with his wife, head bowed, as the friar continued his sermon.

Agnes gazed up into the rafters where a small bird beat its wings briefly and came to rest. Her eyes strayed to the stone walls and the two high windows funnelling shafts of bright light onto the hard ground. Effie leaned closer, sucking a finger, her eyes almost closed as she listened to the friar speak.

'For the Lord's words were written for our guidance and these are hard times, but we must uphold his commandments. We are instructed to be loyal in Revelations Chapter 2, verse 10. "Do not fear what ye are about to suffer. Behold, the devil is about to throw some of ye into prison, that ye may be tested, and for ten days ye will have tribulation. Be faithful unto death, and I will give ye the crown of life." Indeed, these times are not what we might choose, but we must be steadfast...'

Agnes pushed his words from her mind. She didn't want to imagine being thrown into prison and tested for ten days. She cast her eyes to the ceiling again, wondering if the body of the smith was above them in the tower. Opposite, across the chapel, An-Mòr and Rhona were standing together, heads bent. An-Mòr was a good man, a man of peace who did his duty: he would only have assisted in the slaughter of the smith unwillingly. Rhona was fierce and loyal; her son Hendrie was the same: they hated the English and were unafraid to fight. Agnes was thinking about the dark-haired warrior, imagining him in battle, wondering about the risks he took to remain loyal to the king.

The friar was still talking quietly. 'I ask ye all to pray today for Ross McNair, who must each day make difficult decisions as master of this castle. The Lord says in Psalms 59, verse 5, "You, O Lord God of hosts, the God of Israel, Awake to punish all the nations; Do not be gracious to any who are treacherous in iniquity."'

Agnes closed her eyes, listening to the friar talking about guidance from God; he mentioned the book of Genesis, the peace of the brethren, the peace of the flock, and she imagined herself with the warrior, wrapped in his arms. Her pulse quickened as she saw them smiling into each other's eyes, at peace, walking in the dappled forests, living in a small hut with a smoking fire, spending each day laughing together, each night side by side beneath a warm blanket, her head against his chest.

She felt a small hand take hers and when she opened her eyes, she met Effie's questioning gaze. The service was almost at an end;

everyone had bowed their heads in final prayer. Agnes did the same, her thoughts returning to the warrior as the friar's prayer drifted away.

* * *

On Monday morning, Agnes rose early as usual, smoothed her tunic and apron, collecting the buckets, rushing outside across the quiet courtyard to the well. A rooster crowed as Agnes bent to fill the pails in the grey light of the dawn. She listened hard; a solitary bird cheeped in the distance, a repetitive creak like the sound of a cartwheel turning. Agnes left the filled pails on the hard ground and hurried towards the calm stretch of loch, breathing lightly, nervous as she ran.

She saw him in the grainy light, she was sure it was him; a movement in the water, the familiar round head gliding through the still loch. She stared, watching the dip and rise, the strong muscular arms scissoring the water. Agnes realised she was hardly breathing. It was good to watch him swim, the ease of his body's movement, the leisurely pace as if he had nowhere else to be. She thought of the chill of the loch and marvelled at his indifference.

Agnes edged closer: his horse was tethered to a tree; his clothes were piled beneath: a dark tunic, a dagger in a sheath. She held out her fingers towards the horse, who snuffled gently, sniffing the scent of food.

A sharp sound made her turn. He had stopped swimming and was watching her, surrounded by ripples in the water: he threw back his wet hair, droplets cascading, and she saw the pale flesh of his shoulders, the tangled hair of his chest appearing above the surface. He called out to her, something she couldn't make out, but she heard the humour of his tone.

Indecision held Agnes for a moment, then she pulled her tunic over her head, slipping out of her shift, tugging off her cowskin shoes. He was staring at her, and for a moment time stood still, then Agnes rushed into the loch. The first sensation was the intense cold water like a shock to the heart, taking her breath away, needles against her flesh, then the burning sensation of ice. She had no idea how to swim; she thrashed her arms and suddenly the loch swallowed her as she dipped below the surface. Agnes struggled, pushing her arms and legs against the water, gasping and spluttering as her head bobbed up for a moment before she was sucked below again.

Then his strong arms held her, heaving her upright, circling her waist. He was next to her, black hair over his face.

She gasped. 'It's so cold.'

'Most people cannot stand the ice of the loch. It's even colder the further ye swim out, and in the winter, it is unbearable to anything but fish.' He spoke gruffly. 'Can ye not swim?'

Agnes blinked the water from her eyes defiantly. 'No, but if ye can do it, it cannae be so difficult.'

'I could teach ye...' he said. His grip on her arm was firm. She stared into his eyes and again she couldn't tug her gaze away. Then he said, 'You'll freeze. Hold on to me. I'll get us both back to dry land.'

Agnes wrapped an arm around him, feeling the iron muscle tensing in his shoulder. He began to swim, a powerful easy stroke, pushing them both towards to the loch's edge, her eyes staying on him all the time. Then she felt solid ground beneath her feet and stood up, rushing from the water, splashing and laughing. She grabbed her shift from the ground, pulling it over her head in a smooth movement, then she reached for her tunic. She twisted back towards the loch, still shivering, and there he was, looking at her, waist-deep in water. Agnes lifted her chin, then she ran to the tree where his horse was standing and snatched up his tunic, holding it high. 'You'll be wanting this?' She laughed, watching his level gaze. 'Or are ye intending to stay in the cold loch all day?'

For a moment, he seemed unsure, then he said, 'Turn your back for a moment, lassie, for the love of God.'

She threw the tunic on the ground and whirled away from him, listening to the sound of water rippling. She knew he had approached the horse and was struggling into his clothes. Agnes laughed quietly to herself: he was hopping on one leg, then the other, trying to dry himself. Suddenly he was behind her, his arms around her waist. She turned, looking into a serious face as he held her tightly, pulling her against him. Agnes knew he was about to kiss her, so she wriggled free, taking a step backwards. Being close to him was unsettling and compelling at the same time. She'd never been kissed before and the thought of it made her skin prickle.

He frowned. 'Agnes...'

'Ye know my name,' she countered.

'I do. I heard it spoken in the castle. I ken well who ye are.'

'But I don't ken ye well,' Agnes replied spiritedly. 'And I won't kiss a stranger.' She met his eyes boldly. She'd called him a stranger, but there was already a strong connection she couldn't resist. Emotionally, spiritually, it was as if she knew him already. And she badly wanted him to kiss her. But making him wait gave her a delicious sensation of power.

'I'm Cameron Buchanan.' He stepped forward, held her in his grasp again. 'People call me Cam...'

'That's only your name. I still don't ken ye well.' Agnes's eyes sparkled with mischief.

'Aye, but ye will...'

'Then I'll kiss ye when I do.'

She moved back again and he advanced closer. Agnes smiled: it was like a dance; it was ridiculous and she almost laughed out loud. She wanted to tease him, but she wanted to be held even more. He wrapped his arms around her again. His voice was thick with emotion.

'Kiss me – or you'll kill me.'

Agnes squealed with delight; it was the funniest thing she had ever heard someone say. 'Next time I see ye, then perhaps I'll decide to kiss ye, Cam Buchanan. You'll have to survive as best as ye can until then.'

She was off, running back towards the castle, water squelching in her shoes, her wet hair drenching her tunic, still laughing. She heard him call, 'I'll find ye, Agnes, and soon.'

'Maybe ye will,' she called, then she was back in the courtyard, panting hard, lifting full pails, spilling water. Agnes couldn't stop smiling; she had swum in the loch with him and it had been exhilarating, the danger of intensely icy water, the thrill of being held fast in his arms. And he had wanted to kiss her: he had wanted to, badly.

Agnes shivered with a delicious feeling of being desired and being in control. Yes, she'd see Cam Buchanan, and yes, she might let him kiss her. And the thought of it made her skin tingle again.

* * *

Back in the kitchen, Agnes felt Rhona's watchful eyes on her. She clearly hadn't believed that Agnes was soaking wet because she'd spilled water from the well, nor had she accepted Agnes's protestations that she'd wanted to wash her hair so she'd doused herself from a bucket. But Agnes didn't care what Rhona thought. She didn't care what anyone thought of her, except perhaps for one person. She moved around with ease, kneading loaves of bread, winking conspiratorially at Effie as Una piled up more blackened pots for her to wash. Then she hurried over to the ale vat, stirring the grain, singing to herself.

O, where are ye gone, my Scottish warrior?
'Twixt the thistle and the mist o' the morn...

Rhona's eyes glistened as they met Agnes's, but Agnes swirled the ale with more vigour and asked her shamelessly, 'Do ye not like my song, Rhona?'

Rhona didn't answer. She scurried to the fire, staggering back with a hot pan. Agnes joined her, helping her to heave the boiling water towards the vat, and they lifted the heavy pot together, spattering the contents onto the malted grains. The steam rose, rich with warm aroma, and Agnes began to stir as hot splashes leaped to the top of the vat. She felt Rhona's fingers grip her arm. 'Be careful ye dinnae get scalded.'

Agnes stepped back from the steam, indignant. 'I'm used to the brewing now...'

Rhona shook her head. 'I wasnae talking about hot ale...' She moved her mouth close to Agnes's ear. 'I ken the laddie well. He's been asking about ye.'

Agnes's expression was one of exaggerated innocence. 'I've no idea who you're talking about, Rhona.'

'Aye, ye ken well enough,' Rhona hissed and Agnes thought that she seemed sad. 'It'll bring ye both nothing but heartache.'

'I think not.' Agnes tried again, 'What does it matter if I—'

'He fights for the king, lassie. The same as my son.' Rhona's face was suddenly tired. 'Heed my words well, Agnes. I'm sure there will come a day they'll take my Hendrie from me, the English soldiers – they'll hang him from a rope and empty his life on the ground, like they did with the king's brother. I ken it will come to be and it kills me each day to think on it, but I cannae stop it.'

Agnes was momentarily stunned by Rhona's fierce words: she intended to make her point.

'I've no choice but to let him do as he wishes – he's a grown man. It'll break my heart in a hundred pieces, Agnes, but there's nothing to be done – I'm his mother. I do what he needs me to do. I believe in my son; I fight for him each day in my whole being so that he can fight the English. But ye can walk away now, before ye find yourself in the same place as I am. Dinnae give this young man your heart...'

Agnes felt that the breath had been taken from her lungs. She faced Rhona. 'I ken him, Cam Buchanan.' Rhona continued, 'He's a friend of Hendrie's, a brave soldier, a good laddie. And I ken he has a soft spot for ye.'

'I like him well enough.'

'Then it cannot end happily. Of that ye can be sure.' Rhona shook her head, then she murmured to herself sadly, 'But when young ones meet and fall in love, there's nothing that can be done. They willnae listen to older wiser ones.' She sighed. 'Will ye not take a warning from one who knows best?'

Agnes pressed her lips together. 'I'm not sure that I can...'

'He said the same thing when I spoke to him yesterday – he's determined to talk to ye. I'm guessing that's what happened this morning. He won't be told to stay away, to let things be as they are,' Rhona said sadly. 'Well, we can't stop what comes to pass – love, war, death, tears. What will come will come and that's the end of it. But ye cannae say ye havnae been told.'

Agnes took in Rhona's words, then she raised her chin. 'What if it doesn't come to that? What if it's not bound to end in heartache? What if we meet again and we like each other well? What if love can take wings and fly above all the fighting and the hatred for all time?'

Rhona swirled the grains, her head bowed. She didn't answer.

Agnes stared deep into the depths, watching the ale bubble. She'd be fine; she'd see Cam Buchanan again soon, she'd kiss him, she knew it. Their path was already set in stone, it couldn't be changed; she'd known that at first glance and swimming in the loch, his arm around her, had made up her mind. She wasn't afraid to walk along the path, no matter how steep the fall on either side. Love was everything. She began to sing again, her voice tender with emotion.

> *O, where are ye gone, my Scottish warrior?*
> *'Twixt the thistle and the mist o' the morn...*

20

On Monday morning, Zoe was seated at her laptop humming to herself, reviewing a report from the Charities Aid Foundation. She was making notes on her findings for the next video call to Sharon later in the week. She typed rapidly: *The number of people donating to charity has decreased from 69 per cent in 2016 to 62 per cent in 2020 and in the last years there have been 1.6 million fewer donors.* She scratched her head and pondered the problem, glancing towards Leah, who was poring over the new website she had almost finished creating. Zoe watched affectionately as her sister leaned over the desk absently and brought a mug to her lips, replacing the drink down without even noticing. She called, 'What time is your Mr Irving phoning?'

Leah didn't look up. 'This afternoon, about two. Why?'

Zoe glanced at the time on her laptop: it was 11:57. 'I was just wondering about lunch.'

'Mmm.' Leah made a sound of vague interest as she moved the mouse around photos of the loch.

Zoe pushed her chair back. 'I fancy mushroom soup.'

'Have we got any?'

'I mean fresh, made from scratch.' Zoe stood up, stretching her legs.

'Ah,' Leah grunted. 'We might have a couple of skanky mushrooms in the back of the fridge…'

'I'll go in to Rosemuir and get some. I might be able to find some nice bread too.'

'Sounds like a plan.' Leah scrutinised a photograph of the lone deer they had seen in the forest and began to edit the border, bringing the beast into clearer view.

'Do you want to come?'

Leah wrinkled her nose. 'I'm on a roll here, Zo. Mind if I don't?'

'Not at all.' Zoe reached for her jacket, bag and car keys. 'I'll pick up a few other things while I'm out. I won't be too long – an hour, tops.'

'Perfect.' Leah was still examining the photo on the screen.

'See you then,' Zoe called as she stepped out of the warm room onto the cool landing, prepared to make a rush through the chill air of the spiral staircase.

Leah listened to her footsteps and the dull thud of the main door closing. She glanced over the top of the laptop through the window towards the southwest wing. The pale sun gleamed on the loch, making the crumbling wall shine silver. She watched Zoe hurry across the courtyard as she reached across the desk for the set of iron keys on the ring. She'd have enough time to visit the chapel, look around the tower, take some photographs and come back to her laptop before Zoe returned with the shopping.

Leah felt the cold iron of the keys in her hand and a tiny shiver of excitement wriggled down her spine. She reached for her jacket and grabbed a torch: it'd be cold in the chapel, no doubt, and probably dark.

* * *

Zoe's bag bulged with groceries: she'd bought enough vegetables to last a week. The air was fresh and clean, a breeze blowing straight from the loch, and Zoe decided she wasn't ready to return to work yet. She left her purchases in the Mini, parked in the car park of The Canny Man and found her way to the lounge bar. It was almost empty, apart from two men playing darts. The jukebox played an unidentifiable jangly rock song; Kenny was at the bar, singing along to himself, wiping a glass. He recognised her immediately. 'Zoe, good to see you. I didn't have you down as a lunchtime boozer. What can I get you?'

'Just a coffee please.' Zoe sat on a tall stool. 'I fancied a break – I work from home.'

'Anyone would fancy a break from Ravenscraig,' Kenny quipped as he poured coffee from a glass jug. 'It must be very cold in those big rooms this time of year.'

'It is.' Zoe accepted the cup and saucer gratefully. She took a sip. 'Lovely and strong. Thanks.'

'Freshly brewed,' Kenny told her. 'Stay for lunch. I have a good Cullen Skink today.' He saw Zoe's bemused expression. 'Creamy smoked haddock soup. Some might say it's a bit like a chowder.'

'Sounds delicious, but it'll have to be another time – I promised to cook lunch for Leah today.'

'How's your sister managing at the castle?' Kenny arranged his face in an inquisitive expression. 'She's the caretaker, isn't she?'

'Yes. She loves it.'

'She does?' Kenny grinned. 'The last two caretakers couldn't get away fast enough. They lasted less than three months.'

'Why?' Zoe leaned forward.

'The atmosphere of the place. You must have noticed it...'

'It's a bit eerie,' Zoe agreed.

'That's one way of putting it. The last couple were nervous wrecks by the end of their time – and those before them...' Kenny gave a small cough. 'Well, I'm glad your sister seems to be making a go of it.'

'She is. She has all sorts of ideas for the castle. She thinks it would make a great place for a wedding venue.'

Kenny laughed, astonished. 'Hallowe'en, more like.' He composed his face. 'I was just talking about the castle last night. Christie Watt was in here – he has the building company that work at Ravenscraig. You know the main castle has been renovated over the last few years, the great hall and the guest rooms? Christie and his team have done all that. They've made a cracking job of it. He says there's only the southwest wing left to do, but he's in no hurry to start.'

'So, when will that happen?' Zoe asked.

Kenny shook his head. 'Christie says there are plans afoot to rebuild it, but it's a strange building, the southwest wing. I know Mirren Logan's a bit fussy about it – she keeps the place in order, but it has a bit of a reputation, dating back to the time of Robert the Bruce, I believe. I don't know much about it, but a few of the locals think that part of the castle's to be avoided.' He grinned. 'It's probably due to Mirren hanging around the place, scaring everyone off.'

'Oh?'

'Strange lady,' Kenny said. 'A bit eccentric, lives by herself in a wee cottage in the village, crammed with old books and antiques apparently. She doesn't really mix in with the community. She's probably scarier than any spooks you'll find at Ravenscraig.'

'I've met her.' Zoe nodded. 'She seems a bit... cryptic.'

'Aye, that's a good word, cryptic. Like she comes from the crypt.' Kenny laughed once, then he glanced at Zoe's empty cup. 'Do you want another one of those?'

'I'd better be getting back,' Zoe replied. She took out her card and tapped to pay. 'But this is definitely my local go-to place to hang out. Thanks, Kenny.'

'Any time.' Kenny grinned. 'And I'll tell Christie to call in on you both at the castle. Give him a cup of tea and he'll tell you all about the place.'

'That would be great.' Zoe swung her handbag onto her shoulder and slid down from the high stool. 'See you soon.'

* * *

Leah twisted the iron key in the lock, hearing a satisfying clunk. She pushed the heavy wooden door wide and stared into the chapel. A bird flapped high in the rafters as she gazed from the doorway into the empty space. Opposite, a tall window looked out towards the loch, a smaller one on the adjacent wall was circular, both of them unglazed, allowing a slice of bright light and a cold breeze to circulate. The chapel was dingy and bare, and to the right there was a narrow stone staircase winding around a corner into shadows.

Leah stepped inside and flicked on the torch. The chapel was clean: Mirren had obviously swept any cobwebs and dust away. Leah felt a little disappointed: she'd been expecting a pretty place, more friendly, but the chapel was hollow and unwelcoming.

She thought for a moment. With some white paint, beautiful custom-made stained-glass windows reflecting colour and light onto the floor, some tall candles, strategically placed tubs of fragrant lilies, the chapel could be beautiful. Intimate, Leah told herself: it could probably accommodate thirty people at a push for a wedding. And, of course, in springtime, the party could extend into the courtyard; Leah could fill the outside space with tangled garlands of flowers sweeping over archways that the happy couple could walk beneath while the guests threw confetti. She imagined Mariusz and Jordan together in white suits; she, Zoe and Bex would be bridesmaids, flowers in their hair, flinging handfuls of bright petals. Yes, Leah was sure she could make it work.

Something caught her eye on the floor and she moved into the chapel, conscious of the biting draught. As she passed the staircase that twisted up into darkness, she felt a sudden chill that filled her with a strange emptiness. She shone the torch and the beam picked out a single orange flower in the beam of light. Leah rushed over to pick it up. It was a chrysanthemum, a round head of delicate amber petals on a long stalk.

Then she heard the heavy door slam behind her and almost all the light was taken from the chapel. Leah whirled round, staring into gloom. She hurried to the door, tugging the iron latch, but it had closed firmly: the keys were still in the lock outside. She pulled harder but the door would not budge.

She turned back to blink in the meagre light that filtered from the high windows. Holding her breath, she squeezed the torch and shone it towards the ceiling. Something rustled above her, a large bird, a raven perhaps, beating heavy wings. She swept the light around the room, hovering in dark corners where shadows seemed to dissolve and move. Then she recalled the phone in her pocket: she'd call Zoe and explain that she'd locked herself in the chapel. It would be no problem: Zoe would be on her way home by now.

Leah moved the torch to her left hand and the bulb flickered and faded to nothing. She pressed the small switch twice, three times and shook it hard, but the torch would not illuminate: the battery had died. Leah delved into a jacket pocket for her phone; it would serve as a torch and she'd call Zoe.

Then something moved beside her, too close; a hand touched her hair, a light brushing of fingers. Leah whirled around, heart thumping in her throat; someone was in the chapel with her. She called tentatively, 'Hello?' and was suddenly terrified that someone would speak back to her. The echo took her voice and made it hollow. She stared into a corner, where she was sure someone was huddled, breathing. She listened harder: it came again, a low gasp. There was a movement, a grainy shadow lurching forward, a human shape almost, the thrust of an outstretched arm, then the silhouette twisted towards the ground and was gone.

Leah held up her phone, finding Zoe's number, pressing the button to ring, as unseen fingers snatched the phone from her grasp, whirling it across the chapel. Leah heard it clatter against the floor with a dull thud.

* * *

As Zoe was driving towards Ravenscraig, she recognised the person walking steadily by the side of the road; she knew the grey coat, the pale hair over her face. She slowed, winding down the window to call out, 'Mirren, isn't it? Are you going to Ravenscraig?'

Mirren continued walking, her rhythm uninterrupted. She stared ahead. 'I have business to do in the chapel.'

'Of course,' Zoe called. 'I can give you a lift.'

Zoe stopped the car and Mirren hesitated, bringing her face close to the passenger window that gaped wide. Zoe noticed her light blue eyes glittering beneath sketchy brows, thin lips, a hardness around the cheekbones that suggested she rarely smiled. 'I can walk.'

'Of course, but...' Zoe offered her most accommodating expression. 'Let me give you a lift. I'm going back for lunch.'

Mirren scrutinised Zoe's face as if making a decision, then the door was tugged open and Mirren was in the car, huddled inside the old grey coat like a bag of rags. She pulled on the seatbelt awkwardly, refusing to meet her gaze as Zoe began to accelerate away.

They drove in silence before Zoe asked politely, 'Have you worked at Ravenscraig for long?'

'Since Abigail Laing asked me to. Since the new man started bothering himself with all the building work, wanting to bring the castle back to how it used to be.'

'So...' Zoe chose her words carefully. 'What do you do in the chapel?' When Mirren didn't answer, she added, 'Do you clean it?'

'It needs to be left alone.' Mirren's voice was suddenly sad. 'It shouldn't be touched. The chapel is as it was in the days of King Robert. And the tower must never be disturbed.'

'Why? What's in the tower?' Zoe asked.

Mirren turned sharply and her eyes were small and hard. 'My father was David Logan, a man of this parish – he died five years ago, just when the work began on the castle. You know, there have been Logans in Rosemuir since the late twelve hundreds, when they lived in small huts that smelled of smoke because they had no chimneys. I am the last one of a long line.'

'Oh...' Zoe wasn't sure what to say.

'There are stories, tales from long ago, passed down from father to son and mother to daughter. Those stories will die with me, and perhaps that's as it should be.'

Zoe was puzzled. The castle loomed just beyond them, and Zoe manoeuvred the Mini through the gate and over the hump in the track, parking by the stone well. 'Here we are.'

Mirren was already out of the car and on her way to the main gate.

Zoe caught up with her as she stepped through the archway and into the courtyard. 'I'm making some mushroom soup for lunch – can I offer you—'

Mirren stopped abruptly, staring towards the southwest wing. She pointed to the door, where a set of iron keys hung from the lock. Her eyes widened. 'Who's inside the chapel? No one must go in there.' Her face was pinched with shock. 'You have no idea about this castle, about its history, do you?'

'I don't understand. Why are there keys in the lock?' Zoe shook her head. 'Oh, they must be Leah's...'

'Things from the past should be left where they are.' Mirren closed her eyes for a moment, then, when she opened them, her voice was quiet. 'Your sister must be in the chapel. And I warned you both not to go in...'

21

The following day as the first weak rays of the sun filtered from behind the mountains, Rhona insisted thar Effie accompany Agnes to the stone well to collect water. Effie chattered non-stop while Agnes lowered the empty buckets, then raised them full, placing them carefully on the ground. Agnes stared towards the loch through the dim light, wondering if Cam Buchanan was swimming or waiting for her beneath the tree. Agnes was unsure when she would have the chance to talk to him again. She was determined that Rhona would not stop her from meeting him: she was sure that Effie had been sent along to make sure she strayed no further than the well.

Effie twirled a strand of hair in her fingers. 'Your mother once said that I was born at the end of August. So soon I must be seventeen, or even eighteen. That makes me a grown woman now, doesn't it?'

'I suppose it does.' Agnes's mind elsewhere.

'I've had my monthly courses for well over two years now. So I need to find myself a handsome young man, one who'll fall in love with me and ask me to marry him.'

'It'll happen one day,' Agnes replied fondly. 'But there's no hurry...'

'That's what I'd like most in the world, to find someone who'd take me away from Ravenscraig. I hate it here.' Effie sniffed, swishing her tunic. 'If I still had the princess's cloak to wear, perhaps a handsome man would notice me and ask for my hand.' Her brow clouded. 'I liked it when everyone thought me a princess. I was treated so kindly. Now all I have is Una pulling my ears every time I make a mistake. They've become so big, she tweaks them every day.'

Agnes bent towards the well. 'Ye still have pretty wee ears, hennie.'

'But...' Effie was momentarily sad. 'Una tells me no man will want me because of my foolish daffin'. She says I am weak in the head and I wouldnae ken what to do with a man if I had one, but I'm sure I would. What d'ye think, Agnes?'

'I think it likely...' Agnes was carrying the two heavy pails, Effie next to her with the third, water lapping over the sides as she struggled across the cobbled courtyard.

'It would be lovely, Agnes, all that kissing and cuddling, and a man telling me I'm the loveliest lassie in the world. It makes my insides feel all warm to think of it.' Effie's eyes were round globes. 'Someone will choose me. I'm bonnie, I know it. And it matters not what others say in the castle – I'm not half-witted, am I?'

'No, ye are fine, Effie. Everyone comes to things in their own time. One day you'll meet someone you'll love who'll love ye back.' Agnes couldn't help the way her voice thickened with emotion. She tugged her thoughts from images of the too-brief embrace she'd enjoyed yesterday. 'It'll happen, in the fullness of in time.'

'But you're twenty-two, Agnes, and it hasnae happened to ye. Ye didn't love Colban, did ye? We saw his throat cut and it was sad, but it didnae break your heart.'

'He was a friend, Effie, and it was horrible to see it. I'll never forget what the English soldier did to him.'

'Do ye hate the English, Agnes? Do we all hate them?'

'They are our enemies, and enemies of the king.'

They had almost reached the kitchen. Effie put down her bucket, which was now only half full. 'I'm afraid of the English soldiers and it makes me afraid of everyone. Even the men who guard the castle here frighten me, with their swords and their stern faces. I've heard there are traitors who tell the enemy soldiers about us and I've heard they do horrible things to young girls. Una says you'll leave me one day, Agnes, and I'll be alone. Promise me that you'll stay with me for ever and ever.'

Agnes frowned. 'We're sisters, Effie, as good as...'

'But if ye go away, what will become of me? What if I'm alone and old, and Una still tweaks my ears and no one will be there to look after me...' Effie had tears in her eyes.

'We look after each other,' Agnes smiled. 'We always will.'

The kitchen was a hive of activity, meat roasting on the spit, bread baking, vegetables being peeled. Someone called out to Agnes for a bucket of water.

Rhona was by her side. 'I see you're not soaked to the skin today. And you've been a lot quicker about fetching water than ye were yesterday.' Her eyes bored into Agnes's. 'I'll have to send Effie with ye to the stone well every day.'

Agnes met her glare. 'It's all fine by me, Rhona. It will make no difference. I'll do as I please.'

'Aye, ye will,' Rhona replied.

Effie was all ears; she tucked an arm through Agnes's and began to suck a finger. She watched Agnes raise her chin high in defiance as Rhona folded her arms firmly.

'Well, young lassie, tonight you're coming home with me.' Rhona raised her eyebrows. 'I have some weaving to do, Agnes, and I need help.'

Agnes shrugged. 'Why me? I'm no weaver. I have no real skill for it...'

'Then you'll learn,' Rhona said. 'I asked the mistress and she said aye, ye could come home with me and An-Mòr and help me with the weaving, and tomorrow you'll be back at the castle at first light to fetch water.'

Effie's mouth hung open. 'Will she stay at your house in Rose-muir with ye and the giant man?'

'Aye, Effie, she will.'

'And can I come too?'

'Nay, ye cannot,' Rhona replied quickly. 'I just asked the mistress for Agnes.'

'But ye can ask again?' Agnes suggested. 'It would be good for Effie to learn to weave better too.'

'Maybe another time I'll ask for her.' Rhona grasped Agnes's arm. 'Come, ye have loaves of bread to bake.'

Effie had not moved. 'Please let me come with ye, Agnes.'

'Can she come?' Agnes pleaded.

Rhona was defiant. 'I've said it once – nay.'

'Agnes...' Effie's lip trembled as she clung to her arm.

Agnes lifted her hand away gently. 'It's but one night.'

'But I cannae be left by myself. I'm afraid for my own skin.' Effie's eyes brimmed. 'Una will beat me. I don't want to be alone here. I cannae—'

'Please, Rhona?' Agnes asked, but Rhona lifted a hard palm as if she would slap them both.

'Stint, the pair of ye. It's done now. Effie, there are pans to scrape. Agnes, the bread won't bake itself.'

'Aye, Rhona.' Agnes turned to Effie and hugged her, whispering, 'Go to, get the pots scrubbed. And dinnae worry. I'll come back extra early so we can draw water tomorrow...'

Effie's face was streaked with tears that had run into her mouth.

Rhona placed both hands on her hips fiercely and Effie looked away, snivelling.

'If ye say so.' Effie sniffed as she plodded towards the stack of dirty pots, where Una waited, arms folded.

Rhona leaned towards Agnes. 'She's a poor little scrap, that one. What will become of her?' She shook her head. 'I know she's your sister, Agnes, but—'

'Aye, she is, and I'll take good care of her,' Agnes retorted.

Rhona gave her a meaningful look. 'Don't forget, when I leave this evening, you're to come with me.'

* * *

The sun dipped low behind the crenelated castle wall as Agnes followed Rhona across the courtyard, past the southwest wing and through the main gate where the portcullis was raised. They crossed the drawbridge and walked towards the little village of Rosemuir. It had been easier to leave Effie than Agnes thought; she had settled herself in front of the fire as Agnes kissed the top of her head and said she would be back by morning. Effie's eyes were closing already: she was tired from the day's work.

Rhona was talking as she forged ahead. 'It's a hard life, Agnes. I brew beer all day, then I go back home to work my fingers to the bone to cook for An-Mòr, who's hungry and tired from the heat of the forge, and sometimes I have to feed Hendrie if he's there, and then I have weaving and—'

'Will your son be in your home when ye return?'

'Sometimes he's there, aye, but I rarely get the word before he arrives – he has a wife and bairn who wait for him,' Rhona said sadly. 'I fear for him. The English soldiers haven't found their way to Rosemuir yet and it's to be hoped that they don't, but our king is in hiding and they're bound to be searching for him all over the Highlands. The master has good guards here, but ye ken only too well that the country is full of traitors who'd betray him for a piece of gold. Aye,' she was thoughtful, 'being a wife and a mother is a double blessing, but it's a double curse: twice the love, twice the worry...'

'I dinnae concern myself overly much with the English.' Agnes laughed. 'Soon old Edward Longshanks will be dead and his weak son will be king and our soldiers will defeat him in battle and Scotia will be free again.'

'You're young, Agnes, and ye cannae understand fear. You're lucky to have escaped from the burning castle as ye did on the king's brother's horse. Aye, that was a plucky thing to do. But I cannae tell ye some of the horrible things the English soldiers would be capable of, and how they'd treat a bonnie lassie like yourself.'

'I was there at Kildrummy, with the noise of the soldiers fighting all about me and the fire burning outside the walls and the blood spilling on the ground. Aye, I was afraid.' Agnes's eyes flashed with anger. 'But I'd have put a dagger into the heart of anyone before I'd let them lay a finger on me.'

They had walked for a while; the smoke from the fires inside the thatched houses was visible in the distance, curling towards the darkening sky. Rhona smiled, her voice affectionate. 'You're a good lassie, Agnes. I like ye.'

'I like ye too, Rhona.' Agnes met her eyes. 'But I feel sad for ye. Ye have the love of a good man and ye have a brave son. Ye are blessed in life, yet ye worry about so many things that havnae happened'

'You're young and fearless but what ye say is right. I stay awake all night listening; when a rider passes and I hear the hooves of a horse, I hold An-Mòr tight as he snores in his sleep and I think, is this bad news come now? Has something happened to Hendrie? Or are the English soldiers on their way here to kill us all? They have taken our queen and the young princess and locked them away, and

I think to myself, have they taken our king too and murdered our men? Is our country theirs already?'

'Do not fear it.' Agnes stopped walking. They had reached the village now, surrounded by long stone houses with low roofs. 'Your son is a warrior. He and many other brave men will save us from the English. And we women, we ken how to use a dagger. I ken you'd cut an English soldier's throat like you'd chop a rooster if ye had to.'

'I would,' Rhona retorted, her lips tight.

'Aye, me too, if it came to it.' Agnes grasped Rhona's arm. 'I can promise ye that.'

'I believe ye would. Well, here we are.' Rhona paused by one of the houses and hugged Agnes warmly. 'I've done the right thing, bringing ye to my home, lassie. An-Mòr and I talked long into the night about it, but we've made the right decision.'

'To come to Rosemuir and help ye with the weaving?' Agnes was puzzled.

'Nay, that's not why I brought ye here.' Rhona pointed to the door. 'Ye go on inside.'

Agnes hesitated, unsure, then she stepped through the narrow doorway into the house, the thick smell of soot immediately filling her nostrils. She gazed at the fire in the centre of the room that sent coils of smoke into the thatched roof. She noticed the blackened stone walls, the animal rugs on the dirt floor, the pots and simple wooden furniture that An-Mòr would have made himself. Then she heard a voice say her name, 'Agnes,' and she whirled round to find herself in the arms of Cam Buchanan. She caught her breath.

'What are ye doing here?'

'I've come to claim my kiss,' he said simply and his mouth was against hers.

Agnes leaned towards him and kissed him back for all she was worth. At that moment, she was sure something incredible happened to her. In one kiss, she had bound herself to him for ever, given him her heart in exchange for her own.

He murmured into her hair and Agnes closed her eyes, lifted by feelings that engulfed her and swept her away.

They stood together, not moving. Then there was a quiet voice as Rhona stood in the doorway.

'An-Mòr will be here soon and I have his supper to fetch. You'd both better be going.'

Agnes clung to Cam. 'But what about the weaving?'

Rhona shook her head. 'There's no weaving, lassie. I'll do my own weaving. I discussed it with my husband last night and we both came to the same realisation. As you've both said, there's no way out of this now and ye cannae keep swimming in the cold loch each morning – someone will see ye both afore long or you'll catch your death.'

'I don't understand,' Agnes said.

Cam took her hand. 'Thanks to ye, Rhona, and to An-Mòr. I willnae forget that you've done this for us.'

Rhona sighed. 'Have her back at Ravenscraig before the dawn breaks, Cam. She mustn't be missed by the other servants.'

'Aye, I will.' Cam turned to Agnes. 'My horse is outside, and he's strong enough to take the two of us. We're going for a ride together into the forests, lassie. We have much to say to one another.' His eyes shone. 'And I want to kiss ye some more.'

22

Agnes had never felt so alive. Her skin prickled with excitement as she sat astride the horse, Cam behind her, galloping east through open fields and dark forests, the rich scent of earth in her nostrils. They rode for over an hour as night fell, but the horse hurtled on confidently, sure-footed. The wind was behind them and with Cam's arms around her and his mouth against her ear, she was warm and safe. The stallion's sprint slowed to a trot, then a steady plod as they emerged from a dense clump of trees to a winding road that took them down to a beach. The whispering of waves rushed in Agnes's ears as Cam helped her down from the horse's back, wrapping his arms around her. She stared up into a sky crammed with stars and whispered, 'Where is this?'

'A secret place, far from the English armies. It's called Munlochy. We can stay for a while.'

Agnes felt the warmth of his breath against her face. 'What will we do here?'

'Talk, spend some hours. I have brought food to share. I can teach ye to swim in the sea if ye wish it. Then we'll need to rest awhile. Ye must be back to the castle tomorrow and I don't want ye falling asleep in the kitchen.'

Cam kissed her again until Agnes pulled away and they stared at each other for a moment. She noticed the gleam in his eyes, the way his gaze fastened to hers. Then he moved to the horse, pulling something from a side bag attached to the saddle. He took out a woollen blanket and wrapped it around her, then he thrust a piece of bannock bread into her hand. Agnes bit into the crust hungrily. 'It's good.'

He smiled. 'It was made by your own fair hands.'

'How did ye come by it?'

Cam tore off a piece for himself. 'Rhona brings food for me from the castle sometimes. It cheers me to eat something I know you've made.'

'But how do ye live, where do ye sleep?'

'There's a hut in the woods where I stay many nights. But I cannae light a fire there often for fear of being seen. Sometimes I stay with Hendrie and his wife and bairn, and with other men who fight alongside me. We seldom stay in one place; we eat and sleep where we can, away from the English armies.'

Agnes snuggled closer, inhaling the warmth from his body. 'And the king? What of him?'

'I ken where he is. He's safe, in hiding, at a farm not too far from here.' He sighed, and Agnes felt his chest rise against her cheek. 'There will be a battle soon, when The Bruce has enough men to make an army. Until then, we take out a few of the English, mostly at night-time. We attack castles or we hide and wait our chances.'

Agnes thought for a moment. 'Have ye always been a warrior?'

'Far from it...' She heard him laugh softly. 'My father had a piece of land south of here, at Montrose Beach. I've always loved being by the sea. I learned to swim as a child. I worked with horses until the English came. They took our land. I saw them kill my father. It was the first time I used a sword and dagger in anger.'

'What happened?' Agnes felt her grip tighten around his shoulders.

'They burned everything we owned. I got my mother away from the English. They murdered my wee brother too. He wasnae eighteen years old. I killed the soldier who did it. He was my age – I was twenty-three then – but I felt nothing. Then I took my mother and my horse and rode away. I've never been back.'

'And your mother?'

He shook his head. 'I left her with an aunt. She didnae last through the winter. That was almost two years ago. I came north to fight for the loyal men against the English. There's just me now.'

'Ye have me,' Agnes said.

'Aye, that I do, and I want it to stay that way.'

'How will we be able to meet each other?'

Cam kissed her again. 'Ross and Muriel McNair are good people. I spoke to them about ye, that I needed to be with ye, that my feelings were true. They told Rhona to take ye to her home, to say ye were needed to work on the weaving. She'll bring ye there some nights when she can and I'll be waiting. For now, no one must know we meet, Agnes.' Cam's voice was low. 'But we'll make plans, then when the time is right...'

'Then what?' Agnes held her breath, waiting for his next words. She knew what they were before he spoke.

'Then we can be together, like Hendrie and his wife living in the forests. Until the Scots can claim their country as their own again, we'll be in hiding, but we'd have each other.' He pulled her close. 'Aye, that's the chance we take.'

'I'm not afraid of it,' Agnes said defiantly. 'It's what I want.' She closed her eyes. Cam had taken her heart by storm and he loved her. She'd never known such intensity, such a feeling of belonging. In a short time, her life had changed forever and she wouldn't look back now.

'It's what I want too.' Cam took her hand. 'Are ye cold?'

'I am, but I'm warm inside.' Agnes smiled.

'I want to teach ye to swim. It'll be like ice in the sea, but it's tolerable in the summer. I find it helps me – there was so much anger in my soul after my father and brother were killed and the ice in the loch melts it somehow. We'll warm ourselves with a small fire when we come out – we'll not be seen here.' He tugged his tunic over his head and dropped it close to the horse. 'Sealgair will look after the clothes. I trust him with my life.'

'And now you're asking me to trust ye with mine?' Agnes hesitated. 'I cannae swim. I might drown...'

Cam pulled her into his arms. 'Your life is already more precious to me than my own.' He held her face in his palms. 'Who knows how long we have on this earth? I know for sure that the English seek The Bruce to kill him. When I fight for the king, I fight for the land I love and the woman I am growing to love. Agnes, I'm fighting for our future together, that we may grow old in our own land. I'll not let ye come to any harm.'

'I am not afraid,' Agnes retorted. 'Before I met ye, I wasnae.'

'I ken. When I first saw ye and I saw the way the light caught in your eyes, I was sure of it.'

She tugged the tunic over her head, shivering as the sea breeze blew through the thin shift. 'Then let us go together, Cam. Ye cannae teach me to swim while we're standing here.'

She reached out a hand and felt his fingers close around it. They ran towards the sea as it rushed forward to meet them. Agnes lifted her arms and hurled her shift behind her, laughing, increasing her speed, feeling cold water bite her toes and swirl around her knees. Then she was in water to her neck, her flesh almost numb, his arms around her, and she threw back her head and laughed again. In that moment, Agnes was truly happy. While she and Cam were together, she was fearless. Nothing could harm them, not ever.

* * *

Leah stood in the open doorway, the chapel gloomy behind her, and shuddered. 'I don't think I've ever been so scared.'

Zoe hugged her. 'I just pushed the door open – it wasn't locked.'

'I couldn't open it...' Leah took a deep breath. 'It was really terrifying.'

Mirren held the flower that was still clutched in her fingers against her cheek. 'I put this here. A chrysanthemum is an autumn flower. I choose a thistle in summer. This was all I could find, but I always leave a single flower, a sign of peace.' She walked towards the light from the window, standing in the slice of brightness, placing the orange bloom in the centre of the chapel. She picked up Leah's phone. 'Is this yours?'

'It flew out of my hands...' Leah began.

Mirren handed it to her. 'The screen is cracked.'

'I tried to call you...' Leah turned to Zoe, her expression desperate. 'I was only in here for a few moments, but the door slammed and the torch stopped working.' She turned her attention to the torch, pressing the switch. The beam lit up immediately. Leah frowned. 'It was so scary. I didn't even manage to take any photos. I wanted to go upstairs to the tower...'

'You can't go there,' Mirren said quickly. 'I know you're caretaker here, but you shouldn't go into the southwest wing.'

'But why?' Leah asked. 'I don't understand. The chapel is lovely, I mean, it has potential—'

Mirren placed a hand on Leah's arm. Her voice was soothing, the whisper of wind. 'Ravenscraig Castle is very old. It's been in ruins for a long time, and that's no coincidence. No one should live here. My father told me stories that have been passed down about the terrible things that happened. Those stories belong in the past, they're not for this time. And that's why I come to the chapel. I sit by myself to think about what must have happened.' She looked from Leah to Zoe. 'You wouldn't understand.'

'I might.' Leah met Mirren's eyes directly. 'I felt a presence...'

'I'm sure you did,' Mirren agreed. 'Are you happy here at Ravenscraig?'

'I love it,' Leah blurted.

'Then you'll be fine in the castle itself as long as you keep to your private rooms. Past caretakers haven't stayed long. There are stories about all sorts of creaks and bangs and such things.' Mirren glanced at Zoe. 'You should stay away from the southwest wing. Take my word, you don't want to know any more.' Mirren pressed Leah's arm. 'I had business to do here in the chapel, but I've seen enough for today. It's best to lock the door now. Go back to your rooms. Good day to you.'

Then she walked away, across the courtyard and through the main gate.

Zoe watched her go and turned to her sister anxiously. 'Shall we lock up here?'

Leah nodded, closing the heavy door with a clunk and turning the iron key. 'I've no idea what happened in there. It was so disturbing...'

'Let's go inside,' Zoe said calmly. 'I'll make some soup and we'll talk it through.'

Leah frowned. 'What time is it?'

'Ten minutes to two.'

Leah gasped. 'Oh no – Aidan Irving – I have to take his call.' She flapped a hand in front of her face. 'I'll have to get myself calm and professional. This could be my first business deal. Will you sort out lunch, please?'

'Of course.'

Leah was already rushing towards the castle entrance.

Zoe paused, looking back towards the southwest wing, at the heavy wooden door that led to the chapel, the tower above, and she thought again about Mirren's words: *you don't want to know any more.* Zoe began to walk back to the castle, gazing towards the tall gables, the fortified wall and the loch beyond. A raven swooped low, landing on the wall, spreading slick wings, and opened its beak, making a low cry. Zoe felt her heart lurch; she and Leah needed to have a long talk about Ravenscraig Castle. From where she was standing, she could see no future for the place as a wedding venue. In fact, at this moment, she wasn't sure that she wanted to live there at all.

* * *

Half an hour later, Zoe was pouring creamy mushroom soup into two bowls. The kitchenette was warm and the aroma of cooking was comforting. Zoe felt safer as she glanced through the window towards the southwest wing. In the sunlight, the stone gleamed and the courtyard was bright and welcoming. She wondered if she hadn't been hasty before, when she'd felt unsure if she wanted to stay at Ravenscraig. Mirren had been right; they could leave the chapel and the tower to her care and concentrate on their own work.

She carried the bowls of soup to the living room, placing them by the fireside, feeling the warmth of the blaze against her face. Even in summer, the fire would be essential; it would take the chill from the air.

Leah came to sit beside her, lifting a bowl and a spoon, tucking in. 'Thanks, Zo. This is great.'

Leah was completely calm, as if she had forgotten the incident in the chapel. 'How was the meeting with Mr Irving?'

'Aidan. We're on first-name terms now. He's been commissioned by a local whisky distiller, Glencharaid.' Leah grinned. 'He wants to do a photo shoot here.'

'Oh, that's great.' Zoe held her spoon in the air.

'He's coming over to meet me on Thursday.' Leah was delighted. 'I'm showing him round and we'll decide what works best for him. I think it will be all moody shots, views of the loch, rugged men in kilts drinking glasses of amber liquid, that sort of thing.'

'Oh, it sounds perfect,' Zoe said. 'Maybe he won't want to see much of the castle? I mean, he'll just want to do shots outside by the loch?'

'I don't know – I've promised to give him the full tour.' Leah's eyes shone. 'I told him I'll have the new website up before he comes and he should check it out. He was very impressed and I'm sure Abigail will be too when I land this one. He's prepared to pay the full whack.'

'That's great.'

Leah met her sister's eyes. 'I'm going to make this work. I know Mirren said that this place belongs in the past, but I think she's wrong. I'm not surprised it's creepy and creaky, it's still stuck in the fourteenth century. I want to bring it bang up to date, put it on the map. That will drive the ghosts away.'

'Leah...' Zoe began.

'No, I'm not bothered by what happened in the chapel – I won't let myself be. I was really inspired by talking to Aidan on the phone. He was excited by my ideas and I truly believe Ravenscraig has such potential. And,' she leaned forward confidentially, 'I still haven't given up the wedding venue idea.'

'That's good...' Zoe said, but she wasn't so sure.

She collected the empty bowls and took them back to the kitchenette, leaning against the sink to wash them, thinking. She stared out of the window, where a raven plummeted down to the fortified wall, its wings spread, twisting its neck to look around. It opened its mouth and cried out, turning an unblinking eye towards the castle. Zoe thought about what had happened to her sister in the chapel and felt her skin turn to ice.

23

The kitchen bustled with activity, but Agnes turned her back, kneading the bread vigorously, determined to keep her mind on her work. She'd tried to appear normal on the outside for three days now, deliberately helpful to everyone, exaggeratedly positive and cheerful. With Rhona, she talked only of daily duties, ale brewing, asking if An-Mòr was busy in the forge, once commenting on how beautifully the loch shone in the sunshine when she'd fetched water from the stone well. But inside, she was in turmoil, constantly waiting for Rhona to tell her that more weaving needed to be done and to invite her to the hut in Rosemuir.

Agnes was more affectionate and supportive than ever towards Effie, sharing her food, flashing a warning look towards Una every time she pulled Effie's ears or chided her for a mistake. In truth, Agnes felt a little guilty that she hadn't mentioned the night on the beach with Cam Buchanan to Effie. But she told herself that the time would come soon when she could be more open. For now, Cam's safety was most important, and that of their king in hiding: Effie was loyal and sweet, but Agnes wouldn't put it past her to blurt something out in a moment of enthusiasm.

Agnes enjoyed the quiet moments of introspection that often came with her work more than ever. When she was mixing flour with water or stirring the ale in the vat, she could think about Cam. She replayed the wonderful moments of her time with him and pushed other thoughts away. It was unwise to dwell on where he might be, what he might be doing. He was a warrior; he had told her that he took risks and she was determined not to spend her days imagining the worst as Rhona did with her son. Instead, Agnes allowed Cam to fill her thoughts.

The night had been perfect: he had been perfect. He had taught her the rudiments of swimming and she had learned fast. She'd moved strongly through the water, which had been penetratingly cold, colder than anything she had experienced. They had raced back to the beach, laughing; he had wrapped them both closely in a woollen blanket and she had leaned against him, shivering, becoming warmer against his skin. Agnes recalled the feelings that had saturated her at that moment, strong sensations she'd never felt before, and how she and Cam had stared into each other's eyes before he had pulled her shift on over her head and body, kissed her gently and promised that a time would come soon when they would belong entirely to each other. Agnes had been swept on a wave of emotions; passion, happiness, confusion, the thrill of expectation. She knew he felt the same as she did.

Later, he had lit a small fire amid stones and they had slept for a while on the beach in each other's arms. Then, as dawn had dappled the skies, they rode back to the castle. They had kissed too briefly and he had told her he would see her as soon as he was able, that one day, they wouldn't have to part. She had clung to him and he to her, then she had run towards the castle without turning back, her heart pounding with joy. Almost as soon as he'd left, her mind had filled with anxiety about when she would see him next. It was at that point that she had promised herself that she would be strong: she had chosen Cam and he had chosen her. It would be futile to worry about the future: they had the present moment and that was enough.

Agnes shaped the bannock bread for proving, touching the dough lightly with her fingers, wondering if Rhona would take some for Cam.

Then Effie was by her side, her eyes round. 'Is it time for some pottage? I'm tired, Agnes. Una says I can sit by the fire for a while.'

'Let's fetch more water first, hennie.' Agnes dusted her hands on her apron. 'Then it will heat in the pot over the flames while we eat.'

They walked through the courtyard. Several horses were tethered near the main gate near the forge, without their riders. The chapel door was closed and Agnes gazed up towards the narrow window in the tower, wondering if there were any new occupants there, if a traitor had been caught and was being questioned by faithful Scotsmen. She knew from Rhona that although most of the servants were loyal, not everyone could be trusted. A pouch of gold bought the services of a man or a woman whose word could cause the downfall of everyone in the castle. Agnes shuddered, leading Effie through the main gate towards the well, where they bent to fill their pails.

Agnes gazed towards the loch, the shining expanse of water that met the blue of the sky, and she closed her eyes in a brief prayer for Cam. She scanned the loch again; his horse was not there. He was elsewhere; busy doing the king's work.

Effie pulled at her arm. 'What are ye looking for, Agnes?'

Agnes smiled. 'I can smell autumn in the air.'

Effie shook her head. 'It's still the summer.'

'It will soon pass,' Agnes said and immediately her words made her feel sad.

She picked up the pails and walked slowly back towards the courtyard, Effie chattering at her heels.

* * *

Before they had finished eating, Una called Effie over to wash a
bucket of purple carrots. The pottage was unfinished, but Agnes
left it by the fireside. She took her place beside Rhona, picking up
the long spoon, stirring the malted grains. She offered a warm
smile. 'How fares An-Mòr?'

Rhona shrugged. 'Well enough. His belly is full mostly, and the
hut is warm. He is making more armour than ever; the master has
urged him to do so, to make preparations for battle.'

Agnes shivered without meaning to. 'Will there be a battle
soon?'

'The Bruce is gathering an army around him. He fears for
his queen in England. I hear Longshanks has her in severe
conditions of house arrest. He'll be anxious to get his family
back.'

Agnes kept her voice low. 'And her friend, The Earl of Atholl? I
saw the queen ride away with him. Was he taken too?'

'He was hanged by the English and his head displayed on
London Bridge. Hendrie told me he'd heard it from the loyal men
further south. A bloody battle will come before the winter is over,
I'm sure of it.'

Agnes said nothing. She stirred the ale vigorously, concentrating on pushing away the images that already filled her mind.
The memory of the cloying smell of blood, the clash of fighting in
Kildrummy was immediately playing before her eyes, but this time
it was not Niall de Brus but Cam Buchanan who was held captive
and dragged away by the English. She forced a smile. 'I'm sure a
battle will be fought well and the Scottish warriors will win a
victory.'

'Ah, pray God...' Rhona looked away. 'I could do with some help
tonight, and the mistress is glad that I have ye to assist me with the
weaving.'

'Tonight?' Agnes asked quickly, her voice betraying her excitement.

Rhona raised an eyebrow. 'Ye cannae keep the smile from your face, lassie. Aye, tonight, you'll walk home with me. But not a word, not even to Effie. Ye ken?'

'I do.' Agnes nodded and glanced towards the smaller girl. 'And it would be my pleasure to walk back with ye to Rosemuir later: I'm always happy to help ye with a little weaving...'

* * *

It was a perfect November morning, the sun dripping honey rays, giving the loch a bronze lustre. The courtyard sparkled and there was a crisp bite to the air. Leah was secretly excited as she extended her hand towards a tall man in a dark coat and red tartan scarf who greeted her with a smile. 'You must be Leah? I'm Aidan Irving.'

Leah recovered from his energetic handshake and was immediately struck by his good looks and charm. She decided he was a little older than she was; his hair was greying around the sides; he had dark-framed glasses, a direct gaze and a broad smile that suggested that he might be attracted to her. She was glad she'd dressed in a light grey suit with a warm jacket over the top, her hair smartly clipped up: she felt businesslike.

She met his eyes. 'Would you like to tell me about your campaign? We could start outside, I could show you the loch, and then we could go into the castle.'

'I'd like that.' Aidan pointed beyond the gate. 'I've parked the Audi by the Mini. I hope that's okay?'

'Of course,' Leah said, conscious of his low Scottish tones that rumbled attractively.

'The journey from Perth took me just over two hours. There's some delightful scenery.'

'Oh, there is,' Leah said enthusiastically. 'So, the loch is this way

– perfect for photographs in the winter sunlight, I'm sure.'

Aidan gazed around as he followed her through the archway, past the parked cars and the old stone well to the back of the castle, and they stood for a moment contemplating the smooth water. 'Just as I hoped. Breathtaking. I saw the photos of the view and this certainly doesn't disappoint.'

'So, you're looking to arrange a photo shoot for whisky?'

'Glencharaid. It's a relatively new brand. Have you tried it?'

'Yes, I think I have.' Leah recalled the strong drink she'd sipped tentatively in The Canny Man. 'Very quaffable,' she said, offering her most persuasive smile. 'So, do you think you could do a photo shoot by the loch here?'

'If the weather was like this, it would be ideal.' Aidan gazed towards the mountains beyond the lake. 'I'm imagining a muscular Scottish hero in a kilt – think *Braveheart* – coming out of the lake, dripping wet, body gleaming, swigging whisky from a glass in his hand.'

Leah grinned. 'It sounds lovely, but it's not historically accurate. *Braveheart* was set in the time of William Wallace, who died in 1305, and kilts weren't worn until the sixteenth century. Besides, the consumption of whisky began in the fifteenth century in Scotland.'

Aidan smiled. 'We could still have a bold Scotsman swimming in the loch.'

'You could but...' Leah thought for a moment. 'The loch is very deep, and cold water saps body heat. No one would swim in it, certainly not this time of year.'

'We could just put him in there for the photos. I'm thinking, close-ups of water droplets on a beard, sparkling blue eyes, a whiter than white smile. The setting is perfect. And the castle. Tell me a bit about its history, Leah.' He met her eyes directly and Leah wondered if he was testing her knowledge.

She waved a hand. 'Ravenscraig had fallen into disuse and was rebuilt by the owner over the last five years to resemble the way it would've looked in the thirteen hundreds, in the time of Robert the Bruce. Much of it is authentic.'

'Shall we go in?' Aidan asked. 'It's quite nippy out here.'

'It is,' Leah agreed, thinking to herself that it wouldn't be much warmer inside the castle.

As they crossed the courtyard, Aidan paused by the southwest wing. 'What's in there?'

'A small chapel. It's in need of renovation.'

'Up there...' Aidan pointed to the top of the tower. 'I can't see any windows, but the walls are crumbling. It looks quite atmospheric. Could we go up and take a look round? It might be just right for a shot of the whisky bottle, you know, by itself on a stone ledge, making it seem traditional and authentic?'

'Ah...' Leah hesitated. 'Let's see the castle first, shall we?' She decided she'd play for time: he might forget about the tower once he saw the great hall and the view from the window.

'I'm looking forward to it.' Aidan followed her as Leah pushed open the heavy castle door. He hesitated, resting a hand on her arm. 'Let's take a tour of all the old rooms. I'm guessing they'll be perfect for the central character in the photo shoot. A king, perhaps, a regal man and his wife in period costume, toasting each other at each end of a long table with golden glasses of Glencharaid. I can imagine the high ceilings, tapestries, huge open fireplaces, dim light.'

'Oh yes, we have all those,' Leah replied. She glanced at the hand that rested on her sleeve. There was no wedding ring. She smiled. 'Let's go take a look at the great hall.'

'Let's,' Aidan said. 'I have the feeling that everything about Ravenscraig is going to be exactly what I'm looking for. And then, afterwards, we could talk about dates for the photo shoot and maybe you'd let me buy you lunch somewhere?'

'That would be lovely.' Leah met his gaze behind the glasses, the shining eyes. 'I know a perfect little inn in Rosemuir.'

24

The summer drifted into autumn and quickly became a cold early winter, with darker mornings and shorter days. The scent of dampness clung to the earth and a thick pale mist hovered low over the loch. Agnes's life had become that of two different people. By day, she worked hard, baking bread, brewing ale alongside Agnes, and she was well-liked by most of the servants for her cheerful disposition and respected for her spirited remarks: she was witty and good-humoured with everyone in the kitchen, but she was quick to rise to the defence of any injustices. In particular, she made sure that Una knew she would stand no nonsense where Effie was concerned: the tweaking of ears and the constant nagging would have to stop. But, twice a week, sometimes more, Agnes would enjoy a deliciously secret life: while everyone believed that she was called to Rhona's hut to help with weaving, she would meet Cam and they'd travel to their beach, then, as the weather became colder, to his hut in the woods, where they would spend the night in each other's arms, whispering promises of love. Once, she'd joked that there was little linen to show for all the work they had done together, and Rhona retorted that she'd had to work twice as hard herself to keep up the appearance of newly spun clothes and blankets. Agnes's heart was full as she whispered thanks to Rhona. She would be ever grateful for what she and An-Mòr did to enable her to spend precious time with Cam.

It was a bitterly cold December evening, the wind laced with ice, as Agnes and Cam rode deep into the woodlands, stopping at a hut amid a dense growth of trees. He tied his horse next to a tree alongside a black destrier and took her hand, leading her to the doorway. 'There's some people I want ye to meet.'

Inside, a woman was cooking, stirring a pot over the fire, a child clutched in one arm. A fair-haired man was seated on the floor close by, bending over something with a knife, whittling. The man looked up. 'You're here. That's good.'

The woman approached; her hair was in braids and her face was soft with kindness. She spoke quietly. 'Ye must be Agnes. I'm Maidlin Logan. I've been looking forward to meeting ye.' She indicated the baby over her shoulder, a tuft of red hair topping a woollen shawl. 'This is Eaun He's eleven months old, although he's big for his age. He's sleeping now, but his teeth have been paining him today.' She looked towards Cam. 'Ye must both be hungry. Come, sit, and I'll bring ye something to warm ye.'

The man stood up: he was tall and willowy. He met Cam's eyes. 'Sit by the fire. Maidlin has made us a hearty stew.' He grinned. 'She's a great cook, even better than my mother.'

Agnes understood. 'Ye must be Rhona's son, Hendrie – I've seen ye before.'

Hendrie nodded, a frown between his eyes. 'Aye, the business with the smith at Ravenscraig. It's best forgotten now.' Then he smiled. 'There's warm ale. We'll sup soon.'

Maidlin gave her husband a searching look. 'Don't forget, ye promised to fetch logs in before we supped...' Agnes noted the warmth and fondness that passed between them.

'Aye, I did.' He raised eyebrows in Cam's direction, pretending to be pained by the task. 'Come, let's get to it and leave the women awhile... I'm sure they'll have much to jaw about.'

Cam's mouth was close to Agnes's ear as he whispered, 'I'll not be long.' He kissed her forehead.

Hendrie winked towards Maidlin and he and Cam moved through the entrance and out into darkness.

'The stew will all be gone if ye take too long – Agnes and I are hungry,' Maidlin called after him, teasing. She grinned. 'Hendrie thinks we'll chatter, but there's nothing like two men when they get talking. They forget about the time passing and the job they've been sent to do.'

'Can I help with cooking?' Agnes watched as Maidlin began to pour ale, the baby asleep on her shoulder.

'Rest. I'm sure ye work hard all day.' She handed Agnes a cup. 'I'm so glad Cam brought ye here – I've been asking Hendrie for months. I've been wanting to meet ye, to spend time with another woman. It gets so lonely here by myself when he's away.' Her face was suddenly serious. 'But Eaun keeps me busy and I have little time to sit and fret during the day. The nights are hardest. Every wee noise outside keeps me awake.'

Agnes met her eyes. 'I'm sure ye must worry when he's away.' She watched as Maidlin placed baby Eaun in a small crib and covered him with woollen blankets.

'I do.' Maidlin gazed at the child. 'I've just got the bairn off to sleep. Pray God he'll slumber awhile now.' She moved to sit next to Agnes and cradled the cup in her hands. 'I hate being here by myself when Hendrie's away fighting. I wonder constantly about his safety, or that the English soldiers will find this place and harm the bairn.'

'It must be difficult,' Agnes said; it was comforting to be huddled by the fire, talking to another woman.

'I make the most of the time we have when he's here,' Maidlin said simply. 'I love him.'

Agnes nodded. She understood.

They sat quietly for a while, sipping ale. Then Maidlin said, 'You've changed him; Cam's not the same.'

'Och, I hope not.' Agnes was surprised. 'I want him to stay as he is.'

Maidlin raised an eyebrow. 'The other men call him Allaidh. It's said the English soldiers mention him by that name too, and they fear him. Do ye ken what it means?'

Agnes shook her head.

'It means wild one. He is the most fierce of them all in battle. Hendrie says when they fight, Cam is always first into the fray, wielding his sword.'

'I don't see that in him,' Agnes said. 'He is the gentlest and kindest of men.'

Maidlin smiled. 'He is with ye. I've never seen him look the way he looks at ye, the tenderness in his eyes, the gentle touch when he puts his hands on ye. But seeing his father and brother killed in their home put a fire in his belly that won't go out, not while there are enemy soldiers in Scotia. Hendrie says Cam has a fury in him, that he'll fight until The Bruce is back where he belongs. Hendrie is loyal and devoted, but Cam is a true warrior.'

Agnes bowed her head to stare into the cup. She wasn't sure whether to feel proud of his reputation or afraid of what might become of him.

Maidlin rested a hand on her arm. 'Ye love him, and he loves ye. A time will come when this fighting is done, and we'll all move to Rosemuir, we'll have homes in the village and I can put my son in the arms of Hendrie's parents for the first time and watch the smiles on their faces. Ye have met his parents?'

'Yes. Rhona and An-Mòr are good people.'

'I thought as much. I long to meet them. Pray God that time will come,' Maidlin said quietly. 'And then Hendrie and I will have many more wee Logans to fill our home.'

A question formed in Agnes's mouth. 'Was it hard, birthing a bairn?'

Maidlin laughed, a sound of disbelief. 'It was the most terrifying time of my life. I was alone – Hendrie had ridden to Inverness to find a woman to assist me. I spent most of the time on my hands and knees, roaring like a trapped animal, whimpering like a caged one. I feared for my life more than once, I tell ye, Agnes. Then, by the time my husband arrived, Eaun was born and in my arms. The birthing woman came in with her scissors to tie off the umbilical cord and cut it at four fingers' length. I watched as she bathed the child, rubbed him with salt, and put honey on his gums so he'd have a good appetite. I was exhausted, so she took Eaun and presented him to Hendrie. I remember the look on his face, a sort of pride of being a father, mixed with an expression that seemed to wonder where the bairn had come from, then I remember little more. I fell into sleep.'

Agnes's eyes were round. 'I wonder why so many women do it – having a bairn frightens me.'

'We do it because we love our men, and when our bairns arrive, we love them so much that we forget the pain and want to do it all over.' Maidlin laughed. She saw Agnes's incredulous expression, and she lowered her voice. 'Have ye and Cam lain together?'

Agnes closed her eyes. 'We want to, but we are trying hard to wait. Each day, Rhona looks at me strangely and warns me not to get with child. Cam says a time will come soon when we can be truly together, when the war with the English is done, but...' Agnes smiled, feeling her cheeks glow in the firelight. 'I fear neither of us will be able to hold back much longer.' She gave a small laugh. 'When ye love someone, all ye want is to hold onto them as close as ye can and not let them go.'

'Amen to that,' Maidlin replied.

Small snuffling sounds came from the crib as Eaun began to stir.

The baby gave little cries that sounded at first like little coughs, then rose to a full-blown wail.

Maidlin sighed. 'I am afeared when he cries – I'm always anxious someone will hear him and know we're hiding here. Hendrie built us this hut so we'd be far away from the enemy armies.' She bent over the crib and lifted the child and the screams subsided.

'Can I hold him for ye?' Agnes asked.

'I'd be pleased to have my hands free so that I can serve the stew.' Maidlin placed the baby in Agnes's arms and he began to cry again, harsh spiky sounds of protest.

'He wants his maw...' Agnes was a little disappointed.

'Put your little finger on his gum. It will ease the pain.' Maidlin was bending over the pot on the fire, stirring the stew.

Agnes placed her fingertip against his gum, feeling the hardness of a new tooth. The baby's sobs stopped almost immediately. She gazed into the sweet face, a flared pink cheek, and she felt the stirring of a new tenderness as the baby stared back at her, his eyes round with trust.

'Ye are a natural mother.' Maidlin grinned, heaving the pot from the flames. She looked towards the door, where Hendrie and Cam were standing, their arms loaded with fresh logs. 'Just in time. Agnes and I were about to sup.'

'I'm starving.' Hendrie began to stack the logs. But Cam hadn't moved. He was staring at Agnes, watching her as she held the baby. Their gaze met and held. Agnes smiled, her face glowing in the firelight.

* * *

Several hours later, the meal had been eaten and the four of them talked into the night. There was no mention of battles and war against the English; Hendrie steered the conversation to talk of the jobs he needed to do to in the hut to make his family comfortable: he intended to make a coffer for storage from the trunk of a tree, banded in iron. Cam spoke fondly of his family, particularly his younger brother Rabbie who he mentioned in a low voice: he had been a skilful horseman and the kindliest brother ever, and Cam clearly felt the loss bitterly. Hendrie amused everyone by telling stories of his childhood. His eyes crinkled with affection as he talked of his father, always a gentle giant who won many contests of the strong arm but how An-Mòr always did as Rhona bade him in their home, and how he was the same, Maidlin held him in the palm of her hand. The whole time, Agnes felt warm and contented, Cam's arm around her holding her close. She longed for the moment when they could be alone.

Later still, when Hendrie and Maidlin were asleep next to the crib, Cam pulled Agnes to him beneath a warm blanket and kissed her neck. She wrapped her arms around him, whispered his name, clinging to him, finding his lips with her own, hungry for more kisses. His response was immediate, his body warm against hers, and Agnes closed her eyes and passion swirled her into its depths as if she was sinking into an ocean of it.

She wasn't sure who pulled apart first, she or Cam. She heard him catch his breath, then he whispered, 'It's no good, lassie. This must be the last time we hold ourselves apart from each other this way.'

'What do ye mean, the last time?' Agnes was mystified. 'Do ye not love me?'

'Aye, more than ye ken. I cannae keep leaving ye every time with us both feeling like this. It's not right. When I saw ye earlier with the bairn in your arms, something knocked in my heart. I want us to be together properly, ye and me for all time.'

'But how can we?' Agnes was still confused. 'Ye are oft away. We only have now – we should take our chance...' Her eyes were defiant. 'I don't care if I get with child. It's ye I want.'

'As do I want ye...' Cam kissed her again. 'Next time, I'll find a way for us to belong to each other, just as we both want, for the rest of our lives.'

'I don't understand. How can ye talk of a future? Ye know that all we have is this moment – we have oft said it.'

'There are ways we can have both, Agnes. We're young. We love each other.' She felt a sigh shudder from his chest. 'I used to fight in battle and not think twice of my own life. All I wanted was to kill as many English soldiers as I could. But now you're on my mind and in my heart: even when I wield a sword, I think to myself, I have to get safely back to my Agnes, I have to hold her once more in my arms.'

'I am glad of it. I hear the soldiers have a name for ye – Allaidh. The wild one.'

'Aye, I was wild once. Then I met ye. But it hasnae made me soft. It has made me more determined. We belong to each other – we have the same soul.'

Agnes looked into his eyes, reflecting the warm flames of the firelight. 'We do.'

Cam kissed her again. 'And next time we meet, I'll prove to ye how much I love ye, that I always will. Trust me...'

'I do.' Agnes kissed him back.

'The war with the English won't keep me from ye. We'll be together for always – I swear it on my life. The next time Rhona asks ye to go weaving with her, I'll be waiting in her hut and I'll have everything ready. We'll be one for all time, I promise ye. Believe it, Agnes.'

She closed her eyes, nestling in the warmth of his arms, imagining the happiness of spending each night there. 'I believe it, truly.'

25

Leah stood in the great hall, indicating the heavy tapestries, the open fireplace, a smile on her face. 'Well? What do you think? Is Ravenscraig the right location for your adverts?'

'It is.' Aidan's eyes glowed and Leah thought he looked even more attractive. 'I'll go back to my people and recommend it. I think we could do some photos inside the castle, the upstairs rooms that overlook the loch would make for tremendous distance shots, our warrior emerging from the water, fire in his blood and a bottle of Glencharaid whisky in his fist.'

'So you like the castle?'

'It's perfect.' Aidan gazed around the room. 'I want to do some pics in here before I go, so that I can pitch a few ideas about a laird and his lady sitting across the table, these tapestries in the background. Do you think we could even get a fire roaring in the hearth? Maybe roast a boar on a spit?'

'I'd have to check,' Leah began.

'Oh, wait – my phone.' Aidan was rummaging in his pockets. 'I think I must have left it in the kitchen on the table while you were showing me the old water jug.'

'The bronze ewer with the hinged lid?'

'Yes. I'd love to have it featured in a shot next to a bottle of Glencharaid. This is so exciting.' Aidan met Leah's eyes. 'I'll just pop back for my phone, then maybe we'll head off and grab some lunch.'

'Perfect,' Leah agreed. 'I'll meet you in the courtyard.'

'Okay. I'll be with you in just a moment. Then we can drive into the village.'

'Or we could walk? It's a nice day.' Leah imagined that a stroll to The Canny Man would give her and Aidan time to get to know more about each other.

As she ambled through the hall to the open doorway and into the brightly sunlit courtyard, she wondered if she should invite Zoe to go with them. But lunch with handsome Aidan was one of the perks of her job – she'd do this one by herself. She imagined intimate conversation over bowls of cock-a-leekie soup and glasses of white wine; she'd be scintillating company, and after a dessert of Morangie Brie and oatcakes, he'd ask her for a date the following weekend. She smiled: Aidan Irving was a good, strong name.

She was still daydreaming when Aidan rushed from the hall into the courtyard, his phone squeezed tightly in his fingers. He was breathing hard. 'I have to go...' He met her eyes and looked away, shifting his feet awkwardly. 'I-I have to get back to Perth now, to the office...'

'Oh?' Leah was visibly disappointed. 'What happened?'

'My phone...' He glanced at it for a moment and back to Leah. His face was covered with a film of perspiration; he looked unwell and there was an odd glint in his eyes. 'My phone... rang and... I have to be there, so I'm sorry... I have to go.'

'Can you email me...?'

'The thing is...' Aidan was clearly uncomfortable. He was shivering beneath his dark coat and scarf. 'The thing is, I'm not sure this place is right for the Glencharaid brand. I mean – I have other places to view. I'll get back to you... sometime.'

'Aidan?' Leah was perplexed. 'I thought you said the location was perfect.'

'I did...' He began, then he glanced over his shoulder, back into the castle. His voice shook. 'No, no, I don't think I'd want to do the photo shoot here.' His expression was suddenly irritated. 'To be honest, I don't know how you can live in this place.' He began to walk away, then he called over his shoulder, 'It's a no, Ms Drummond. Thanks for the tour, but I'll take our business elsewhere.'

A deeper frown creased Leah's brow as she watched him stride away and disappear through the broad stone arch of the main gate. What had just happened? He had been so keen – they'd almost closed the deal. She wondered if she had said or done something wrong. A familiar feeling of failure seeped into her skin. She wandered sadly into the castle and closed the heavy door behind her with a resounding clunk.

In the living room, Leah sank down beside the log fire. She was filled with bruising feelings of failure – she couldn't make anything work.

Zoe continued to type on the laptop, her back to her sister. 'How did it go?'

Leah didn't answer. Fat tears fell onto her fingers and her lap, darkening the grey material of her suit with blotchy spots. She sniffed, swallowing hard, but no words would come.

Zoe chatted as her fingers tapped. 'I bet he loved the castle. When's he coming back to do the photo shoot?'

Leah couldn't answer. She heaved a breath and, in that time, Zoe realised she had taken too long to reply and whirled round.

'What's wrong?' She saw the tear-stained face and rushed over to the fireside, falling on her knees next to Leah. 'What happened?'

'I don't know, Zo. I've no idea.' Leah took a shuddering breath. 'Aidan said he loved the place and it was just what he was looking for and he offered to take me to lunch in Rosemuir, then all of a sudden he had to go back to Perth and he left.' She snuffled again and Zoe wrapped her arms around Leah, hugging her in a tight squeeze. Leah sobbed on her sister's shoulder, leaving a damp patch of tears. Her words came as quickly as her sobs. 'He just rushed off... I thought I had clinched it... I so needed to make a go of this job but... I'm useless, Zo – just like I was at St Joseph's. Whatever I try to do, it goes wrong. I-I was mad to think it would be a good move to come here... I'm just failing again...'

'No, don't think that. It was just a one-off.'

'Why?' Leah's face puckered. 'I don't understand...'

Zoe grabbed her sister's shoulders firmly. 'Go on – wash your face, get a warm coat. We're going into Rosemuir. We'll have lunch in The Canny Man,' she said determinedly. 'You were promised lunch and you're going to have it.'

* * *

Half an hour later, they were dipping spoons into creamy Cullen Skink. Leah was still introspective as she stared down at the chunks of haddock, potatoes and onions, the liquid flecked with green parsley. She sighed. 'I was sure Aidan wanted to use the place for his photos.'

'It does seem a bit weird.' Zoe shrugged. 'I wonder what made him change his mind?'

'He was fine before he went back to get his phone, then he came outside and he looked freaked out. I couldn't understand it.'

'Leah...' Zoe held her spoon in the air. She recalled being alone in the kitchen herself, holding a goblet, feeling someone standing close behind her. She took a breath. 'You don't suppose he... felt something?'

'What do you mean?'

'I've... sensed something weird. You know, like someone else was there with me when the room was empty.'

Leah looked up, meeting her sister's eyes. 'Really?'

Zoe nodded. 'In the kitchen...'

'I felt something a bit strange in the chapel – like you said, as if someone else was in the corner, watching me.'

Zoe lowered her voice. 'Do you think the place is haunted?'

'It's definitely old and a bit creaky. It plays tricks with the imagination.' Leah returned her attention to her soup. 'Mirren told us the chapel had a strange atmosphere, but she promised we'd be all right in the castle.' She was suddenly troubled. 'We will be all right, won't we, Zo?'

Zoe sat up straight. 'We will. Let's stop focusing on negatives and make a plan.' She reached out and patted Leah's hand. 'You're doing a great job. The website is fantastic now you've upgraded it. So what are you going to do next?'

'I don't know.' Leah made a sad face. 'I feel a bit low now I didn't get the whisky photo shoot, like I failed...'

'You haven't.'

Leah sighed, lifting a spoonful of soup from the bowl and allowing it to dribble back with a splash.

'You know all about the history of the place. What about doing a tour – an open day, inviting local people?' Zoe was thoughtful. 'It's November now – is there any date this month we can celebrate to do with Scottish history? Or next month?'

'I'm not sure.' Leah pulled out her phone, pressing buttons. Her brow creased. 'What about this? On 17 November 1292 John Balliol acceded to the Scottish throne...'

'Why is that important?'

Leah's voice thickened with interest as she read: 'He was known by the nickname "Toom Tabard", usually understood to mean "empty coat", in the sense that he was an ineffective king.'

Zoe pressed her hands together. 'But how does that celebrate Scotland?'

'He was a puppet for the English king, Edward I. The loyal Scots tired of him and started rebelling. Edward wanted to have legal authority over Scotland and they clashed big time. There was no king after John Balliol until the accession of Robert the Bruce in 1306. And then there were some real battles.'

'How can we tie that into a guided tour?' Zoe asked.

'Easy-peasy.' Leah beamed. 'I'll call it The Bruce Tour. I'll put an information leaflet together, starting with Balliol and ending with Robert.' She was suddenly animated. 'I wonder where I'd find the information about who lived in the castle in the thirteen hundreds, and how far the occupants were involved in the anti-English rebellion. That would be so exciting.' She rubbed her hands. 'I'll talk to Abigail and ask her what she thinks...'

'The seventeenth is just fourteen days away.'

'Well, maybe the date is less important than the idea.' Leah began to tuck into her soup. 'We could advertise it here in the pub – get the locals really interested, then spread our information out to Inverness.'

'It could work...' Zoe said thoughtfully.

Leah put down her spoon. 'Finish up, Zo – I need to get home. I have some research to do and I need to phone Abigail.' Her eyes gleamed. 'I'll start on the Bruce project straight away. I could invite people from the university in Inverness, the Highlands and the Islands.' Leah was on her feet, reaching for her coat and bag. 'Lunch was great – really great. Now let's head back – I have so much work to do.'

26

Agnes watched Cam ride into the distance, horse and rider as one. It was still dark; a crack of crimson light fractured the sky beyond the loch, streaking the water with a line of shimmering colour. Dawn was breaking and she paused for a moment, inhaling the peacefulness of the water and the mountains beyond. She could sense a sharpness in the air: snow would come soon. She imagined Cam's kisses still on her lips as she rushed through the portcullis towards the courtyard. One of the soldiers on guard nodded to her as she walked past and she wondered if he knew that she had just dismounted by the loch as Cam whispered a promise in her ear and rode away on Sealgair. Agnes couldn't help smiling. She would see him soon; it was mid-December and by the new year, Cam would find a way for them to be together forever. He had promised it.

She hurried through the castle doorway towards the kitchen, where she could already smell oats being cooked over the open fire for the master's breakfast. Her stomach rumbled; there would be brose for the servants, a hearty meal of oats, barley and pease.

Agnes heard a high shriek and knew immediately that it was Effie's. She ran into the kitchen. Effie's face was contorted in fear;

she had dropped a dish full of eggs on the rush-covered floor, a mess of gold yolks and cracked shells at her feet. Una was next to her, red-faced, fists clenched. The other servants had stopped working to observe the quarrel, their faces etched with interest.

Effie cried out. 'I didnae mean to drop them, Una...'

Una's voice came from deep in her throat. 'They were collected for the mistress minutes ago and now ye have smashed them all.'

'I'm sorry for it—'

Effie had no more time to speak. Una slapped her face hard with the back of her hand. Effie fell to her knees, cringing and snivelling, and Una lifted a long-handled wooden spoon and hit her across the shoulders. Una shrieked, beating Effie with each alternate word. 'Ye broke them all and now I'll break ye, ye foolish daffin' useless hen.'

Effie's wails rose to a higher pitch. 'Stop, Una, I beg ye. Can't ye see I'm scunnert? I hardly slept last night after ye made me work until the late hours...'

'And you'll work the whole of tonight, scrubbing pots, until morning...' Una raised the spoon again, but Agnes was in front of her, clasping her wrist with a firm grip.

'Leave her be.' Agnes's voice was a harsh whisper. She noticed Una's skin beneath her grasp turn white.

Una met her eyes, her own small and fierce. Agnes could see the thin slice of her cheekbone standing out against her skin. 'Why? What will ye do, Agnes?'

Agnes increased the pressure, her face not flinching. 'Ye won't want to find out.'

Agnes released her grip as Una lowered the spoon. 'What is it to ye if I give the foolish lassie a good beating? She's not your sister. She looks nothings like ye.'

Effie leaped from the floor, cannoning into Agnes, grasping her waist with both arms. 'We are sisters, we are. Tell her, Agnes.'

Agnes noticed the red weal across her cheek and she moved

even closer to Una. Her voice was hushed. 'Don't ye ever touch Effie again. If ye lay a finger on her, I'll give ye a hiding ye won't forget.'

Una stared back, scowling, then she turned away and muttered, 'I'm not afraid of ye...'

'You've no need to be,' Agnes replied simply. 'Unless ye try to hurt Effie again.'

Agnes noticed the gleam in Effie's eyes, the adoration and gratitude. She felt a pang of guilt for leaving her overnight; had she not been with Cam, Una would not have beaten Effie.

Then there was a harsh voice behind them. 'What's happening here?' Rhona was standing with her arms folded, looking from Una to Agnes and back again.

Una piped up. 'I was just instructing Effie that she cannot smash all the mistress's eggs with her clumsy ways.' She glanced towards Agnes. 'Then *she* threatened me – Agnes told me she'd give me a hiding. Everyone heard it.' Una whirled round to the other servants for support, but they were back to work, stirring pots, pouring water, shelling peas. 'Are ye going to let her threaten me, Rhona?'

'Agnes?' Rhona asked.

'Aye, I said it. She'll not hit Effie while I stand by and watch,' Agnes said quietly, but her eyes flashed with anger.

Rhona nodded slowly. 'Una, Effie will work alongside me today. I'll instruct her how to be an alewife...'

Effie's face crumpled. 'No, it's too hard with all the heavy water and stirring, and the ale reeks and I'll reek of it too...'

Rhona silenced her with a raised finger, then she turned to Agnes and spoke quietly. 'The bread willnae bake by itself.'

'Aye, it won't, Rhona.' Agnes felt immediately grateful; there was no hint from Rhona's expression about where she'd been overnight, and she was thankful for her presence of mind and her calmness. She stood where she was as Effie followed Rhona to the large vat, her small shoulders hunched humbly, then she noticed Una glare angrily in her direction before turning away.

Agnes walked slowly to the pantry and heaved a sack of flour. She returned to the table and began to mix bannock bread, kneading with all her energy, shaping loaves. Her thoughts shifted to the night she had spent with Cam, in his arms, and in her heart she was back there once more. He had promised her that they'd be together, living as Hendrie and Maidlin did in a smoky hut deep in the forests, hiding from the English soldiers, but the thought of it excited her. She'd learn to make things, a stool, a coffer for the bedding, while Cam was away fighting for The Bruce. She'd make bread, stew, beer; she'd get hold of a wooden wheel and spin wool, making blankets and clothes. With practice, she'd soon improve her weaving skills.

Agnes glanced towards Effie, who was gawping at Rhona as she showed her how to stir the grains in the large vat. Effie was slight and frail, and the huge stirring spoon made her seem more fragile than ever. Agnes was thoughtful: when she left the castle to live with Cam, she would need to take Effie with her. She vowed she would speak to Cam about it first, then she would tell Effie everything.

Agnes turned to fetch more water to mix into the flour and she met Una's glare. Una was skinning a rabbit, raising the knife skilfully, paring the fur from the flesh, and her eye glinted with a new malice. Agnes fastened her eyes on Una a moment too long, as instinct told her she must, then she moved away. She had made an enemy now and she knew she would need to be careful.

Leah was sitting at one side of the living room researching on the laptop, moving the mouse around, her brow creased in a frown. She had found superficial facts about Robert the Bruce, his family, the details of his life, some of which she knew already. She'd compiled several pages of information, and had just typed the dates he'd reigned,1306–29, and that he'd freed Scotland from English rule, winning the decisive Battle of Bannockburn in 1314 and ultimately confirming Scottish independence in the Treaty of Northampton in 1328. But what she sought were the real stories, the local colour, linking him to Rosemuir. There were a few facts online about Ravenscraig Castle: it had been built by Malcolm McNair in the late twelve hundreds and handed down to his eldest son, Ross. But Leah was desperate to find a connection between the castle and the king; wherever she searched, she drew a blank. It was the link she needed to make the open day leap from the page. Robert the Bruce: from the page to the battlements. That was her strapline for the tour.

On the other side of the room, Zoe was preparing some research for Sharon, which she'd been told would find its way into an article in *The Observer* soon. Zoe blinked at the blurring screen. It was past eleven; she was ready for a coffee break.

They heard the resounding knock at the front door at the same time, and Leah pushed back her chair. 'I know who that is. I'll go.'

Zoe immersed herself in her research, finding a graph showing that donations among the top 1 per cent of earners had plummeted dramatically. She saved the document as she heard a familiar voice behind her. 'Hello, Zoe. Leah and I have a brief meeting. We'll go downstairs – we won't disturb you.'

Zoe whirled round on her chair to see Abigail Laing, smart in a black coat and tartan scarf, standing with Leah. Zoe shook her head. 'Not at all. I'm due a break and I was about to make coffee. Shall I make some for us all?'

'Oh, yes please,' Leah enthused.

'Tea for me, no sugar,' Abigail said.

Leah watched as Zoe rushed towards the kitchenette, then she indicated the small sofa. 'Shall we sit?'

She and Abigail sat down and Abigail produced some documents from her briefcase. She offered Leah a professional smile. 'Firstly – I know I didn't come here to discuss this – but I had an email from Aidan Irving, who wanted to do the whisky photo shoot here. I checked up on him. Apparently, he has some kind of business degree and was given free rein by his father's firm to follow his whimsical ideas for advertising the product. Not the way to run a shrewd business. Suffice it to say, he won't be back here.' She nodded towards Leah, her mouth firm. 'I have no patience with these timewasters. Foolish talk about supernatural sightings only gives this place a bad name and I want to quash it. I have replied to him to this end. I'm sorry you had to put up with him, Leah. He was clearly the disorganised type who has too much imagination and not enough acumen.' She offered a tight smile. 'Shall we agree not to mention him again?'

'Oh – all right.' Leah was surprised that Abigail wasn't annoyed with her. More puzzling was the fact that she'd never said much about the castle being haunted before. Leah assumed that she was too down-to-earth to believe in ghosts.

'Now, on to your idea for an open day. That's why I'm here, as per my email.' Abigail almost smiled. 'I think it's a splendid idea and I think we should make some sort of plan. I've spoken to the owner of Ravenscraig, and we've agreed to pursue it.'

'Oh – that's great.' A wide grin spread across Leah's face.

'December the tenth is a Saturday and it gives us a whole month to plan it. Now, I know you're keen, but I thought we'd make the first event small and select, invitation only, to make sure we get the sort of clients we want.'

'Oh – not the general public?' Leah was surprised.

'We can work up to that. But I thought we'd ask some local academics, writers, professional people who could be good for Ravenscraig's reputation and subsequent business.'

'Is that what Da— what the owner is looking to do, build the business?' Leah was furious with herself. She'd almost mentioned Daniel Lennox's name and, since Abigail seemed to want to ensure his anonymity, she didn't intend to reveal that she'd found it out.

Abigail was quiet for a moment. 'He's keen to make the castle a going concern, yes. On a professional scale, not as a B&B or some sort of ad hoc tourist attraction, but a place where it has some status. That's why I'm going to invite ten influential people to an open day.'

'Okay...' Leah nodded.

'I'll organise invites, get the place tidied. Leave all that with me. But December should bring a sprinkling of snow and the proximity to Christmas means if we have all the fires roaring in here and I get caterers in to do an elegant buffet, your role would be to provide an hour-long tour that focuses on the history of the castle. I mentioned your background in history to the owner and he's of the same opinion as I am, that it would be a shame not to use your expertise. Do you think you could do that?'

'I'd love to.' Leah beamed.

'Right.' Abigail looked over her shoulder as Zoe brought in a tray of tea and coffee and a plate of biscuits. 'That's agreed then. We'll liaise on the details as we go, but leave the organisation to me.'

'December the tenth it is. Our first proper tour.' Leah nodded.

'Thank you.' Abigail accepted a cup of tea from Zoe. 'A serious tour would be very useful and it might pave the way for future events. The owner will be very grateful. I'm anxious to dispel some of the silliness that surrounds Ravenscraig.' She sipped her tea. 'Some of the locals have a lot to answer for.'

'Oh?' Zoe perched herself on the floor, coffee mug cupped in her hands. 'In what way?'

'There have been rumours over the years, long before the place was taken over and renovated.' Abigail wrinkled her nose as if something was distasteful. 'You know, there are people who believe the castle has a ghostly atmosphere.' She scoffed. 'Quite ridiculous in this day and age.'

'Oh, indeed,' Leah agreed heartily, then she met Zoe's eyes and she knew they were thinking the same thing.

Zoe gazed through the window towards the turret of the south-west wing as a raven perched, stretching its wings in the sunlight, opening a wide beak to caw. She sipped her coffee and said nothing.

27

For the next few days, Leah was hunched over the computer, desperate to find out more information about the history of Ravenscraig. She noted down what she discovered about Ross McNair, who owned the castle at the beginning of the thirteen hundreds. His wife had been called Muriel; they'd had a son, William, who'd only lived for a few years. But any information about them seemed to run out after 1307; after that, the next historical detail about Ravenscraig was that the MacDonald clan had raided the castle and had stolen 'two hundred bolls of oats, with fodder; one hundred bolls of bere; one hundred cows; one hundred calves; forty young cows; ten one-year-old stirks; eight horses and four mares'. Leah wrote it down, but she was puzzled by the lack of information available about the castle around the time of King Robert. She tried a new angle: she emailed a professor at the University of Stirling, Dr Alison Wylie, who had a background in medieval Scottish history. She hoped that Dr Wylie would have a great deal of information at her fingertips and be willing to share it.

Zoe was so immersed in her own research that she and Leah hardly spoke, both so absorbed in their separate worlds. So, on

Friday afternoon, Zoe tugged down the lid of her computer with a flourish and said, 'Right, Leah. We're going for a walk.'

Leah didn't look up from her work. 'Abigail has just emailed to say that six people have said yes to coming on the tour – two academics from Inverness, a historical author, a newspaper editor, a local businessman and a depute provost.'

'What's one of those?' Zoe asked.

'Someone from Inverness from the local authority – an elected civic person from the community councils...'

'Oh, that's great,' Zoe replied. 'Let's go for a walk. It's a beautiful day and the outdoors will do us good.'

Leah switched off her laptop. 'Brilliant idea. My brain is buzzing. Let's go and inhale some Scottish air.'

They dressed warmly, woollen hats and scarves, thick coats, but the wind still found a way to whisk around their ankles and make them shiver.

Leah linked her arm through Zoe's as they strolled along the path beside the loch. 'I'll never tire of this view.' Leah gazed across the water. Tiny ripples dimpled the smooth surface.

'It's almost winter...' Zoe gazed towards the mountains in the distance. 'We'll be looking at snow caps soon.'

Leah's cheeks shone in the cold wind. 'I can't wait.' She squeezed Zoe's arm. 'It'll be totally beautiful here. You won't want to go back to Birmingham in January.'

Zoe paused for a moment, then she sighed. 'I was chatting to Bex yesterday and she was telling me that they had a fantastic Hallowe'en do in The Red Cellar. Martinis and dancing and lots of fancy dress. Apparently Mariusz and Jordan went as Morticia and Gomez Addams. She sent photos – they were hilarious. It looked like such a good time.' She chewed a lip. 'I have to admit, I felt quite homesick.'

'Oh, I'm sorry.' Leah's expression was one of genuine sadness.

'Am I totally selfish, dragging you here when your heart is back in the Midlands?'

'Not at all... I was tempted to tell Bex that we have the real Hallowe'en deal up here.' Zoe winked.

'What do you mean?'

'Our castle has a ghost.'

'Do you really believe that, Zo?'

'Yes, I do.' Zoe turned her attention to her sister. 'Don't you? I'm sure that's why your Aidan Irving ran away. And you know you felt something when you were locked in the chapel – you weren't even locked in, the door opened easily.'

Leah was thoughtful. 'Abigail said she didn't like the locals giving Ravenscraig a reputation as a haunted castle... but I suppose there's no smoke without fire.'

'So – who do you think the ghost is?' Zoe turned back to gaze at Ravenscraig.

'I don't know, but I might ask the professor from Stirling what she thinks. She might be able to throw some light on it.' Leah closed her eyes. 'I'd like to imagine it's the ghost of a young woman who died of a broken heart, but it's more likely to be just residual energy from all the battles and murder from the various power struggles in times gone by.'

'Energy?' Zoe asked.

Leah gave a short laugh. 'As historians, we're always faced with making decisions about relics of the past. Archaeologists uncover graves, we examine artefacts. Most people are too interested in reality to be caught up in an imaginary atmosphere, but I've heard lots of stories. I remember once a lecturer told us about a pub in Chester where a whole Roman army is often seen marching through the walls.'

'Really?' Zoe was incredulous. 'I suppose there must be some truth in ghosts if they are experienced by so many people. But I wonder if it's really a ghostly presence or just imagination and we should look for a rational reason behind it all.' She paused, remembering. 'It felt real enough when I stood in the kitchen...'

'I think a ghostly presence might be quite useful, especially if the castle became a wedding venue – you know, I could put an extra seat in the chapel for the ghost, lay an extra table setting. It could become a selling point.' Leah raised an eyebrow. 'Mariusz hasn't decided where to have his wedding yet. There's a place he's looked at in Birmingham, and he messaged me that he doesn't need to confirm until January, so I've asked him to hang on in case I can sort something out. I'm sure once we've done this tour in December, I'll be able to ask Abigail and, off the back of a great success, she'll let me trial a wedding for the boys.'

'I suppose it's worth a try.' Zoe grinned. 'They might come up for Hogmanay, Bex too. I thought it might be nice. They can all stay at The Canny Man.'

'They can stay with us, in the guest rooms. It would be good to air them,' Leah said cheerfully. 'I'll ask Abigail.'

'That would be lovely, all of us together,' Zoe agreed. 'We could go to a great Hogmanay party.'

'There'll be one in The Canny Man. Oh, just imagine Christmas in the castle,' Leah sighed. 'And then a February wedding. You know, I might even get married myself at Ravenscraig.'

Zoe spluttered laughter. 'You'll have to find someone to marry first.'

'Oh, I know I'll find the perfect person in Scotland – it's my destiny.' Leah rolled her eyes, teasing. 'It's you I'm worried about. You might turn into an old maid living for nothing but your work.'

Zoe gave a long hoot. 'There are worse things, Leah. Like being stuck at the kitchen sink in a tiny, cramped terrace with six screaming babies chomping at your ankles.'

'I'll be living in Rosemuir, or somewhere equally beautiful, overlooking a loch and mountains. I won't settle for anything less.

And Blair or Hector will adore me, and we'll have well-behaved children and a nice kitchen sink.'

Zoe was about to reply with something ridiculous, when she paused, pointing across the loch towards the sky. 'Look, Leah – there's a band of weather coming in.'

In the distance, dark clouds hung low over the mountains and the sky had become a brooding grey. The air was suddenly colder, laden with ice, as the clouds closed in, shifting quickly towards the castle, and the first drops of rain started to spatter.

'We'd better head back quickly. We'll get soaked,' Leah urged.

'It's a twenty-minute walk or a ten-minute run.' Zoe grinned. 'Come on, Leah.'

'I can't run...' Leah protested. 'Go without me...'

'Never.' Zoe laughed, grabbing her sister's arm, rushing back towards the castle, head down.

Leah allowed herself to be dragged along as laughter spluttered from her lips. 'I'll make the hot chocolate when we get in,' she yelled as the wind took away her words and the skies split, lashing hard rain. As the downpour began, full drops bouncing on their heads, the earth beneath their feet squelching, Zoe and Leah whooped with delight.

When they crossed the grassy hump where the drawbridge had once been, they noticed a white van parked next to the Mini. There was a name on the side in black lettering and a silhouette of a man carrying a brush: K Robertson and Son, Chimney Sweep. A man emerged from the van, middle-aged, slim, a cap on his head. He said, 'Are you the caretakers?'

Leah beamed, her face shining. 'That's me.'

The man nodded. 'I'm Keith Robertson. Ms Laing sent me to do the chimneys.'

'Oh, all right,' Leah replied. 'She didn't tell me you were coming.'

'She asked me an hour ago and I said I'd fit you in. She said she'd email you.'

'I must have missed it.' Leah led the way through the main gate to the courtyard. The pebbles were shining in the downpour. She delved in a large pocket for the keys.

The sweep stood next to her. 'No problem. I was about to leave, but then you turned up. Ms Laing was keen to get it done; she said I was to do the two chimneys downstairs, in the kitchen and the great hall. She said they are original; they haven't been swept since the castle was rebuilt.'

'Oh, you'd better come in.' Leah opened the heavy door and stepped into the dark hall, glad to be dry.

'Would you like a cup of tea first?' Zoe offered.

Keith stared at her, water dripping from the end of her nose, and shook his head. Then he gazed over her shoulder into the hall, a frown between his eyes. 'Funny place this, very cold. I've not done a castle before.' He gestured with his thumb towards the courtyard. 'I'll get my gear in and you can meet me here when you're dry.'

'It's a deal,' Leah agreed, watching him turn and lumber away through the courtyard. 'We'll see you in five minutes.'

Leah and Zoe stood in the hall ten minutes later, their hair still wet, watching Keith stack his equipment against the wall: brushes, tall rods, large pale sheets folded tightly. Leah said, 'Shall we do the great hall first?'

'Whichever is nearest,' Keith replied casually. He followed them into the large room and moved towards the huge fireplace. 'You'd need something big to keep this place warm.'

'We don't use this room,' Leah explained.

'We have a flat,' Zoe added. 'The chimney up there is rebuilt – it's swept regularly, I think.'

'I've never been here before,' Keith glanced around. 'Most people around here aren't so keen on the castle. But Ms Laing said there was going to be a big do and the chimneys had to be clean. She wants the fires lit.'

'That's right,' Leah said proudly. 'I'm doing a tour.'

'Why aren't the locals keen on the castle?' Zoe was inquisitive.

'If you don't know, I won't tell you,' Keith said simply. 'You have to live here, I don't.'

Keith laid out a pale cloth across the hearth, pushed a broom up the chimney, then started up a machine that resembled an industrial vacuum cleaner. It made a loud noise and Zoe and Leah moved to the window, listening to the sweep banging about in the fireplace, turning his machine on and off, grunting as he pushed the broom up the flue. Beyond the window, the rain was pelting, making deep dimples in the loch, water splashing upwards with the force of the droplets.

Leah grinned. 'This will be lovely in here when we have the fires blazing, all the guests chatting, a nice buffet on the table. It won't matter what the weather does.'

'Typical Scottish weather, rain,' Keith quipped over the noise of the soot vacuum. 'Next month we'll have snow.'

'Oh, that will be nice,' Zoe said.

'Not if you get snowed in here.' Keith turned and switched the machine off. 'I doubt there will be many from Rosemuir prepared to come and dig you out.'

Zoe shrugged. 'Are you from Rosemuir?'

'Dingwall,' Keith replied without explanation. 'No locals will work here,' he grunted. 'Only people from outside the area are mad enough.' He straightened. 'There's another chimney in the kitchen, you say?'

'There is,' Leah replied.

'Right, let's do that one and I'll be off. I finish early on Fridays.' Keith looked around, gazing into corners, towards doors. Zoe wondered if he was looking for an escape route.

'This way,' Leah said and she and Zoe led the way. Keith lugged his equipment, and followed hesitantly.

The kitchen was cold and Zoe shivered. She looked around, taking in the iron cooking pans that hung from the ceiling on large hooks. Shelves were stacked with plates, trestle tables held huge pots, ladles, knives, a primitive grater. Zoe noticed the mottled goblet made of bluish-grey clay with a dull green glaze. She recalled the ornate decoration, a bearded face, a woman with curls. It gave her a strange feeling; she wouldn't pick it up again.

Keith was fascinated by the vast open hearth with adjustable hooks for hanging cauldrons. He gave a short exclamation of surprise. 'This has to be the biggest fireplace I've ever seen.' He laid out another huge sheet and adjusted his broom, attaching a longer rod, bending down to gaze up into the void. 'Huge chimney up there, original stone, black as the very devil.'

'The kitchen provided food for the whole castle, so it needed a huge fire,' Leah explained. 'There would have been meat, vegetables, bread, pastries, all baked here.'

Zoe shivered. 'We could do with a fire now. It's freezing.'

'It is,' Leah agreed. 'It must be the coldest room in the castle.' She gave a small laugh. 'I bet it wasn't so cold in here in the thirteen hundreds, when the kitchen maids were bustling around roasting wild boars on spits.'

'Bloody hell,' Keith grunted as he struggled to push the brush upwards. 'It's hard work to get all the way up this chimney. It hasn't been cleaned for years. There's enough soot up there to fill half a dozen trucks, I'd say. It's all caked on hard.'

There was a tumbling sound as soot descended in clumps.

Leah shrugged. 'Castle kitchens had fires burning all day and most of the night. Some of the staff even slept by the fire, the servants who didn't live locally. It would need to be a ferocious blaze to cook all the porridge and bread...'

There was another rush of plummeting soot, another grunt

from Keith, who jerked back as more soot sprayed outwards. 'Never seen anything like it.'

Zoe's skin prickled; her voice was hushed. 'It's so chilly in here, Leah. I wish I'd brought a coat.'

'It is perishingly cold,' Leah began, then Keith shouted a warning and there was a rattle from inside the chimney. Something hurtled down, hitting the hearth and flying onto the floor with a clatter. It was followed by a fast rushing of soot and, with it, another blackened shape that flopped into the hearth like a dead crow and lay on the pale sheet surrounded by murky water and clumps of carbon.

28

Agnes couldn't sleep. She huddled by the fireside, gazing into the glimmering embers as Effie snuffled beside her. For a while, she was hypnotised by the flickering of the flames, thinking. Then she heaved another log onto the fire; it was best if it didn't go out, it would be easier to coax at dawn, and there would be trouble if she and Effie didn't have a blaze ready to boil water and cook porridge the next morning.

She wrapped her arms around her knees, listening to the nasal buzzing of other servants as they slept in various corners of the kitchen, ready to rouse themselves into action at first light and begin the busy castle routine.

Then she looked at Effie, her eyes closed, her face lit by the fire's glow. She was innocent as a cherub but for the indentation of tension that hovered between her brows as she slumbered. Agnes was planning how she'd tell Effie about Cam, how they met and fell in love several months ago, back in the summer, and she was troubled by the fact that she'd held their relationship in her heart for so long and said nothing of it. Effie would feel betrayed; she was used to being first in Agnes's priorities and she would be hurt that Agnes had kept a secret unshared for so long. Agnes was not sure how to explain that she had said nothing of it for Cam's safety, for fear that Effie would blurt something out unintentionally.

Agnes wondered where Cam was now, and she pictured him on horseback, Sealgair rearing high, Cam clutching a sword, raising a shield that glinted in the moonlight. He was probably cold and hungry somewhere south of Inverness, hiding in a thicket with Hendrie and many more, watching the English army setting up camp, planning a night raid in the darkness. Her thoughts moved to Hendrie's wife, Maidlin, waiting in the hut in the forest, holding her child as he whimpered. She marvelled at how they lived, foraging for food, depending on handouts from family and friends; Agnes guessed that Ross McNair also supported the Scottish warriors and their families. Cam had said he'd eaten bread that Agnes had made. It was a connection between them now, linking them across vast distance, and she clung to the idea that his rough hands held the bannock she'd baked, that he put it to his lips and thought of her. It occurred to her that life would be hard once she and Cam lived together. She'd be alone a lot of the time. But she'd have Effie for company. They'd manage.

There was a shadow in the doorway and Agnes turned sharply. Someone was standing beyond the entrance and Agnes called out, 'Who is it?'

A low voice, guttural and hushed, murmured, 'Dinnae ye fret, lassie,' and a soldier took a step forward. He was tall, broad-shouldered, his head and torso covered with chainmail armour. He didn't move. 'I came in for a cup of ale. It's cold outside and a warm ale cheers the soul.'

'I'll fetch some for ye.'

Agnes shifted her legs, about to clamber up, but a voice from the other side of the kitchen called, 'Dinnae trouble yourself, Agnes. I'll do it.'

Agnes watched as Una moved quietly to pour ale from a pitcher.

She handed the cup to the soldier, gazing up at him, and they crept into the corridor together, talking in hushed voices. Agnes wondered if Una had a sweetheart and she hoped that she had. Love might sweeten her disposition and perhaps she'd be kinder to Effie. Agnes had to admit that Una bothered her; she held a grudge in her face that revealed a deeper one in her heart, Agnes was sure of it.

Effie jerked suddenly and shrieked once. Her eyes opened wide and she began to tremble, a gulping sob in her throat.

Agnes threw her arms around her, holding her still. 'What is it, hennie? Have ye been dreaming?'

'It was horrible, Agnes. I was drowning in the big vat and Una and Rhona were stirring the pot like witches and laughing at me. And I was going under and my mouth was filled with a bitter taste and I was covered in that reekie smell. And I looked for ye and ye were gone away for ever.'

Agnes pulled her closer. 'It's only a mare – ye are awake now and it's not real.' She pressed her lips against the top of her head. 'It's gone now. There's no need to be afeared.'

'I'm afeared all the time,' Effie whispered. 'I'm afeared that Una will beat me and that Rhona will scald me with hot water and that I'll fall into the ale vat and be drowned.'

Agnes pressed a hand against Effie's back, rubbing with a circular motion. 'No one will hurt ye while I'm here.'

'But what about when ye are away with Rhona, doing the weaving? Una pinches me sometimes and I have a sair arm for days.'

Agnes rocked Effie as she would a child. 'Be bold, Effie. All will be well. I'll take care of ye awhile.'

'I hate it in this castle.'

'Dinnae say that,' Agnes whispered.

'I do. I hate Ravenscraig. I wish we'd stayed at Kildrummy.'

'Nay, ye mustn't say that,' Agnes's voice was edged with warning.

'The English solders might have been nice to me if I was kind to them.'

'They aren't nice, Effie, they are our enemy.'

'But one might have liked me and been my sweetheart.'

'Shhh.'

'I hate it here more than ever,' Effie spoke loudly. Her small face was filled with cunning. 'Let's run away, Agnes.'

'Stint, Effie – someone will hear ye.'

Effie whispered, but the sound came as a loud hiss: 'I think about it all the time when you're not here. I think about killing Una with a kitchen blade and running away. I'd go back to Kildrummy and find someone who'd be kind to me.' She raised her eyes pleadingly to Effie. 'I thought ye were my sister and you'd take care of me, but I'm afeared here in Ravenscraig.'

'Hush.' Agnes hugged her again. 'Trust me, Effie. It willnae be for long.'

Effie pulled away to examine Agnes's expression, her eyes round with trust. 'Are we going to leave here?'

Agnes took a breath. 'In time, I promise. Ye have to trust me, Effie, and ask no questions, do ye hear? Say nothing and leave it to me.'

Effie nodded and Agnes noticed the hope in her eyes, the faith of a child. 'I will. Thank ye, Agnes. I know you'll look after me. Ye are my sister and my best friend in the wide world.'

Agnes took her hand. 'Go back to sleep, Effie. It'll soon be dawn and we'll be awake again fetching water.'

She watched as Effie snuggled down, curled up like a baby, and she sighed. She should try to sleep too. She wondered about her words to Effie; she'd made a promise to her that they would leave together, and she hoped that it would come soon. Rhona would bring word from Cam in a day or two, Agnes would meet him, then she and Effie and Cam would spend the rest of their lives in happiness and peace. Effie would go with her: she couldn't leave her behind.

Agnes clasped her hands in prayer and whispered words of hope, for safety, for an end to war, and she murmured deep thanks for the love she held in her heart that she prayed would be forever hers.

As she opened her eyes, she heard shuffling and whispering in the corridor, then Una was back in the kitchen, looking around. She turned sharply towards the fireside, whispering to Agnes, 'Ye didnae see me leave here tonight, Agnes. Ye understand?'

Agnes frowned. 'What do ye mean, Una?'

'I have someone important to me, one of the master's soldiers. We meet from time to time.' Una dropped her voice. 'I ken ye hate me, Agnes, and you'll want to spoil it for me... but I willnae let ye do it.'

'I dinnae hate ye.'

Una looked down from where she stood, her face bitter. 'If ye speak a word of it, I'll kill Effie while she sleeps with the knife I use to gut rabbits, I swear it.'

'You'll leave Effie alone – and you'll not threaten me or her...'

'It's just words,' Una whispered with a sarcastic smile. 'And if ye heed my words, there'll be no need for anything else between us... ye mark me?'

Agnes watched as Una walked quietly to the other end of the kitchen, as she lay down on the reed floor, sighing once, then wrapping herself in a blanket. The room was filled with the sounds of sleep, a groan, a grunt, then silence. Agnes stared into the embers and wondered what the new day would bring.

* * *

Leah and Zoe stared at the dark fireplace, the heaped soot and water stains on the sheet, at the large metal object and damply folded heap lying amid the rubble.

Keith Robertson was wild-eyed and furious. 'That thing nearly killed me. I felt it hit my shoulder. What is it? Is it a body? A head?'

'No, it looks like some kind of knife, the metal object. I'm not sure what the other thing is – it's a bundle of clothes, rags, or something else...' Leah's voice was calm.

'It's probably a dead raven.' Keith sniffed. 'They often get stuck up in these big chimneys.'

He put a cloth over the cavity of the fireplace and switched on his industrial vacuum cleaner, the motor whirring deafeningly.

Leah leaned forward and picked up the long metal item, showing it to Zoe. It was clearly some sort of weapon with a wooden hilt, two oval swellings at the guard where a hand might have held it. The blade was corroded; it may once have shone, but now it was encrusted with something that looked like concrete.

Leah's eyes widened. She raised her voice over the guzzling motor. 'This is a real find. It's a dagger. I think they were called ballock daggers. I read somewhere that Macbeth used one to kill King Duncan.'

'Ballock?' Zoe smiled. 'It sounds rude.'

'It's meant to.' Leah indicated the two bumps on the handle. 'They were called ballock daggers because these were shaped like testes and the warriors would wear them dangling in front of the girdle to look macho. Medieval culture was full of phallic imagery.' She waved the old dagger provocatively and winked. 'This is quite special though. I can't wait to show Abigail.'

'What about the other thing?' Zoe asked, poking the folded bundle of rags precariously with her finger. 'It's not a creature. It feels a bit like metal or some sort of stiff material.'

Leah started to unwrap it. Beneath the damp, soot-stained outer fold, it was copper-coloured, rusty, with a few patches of silver. A smile filled Leah's face. 'I don't believe it! It's a hauberk.'

'A what?' Zoe frowned.

'A hauberk is part of the chainmail armour a soldier would have worn centuries ago. And look...' An extra piece flopped in her hand. 'A coif too – the headgear. This is a proper piece of fourteenth-century armour, I'm guessing.'

'My goodness...'

'We've made a find here, Zo. Armour and a dagger. They must have been in the chimney for seven hundred years.'

'Incredible.'

'This will attract the punters. Imagine the headline we'd get in the newspapers – *Fabulous Fourteenth-Century Find at Ravenscraig.*' Leah was still shouting as Keith switched the vacuum cleaner off. He gave her a glance, then began to fold up his dirty sheet, along with its contents. 'Wait... Leah yelled. 'We're keeping these.' She clutched the two items, looking around, but there was nothing to put the armour and the dagger in.

'I'll fetch a towel,' Zoe said and rushed towards the stone staircase.

Keith was puzzled. 'We find all sorts of old rubbish up chimneys all the time in old places – what did you say you'd got there?'

'Armour, I think – and a dagger.' Leah was pleased.

Keith began to pack away his equipment. 'I'll have to add a few pounds onto the bill. Danger money. That metal thing clipped my head.'

Leah wasn't listening. She held the dagger flat in her hand, turning the encrusted metal over, examining the handle. 'This must have done some damage in its time. I wonder who owned it and how many times it was used...'

Keith was unscrewing brushes, stowing away long poles, not listening.

Leah gazed at the dagger again, then turned her attention to the armour. 'I wonder what stories these items could tell...'

Then Zoe rushed into the kitchen and Leah could tell something was wrong. She clutched the towels too tightly, her face was a strange pallor, her breath came in short gasps. Keith grabbed some of his sweeping equipment and made for the door, leaving both of them alone. Leah moved closer to Zoe, taking the towels, wrapping the dagger and the dirty armour carefully. Then she met her sister's eyes. 'What is it?'

Zoe shook her head in disbelief. 'I'm being silly...'

Leah gave her a questioning look. 'What do you mean?'

'It's always chilly on the spiral staircase, Leah, and on the landing, but...'

'But what?'

'The cold on the stairs was penetrating. I mean, it was a type of cold that I haven't felt before – deathly cold, down the back of my neck... as if it was someone's breath...' Zoe hesitated.

'Zo?'

'Leah, someone followed me as I came downstairs – I'm sure of it. I felt them moving, right behind me, as close as we are now... but there was nobody there.'

29

'What do you think?' Leah asked Zoe, pointing to the laptop screen. 'There it is – my information sheet for *The Brus – From Page to Battlements* tour. Abigail thinks it's great.'

'It looks fab.' Zoe glanced at the work Leah had been doing. It was a leaflet with photos of each room of the castle, a few lines of information, some historical detail. There was no mention of the southwest wing or the chapel.

Zoe gazed over her shoulder. It was Friday lunchtime; she had just finished work and the fire was roaring in the living room. She was in the mood for a light lunch and then she'd sit awhile and read a good book. But Leah was full of energy.

'The photos of the chainmail and the dagger have come out well on the back page. Abigail says she has a few other things that were found here when the builder was working. I know there was some bone gaming pieces found in the soil. Tablesmen, they were called. I expect they belonged to Ross McNair. It was a game a bit like backgammon. And Abigail says a bronze brooch was found. I bet that was Muriel's.'

'You're on first-name terms,' Zoe quipped.

'The artefacts are with Alison Wylie from Stirling University. Apparently, she drove up to collect them from Abigail earlier this week. She's going to examine them and let us have a full report.'

Zoe tried to share Leah's enthusiasm. 'I expect it's what you said – chainmail armour, a dagger.'

'She'll be able to get a date, all sorts of details. Abigail has invited her to the tour I'm doing on the tenth and she's going to arrive early so that we can chat about her findings. Isn't it exciting?'

'It is...' Zoe put a hand across her mouth, stifling a yawn. 'I'm sorry – I haven't been sleeping well.'

'I sleep like a top.' Leah looked concerned. 'You haven't been... you know, too freaked out to sleep, after what you felt on the stairway?'

'I'm all right in this part of the castle. No, don't worry,' Zoe said, hoping that she sounded convincing. She shivered at the memory. She'd never be able to walk down the steps again without feeling uneasy. 'It's just bitterly cold everywhere. It's December next week, and everyone keeps saying it will snow and they can't wait. I'm dreading it – I'll perish.'

'I'll buy you an extra duvet, Zo – and some more gloves.'

Zoe frowned. 'It's not like me to feel the cold all the time. I've always been quite hardy, out running all weathers. But I have to admit, this morning I almost stayed in bed.'

'That was in Birmingham though.' Leah brightened. 'It was warmer there. I'll get us some thermal undies. That will keep us toasty.'

'I've never seen myself as a thermal undies kind of girl...'

'Needs must,' Leah said, ever practical. 'I'm getting so excited about the tour, Zo. We'll be able to display the artefacts we found up the chimney, and Professor Wylie – Alison – said she'd give a brief talk. All ten guests have agreed to attend, plus Abigail and Alison, that's twelve, and you must come too. Abigail said—'

'Unlucky thirteen?' Zoe raised an eyebrow.

'And me...' Leah looked back at the screen, frowning. 'I just need some local colour in this leaflet, some primary evidence that I've researched myself, that's fresh and cutting edge.'

'Primary evidence?' Zoe guffawed. 'They are all dead, the people who lived here in 1300.'

Leah screwed up her face, thinking, then she said, 'Mirren Logan...'

'I haven't seen her for a few days – perhaps the cold is keeping her indoors.'

'I hope so.' Leah leaped up. 'You've finished for the day. What are you thinking of doing now?'

'I was going to have some lunch, chill, read a bit...'

'Let's go to The Canny Man – I'll buy.' Leah grabbed her sister's hand. 'We'll ask Kenny where Mirren lives and pay her a visit.'

'I can't imagine her being pleased to see us,' Zoe said slowly.

'We'll tell her about the things we found in the chimney. She's bound to be interested. What did she say – her ancestors date back to the time of King Robert? She'll be thrilled that we've called round with the news.'

Zoe wasn't so sure. She looked towards the fire and let go of all thoughts of relaxing in the warmth and drifting into the enticing story of her book. She smiled. 'Right, let's get our coats. Lunch it is.'

* * *

Two hours later, after a glass of red wine each and a bowl of stovies, a meaty stew, Zoe and Leah found themselves walking through Rosemuir down a narrow backstreet crammed with stone-built terraces, huddled together beneath staggered low slate roofs. In the distance, tartan fields of earth colours and pine forests melted into a silver sky. They passed a neat cottage with tidy flower baskets, the blooms all gone, waiting for the coming spring, and another with a bright red door. Zoe glanced at it with interest.

'This is fifty-three Culduthel Terrace. So, Mirren's is number sixty-one...'

They passed three more pretty terraces, and they paused: they knew which house was Mirren's before they reached number sixty-one. The grey stonework was covered with clambering ivy, twisting towards the small top window. The door was green, the paint peeling to reveal its previous salmon colour.

Leah grasped the brass knocker, a horseshoe perched over a tarnished thistle. She rapped twice and waited. The downstairs curtains were half open and, behind them, the room appeared unlit and gloomy. Leah knocked again.

'Perhaps she's out?' Zoe suggested. 'Maybe she's up at the castle, cleaning and preparing for the tour?'

'The southwest wing isn't included in it,' Leah said sadly. 'I'm going to try to persuade her to take us in there, show us what's upstairs...'

'We've been advised to stay away...' Zoe had no intention of returning. It was a strange, unsettling place. The thought of going back there turned her bones to ice.

'But what about the chapel as part of the wedding venue?' Leah's face was hopeful just as the door opened and Mirren peered through. She was dressed casually, a dark jumper, black trousers, her hair tied in a loose knot. She frowned. 'What do you want?'

'It's me, Leah Drummond, and Zoe, from the castle.'

'I know who you are.' Mirren's tone was flat, not unfriendly. 'Why are you here?'

'Leah's doing a special tour of the castle...' Zoe began.

'I know.' Mirren's face was closed, unimpressed. 'I heard about it.'

Leah leaned forward. 'We found some things in the chimney from centuries ago and I wanted to let you know, to ask about them. I wonder if you'd be able to tell us anything...'

'What things?'

Leah was suddenly animated. 'A dagger – a ballock dagger – and a hauberk.'

Mirren paused; her eyes were dark blue in a pale face. 'You'd better come in.'

Zoe hesitated in the doorway, surprised to be invited inside. Leah was already in the hallway, gazing around, fascinated. Mirren led the way into a small room where a fire burned in a miniature woodburning stove. A dark red damask sofa covered in a variety of patchwork throws took up most of the space in the sitting room. Brown wooden shelves held volumes of books, mostly large dark ones. Leah immediately spied several about the Logan clan and another about the reign of Robert the Bruce. There were knick-knacks in all corners, a goblet with red dragons and blue thistles. On the wall, there was a dark-framed painting of a man with a rough red beard wearing a metal helmet. He held a sharp black battle-axe, his eyes piercing blue as they stared into the distance.

'Sit yourselves down.' Mirren's voice was husky. 'Will you want tea?'

Zoe was about to refuse politely, but Leah waved a hand in assent. 'I'd love one.'

Zoe nodded. 'Thanks.' Mirren left the room and Zoe made a face. 'At least it's warm in here.'

Leah nodded, gazing around. She was fascinated by all the objects that cluttered the room and she held herself back from leaping up and examining the many figurines of men in silver armour on horseback or in battle positions holding swords aloft. There were various tartan tea towels in clan colours folded in a pile, maps, framed bronze pennies and even a Ladybird book called *Robert the Bruce*.

Then Mirren arrived carrying a tray, handing a mug to Leah, then to Zoe. She sat down by the fire on the floor and folded her hands in her lap.

Leah sipped strong tea. 'I love your house. You have so many interesting things.'

'So – I want to know...' Mirren closed her eyes for a moment. When she opened them, she said, 'Tell me about what you found in the chimney.'

'I'm waiting for the report to come back from the university but...' Leah leaned forward excitedly. 'I'm pretty sure the dagger is a ballock, from the thirteen hundreds—'

'I would like to see it...' Mirren pressed her lips together. 'One of my ancestors used to make them. He was a smith in the castle, apparently.'

'Was that when Ross McNair was alive?' Leah blurted, full of enthusiasm. 'I read that he owned Ravenscraig in the time of Robert the Bruce.'

Mirren was thoughtful for a moment. 'I know only what has been passed down by word of mouth, over the centuries. The Logans have lived in Rosemuir for over seven hundred years and one of them was a smith. He was very tall: my father told me that a tall red-haired Logan man was born every second generation. There's some talk of one of my ancestors fighting for the king. His name was Hendrie Logan, apparently, and he was quite an important character in the battle against the English.' She paused, looking from Zoe to Leah. 'I remember my father telling me the story of Hendrie Logan. I used to be fascinated by it as a child, but nowadays, I don't like to think of it.'

'Perhaps the ballock dagger belonged to him?' Leah tried hopefully.

Mirren shook her head. 'I doubt it.' She was silent for a moment, lost in thought, then she said, 'You found armour, you say?'

'The sweep was cleaning the chimney in the kitchen – it clearly hadn't been swept properly in a long time. There was chainmail armour, a coif and a hauberk.'

'Inside the chimney?' Mirren repeated, staring into the fire.

Leah nodded. 'Why would someone put it there?'

'Hidden there for some purpose? Or perhaps some soldier was once wearing the armour and he was buried alive in the chimney?' Mirren's eyes narrowed. 'They were cruel times.' She heaved another sigh.

They sat quietly for a while, Leah sipping tea, Zoe realising that she hadn't felt so warm in ages. Then Mirren lifted her head.

'I want to see the armour, the dagger. May I?'

'I don't see why not,' Leah replied brightly. 'I think Abigail likes to keep the artefacts under lock and key most of the time, but she'll let me display them on the open day. Why don't you come along?'

'Perhaps I will.' Mirren glanced at their mugs, checking if the tea had been finished. Both Leah and Zoe had half a cup left. 'Do you like living at the castle?'

'I love it,' Leah enthused. 'It's my dream job...'

'And you?' Mirren faced Zoe.

'It's cold,' Zoe replied without thinking.

'Bone cold,' Mirren said, and was quiet again.

'Do you like working there?' Leah asked politely.

'I like being in the garden, walking outdoors in the grounds in the spring and summer, remembering that people who might have looked like me who once lived and worked there.'

Zoe lifted the mug to her lips. 'And what about the southwest wing?'

'What about it?' Mirren asked sharply. Her eyes narrowed.

'It's a strange place.' Zoe couldn't help herself. 'You know that, Leah, from the time when you were locked in there...'

'Yes,' Leah admitted. She met Mirren's eyes. 'Both of us have witnessed some strange things in the castle.'

'What things?' Mirren's voice was an echo.

'A presence, as if I'm not alone,' Zoe admitted.

'I was sure someone was in the chapel with me,' Leah added.

'And there have been other strange things – lights in the south-west wing, orbs on photographs, the laptop switching itself off...' Zoe explained.

Mirren pressed her fingers together. 'Most caretakers usually leave after a few weeks.'

'I don't want to leave,' Leah said. 'I want to make it work.'

'But we do need to find out about the castle,' Zoe persisted. 'What's going on in there, Mirren? Help us to understand.'

'I only know what has been passed down to me.' Mirren's tone was hushed. She hesitated, then said: 'For a long time, a Logan woman has always visited the southwest wing. We lay down a thistle in the spring and the summer, other flowers in the winter, to remember.'

'To remember what?' Leah asked nervously.

Mirren took a breath. 'Things happened inside the castle walls that should never be spoken aloud.' She stood up slowly, her expression grave. 'The walls of the wing must stay untouched. I know only a few tales my father passed down. After me, all knowledge of the castle will be lost forever. But something terrible happened in the southwest wing all those years ago. And now it must be left alone.' She narrowed her eyes. 'It's time for you to go.'

30

The December snow had arrived in thick rumpled blankets, piled in the courtyard, banked up high against the crenelated wall. Agnes was alone with her thoughts as she carried two empty pails through the raised portcullis towards the well. The Christmas feast had come three days ago, but Agnes had not been able to enjoy it. She'd prayed silently in the chapel on Christmas morning, her eyes heavy, her limbs weary from all the baking she had done. The servants had cooked into the early hours, Agnes with them, preparing the feast that the master and mistress allowed all servants to share the following day. There had been much cheer on Christmas Day in the castle, drinking of ale and revelry, games, dressing up in disguises, and they had huddled around trestle tables in the great hall and shared a boar's head, carrots, peas, turbot and an abundance of bread. Effie had dressed in a long red woollen cloak Rhona had found for her and danced, smiling all the time, calling to Agnes, 'See, I'm the wee princess again.' Agnes had smiled back affectionately, but her thoughts were elsewhere.

She had not received word from Cam for thirteen days and now she was fetching water from the icy well in the early hours, hoping that she'd glimpse a rider on horseback approaching fast and it would be him. She knew Rhona was worried too: she had been tight-lipped as she worked with Effie at the vat, lost in her own world. Even An-Mòr, who could be relied on to give good cheer, turned down several invitations to compete in the strong arm on Christmas morning. His face was a mask of sadness. There had been no word of Hendrie either, and Agnes's heart went out to Maidlin, alone with her child in the hut in the forest for almost two weeks.

Agnes filled the pails slowly; the water at the bottom of the well was crusted with snow, and she heaved the contents distractedly, her eyes on the horizon, hoping for a speck in the distance that might be Cam coming back for her.

Tears filled her eyes and she wiped them away on her sleeve. She could not cry. He had not abandoned her. He was still alive. He was on his way to her now, and before the new year came, she would hold him close to her and they would cover each other's faces with so many kisses. She was sure of it.

The white mountains were tinged ice blue beyond the water of the loch, and Agnes wondered if he was up there in the hills, if he felt the bite of the wind, if he was hiding or fighting or lying in a ditch, his head bloodied. As her eyes closed, Agnes realised that the wind had turned her fingers red and numb around the handle of the bucket.

Aimlessly, she trudged back to the kitchen, where the servants bustled about their work. She placed the water on a hook over the fire to heat, warming her fingers for an instant before fetching flour to make bread. Effie was chattering to Rhona as they bent over the vat brewing a new batch of ale. She was asking if she could wear the red woollen cloak again, where Rhona had got it and, although it wasn't nearly as nice as the one the wee princess had worn, could she keep it for her own.

Agnes pummelled the bread, kneading it energetically; she could see Una seated on a stool nearby plucking a grouse, her lips tight in concentration. Then she thought of Cam and Hendrie again and she tried to catch Rhona's eye, to offer her a brave smile of hope, but Rhona's head was bowed over her work, her mind was occupied.

The loaves were shaped; Agnes placed them in the clay cooking pots ready for the oven. Then she became aware that someone was standing close to her. She turned to see a servant she didn't know by name but who she had seen before. It was the same young woman who had brought her and Effie to the comfortable bedroom when she had first arrived.

Agnes studied her expression: she was waiting for Agnes to finish her work. Then the maid said, 'Ye are Agnes Fitzgerald?'

'I am,' Agnes replied.

'You've to go to the great hall straight away.'

The maid turned to leave and Agnes called, 'Why? Who seeks me there?'

'The mistress has asked for ye. You'd better hurry along.'

Her thoughts crashing together with anxiety, Agnes wondered why she had been summoned. She couldn't recall doing anything wrong. The memory of the smith came back to her, the day she'd been asked to identify him before he'd been dragged away to suffer a horrible death. Cam had been there then; he'd spoken to her with the slightest movement of his eyes. She had loved him from that moment.

Agnes left the kitchen and rushed towards the great hall, where the mistress was seated by the hearth, staring into the roaring fire, alone. She was wearing a blue dress and a bronze brooch with a fine clasp, and her hair was coiled in plaits. Agnes curtsied low and Muriel McNair's voice was kind. 'Agnes? Would ye come and stand by me? What I have to say is only for ye to hear.'

Agnes shuffled forward and waited. 'Madam?'

'Ye know of a young man whom the others call Allaidh?'

Agnes's heart leaped. She said quietly, 'I do.' She examined Muriel's face for any information about Cam, but her expression was calm.

'Tell me about him...' Muriel said.

'He's called Cam Buchanan. He and I are sweethearts.'

'So I believe.' Muriel pressed her lips together. 'He is also one of King Robert's men. He is a fearless fighter for the king. Two weeks ago, he came here to talk to my husband about ye, asking if he could take your hand. He loves ye very much.'

Agnes nodded. 'And I him. Do ye ken where he is, Madam? I've heard nothing for a while now—'

Muriel raised a finger and Agnes was silent. 'Ye ken that it's a hard life, being a soldier's woman.'

'I'm not afraid.'

'I can see that.' Muriel took a breath. 'My husband gave his permission for ye both to join hands. But I suggest ye stay here and work in the castle for the time being. Things are very difficult now for us all. And, of course, there is the matter of your sister.'

'Effie.'

'I believe Rhona is keeping an eye on her, making her into an alewife.'

'She is, aye.'

'Agnes...' Muriel began and her face was sad. 'I have to tell ye the English armies are moving north. Word came to my husband yesterday that they are close to Inverness and your young laddie and Rhona's son are in the thick of the fighting there.'

'Have ye news of Cam? Is he well?' Agnes could not help herself.

'Yesterday,' Muriel folded her hands in her lap, 'a messenger arrived and told us that the battle is hard but both men are still alive. I should hear more news soon and, pray God, they will both return unharmed.'

'Pray God,' Agnes repeated, closing her eyes. Then a thought became words in her mouth. 'Madam, Hendrie has a wife, a bairn in the forests...'

Muriel smiled. 'I ken. I keep them both well fed. Ye need not worry about them. My husband and I are true to the king and we do all we can. But the English want our lands for Longshanks, their own king, and the Scots will fight to the last man to stop them. We are full of fear in the castle; there are traitors to Scotia among us, who would betray The Bruce – ye ken that, Agnes, ye have seen it with your own eyes.'

'I have.'

'Be vigilant at all times. A wrong word would see us all dead.'

'Aye, Madam, I ken.'

Muriel sighed and turned back to the firelight, staring into the sparks. 'That is all.'

Agnes didn't move. 'Madam...'

'What is it?' Muriel was still staring into the flames.

'Ye will tell me if ye hear news of him, my Cam?'

Muriel turned to her and tears shone in her eyes. 'Aye, I will.' She paused for a moment, as if unsure, then she said, 'I had a son, William. He would be twenty-five now, the same age as your sweetheart, had he lived. He too would have been loyal, fighting for his king. He is always in my heart...'

'Madam, I am sorry to hear it.'

Muriel took a breath and she was composed again. 'My husband and I wish ye both long lives and many children. If I hear word of your sweetheart, I will call ye here to speak with ye. I have already summoned An-Mòr to tell him that his son is well, but if ye will, ye might mention it quietly to Rhona in the kitchen.'

'Aye, I will.' Agnes curtsied.

'Agnes...' Muriel's voice became hushed. 'If my husband finds out about those who work here who would betray the king, he will deal severely with them. Ye ken that?'

'Aye, Madam, I do.'

'So, if ye should hear anything untoward...'

'Aye, I'll speak only to ye of it.'

Muriel inclined her head. 'I am keeping ye.'

'Madam,' Agnes replied, and as she turned to walk away, she muttered to herself, 'I ken – the bannock willnae bake itself...'

Instead of returning directly to the kitchen, Agnes walked quickly to the dark hall and through the doorway into the courtyard. She wanted to look out towards the loch once more, to imagine where Cam was, what he was doing. No one would miss her for a moment.

It had started to snow again, light flakes curling as they fell, soft as swan's down. She lifted her face, feeling the dampness on her cheeks, and imagined kisses there instead. The snow dampened her cap and the curls beneath as Agnes turned towards the loch. Flakes fell more thickly, clouding her vision. Cam was out there somewhere, he and Hendrie and the other men, and her heart sang with the hope that he was alive and safe, soon to return.

She glanced towards the main gate; the portcullis had been lowered and there were more guards standing by, their bodies stiff in hauberks, chainmail coifs covering most of their faces. Muriel McNair's words came back to her: *the English armies are moving north*. Agnes could sense it in the edgy stance of the soldiers, the lowered grid of the portcullis. There was a tension in the air and Agnes shivered with the thought that the English could move towards Rosemuir. Her heart sang that Cam was alive, but it was gripped with the fear of what might come.

As she rushed into the warmth of the kitchen, Agnes almost bumped into Una, who was going in the other direction, holding a pitcher of ale and food wrapped in a cloth. 'Agnes,' she grunted and indicated the food. 'The soldiers need to eat.'

Agnes nodded agreement as she headed towards the roaring fire; she was comforted by the sudden dry heat. Rhona and Effie didn't notice her. She'd speak to them both soon. Her hands were best kept busy; she picked up the proved loaves, but her thoughts were elsewhere as she began to sing softly to herself.

> *O, where are ye gone, my Scottish warrior?*
> *'Twixt the thistle and the mist o' the morn...*

31

It was past eight in the morning. Zoe was due back from her run at any moment. Leah was in the kitchenette preparing porridge and toast. She looked out of the window onto the courtyard; there was a light dusting of snow below, sparkling like fine sugar. She gazed up at the sky, white as blank paper, heavy with a blizzard. A movement caught her eye; someone was approaching through the main gateway. Leah frowned, leaning forward, screwing her eyes for a better look. She'd assumed it was Mirren Logan who'd come to clean the chapel and she'd already decided to rush downstairs and invite her in for a warm drink. But it was a man, warm in a heavy jacket and scarf. Leah noticed his thick hair, a tidy beard. From a distance, he might be quite good-looking. She watched him approach the southwest wing, try the chapel door, tugging the latch. It was locked. He moved around to the far side and peered over the crenelated wall, where stones had crumbled to rubble. Leah grabbed a coat and pushed her feet into warm boots. It was her job as caretaker to find out what he was doing, she thought with a smile.

She rushed down the spiral steps, feeling the cold air against her face, and out into the courtyard where the chilly wind made her eyes water. She hurried over towards the man. 'Can I help you?'

He gave a confident grin, friendly and warm. 'You must be Leah Drummond?'

Leah gave a half-laugh, a little embarrassed. 'You're ahead of me.'

His eyes crinkled in another smile and he held out a gloved hand. 'Christie Watt. I'm the builder – my team have done all the work to the castle over the past few years. I'm sure Abi Laing has mentioned me?'

Leah was momentarily flustered: she couldn't imagine anyone abbreviating Abigail Laing's name and getting away with it. But this man was very charming. She tugged her cold hand from his gloved fingers. 'So, are you here to do some tidying up before the tour on Saturday?' She gazed around at the frosting of snow. 'I can't imagine the weather is suitable.'

'It's not, but I wanted to take a look at this part of the castle. It's the last piece of the jigsaw and I know Dan Lennox is keen to get the place finished.'

'Is he?' Leah marvelled: the builder knew the owner; he'd abbreviated his name too. He was casual, very familiar. The words tumbled from her mouth. 'Do you know the owner? Have you met him?'

Christie nodded. 'My sister was in his class at school. He's a local boy. His parents weren't short of a bob or two, though, and Dan took it up several levels. It's the Asian Tiger economy.'

'It is,' Leah agreed. She had no idea what Christie was talking about. She took a breath and tried her best not to stutter: despite his good looks, he was a builder and she was a caretaker. She would be professional. 'So, how can I help?'

'I need to work out what to do with this part of the castle.'

'The southwest wing?'

'Exactly. The outside wall needs rebuilding and I'd have to access it from the other side, put up some scaffolding.'

'When will you start?'

'February, I think...' Christie met her eyes.

Leah's immediate thought was that Valentine's Day was in February and she'd planned to hold Jordan and Mariusz's wedding in the castle, although she hadn't mentioned it to anyone. Scaffolding would spoil the wedding photos. She said, 'Maybe later in the spring the weather might be nicer?'

Christie gave a short laugh. 'This is Scotland; I'm a builder.'

'And?'

'And the weather has to be very inclement to stop work.'

'Oh...' Leah was a little disappointed.

'Could I take a look inside?' Christie indicated the southwest wing with a movement of his head.

Leah pressed her lips together. 'That's usually Mirren Logan's responsibility.'

He shrugged. 'Ah, she's a sweetie – Mirren won't mind.'

Leah was astonished. She hadn't thought of Mirren as a sweetie – at least he hadn't abbreviated her name. She took a breath, and the cold air that filled her lungs gave her an idea. She'd play for time.

'Can I offer you a warm drink, Mr Watt?'

'Christie...'

'Christie...' Leah's glance moved to his left hand; there was no wedding ring there. 'It's freezing out here. Let's grab a cuppa and we can get the keys and come back and take a look.'

'Okay, tea for me, one sugar, please,' he agreed. 'Lead the way, although I know every room in the castle like the back of my hand. I hope the flat is comfortable enough for you and your partner.'

'My sister.' Leah turned towards the castle door, feeling a little sad that their feet were marking the smooth perfection of the snow. She gazed up. There would be more.

'Two sisters as caretakers.' Christie nodded. 'That's a nice idea. Usually, it's an older pair who like to do a bit of house sitting. They don't stay long. People find the place too cold.' He raised an eyebrow.

Leah wondered if he knew about the ghostly presence. She decided that he didn't look the type to believe in the supernatural. It occurred to her that he might be the perfect person to accompany her to the southwest wing. She smiled. 'Right, I'll make us a quick drink and we'll grab the keys and have a look round.'

Christie's brow creased. 'You haven't been in there before...?'

'No, Mirren doesn't really like...'

'Ah, of course.' He grinned. 'She's a wilful lass, our Mirren, and her roots are here, in Rosemuir, so she's quite protective of Ravenscraig.'

Leah took in his accent, the Scottish burr, and decided it was very attractive. They clambered up the winding steps, across the landing and stood together in the kitchenette.

Christie said, 'It's always deathly cold in this place.'

Leah nodded, the word deathly lingering in her ears. She busied herself with the kettle and mugs. Christie sat at the small table, gazing through the window. 'I love the view from here, but my favourite one is from the great hall, that aspect of the loch and the mountains. It's breathtaking.' He rubbed his hands together. 'Dan's picked a lovely place.'

'Oh?' Leah's back was turned and it made her feel more daring, asking more probing questions. 'What does he intend to do with it, I mean, when it's finished?'

'He's a proud Scot. He wanted to put something back. I wouldn't be surprised if he doesn't open it to the public as a piece of Scottish heritage.' She heard Christie laugh. 'Or he might just live in it. He's that sort of guy...'

'What sort?' As Leah poured water, she heard the interest in her own voice.

'He's a character...' Christie began.

The door flew open and Zoe was standing in the opening, bright-faced with cold.

'Bloody hell, it's brass monkeys...' She stopped short, staring at the handsome man who sat at the table, long legs stretched out, work boots on the end. Zoe saw the smile spread across his face and her eyes seemed to be stuck to his lips, the soft curve of flesh there. She decided on the spot that she'd never seen such kissable lips.

Christie looked towards Leah for assistance. 'Is this your sister?'

'Zoe, this is Christie Watt, the builder,' Leah began.

'Oh, sorry, yes, I mean – I've been out jogging,' Zoe gabbled, conscious that her cheeks were glowing hot.

'Do you want a cuppa?' Leah asked. 'Then we're going to take a look in the southwest wing. Why don't you come with us?'

'Yes, no, I need a shower... I stink,' Zoe stuttered, painfully conscious that she didn't look her most attractive.

She turned round too fast, blundering into the door post. She rushed towards the bathroom, switching on the hot shower, peeling off her wet trainers, damp leggings, sweat-coated top. Leaping under the scalding spray, she reached for shampoo. Zoe was furious with herself: she had just told the handsome man with delicious lips that she stank. As she lathered herself with something that smelled of fresh herbs, she asked herself what on earth was wrong with her? It was unlike her to fall into a babbling heap just because a man was pleasant to look at. For a moment, she wondered if she could hide in the shower until he'd gone away. But there was a rising feeling of inquisitiveness, fascination even. She had to go back and speak to him again, show that she was calm, unperturbed. After all, she told herself, taking deep breaths, he might not be so good-looking the next time she saw him. He might even be quite ordinary. So why, she asked herself with irritation, was her heart thudding?

* * *

Half an hour later, Leah led the way across the courtyard, clad in a warm coat and scarf, thick mittens clutching the metal key ring. Christie walked next to her, his breath a mist in the cold air. Zoe straggled behind, her curls damp, her hands deep in her coat pocket, watching the sway of his shoulders as he moved. She decided that he was even better looking than she'd thought, and she felt suddenly awkward. She wasn't sure why she'd tagged along. She shook droplets from her head: she wasn't sure why she was there at all. She could have made the excuse that she had to work: it was true, but the appearance of the builder intrigued her more than she was frightened by the idea of being in the cold eerie chapel. They huddled closely together, three chilly bodies in the whipping wind, as Leah pushed the heavy door.

Christie looked at Leah, then Zoe. 'Shall we go in?'

'It's dark inside...' Zoe muttered, hovering a few paces behind. Dismayed by the fact that she was stating the obvious, she closed her mouth with a snap of teeth.

'I have a torch...' Leah flicked the beam on and ushered Christie inside.

Christie stepped into the chapel. 'Well, this is quite lovely. A nice space, very solid stone, totally original.' He walked into the centre, illuminated by the light from the window. 'What's this? Dried flowers on the floor?' He bent down.

'Mirren puts them there...' Leah began.

There was a heavy beating of wings; a dark bird swooped over their heads and curved upwards towards the rafters.

'That was a raven...' Zoe spluttered.

Christie agreed. 'The raven of Ravenscraig. There's always one around here, usually sitting on the battlements, watching.'

'That's creepy,' Leah remarked.

Christie sniffed. 'I suppose so. I've done a lot of work on this place over the years. I'm used to all the foibles.'

'The chapel is perfect...' Leah was dreaming of weddings again. 'How easy would it be to put stained glass in?'

'Very easy,' Christie said. 'The light into the chapel would be limited, but it would look stunning.'

'And we'd have candles, wall sconces,' Leah suggested.

'Very nice.' Christie turned to Zoe. 'Are you okay? Your hair is still damp. You'll catch a chill.'

Zoe nodded. 'I'm a bit cold.' She was stating the obvious again.

'Let's go upstairs and have a quick look around, shall we? We won't stay long, then we can head back to the castle and warm up,' Christie said.

Leah felt her spine stiffen with fear. 'What's up there, do you think?'

'I've no idea...' Christie moved towards the stone spiral steps and gazed up. 'Bats maybe, some sort of chamber. I've seen a small window on the outside up there. Shall we go and find out?'

Leah was relieved that Christie was oblivious of Mirren's demand that no one should go up the steps. She handed him the torch – he was welcome to go first – and she and Zoe were at his shoulder as he strode upwards into shadows, his feet ringing on the hard steps.

They stood in a square room that was so dark they could hardly see. A high vertical window cast a slice of white light on the stone floor. The walls and towering ceiling were heavy stone, and there was an overpowering smell of damp, a fustiness that stifled the throat and made breathing more difficult. There was another smell, an oppressive stench of something rotten.

Christie raised an eyebrow. 'This is a cheerless place.'

Zoe shivered. 'What do you think this place was, back in the day?'

Christie lifted the torch; he was examining stones, checking the solidity. The beam of light cast eerie shadows. 'A priest's chamber, maybe?' Christie shook his head. 'It's damp in here and perishingly cold. All the wind from the mountains blows in, but the air isn't fresh. It's putrid.' He shook his head. 'I can't work it out.'

'I don't like it up here.' Leah was thinking of the space for a wedding, but there was an overbearing feeling of something being not right. She couldn't work it out. Mirren had said they should not come into the upstairs room and Leah knew why. She felt as if she was intruding; worse, she felt that her presence there was wrong, unsafe.

'This place is awful.' Zoe was feeling intensely cold. It was not just her damp hair and the ice and snow in the wind: she was shivering from somewhere deep in her bones. She gazed around, shaking, her hands pushed in her pockets. There was a sadness in the room, and it was difficult to breathe. It was as if her chest was compressed by overwhelming grief. Something had happened in the room, something dreadful.

Then they heard a noise from the far wall, the one that faced the loch, once, twice. It was as if unseen fingers scraped behind the stones, a blunt repeated scratching that set their nerves on edge.

Zoe's eyes were wide. 'What's that?'

'Rats, I guess,' Christie said calmly.

Leah had seen enough. 'We should go...'

'I think so.' Christie lifted the torch, pointing towards the stairs and began to descend. Leah was behind him, at his elbow, her footsteps hurried.

Zoe followed them, turning to look back into the dark chamber. Shadows shifted before her eyes, moving, huddling in corners and, as she twisted away to bolt down the steps to safety, she heard a noise like the low whimper of the wind. But it wasn't the wind; she was sure it was a voice, a single breath of sadness. From behind the wall came a deep, soulless sigh.

32

Agnes observed Effie carefully. Something about her had changed since she'd started learning to be an alewife. She was flourishing under Rhona's guidance, and she seemed more contented, more confident. Each day, she'd pull on the red cloak Rhona had given her, picking up a pitcher of ale and several trenchers, rushing off towards the forge through the cold to deliver some food to An-Mòr. Agnes wondered if she had met a young man in the forge who had caught her eye; Effie always returned with a secret smile on her lips, as if she was hiding a treasure in her heart. Agnes resolved to ask her about it.

She was grateful that Una kept her distance now. They rarely spoke, apart from the times Una came to her to ask for bread for the soldiers. The cold weather made them hungrier than ever; they were guarding the castle grounds for longer hours now.

Agnes watched the yeast froth in the bowl and inhaled the sweet-stale smell of fermentation. She sifted flour and thought of the falling snow outside, of Cam in the mountains fighting the English army. It was the last day of the year today and she prayed in her heart that he was safe and that she would hear from him soon.

Effie caught her eye and they shared a smile as Effie passed by. She made her way slowly to the kitchen entrance, past the leaping flames of the fire where a cauldron of pottage steamed. Agnes felt her stomach growl; she was ready for something to eat. Then Rhona was by her side. 'Effie is on her way to the forge again.'

'Aye – the men there must be hungry. It's bitterly cold.'

'That's true. But she has a sweetheart there, a man twice her age.'

Agnes frowned. 'Who is it?'

'Bròccan Millar. He works with An-Mòr. His wife died giving birth two years ago – the bairn died too. Now Brccan's turned his sights on wee Effie. She's fair taken with him, too.'

'Is he a good man?'

'I dinnae ken him well.' Rhona shrugged. 'He's fairly quiet. An-Mòr says he rarely hears anything from him the long day. He lives in the village; he has his own small house. Effie takes food to him in the forge and they sit with their heads together and talk, and he holds her hand in his like it's made of precious cloth. Aye, I think Effie seems happy enough with him and perhaps Bròccan will take care of her.'

'That's good,' Agnes said quietly, but she was surprised that she felt otherwise. She was protective of Effie, who had been secretive and said nothing of this man. Agnes wanted to meet him. She hoped Effie was making a good choice, that Bròccan would treat her well.

Rhona interrupted her thoughts. 'How are ye feeling, Agnes? This cold weather and snow chills to the bone.'

'I'm warm enough,' Agnes replied, noticing Rhona's enigmatic smile.

'Then you'll not be too tired to walk to the village with me tonight. I have some weaving that needs to be done.'

Agnes almost squealed with delight. Her eyes were round as she leaned towards Rhona, her voice a whisper. 'Is he come back?'

Rhona teased. 'I've ale to brew now so I cannae spend time talking. But mark ye that ye come home with me tonight. And we'd better not keep the laddie waiting...'

Agnes's heart was light as she pummelled the bread. Each moment that passed was loaded with excitement, the thrill of waiting, the ache of longing. In several hours she'd be in Cam's arms again and the mistress knew of their love; she had given her blessing. They would be reunited and they'd have the whole night together. Cam had promised they'd be together for ever. Agnes imagined kisses on her neck, the warmth of his breath, and she smiled.

'I have food for ye, Agnes – ye havnae eaten yet.' It was Effie, holding out a bowl of pottage.

'Thanking ye.'

Effie tugged her sleeve. 'Come and sit by the fire and tarry a while. Let's sup together.'

Agnes followed Effie to the hearth and they watched a grouse spit on a skewer.

Effie's eyes gleamed. 'I need to tell ye, Agnes – I have a sweetheart.'

'I'm glad for ye, Effie.' Agnes did not want to lie, but she added, 'Is he a good man? Tell me of him.'

'He says he loves me, that he'd die for me.' Effie closed her eyes dreamily. 'And I love him too. He's going to ask the master if we can wed next year and I'll live with him in his house in Rosemuir. We'll have bairns and be happy together.'

Words sprang to Agnes's lips; she was desperate to share that she too loved a man who was brave and kind and loyal, but she dared not speak of Cam, not yet, not while the king was in hiding and the English armies were so close.

'That's good, isn't it, that I have a sweetheart? He's called Bròccan Millar and I am to be Effie Millar next year, no longer Effie Gale.' Effie's small face was flushed with excitement.

Agnes wrapped an arm around Effie. 'Can I meet him soon?'

'Och, I've told him all about ye, Agnes, that ye are my sister and that we escaped from Kildrummy together with the princess's cloak, and he asked me if ye had a sweetheart and I told him nay, and he says he'll meet ye when the time is good and right. He says one day he'll buy me a cloak, not like the old red one Rhona gave me, but a fur one like the Princess Marjorie's. He says one day we'll be together and he'll buy me clothes and brooches like the mistress wears and we'll be happy, rich as kings and queens.' Effie clasped her hands. 'I've always wanted to be treated like a princess.'

Agnes frowned. 'How will he do that?'

'He's canny and wise. We talk together every day and he tells me that he loves me and I believe him too.'

Agnes nodded slowly, suddenly protective. 'I'd like to meet him.'

'Aye, and ye will, when he's ready.' Effie offered a secretive smile. 'But I must go back to brewing ale or Rhona will lug my ears. I tell Bròccan that I dinnae like the reek of it, but he says he loves the smell of it on me. He likes to drink ale a lot and says a brewster woman will make the best of wives.'

Agnes watched as Effie rushed back to the vats of ale, picking up a long spoon, whispering to Rhona and gazing furtively towards Agnes. Agnes nodded once, wiped her hands on her apron and went back to her table to work, passing Una on her stool, a bowl at her feet. Una shot her a hostile glance, muttered 'Agnes' gruffly and returned to skinning a rabbit. Agnes paid no heed; she had a lot on her mind.

* * *

Agnes was still anxious as she followed Rhona back to Rosemuir. The sky was pitch black but for a hooked sliver of moon. 'I'm troubled, Rhona. Effie says that Bròccan drinks a lot and he seems a wee

bit canny for her. She says he's making her promises to buy her a
new cloak and—'

'Dinnae fret,' Rhona soothed. 'I'll speak to An-Mòr. It may be
that an older man will care for Effie – she's a bairn still, and
maybe that's what she needs, someone who kens the ways of the
world.'

'Ye may be right.' Agnes was unsure.

'Here y'are, we're almost home and ye have a lot to think about
now...'

Agnes smiled. 'I long to see Cam. It has been an age.'

Rhona nodded, her face grave. 'And there has been much bloodshed. Those poor men fighting with The Bruce have seen so much
of death. Who kens how they must live each day, always in fear of
the next battle?'

'Aye,' Agnes sighed. 'Are ye thinking of Hendrie? I oft times
wonder about his wife Maidlin and the bairn, alone in the forest.'

'It's no life for a lass...' Rhona stopped herself. 'I would have
them with me here, but Hendrie is a wanted man, Cam too, and the
others. It isnae safe...'

They had arrived at the timber and wattle house, ducking
through the low doorway. Inside, the smoke from the fire curled
towards the thatch and hung there thickly.

A figure stepped from the shadows and lunged towards Rhona.
'Maw.'

Rhona turned and saw her son. 'Hendrie...' Then she gasped.
His face was covered in blood, one cheek sliced open, the flesh livid
beneath. She rushed to fill a bowl and hissed, 'What happened? Sit
and I'll tend to ye...'

'I cannae stay...' Hendrie flopped onto the stool that Agnes had
fetched.

Rhona was already bathing the wound; the water in the bowl
was red with gore. She breathed heavily. 'An-Mòr will be here too
and he'll tell ye to stay. Ye are hurt badly.'

'I have a wife and bairn to see...' Hendrie groaned, closing his eyes for a moment. His body slumped forward, weak and weary.

'What happened?' Agnes asked.

'The English armies are strong now – there are so many of them and we are so few. Cam was behind me, fighting the ones who gave us chase, but pray God he'll be here soon.' Hendrie's eyes moved to Agnes, who took a pace back, her heart in her throat. Already she was fearing the worst. Hendrie tried again. 'Longshanks' soldiers are moving forward all the time and it's all we can do to hold them back.'

Rhona frowned. 'This wound needs a stitch, or I could clean it with vinegar and change the dressing every couple of days. It'll leave a big scar...'

'Maidlin loves me, ugly or no.' Hendrie grinned, then he flinched beneath his mother's arm.

The sound of hooves clattered outside and Rhona spoke to Agnes without turning. 'It's Cam. Grab the bundle in the corner, lassie, and be on your way now.'

'Bundle?'

Rhona indicated a bundle of cloth with a nod of her head. Agnes grabbed it and Rhona hissed, 'Go, Go.'

Agnes ducked beneath the doorway and Cam was waiting, seated high on Sealgair. He pulled her in front of him as she clutched the bundle, spurring the horse onwards, his lips against her ear. 'I've missed ye, Agnes. So much. Ye are in my thoughts every moment, day and night. But I promised ye this, and here I am now.'

They rode through the snow, climbing high into the forests. Agnes was warmed by his arms around her. She noticed Cam's hand that held the reins had a deep slice between thumb and forefinger that gaped and hadn't yet become a scar. She ran her finger over it and felt him wince. 'What happened?'

Sealgair's paces slowed as they entered a clearing thick with fallen snow, branches laden with it, sparkling in the light of the curved moon.

'A cut from an English dagger. But he'll cut a Scotsman no more.'

'And The Bruce? How fares he?'

Cam was silent as the horse plodded on. 'He fights hard. He wants this done, his wife and child returned to him, Scotia ours again, the English gone. I fear it'll be a while coming. There are more of them than of us. But we gather more loyal men each day.'

They had arrived at a clearing and Agnes saw a small hut in the shadows, a palfrey horse stood a few feet away tethered to a tree; its back was covered with a simple saddle cloth. Sealgair stopped and Cam helped her down.

'Whose hut is this?' Agnes asked.

Cam smiled. 'Mine. Ours.'

Agnes was puzzled.

A familiar man emerged from inside the hut. He held out his arms in welcome. 'Cam. Ye are later than I thought you'd be, but I've a good fire going inside and some food in the pot.'

'Thank ye, father,' Cam said quietly, and Agnes recognised Friar John, the Franciscan monk who often held a sermon at the chapel at Ravenscraig.

She frowned. 'I don't understand...'

'Go, change your clothes.' Cam's eyes glimmered as he indicated the bundle she hugged closely. 'I'll be waiting here.'

Friar John smiled. 'And be quick about it, lassie, for it's bitter cold and I've a long way to travel tonight to get back.'

Agnes rushed inside the hut, confused, opening the bundle, inhaling the smoke of the room and the aroma of a stew bubbling. She glanced around; a pile of warm blankets was heaped in the corner. Inside the cloth Rhona had given her was a linen dress, embroidered with tiny thistles. She knew instantly that Rhona had woven it painstakingly for many weeks, and her eyes filled with tears of gratitude as she pulled off her tunic and shift, tugging the dress over her head. Her skin tingled with excitement. She was going to be wed. It was what she and Cam wanted more than anything on earth. Agnes paused, closing her eyes for a moment, allowing the deliciousness of it to sink in. She and Cam loved each other – and in a few moments' time, their hands would be joined. Nothing could separate them now. As she dragged her fingers through her hair, untangling the curls, she wished she had a fine comb like one she'd seen that belonged to Muriel McNair, carved from an antler. But it didn't matter. Nothing mattered except taking the hand of the man she loved and promising to be his for eternity.

Cam was waiting outside, his face shining with love as he gazed at her. He held out a hand and Agnes faced him, placing hers inside, both right hands, pulses touching. Their eyes locked as the friar spoke softly. 'These are your two hands, young and strong, as ye promise to love each other today, tomorrow and forever. These are the hands that will work alongside each other, as ye build your future together. These are the hands that will ne'er let go.' Friar John wrapped their hands in cloth and knotted it, then he smiled. 'Speak your vows, Cameron.'

Cam's eyes burned into Agnes's as he spoke, his voice low and thick with emotion. 'Wherever I go, whatever I do, I am yours, Agnes Fitzgerald. Today I swear it, my life, my body, my soul are yours and I will love ye from this day onwards, come what may. Through sorrow and happiness, life and death, I will reach my hand to ye as I reach it now, and we are bound together for all time to come.'

Agnes swallowed tears.

The friar inclined his head. 'Say your vows, Agnes.'

She took a breath, her voice a whisper. 'As ye to me, the same am I to ye, Cameron Buchanan. Ye are my life and my soul and we will never be parted, come what may.'

The friar bowed his head. 'Praise God, may this cord draw your hands together in love, never to be used in anger. May the vows ye have both spoken never grow bitter in your mouths. May the love ye share today grow with each new morning.'

Cam and Agnes bowed their heads and when they raised them, their eyes met and locked. They heard the good friar murmur blessings and kind wishes as he clambered onto his horse. They heard him ride away into the forest, hoof beats becoming quieter, and then they stood in silence, facing each other, their breath mingling in the cold air. Neither of them spoke as they gazed into the face they loved most in the world. Then Cam whispered, 'I swore to ye that we would be together.'

A tiny frown appeared between Agnes's brows. 'But the mistress said I am to stay in the castle for a while and work on...'

'I ken.' Cam's arms were around her. 'Only while I'm away. But our hearts are together here. This is our home for now, mine and yours.'

'When will we live here?'

'Whenever we can. Often. And then when the fighting is done, we can live in Rosemuir, next to Hendrie and Maidlin, our families together, and we'll be content.' He pulled her against him. 'It will be our time, Agnes, now ye and I are one.'

They kissed, tugging each other into the warmth of the hut, pulling off clothes, fumbling, tumbling onto the heap of rugs and blankets. Agnes clung to Cam as she would cling to life. As she held him against her, she delved into a place deep within herself as if she were diving to the bottom of their loch, his arms entwined around her, their souls in their mouths, passing one to the other.

She was his, he hers, and she believed the feeling would last forever.

33

Leah woke abruptly on Saturday morning and, as she sat up in bed, she felt a delicious mixture of fear and excitement, a thrill that made every nerve of her body tingle. Today was the day of the tour, and she had rehearsed what she would say over and over until it was perfect, but the thought of speaking to the academics and local luminaries who would follow her round the castle and hang on every word made her fingers tremble in anticipation.

She eased herself out of bed; it was past eight. She could hear Zoe moving round, the clanking of cups, the aroma of toast filling the air.

Her feet bare and cold, Leah padded into the kitchenette in pyjamas, where Zoe, in damp running gear, handed her a cup of coffee and said, 'Welcome to your special day. How are you feeling?'

'Really nervous, Zo.' Leah perched at the small table, reaching for toast. 'I've prepared and prepared for this. But what if I mess up?'

Zoe smiled. Leah had been obsessing for days over minor details, finding out new nuggets of information. 'You won't.'

'But they are all experts. They are much more knowledgeable than I am. I'm bound to make mistakes.'

Zoe shook her head. 'You are the castle caretaker. You know about this place. They will be fascinated by everything you tell them and you can ask them questions, use their expertise, get them to tell you more about what they know about the history.' Zoe reached for her hand. 'We can do this.'

'We?'

'I'm not missing it – I have my smart suit ready. I'm going to stand at the door, meet and greet, hand out canapés...'

'You're amazing.' Leah hugged her sister gratefully, feeling calmer already.

Zoe made a mock-bashful face. 'I'm your twin.'

'You're the best.' Leah gazed over her shoulder through the window. The snow in the courtyard had gone, although beyond the loch, the mountains were gleaming white in the winter sunshine. It was a bright day, cold and crisp, frost crusted on the edges of the windows, a delicate feathery etching. 'The tour starts at two. Abigail says she will be here for half past one to orchestrate the parking.' Leah sipped her coffee. 'The professor from Stirling is going to say a few words about the dagger we found in the chimney, and the chainmail hauberk and coif. She emailed me that they are typical of the armour worn in the time of Robert the Bruce.'

Zoe was suddenly alarmed by a thought. 'What if they ask to go in the southwest wing?'

'I'll say it's under repair,' Leah said quickly. 'That's sort of true – Christie Watt is intending to do some building there.'

'Even after what happened?' Zoe recalled the bone-cold upstairs chamber, the low scratching sound of rats scraping behind the wall, the sigh she was sure she had heard as the other two had descended the stone steps.

Leah fanned her face with her hand. 'I won't be going up there again.'

'But what about your wedding venue plans?'

'Christie seemed to think we could do the chapel up to look nice. That part might be okay.'

'Christie...' Zoe recalled the easy grin, the kissable lips.

'He was nice. I liked him,' Leah agreed.

'Liked as in...?'

Leah pulled a face. 'Oh, he's handsome and pleasant, but I don't think he's my type – Zoe?' She suddenly grinned. 'You like him, don't you?'

Zoe was alarmed to feel her cheeks tingling. This wasn't how she behaved normally. She gave an expansive shrug and grinned mischievously, hoping it would cover her feelings of awkwardness. 'I thought he was okay...'

Leah winked. 'I remember when you told Mum and Dad that I was trying to chat up Kevin Freer in history. I was mortified for a month.' She grabbed her sister's arm. 'It's my turn now – revenge at last.'

Zoe was deliberately frivolous. 'I don't know what you mean, Leah...'

'You like him.'

'I didn't say that.'

'Your face did – you're blushing.'

'I've been running...' Zoe's voice rose in a poor imitation of an excuse, then she laughed. 'Yes, all right, I think he's attractive.'

'I need to find out if he's single then.' Leah was suddenly excited. 'He wasn't wearing a wedding ring.'

'How do you know?'

'I peeped.'

'That doesn't mean—'

'Oh, romance is definitely in the air.' Leah rubbed her hands together. 'I haven't seen you this interested in a man in ages, Zo.'

Zoe stood up, collecting crumb-filled plates. 'I'm not at that stage yet – just mildly attracted. He's probably got a wife and kids.'

'We'll see.' Leah stretched her arms above her head and sighed. 'But I'll have to put playing Cupid on the back-burner for today. I have a tour to organise.'

'Then let's do it,' Zoe said firmly. She raised a hand for Leah to slap. 'Sisters first, men later.'

'Sisters first,' Leah agreed with a grin. She reached out a hand and pinched her sister's arm playfully. 'Bags the shower first. You can wash up.' And with that, she whirled out of the door, heading to the bathroom, shrieking with laughter.

* * *

By ten minutes to two, Leah's smile was purely professional as she greeted the visitors. Mirren had not accepted the invitation to join the tour: she'd said there would be too many people there. Abigail Laing lurked in the background, talking in a hushed voice to each guest. Zoe ushered the new arrivals into the great hall, where a huge fire roared in the hearth, and Leah shook hands, grinning effusively.

Dr Alison – 'call me Ally' – Wylie was the first to arrive, impeccable in a long black coat, silver hair tumbling beyond her shoulders. She was bubbling with excitement, keen to talk about the hauberk and coif. Then other guests appeared: Leah identified the historical fiction author, a young woman with crimson lipstick; the newspaper editor, a well-spoken man in a stiff suit; the local businessman who arrived in a kilt; and the depute provost, a neatly dressed woman with a firm handshake. Leah scanned the others: a friendly man called Huang, a quiet woman called Zelda, another man whom she thought was an academic from Inverness whose name was Patrick and three more men whose names she missed. Then, as she was about to begin, Zoe rushed in with another guest, a lean man with round glasses, his fair hair parted to the side and swept behind his ear.

Leah frowned: she counted again. There were twelve guests, not the ten plus Dr Wylie. She gazed towards Abigail for an introduction, but she was talking with the new arrival. Leah assumed it was her husband and began the tour immediately.

'Well, good afternoon...' She immediately recalled an English teacher telling her never to start a speech with the word *well*. 'And welcome...' She took a breath, trying to stop the quake in her voice.

The group gathered in a small circle around her.

'I'm Leah Drummond, and I'm delighted to welcome such an exciting group of interested people to Ravenscraig Castle. I'm sure you'll know much more than I do about the history, but since I arrived as caretaker, I've fallen in love with this place, and it's my pleasure to show you around. Do ask questions as we go – and when we reach the kitchen, we'll have the chance to talk about an exciting recent discovery in the fireplace.'

Leah gazed towards Ally Wylie, who nodded encouragingly. The history writer stood at her elbow, smiling, as she pointed to the tapestries and began to talk about the renovation of the great hall. She noticed Zelda taking notes; the newspaper editor and the history writer were scribbling on memo notepads. Huang was following her every word with interest, but, as the group moved forward, Leah noticed the fair-haired man in glasses had paused to take a phone call. Leah rolled her eyes without meaning to and she continued with the tour.

She raised her voice. 'It's nice and warm today – it's usually cold in here, but if you follow me, we'll go into the kitchen. Dr Wylie will tell you about two fascinating artefacts we found there. And the fire's been lit, so you just need to imagine the place, many years ago, when it was bustling, very warm and full of the aromas of baking...'

* * *

Agnes, wearing her work clothes, made her way across the drawbridge, beneath the arch of the main gate, towards the kitchen. It was almost light, the sky and the loch merging in a blend of dusty grey. Soldiers stood around the courtyard, still as stone statues. Two hours ago, she had been in Cam's arms, and in her imagination, she was still beneath warm blankets, sharing one breath, hurried promises. They had ridden quickly through the forests before dusk and he had dropped her by the loch, whispering words of love before riding away on Sealgair. She recalled their conversation in the darkness: he'd told her the fighting was fiercer now, the English were moving north; The Bruce had recruited more loyal Scots, but there were not enough men to push back the English armies. But the hut in the forest was their home, their place of private refuge.

Agnes smiled secretly; it was the first day of the new year, 1307. Things were changing: she had left the castle a maid and now she had a husband whom she would love for eternity.

A familiar figure nodded towards her as she crossed the courtyard. Una was talking to the soldier again, under the pretence of bringing him food. Agnes wondered if Una had seen her arrive with Cam and, if she had, who she would tell. She nodded curtly in reply and was about to step into the hall when she heard a low voice call her name.

A short man with a dark beard scuttled towards her. Agnes had seen him before. His expression seemed over-friendly, but his eyes mocked her, as if he knew something she didn't.

She paused. 'Do I ken ye?'

'I'm Bròccan Millar...' Agnes didn't reply, so he added, 'Your sister's promised to me.'

Agnes curled her lip, unimpressed. 'You're Effie's sweetheart?'

He spoke loudly, carelessly. 'She and I are to wed in the spring. We thought by then that the English army will have retreated. Old Longshanks is past his prime; he'll be long in his grave and his son will have taken over and everyone knows that the young Edward is just full of foolish daffin'.'

Agnes took in his gleaming eyes, the fresh spittle on his beard, and she shrugged. 'I know nothing of battles. I work in the kitchen. So, I'll trouble ye to—'

Bròccan moved closer. 'Where have ye been the night, Agnes? I'm guessing you're just returned from the arms of some sweetheart...'

Agnes stared at him, annoyed by his boldness. 'You'll be guessing away until bedtime...'

'I just heard a horse gallop away.'

Instinctively, Agnes didn't trust Bròccan. The thought of him with sweet, vulnerable Effie disturbed her. She faced him, her chin raised. 'I suggest ye gallop away back to the forge, Bròccan. Ye have work to do, and I've no time to spend with idle gossips.'

She turned to leave and heard him laugh behind her. 'We're almost family, Agnes. Ye and I are to be brother and sister. Ye can tell me your secrets...'

She ignored him and hurried towards the kitchen. It was dark inside; bodies were still slumbering on the floor and Agnes noticed to her horror that the fire had become a flicker in the grate. She rushed across to grab kindling and logs to feed the embers, when Effie stepped from the darkness inside the hearth, clutching her cloak.

Agnes frowned. 'You've let the fire go, Effie....'

'Aye, I was just...'

'What do ye have there?'

'It's nothing.' Effie pulled the cloak to her, hugging it closely, her face guilty.

'What do ye have?'

Effie met her eyes for a moment, her expression cunning, then she said, 'It's a secret.'

'What secret?'

Effie clutched the cloak to her chest. 'Something Bròccan gave to me to hide away...'

Agnes put a hand on the cloak. 'What are ye hiding, Effie?'

Effie's small face was creased with doubt, then she whispered, 'Bròccan has given me armour from the forge – and daggers. Two of each.' She leaned closer. 'It's for ye and me to hide...'

'Why would he do that?'

'He loves me. And you're my sister.' Effie lowered her eyes. 'Bròccan says the English armies may come here and if they do, they like to harm young women in the most horrible way. He told me to put these things inside the chimney for safekeeping. Then, when the enemy comes, he'll find us a horse and we can put on the armour and ride away unseen.' Her eyes were pleading. 'Agnes, he gave me this with the promise that we'd be away on a fine horse like the king's brother's destrier. He means well, to keep us safe.'

'He gave ye this?' Agnes watched as Effie opened the cloak. There were two fine daggers and chainmail armour from the forge. She felt immediately suspicious; she recalled her earlier conversation with Bròccan. Effie's unswerving trust was unsettling. His motives troubled her.

'He loves me – he's so desperate to keep me from the hands of the English.' Effie gave a slight smile. 'Say you'll help me do it.'

There were sounds of people stirring from sleep. Agnes seized the bundle quickly and reached into the wide chimney. She felt Effie push her as she clambered inside, scrabbling and stretching up until she found a thick ridge in the stones. She pushed the armour high, lodging the daggers on top, and struggled down. Then she piled logs onto the fire, grasping bellows, fanning the blaze. 'It's done now. I'll fetch some water ...'

Effie laughed, the open laugh of a child. 'Ye have soot on your face. And your apron reeks.'

'It'll wash off...' Agnes collected pails, pushing one into Effie's hand. 'Come, let's leave the fire to roar away and we'll go to the well.'

She set off at a pace and Effie was at her elbow.

'Bròccan means no harm, Agnes. He will look after the both of us. He is a good man... he told me I have to tell ye how good he is.'

'Aye, he may well be...' Agnes was striding ahead, anxious to clean her face and her apron, to return with water. She was thinking about talking to Rhona secretly about how she and Cam had joined hands. She wanted to thank Rhona for the embroidered dress and tell her how her heart was bursting with happiness. She wondered about confiding in Effie, but something about her sly expression, how she talked about Bròccan and the episode with the daggers and the armour troubled her. Something had changed in Effie, and Agnes was filled with a new sense of unease.

34

Leah stood smiling in the doorway with Zoe, both now dressed in warm coats, as the guests filed out in turn. They had followed her around the castle, visiting most of the rooms; they had listened, questioned, eaten canapés, and now they were shaking hands and offering warm thanks. Abigail was still in the great hall talking to the last remaining guests as Ally Wylie assured Leah that she'd email her soon and they'd catch up to talk about the history of Ravenscraig. The historical fiction writer was profuse with her thanks, promising that the castle would be mentioned in the acknowledgements of her next book. Huang was delighted with the tour and asked when the next one would be; he would come back with his family.

Zoe whispered in Leah's ear, 'I didn't know that Lady Macbeth's first name was Gruoch and that she was born in 1005. You really set the context for Robert the Bruce so well.' She hugged her. 'I'm proud of you.'

Leah was beaming. 'Did it go okay, Zo? Oh, I hope it was all right.'

'It was a great success...' Abigail's voice was syrup smooth behind her. 'Thanks so much for this afternoon, Leah.'

Leah was about to reply, when she noticed the man standing next to Abigail, his floppy fair hair, round glasses, an awkward smile.

Abigail said, 'Leah, I'd like to introduce you to Daniel Lennox.'

'Call me Dan – or Danny, it doesn't matter...' The fair-haired man extended a hand with a lopsided grin. 'I just wanted to say that I thought your tour was really brilliant. Thank you so much.'

'You're the owner of Ravenscraig...?' Leah stammered, feeling foolish because she was stating the obvious, so she added, 'I didn't expect you to be here...'

'Mr Lennox has some business in Scotland...' Abigail offered.

'Well, yes, I do...' Daniel Lennox looked at his phone and back to Leah. 'I just love how you have all the facts at your fingertips. The visitors were hanging on every word.'

'Leah is a historian,' Abigail said. 'She's a tremendous find.'

'She is...' Daniel beamed, then he blurted, 'Would you like to come on a boat ride around the loch?'

'Now?' Leah looked at Zoe, who seemed equally surprised.

Daniel scratched his head. 'I've organised one. I'm meeting someone and we're taking a look at the castle from the perspective of the loch, and we'll be leaving at four o'clock. I've hired a boat. So...?' He looked from Leah to Zoe and back to Leah. 'What do you think?'

'It would be a good angle for photographs for the website,' Abigail said curtly, then she inclined her head. 'I'm so sorry, Daniel, but I have to go. I have to be back in Inverness for an engagement this evening.'

'Oh, no, not at all, not at all.' Daniel watched her go, then he turned back, all smiles. 'The tour was such fun. It reminded me how much I miss Scotland. It's good to be back.'

'You work in China?' Leah remembered.

'Yes, I develop property there.' Daniel seemed suddenly bored. 'Too much work, not enough downtime.'

'So how long are you staying in Scotland for?' Zoe asked politely.

His smile broadened. 'I can stay as long as I like – I'm my own boss.' He shrugged. 'I might stay for Christmas...' He gazed towards the car park. 'Oh, he's here now. That's good.'

Zoe watched as a tall figure strode towards them, a man in a dark coat and a red scarf, the wind ruffling his hair. She recognised the physique, the face, the mouth. 'It's Christie...'

'It is.' Daniel was delighted. 'We go back a long way. He does my building work for me. He's done an incredible job of the castle. We wanted to take a look at the southwest wing from the loch.'

'We went in there together recently,' Leah explained. 'It's a strange place.'

'He told me. That's why we're going to check it out from the loch. We'll get a good view.' Daniel held out a hand as Christie arrived. 'Christie, good to see you.'

'Dan.' Christie enveloped him in a bear hug.

Zoe and Leah exchanged glances.

'The girls are coming with us,' Daniel added excitedly.

Zoe couldn't remember if she'd actually agreed to go and she was unimpressed at being called a girl at thirty years of age. She glanced at Daniel – he was at least thirty-five, probably older, and she decided he should know better. But Leah was already smiling and agreeing that it would be lovely to see the castle from the loch, and Daniel was pointing to where the boat was due to arrive at any moment.

Christie turned to her. 'Are you coming, Zoe?'

Zoe shrugged. 'I may as well.' Then she felt an immediate pang of dismay; in her attempt to be cool, she had sounded indifferent, bored even.

'You might enjoy it,' Christie insisted with a grin and set off after

Daniel and Leah, who were already forging ahead, deep in conversation about the history of the castle and Robert the Bruce.

Zoe sighed sadly and trudged along; she was certainly keen to spend the rest of the afternoon with Christie, but she needed to get a grip on herself and try to behave normally.

They were greeted at the lochside by a tall, bearded man who introduced himself as John Aitken. He shook hands warmly with Daniel Lennox and then became all-efficient as he handed life jackets to everyone with a curt: 'Put these on – it's a fast ride.'

Leah tugged a woollen hat from her pocket and pulled it on, tucking shiny hair underneath. Zoe wished she had brought a hat too as she clambered into the boat and took a seat next to Christie. He mouthed, 'Are you all right?' and she nodded and muttered, 'Cold...'

He lifted the scarf from his neck, wrapping it carefully around hers. 'You'll be fine.'

'I will,' Zoe muttered and added, 'thanks.'

He smiled and the speedboat took off, slicing through water, a fast forward thrust that took Zoe's breath away. Then she relaxed as they headed out into the open loch.

In the front of the boat, Leah was still chattering to Dan Lennox. 'I suppose it must be lovely to live in China.'

'It is... well, I thought so, yes.' He seemed perplexed. 'I've been there for over fifteen years and it's turned out well, so I'm very grateful. But I'm thinking about retiring.'

'Retiring?' Leah was astonished. 'But you're young.'

'I'm forty next year.' He sighed as if it was a great age. 'My parents were property developers, buying places in London, and they started me off when I was in my early twenties, and I went to China to invest in more property, there was money to be made and...' He grinned. 'I made it without trying too hard.'

Leah wasn't sure what to say, so she said, 'That was lucky.'

'It was,' Dan agreed. 'But I can be a bit driven, to say the least, and I miss out on things.'

Leah had no idea what he meant, so she asked, 'Such as?'

'Friends, a social life...' Dan shook his head. 'All my social life is business meetings and networking. I think it's time to slow down and do something different, something I can fall in love with.'

'Are you coming back to the castle?' Leah blurted. She was suddenly afraid she'd have to move out.

'Scotland is in my blood,' he said. 'The castle is a business – it's history, our heritage, it belongs to Scotland, and I want to help share it with local people...'

Leah was relieved. 'I agree. I'm half-Scottish.'

'Which half?' Dan guffawed too loudly, and Leah frowned at his clumsiness.

'My father's side.'

'Is that why you want to work here in Ravenscraig? I could tell when you were talking during the tour that your heart is in Scotland.'

'We used to go to Gairloch as kids, Zoe and I,' Leah explained. 'They were the best times.'

'Gairloch.' A wide smile crossed Dan's face. 'I haven't been there in over – what? – twenty-five years. I bet it hasn't changed a bit.'

Leah examined his face, his green eyes behind glasses, his fair hair that lifted in the wind. He seemed nice enough, but he was her boss, a millionaire, and she couldn't reconcile the fact of his wealth with the ordinary, pleasant man who was chattering to her. She wasn't sure of her footing with Dan Lennox, whether she should try to impress him, be grateful that he'd given her a job she loved, or treat him as just any other person. But he wasn't any other person, he was rich and privileged. She watched thoughtfully as he called casually to John Aitken, 'Can you pull the boat in over here, John? Close to the side of the castle, where the stones have started to crumble. Yes – here. Good.' He turned round. 'Christie, what do you think?'

Leah thought Dan Lennox seemed used to giving orders and expecting people to do as he asked; it was second nature for him to please himself. She wasn't sure if she liked him or not.

The speedboat came to a standstill, the engine rumbling beneath them in the deep water.

Christie spoke quietly to Zoe. 'It looks very different from the outside. When we went in there, it was oppressively dark. From out here, it just looks like an old castle building in need of a little repair.' He raised his voice over the stuttering engine. 'The condition of the stone looks reasonable from here, Dan. I could rig up some scaffolding without too much trouble on the other side and wrap it over the top and round here. We'd access the wall to renovate it easily.'

'What would you do with the southwest wing when it's rebuilt?' Leah asked.

Dan shrugged. 'We'd discuss it as work progresses.'

'It's a soulless place,' Christie said. 'I have no idea what you could do with it.'

'Gut it completely, turn it back to how it used to be.' Dan wrinkled his nose. 'Do you think the upstairs was part of the chapel?'

'Mirren would know,' Leah suggested. 'We should mention it to her. She'll be upset about it being renovated. She wants it left alone.'

'I'll talk to her about it,' Dan began. 'It's a lovely tower. Are you sure it won't be a problem to rebuild it, Christie?'

'On the outside, no.' Christie shook his head. 'Inside is your problem. It's quite eerie in there. It feels almost as if it's best not disturbed.'

'I felt that too,' Zoe agreed.

Leah took her chance. 'I always thought that the castle would be a wonderful wedding venue. It strikes me as an extra business opportunity; with the chapel renovated with stained-glass windows and upstairs refurbished, it could be a space for a choir...'

Dan met her eyes. 'It could.' He was thoughtful for a moment. 'Go on, Leah – tell me what you've been thinking...'

'Weddings in the chapel, using the courtyard in spring and summer for extra people, the great hall as a reception room, guest bedrooms upstairs. We wouldn't need to disturb the original lay out or jeopardise the history. We could still hold tours and use the castle for photo shoots and films. People would be so thrilled to have a wedding in a castle by a loch.'

'I think it's a good idea...' Dan was thoughtful.

Leah's smile filled her face as she offered her final suggestion, which she hoped would seal the deal. 'We could try it out in February – a trial run. I have friends who are getting married on Valentine's Day and they haven't found a venue yet...'

'Brilliant.' Dan was impressed. He turned to Christie and Zoe. 'Please – let me take us all out to dinner somewhere. We can talk about this. I mean – it's not just a business dinner – I have so many business dinners. Let's go somewhere really nice, the four of us, and have some fun.'

'I might be able to...' Christie thought for a moment. 'I'd have to make a phone call first.'

'Leah? Zoe?' Dan asked.

'All right, yes, thanks very much.' Leah decided it would be a perfect opportunity to move her plan forward.

'Zoe?' Dan asked. 'We could have another quick spin around the lake in John's boat, take in the clear Scottish air and the views, then we can discuss where we should eat...'

Zoe was staring up at the tower. Her voice was suddenly small. 'Is that a window?'

'I hadn't seen it...' Christie followed the line of her finger. 'Yes, it is...' He understood immediately what was worrying her. 'It's a narrow window, high up. That's odd...'

'Why so?' Dan asked.

'We were in there recently and there was no window...' Zoe breathed.

'I'm sure of it,' Christie added. 'There was just one window facing the courtyard, a narrow one – but no second window looking out on the loch. Just a stone wall and darkness.'

'And rats,' Leah remembered uncomfortably.

'We'll have another look around,' Dan suggested.

'Not now, please.' Leah shivered. 'I prefer your idea of dinner.'

'And a tour of the loch, before it gets dark,' Christie added.

'John, can you take us back please, but give us a quick spin around the loch as we go?' Dan asked.

The engine growled and the boat pushed forward as John Aitken shifted the throttle. They sped across the loch, the front of the boat tilting upwards, cutting through water, sending spray soaring.

Zoe glanced over her shoulder back towards the tower in the southwest wing. She narrowed her eyes, staring at the vertical window at the top – it was her imagination playing tricks, but she was almost sure she saw a hand, stretched upwards, fingers extended through the gap as if begging or calling for help. She stared again. There was nothing, just a tower disappearing into the distance.

35

Over the next few days, Agnes was filled with troubled thoughts. Each morning as she made her way to the well, she saw Una taking food to the soldiers, whispering quietly with the same sentry. She would nod to Agnes brusquely as she passed, a brief acknowledgement. Agnes wondered if she was being watched, if others knew that Cam and she had joined hands and that he was away fighting hard against an advancing enemy. Her heart leaped to her mouth whenever she thought about him in battle, as if the safety of her arms around him on their wedding night could save him from future danger in the fray. She knew it would not.

She tried to think only of her work in the kitchen, watching as the yeast frothed in the bowl, shaking flurries of flour, but Effie was always at her elbow, chattering constantly about Bròccan Millar and how they would marry in the spring, how he had so many plans for their future. Agnes said nothing in reply, although she wished she could tell Effie what she felt in her heart. Bròccan wasn't a trustworthy man; he wasn't the best suitor. In truth, Agnes didn't like him. He was deceitful and selfish, and she feared he'd take advantage of Effie's good nature.

But her thoughts always came back to Cam. Only Rhona understood how she felt as the wife of a warrior. Agnes had thanked Rhona profusely for the gift of the embroidered dress. She could never repay her kindness. Rhona had taken something from her apron and pressed it into Agnes's hand. It was a goblet, made by An-Mòr in the forge, a wedding gift. It was engraved with a rough image of Cam and Agnes, side by side, and Agnes had found it hard to stop tears filling her eyes. She hid it in a large drawer at the table where she worked each day, imagining it in their small home, she and Cam sharing water from the same cup. Later, she had rushed to the forge to thank An-Mòr, who had laughed, embarrassed by the hug she gave him. As she'd pulled away, she saw Bròccan in the shadows watching her suspiciously.

Several more days passed. Agnes was on her way back from the well, pails full. Effie was busy helping Rhona that morning, but Agnes was glad to be alone. She stood quietly with her thoughts of Cam, hoping he'd soon send word, that she could meet with him again before many more days went by.

As she passed the forge on her way across the courtyard, Bròccan Millar appeared from the shadows, his arms folded, his lip curled. He was watching her again.

Agnes ignored him.

He called out, 'What is the news of the war with the English, Agnes? Have ye heard how The Bruce is faring?'

Agnes froze: she thought immediately that Bròccan must know something about Cam. She glanced away and he raised his voice.

'I hear ye like to go weaving some nights, Agnes.' He gave an unpleasant sneer. 'Effie and I like the weaving too. Last night, she and I were at the weaving together until past midnight.' He laughed again.

Agnes put down the pails and walked over to him. 'Ye should mind your mouth, Bròccan.'

'Aye, and what will ye do?' Bròccan sneered.

Agnes showed him a hard fist. 'Mind what ye speak. Effie is your sweetheart, she is trusting, and ye should treat her with more respect. Those are bad words you're saying about her...'

'Ye think ye are so high and mighty, Agnes.' Bròccan's face clouded. 'I ken what ye do. Ye cannae keep things a secret for long, not in this castle.'

Agnes fixed her eyes on his. 'Ye are a feartie fool, a coward who's not worthy to call himself a Scotsman...'

'And I ken what ye are too, out nights in the forest, coming back in the darkness on a warrior's horse...'

Agnes turned her back on him. 'Ye ken nothing.'

'I havnae told Effie yet about the man who has been your sweetheart these many months...' Bròccan taunted. 'I wonder what she would say of it, that ye hadnae told your own sister that ye were always at the weaving with a warrior of The Bruce.' He scoffed. 'Weaving, indeed.'

Agnes ignored him, picking up the pails. She was almost inside the door when he called, 'If ye give me a kiss, sweet Agnes, I'll say no word to Effie or to anyone of the man they call Allaidh...'

Agnes continued walking, but her mind was racing. Bròccan knew about Cam, that they spent time together. She wondered who else knew, and the thought terrified her. There were traitors everywhere: the mistress had said as much. Agnes wondered if she should confide in Muriel McNair, but she had no evidence, just unpleasant gossip from Bròccan. She saw Una, who was busy stirring oats in a pan, who glanced up and muttered, 'Agnes...' as she passed. Agnes wondered if Una talked to the soldiers, if she was a spy who passed on information to the English. Agnes ignored her, turning her back, placing the pails on hooks over the fire. Then Effie was by her side.

'Agnes – Agnes, did ye see Bròccan when ye were out at the well? Did he speak of me?'

Agnes sighed: she did not know how to reply. She did not like

Bròccan; she suspected him of disloyalty and he was clearly a bad match for sweet, trusting Effie. She wrapped an arm around the younger girl. 'D'ye love him, Effie?'

Effie's face flushed with delight. 'With all my heart.'

'And how long have ye and he been sweethearts?'

'These four weeks, since before Christmas Day...'

Agnes hugged her. 'Ye have little experience in these matters of men and love.'

Effie's brow puckered. 'Are ye jealous, Agnes? Do ye want him for yourself?'

Agnes suppressed the urge to laugh for a moment then she became serious. 'I just want to be sure he loves ye.'

'We are to wed and...' Effie lowered her voice. 'He told me to place the daggers and the armour in the chimney so that we can run away.'

Agnes frowned. 'Ye and Bròccan?'

'Aye...' Effie thought for a moment. Agnes saw her expression change as she realised that she had made a mistake. 'Or for ye and me to run away, Agnes, if the English come...'

'So the armour in the chimney is for ye twain? Not for ye and me?'

'Do not be vexed.' Effie's eyes filled with tears. 'He asked me to hide it for us. We want to escape from the castle together and live on an island safe from the armies...' She lowered her voice. 'I have lain with him already. What if I get with child?'

'Oh, Effie...' Agnes had no idea what to say. Effie was a victim in Bròccan's deceitful games. She wanted to tell Effie about Cam, but Bròccan knew too much already. In an effort to calm the moment and to safeguard any future situation that might arise, Agnes said, 'Ye and I have so much to speak of as sisters. We need to sit awhile and unfold the secrets of our hearts by the fireside.'

'We do,' Effie agreed. 'But I cannae speak now. I have to help Rhona...'

They turned to look towards the huge vat, where Rhona had paused from work, the long spoon in her hand. She was talking to someone Agnes recognised: it was Muriel McNair's maid. She was speaking in a low voice as she and the maid glanced towards Agnes, who felt her blood chill as she saw them both walking towards her.

Rhona was at Agnes's elbow when she spoke to Effie sternly. 'Ye must tend the vats now. There's work to be done. The beer won't brew itself.'

'Aye, Rhona,' Effie said quietly and scuttled away.

Rhona took Agnes's hand and her grip was vice-like. 'We've been summoned to speak to the mistress, ye and I both.' Her expression was anguished. 'I hope she doesn't bring bad news.'

Agnes squeezed Rhona's hand and realised that they were both trembling. Words would not come.

Rhona urged her forward. 'Pray God it's something of no importance, some detail of a feast the master wants us to prepare or...' Agnes felt Rhona tremble as she added, 'But I always fear bad news. There are traitors among us, Agnes. Who knows what ill they do each day?'

'Indeed...' Agnes was thinking of Bròccan, of Una. She wondered if this might be the moment to share her fears with Muriel McNair, but she had no idea what to say without implicating Effie.

Agnes's legs were weak as she followed Rhona into the great hall, where Muriel McNair was standing in front of the fire. She glanced towards them and Agnes saw from her frown that something was wrong. Somehow, her feet carried her towards the mistress and she curtsied. She felt Rhona bob down beside her. Both of them were trembling with fear.

'I asked ye both to come here...' Muriel glanced from Rhona to Agnes and back to Rhona. She took a breath. 'I have already spoken to An-Mòr. He has gone back to Rosemuir.'

'What has passed?' Rhona's voice was weak with fear. 'Madam, what news?'

'Agnes will go back with ye now, Rhona, where your husband is waiting. It is not good news I bring...'

Rhona's voice was strangled in her throat. She knew already. Agnes's arm circled her waist and held her close.

'Hendrie has been killed in battle, Rhona. He has been brought home for ye and An-Mòr to lay in the earth.'

Rhona's blood-curdling howl quickly dissolved into heaving sobs. She sank to her knees, gripped by the agony of a mother whose child had been wrenched from her. Agnes pressed her lips against Rhona's hair, muttering words of kindness.

Muriel's voice trembled. 'Please take her home, Agnes. Stay with her for a day, two, whatever she needs. Ross and I are in her debt – we are all in the debt of her brave son and all he has done for Scotia and for our king.'

Rhona's sobs shook her entire body, then her howls become groans of acceptance.

'I'll leave ye to your grief,' Muriel said quietly and swept towards the spiral steps.

Rhona looked up, turning an anguished face to Agnes. 'My sweet wee bairn, my Hendrie...' She began to whimper, a broken sound unlike anything Agnes had heard before.

Agnes grabbed her arm. 'Can ye stand, Rhona? Shall we go to An-Mòr?'

'To see my child lying dead and bloodied on the ground, to put him in his grave for eternity?' Rhona was weeping. 'I told An-Mòr, I said to him, I ken how this war will end... I ken full well how it will come to be... my son... my own sweet laddie...'

She could not finish her words; her body was racked with more sobs. She clung to Agnes, who led her gently from the great hall towards the door. As they walked across the courtyard, people had emerged from the kitchen and the forge, other servants gathered, the soldiers, all watching. No one spoke a word as Rhona and Agnes passed through the main gate. Everyone knew.

Each step they took on the silent walk to Rosemuir was filled with sadness. Rhona gasped as she saw her hut beyond other houses in the distance. People from the village stood outside their doors, their heads bowed. When they reached the house, there were two horses tethered nearby, Hendrie's mount and Sealgair.

Rhona caught her breath. 'I cannae go in, Agnes.'

Agnes nodded, waiting by her side. Then An-Mòr rushed from within, clasping his wife in his huge embrace as she slumped into his arms, tiny as he held her, his own face contorted with tears. They stayed locked in an embrace until An-Mòr took her hand in his bear paw and led her inside. Agnes heard her gasp and begin to sob aloud again.

She followed slowly into the smoky room and Cam was beside her from the shadows, taking her hand. He whispered, 'I brought him home.'

Rhona sank to her knees beside her son, whose head was bloodied, his body twisted and unmoving, a wound in his chest large enough to place a hand inside. Agnes gazed at his face, the recent scar across his cheek still livid, the strange silence that surrounded him. But what terrified her most were his eyes, open, unseeing as glass. There was no movement, no breath, no life. Agnes could not help but stare.

An-Mòr put a hand on Rhona's shoulder and his voice was low with emotion. He didn't turn. 'Thank ye for bringing our laddie back to us, Cam.'

Cam nodded. 'I am truly sorry for it...' His voice trailed away.

An-Mòr took a deep breath and his giant chest shuddered. 'Will ye... can ye go to his wife, tell her...?'

'I will.'

An-Mòr put a hand to his wet face. 'The master said he will

send horses tomorrow, fetch her here. I was promised it. She and the bairn will stay with us...'

Rhona's sobs began anew.

Cam nodded. 'Will ye come along with me, Agnes?'

'Aye, I will,' Agnes said, her voice hushed.

She met his eyes, her own sad. She had no idea what she would do to help, but she would do her best to support Maidlin and her child, to help Cam tell her the terrible news. But, in her heart, she had no words of comfort. There were none to be said.

36

Zoe couldn't sleep. The events of the evening, the dinner shared with Leah, Dan and Christie in a small country inn just outside Inverness, kept playing over in her mind like a film reel. She'd enjoyed the warmth of their conversation, the feeling of new friendship. She liked Christie instinctively. They had laughed, shared memories; he was genuinely interested in her, her job, her life in Birmingham and he told her a little about himself, where he lived and grew up. But she still held her feelings back; something told her he wasn't free to pursue a relationship. She wasn't sure what it was. Leah and Dan had talked non-stop about ideas for a wedding venue at the castle, despite Dan's protestations that it was to be a fun dinner. Zoe wondered if Dan had spoken about anything other than business or let his hair down in years.

Zoe rolled over into the warmth of the duvet. It was past two o'clock. She couldn't sleep. She'd drunk two glasses of wine during dinner, which had left her feeling thirsty, so she decided she'd go to the kitchenette for some water. Then she heard a scraping sound from one of the nearby rooms. Zoe frowned, listening harder. There were moments in films, she recalled with a grimace, where the heroine pursued a strange noise in the house with disastrous outcomes. Zoe would scream warnings at the screen, wondering why someone would follow an ominous eerie creak or bang and put themselves at risk.

Zoe needed water. She took a deep breath and slipped out of bed anyway, wriggling into furry slippers, a heavy dressing gown, flicking on the lamp. She heard it again, a dull grunt this time. It was coming from the living room. Zoe stepped onto the cold landing, holding her breath; beneath the door, there was a light on, a slice of brightness. She pushed the door open and saw Leah hunched over her laptop, her face puckered in a frown.

Leah looked up. 'What are you doing up, Zo?'

Zoe laughed. 'You're up... it's late. Or early. I heard noises.'

'I'm sorry I woke you. I'm writing a business plan for the boss. I've nearly finished. It's called *Ravenscraig Weddings – A Match Made in a Heavenly Scottish Castle*. What do you think?'

'I think you're a dab hand at this stuff. A natural.' Zoe shoved her hands deep into her dressing gown pocket. 'Aren't you cold?'

'A bit, I suppose – I didn't really notice.'

Zoe grinned. 'I'll make us a hot drink. You finish up here, eh?'

'Awesome.' Leah was typing again, her eyes fixed to the screen. 'I've only got a couple more sentences to write.'

Zoe drank two glasses of water, then she heated milk for hot chocolate, making it especially creamy and unctuous, adding the chocolate sprinkles on top that Leah loved. She took the mugs back to the living room and Leah saved her work with a flourish, grabbing the drink and slurping greedily.

'Mmm. You make the best hot chocolate. Just like Mum used to when we were kids.'

Zoe raised an eyebrow. 'It was an interesting evening. Great food, great company...'

'It was,' Leah enthused, wiping away a chocolate foam moustache with the back of her hand. 'I want to ring Mariusz tomorrow and tell him that the wedding here is on. He'll be delighted, Jordan too.'

'Dan Lennox seemed very taken with the idea.'

'He was, totally.' Leah thought for a moment. 'I think he's a strange man. I mean, he's so rich and all he seems to think about is work.'

'That's probably how he made his money, Leah. He's very – focused.'

'I was just so keen to show him that the wedding idea is a winner...' A thought occurred to Leah. 'Did you enjoy the dinner? You seemed to be getting on well with Christie.'

'He's nice.' Zoe wasn't sure what else to say. She didn't want to tell Leah that she'd watched his lips for most of the evening.

Leah asked the question that was in Zoe's mind. 'Do you think he's single?'

'I don't know. I did wonder about it. I mean, it doesn't really matter—'

Leah hesitated, examining Zoe's face, gauging her reaction, her pretence of indifference. She knew that Zoe liked Christie more than she wanted to admit. 'There was something he said when Dan mentioned us all having dinner together – he said, "I might be able to." Then I heard him on the phone in the car park and I'm sure he was talking to a woman.'

'How could you know that?'

Leah sniffed. 'He said something like, "It's just dinner, a one-off..." and that he wouldn't be late. You don't say that to anyone but a partner, do you?'

'I suppose not.' Zoe shrugged, disappointed. She changed the subject. 'Is Dan married?'

'I doubt it. He's almost forty years old, he said, but who'd have him?' Leah laughed.

'He's rich...' Zoe protested.

'Yes, but he's a goofball...' Leah countered. 'And he's all work and no play, a typical workaholic.'

'He's certainly not a playboy,' Zoe said.

'We might get to know him a bit better, though, now he's staying in the area for a while. He said he's looking for a house too. I expect he'll move between here and China.'

'I thought he wanted to retire?' Zoe remembered.

'Can you imagine Dan Lennox living a life of leisure? He wouldn't know what to do with himself...'

'Yesterday was lovely though, the speedboat ride – I could get used to that.'

Leah agreed. 'And it was nice to get a view of the southwest tower from the loch. What a view that is.'

'But not from inside...' Zoe said quietly. 'I wonder why it's like that, with stones bricked up over the window.'

'I expect there was some building work to keep the walls in place over the years.' Leah shrugged. 'Anyway, I'm hoping Christie and his team will pull it all down... I thought we'd make space for something, maybe a table where a couple can sign a register or – get this – I thought we might even add handfasting ceremonies to our repertoire.'

'Handfasting?'

Leah leaned forward, full of enthusiasm. 'Yes – it's an ancient Celtic ceremony. A couple stand face to face as their hands are tied together with a ribbon or a cord – hence the phrase tying the knot.'

'It might work... It does sound symbolic and romantic.'

'It would be great as a side-line – we could even offer it as part of a wedding ceremony. I'd have to research it properly...'

Zoe stretched her arms above her head and yawned. 'It's bedtime for me. The hot chocolate has done its trick. I'll be off to sleep like a tot.'

'I just have to write it down before I go to bed,' Leah said, and Zoe laughed.

'Maybe there isn't much difference between you and Dan Lennox.'

Leah laughed and gave her sister's shoulder a gentle punch. 'You go ahead, Zo. I'll be half an hour here and then I'll turn in. Tomorrow's Sunday and I deserve a lie-in after the tour today.' She grinned. 'I think it all went very well.'

'It certainly did. You were awesome. So, what shall we do tomorrow?' Zoe was thoughtful. 'A walk might be nice. It might snow...'

'Shall we decide over a leisurely breakfast?' Leah turned back to the laptop.

'Okay – night, sis.' Zoe placed a kiss on Leah's hair and made for the bathroom. She'd brush her teeth and slink back to the warmth of the duvet.

Zoe was asleep in moments, slipping into dreams about lochs, snow-peaked mountains, speedboats slicing through inky water. Then, in her dream, she glimpsed the tower of the southwest wing, the vertical window, an arm outstretched, begging. Then she fell overboard, out of control. She was being sucked into the water, into the depths, sinking, reaching out for help, plummeting down. She woke with a start and caught her breath. She was suddenly wide awake.

Zoe glanced at the clock. It was three forty. She heard the creak of a footstep on the landing outside the room: Leah was still up. Zoe rolled her eyes from the warmth of the duvet, filled with affection. Months ago, back in Birmingham, she had been so worried about Leah, her apathy: she had focused on what her sister couldn't do, not on her potential to succeed. Leah seemed to be failing at so many things then, her job, relationships, her social life, and Zoe had invested in that belief, thinking that she herself was somehow responsible, the first twin, the one Leah compared herself to. But Zoe should have focused instead on the positives, on what Leah could do: she was intelligent, talented, she was like a dog with a bone when something caught her interest. It was only to be expected that Leah was flourishing now. It was her time to shine, and Zoe was delighted.

The creak on the landing sounded again, and Zoe knew that Leah was outside the bathroom. She decided she'd let her sleep in later; she could bring her breakfast in bed, coffee, croissants. Leah loved those little treats and luxuries. She called out affectionately, 'Goodnight.'

There was a rustling beyond her door, then silence. Zoe could picture Leah padding past in slippers and pyjamas, her hair freshly brushed, tied in a loose plait. She was singing softly, and Zoe smiled. She could hear the light melody, a snatch of words.

> *O, where are ye gone, my Scottish warrior?*
> *'Twixt the thistle and the mist o' the morn...*

Zoe heard the light feet move beyond Leah's bedroom; she was going down the stone steps, she was sure of it. Zoe frowned: perhaps she had left something downstairs after the tour.

Zoe slithered out of bed and pulled on her slippers. 'Leah?'

There was no reply.

Zoe opened the door and stood on the landing, flicking on the light, a dim glimmer overhead. Then she heard the song again.

> *O where are ye gone, my Scottish love?*
> *Will ye come back to me at dawn?*

Zoe hesitated at the top of the stairs. It wasn't Leah: it wasn't her voice. She froze, standing still as stone in the aching cold, listening. The whispering sound of footfall came to her, the lightest tread, then she heard the grating sound of the main door being opened. It wasn't possible: Zoe had locked it herself earlier, turning the large metal key, pulling the heavy bolt across. She shivered in the penetrating ice of the air, unsure what to do.

She rushed into the small kitchenette, over to the window, staring down into the courtyard where nightlights glimmered. Then she saw a movement from the shadows, the outline of a woman in a translucent dress, her hair over her face. She turned to stare directly up towards Zoe, who caught her breath with the sudden shock. Zoe's heart knocked as she tried to take in the details, the hazy form, the arc of the arm as the figure raised it towards her, the same outstretched fingers she had seen in the vertical window from the loch.

Then the pale silhouette turned, moving away towards the southwest wing, light as if lifted on air. Zoe watched and shivered as she paused in front of the door to the chapel for a moment. Her outline seemed to merge with the wood and she became the texture of grain.

Then she vanished.

37

Agnes wriggled from Cam's horse into his arms and they stood outside the hut as he tethered Sealgair to a nearby tree. The muffled sound of a baby's cry came from inside the hut, and the soft clucking of Maidlin comforting him. Then her voice called from within, 'Will ye come on in out of the cold? I have warm food in here to sup, and ale.'

Cam took Agnes's hand and they stepped inside. The room was warm, smoke rising towards the thatch in a grey curl, clinging to straw. A pot bubbled on the fire.

Maidlin straightened from placing Eaun in his crib, then she turned, pushing back her hair. 'Cam, Agnes – I thought Hendrie was come home. I was expecting him...' Her voice trailed and she stood still, her hands rising to her face.

Cam approached her gently. 'I'm sorry, Maidlin. It's the worst news I have for ye...'

Agnes watched as Maidlin stiffened, her mouth open, gulping air. Then she held herself tense, her chin in the air. 'Is he gone then?'

Cam nodded. 'He is, aye.'

'When did it happen? What befell him?'

Agnes was seized with the urge to rush over to Maidlin, to wrap her in her arms, but the young woman took a step back.

'Was it quick? Tell me, did he take many of the English soldiers with him?'

'Aye.' Cam's voice was thick with emotion. 'We were fighting side by side. Hendrie...' He paused, as if speaking his friend's name was difficult. 'Hendrie was fierce in battle, as he always is. The Bruce has collected many more soldiers and we surprised the English as they slept at night. It was a bitter fight, and there were more of them than we. Then Hendrie faced five of them together and one of them cut him with a sword and he went down.' Cam swallowed, composing himself. 'I took three of them after that, but it willnae bring Hendrie back...'

Agnes stared at Cam, reliving the battle in her imagination. She saw it all, Hendrie falling to the ground, Cam fighting on furiously. This time, Cam had come back safely and Hendrie had not. Agnes couldn't bear her next thought – what if it had been Cam who hadn't returned? She watched helplessly, her heart aching for Maidlin. But there was nothing to be done about it now.

Maidlin hadn't moved. Her face showed no emotion. 'I didn't think on it happening so soon...'

Cam shook his head. 'He was the best of warriors, the best of men.'

'The most foolish of husbands,' Maidlin said bitterly. 'And I shall never see his like again.' She turned to Agnes. 'I am with child once more. He will be born late in the autumn. I will name him Hendrie.'

Agnes nodded. 'I am sorry...'

Maidlin shook her head vigorously. 'I made some pottage ready and warm for Hendrie when he came back. I thought to see him here tonight... Will ye stay here and share it with me now?'

'Nay, do not trouble yourself...' Cam began, but Maidlin raised a hand.

'Stay, I beg ye. I have need of company. I'll fetch ye some blankets and warm food.' She turned large eyes towards Agnes. 'I cannae be alone this night...'

Agnes nodded. 'We will stay.'

'Eaun is not sleeping well...' Maidlin waved a hand. 'And now he will not remember his father, and the new bairn in my belly will never meet him...'

'He will hear of him in your words. He will come to love him that way,' Agnes said quietly.

'I willnae ever let a son of mine become a warrior.' Maidlin whirled on Cam. 'Ye make sure the English are beaten and old Longshanks is put in his grave, and many more with him, so that Scotia is ours again and The Bruce is back on his throne. I willnae have my man slain for nought. I willnae allow it, ye hear?' She sniffed once, wiped her face with the back of her hand, and Agnes was by her side.

'Can I help ye, Maidlin?'

Maidlin seized her wrist in a vice-like grip. 'Aye, Agnes, ye can. Hold on to Cam with everything. Tell him to come back to ye after the wars and make sure ye have many children. Hold him in your arms forever and dinnae let him go.' Her eyes were furious. 'I always thought I'd lose my Hendrie. With his daffin' ways and his smile and his fond words. I couldnae keep him long; I told him many times he'd die fighting and he'd laugh his laugh as if it didnae matter. I hoped we'd have longer.' Her eyes hardened momentarily. 'Ye are all foolish daffin' men off to the wars, and we woman are left here alone with growing bairns to feed and broken hearts that will not mend as long as we shall live...' Cam and Agnes watched in silence as Maidlin turned an angry face streaked with tears towards them. 'I am to go to Rosemuir then with Eaun, to live with his mother there?'

'Aye, it is arranged, someone will come for ye tomorrow,' Cam said, his voice low.

'Rhona is the best of women.' Agnes's hand was around her shoulders. 'She will care for ye.'

'She cannae bring her son back to me. Where is he now?'

'I brought him home to Rosemuir.' Cam didn't move. 'He will be laid in the earth there.'

'Then I will see him once more, to say my farewell.' Maidlin wiped her face quickly once more. 'He was just a man and I was ever more foolish for loving him and losing him too soon.' She leaned against Agnes for a moment, stifling a sob.

There was a snuffling sound from the crib; the baby was stirring.

Maidlin's voice was strained. 'Agnes, please, could ye help me with the food. I must feed the fire and tend to my child. I forget myself – Cam, ye are tired from the fray. Ye must sit and sup. Come, Agnes... the food is prepared and we grow hungry.'

Agnes looked towards Cam, then she moved towards the fire, stirring the soup with a long spoon as Maidlin bent over the crib, settling her child, staring at his face with tears in her eyes.

* * *

Hours later, the flames from the fire casting leaping shadows on the walls, Agnes could not sleep. She could hear Maidlin across the room, lying next to the crib, sobbing quietly, the sound turning into a single heavy gulp before she slipped into sleep. Agnes and Cam had held each other closely, Cam whispering tender words in her ear, telling her that he loved her more than life itself. Tomorrow, they would go to Rosemuir at first light and offer comfort to Rhona and An-Mòr. Cam would occupy himself with practical tasks, while Agnes stayed close to Rhona. He'd promised they would spend time in their hut in the forest before he took her back to the castle. But it would not be for long: the fighting would be over soon, the English would be defeated, and their life together would be a long one, filled with peace and joy: it was coming, he was sure of it. He'd told Agnes he often imagined her with their first child in her arms, and he'd put a hand on her belly and closed his eyes. He was asleep in moments.

But Agnes's head was crowded with so many thoughts of terrible battles and bitter fighting. Hendrie's death had shocked her, and she remembered his corpse, a blood-spattered image that froze before her eyes, and then, in his place, Cam lay on the mud floor, his eyes glazed and open, a gap in his chest big enough to put your hand into. Maidlin's words came back to her. *Hold on to Cam with everything. Tell him to come back to ye after the wars and make sure ye have many children. Hold him in your arms forever and dinnae let him go.*

Agnes wriggled closer to Cam; she laid her head on his chest. In his sleep, he lifted a hand and tangled his fingers tenderly in her hair. She could hear his heart beating steadily as she breathed out and closed her eyes.

* * *

Leah woke, her head buzzing with thoughts of business plans, weddings, handfasting, how she'd go through everything she wrote last night one more time before she sent it to Dan Lennox. She would ask him for an email address.

She glanced at her phone. It was just after nine o'clock, so she padded on bare feet in pyjamas to the kitchenette. Zoe was back from her run, but bleary-eyed, her movements stiff and tense. She handed Leah a bowl of porridge and watched as Leah spooned honey on top. 'I was going to bring you breakfast in bed, but you're up...'

'Thanks, Zo. Mmm, just what I needed.' She grinned, lifting a

spoon of creamy oats in the air. 'I should make breakfast for you
sometime, but you're always awake first. How was the run around
the loch?'

'Cold.' Zoe shivered to prove it. 'Everything's cold. That's why
I'm rushing around to warm myself up.'

Leah examined her eyes, the dark circles beneath them. 'Didn't
you sleep well?'

Zoe shook her head, settling down with porridge, sprinkling
blueberries on top. 'No, not really.'

'Was it because I stayed up late working? Sorry.'

Zoe took a breath. 'No, it's because I saw the ghost.'

Leah laughed once in disbelief, then she saw that Zoe was serious. 'You saw the ghost?'

'I heard her singing. I thought it was you. She sounded really
sad, then I heard her go downstairs and out into the courtyard and I
peered through the window and she looked up at me.'

'Are you joking?' Leah shook her head. 'I know this place has a
presence, but a real ghost? Are you sure it wasn't Mirren?'

'A spirit, Leah – a young woman, standing outside. Then she
went into the southwest wing and vanished.' Zoe felt her skin go
cold all over again.

Leah leaned forward. 'What should we do?'

'I think we should leave the southwest wing alone, like Mirren
says.'

'But what about the weddings...?' Leah's face crumpled.

Zoe let out a deep sigh. 'I think we should go back to Mirren, talk to
her, tell her everything and ask her what she knows. I mean, we need
to find out the details, the stuff she says her family have passed down.'

'Or we could just ask Dan to get Christie to knock the whole
southwest wing down and rebuild it. Maybe the ghost will go away
then?'

Zoe hadn't touched her porridge. 'I'm definitely not going near the place again. I'll be honest with you, Leah, last night I wished I was back in Birmingham, I was so scared.'

Leah reached out, grabbing her hand. 'Please don't leave, Zo. You promised you'd stay until January. It's only another month or so...'

Zoe forced a smile. 'I promised, and I'll stay. Plus, I had a message from Mariusz this morning. He says things are going really well with Jordan's business, and my flat is full of all sorts of stuff, upholstering, soft materials.' She sighed. 'I did tell him you had some news about the wedding plans, though, and he's going to ring you tonight.'

Leah clapped her hands. 'I can't wait to tell him he'll be the first to have a wedding here in the castle. He'll be so thrilled.'

'Aren't you getting ahead of yourself?' Zoe asked.

'Oh, I'm sure Dan will agree to my ideas – he's as good as said so.'

'I mean the ghost...'

There was a thundering knock downstairs, someone rapping at the wooden door. Zoe and Leah both leaped in their seats. Zoe felt her body tense.

Leah stood up. 'I'll go. Whoever it is will have to suffer me pre-shower, pyjamas and all.'

Zoe hadn't moved. 'Do you want me to come down with you?'

'No, don't worry.' She winked. 'With a bit of luck, it will be Mirren and we can drag her up here for a coffee and pick her brains about the ghost. Now that *would* be a bonus.'

Zoe watched as Leah gulped another mouthful of porridge and set off for the door, her feet thudding on the landing as the knock was repeated even louder. Zoe rested her chin in her hands, amazed at Leah's ability to recover. Zoe was still trembling; a few moments ago, they had both been talking about ghosts, and now Leah was lunging towards the door as if there was nothing amiss. Zoe reached for her coffee, wrapped cold hands around the mug and shivered again.

Leah flung the door wide and looked into a pair of green eyes behind glasses, different ones, black-framed, his fair hair lifted on the wind and he had a wide smile.

Dan Lennox shoved his hands in his pockets and looked awkwardly at Leah in pyjamas. 'Am I too early?'

Leah frowned. She didn't really understand his humour. 'For what?'

His grin broadened. 'We're going to Gairloch.'

'We are?'

'I hired a car, a four-by-four, so that we could take a trip, all of us. Dinner was such fun last night and I thought since you said you used to go to Gairloch years ago, we'd all go today.' He showed her a set of keys. 'I hope you and Zoe haven't made plans...'

'No...' Leah's voice was full of doubt. She hadn't made her mind up whether to go.

Dan was suddenly embarrassed. 'Have I been a bit presumptuous? I'm sorry... I should have phoned in advance, but... but I don't have your number.' He looked hopeful. 'I spoke to Christie and he's coming with us – we'll pick him up – and...' He waved a hand towards the bright sky. The winter sun sparkled on the courtyard. 'It's a lovely day and we'll have such a good time...'

Leah studied his eager face, the round green eyes filled with hope behind the glasses, the wide grin of spontaneous optimism, and suddenly she knew that he had little experience in making friends outside of business deals and he clearly wasn't used to having fun. She offered a warm smile. 'We haven't anything planned today, and I'd love to go to Gairloch – but I'd have to check with Zoe first.'

'Oh, I hope she can come too...' Dan blurted, full of excitement.

'I'll go up and talk to her now.'

'That's wonderful...'

Leah made to close the door just as Dan stepped forward into the hallway, and she flinched as she caught his foot in the gap.

He winced, laughing uncomfortably. 'I'll wait in the car, shall I? Oh, that was awkward...'

Leah was mortified. 'Um, it was – I just shut you out of your own castle... I'm so sorry.'

'No, *I'm* sorry...' Dan insisted, and waved the keys again. 'I'll be in the car. I'll wait there until you're ready?'

'All right,' Leah mumbled. 'Give me ten minutes? Fifteen...'

'Yes, no, not a problem. See you then...'

Leah watched as he turned, strolling across the courtyard towards the main gate. She took in his expensive coat, the tartan cashmere scarf and frowned. She'd just squashed her millionaire boss's foot in the door of his castle and made him stay outside. Feeling foolish and suppressing the embarrassed urge to laugh, Leah fled through the hall and up the spiral steps, wondering why she hadn't simply invited him in for a coffee.

38

Zoe and Leah stretched their legs in the back of the Range Rover, which Dan insisted was his favourite hire car to drive as he had one just like it in Guangzhou and it was perfect for the extreme Scottish weather. Snow lay in drifts on pine branches and high in the mountains, but the skies were ocean blue. Dan left Rosemuir, driving up a hill, turning up a narrow lane, pausing at a beautiful old cottage beyond a wicker gate. Zoe watched as the front door opened and Christie emerged in a warm coat and woollen beanie. He turned to a woman in jeans who held a small wriggling girl with dark hair in two high bunches. He kissed the child's cheek and she waved frantically as he rushed to the gate and leaped in the car beside Dan, who accelerated away.

Zoe exhaled slowly: Leah had persuaded her to come along, but she wasn't convinced that she wanted to spend the day with Christie. It wasn't a good idea: he had a family, a daughter, and Zoe found him incredibly attractive. It would have been better to stay home. She was momentarily surprised that his wife didn't mind him spending most of Sunday in the company of friends, especially two single women, but she shook the thought away. It didn't matter

– it was a day in Gairloch, nothing more. Then the car was filled with conversation, Dan pointing out the view on each side of the road, Leah was taking photos, leaning through the open window, cold air blasting into the car mixing with the warmth from the heater. Zoe heard Christie talking about a local contact of his, a talented artist in her early seventies who made incredible stained-glass windows, and she'd gladly design something for the chapel. Leah gushed that she'd love a panel in gold and blue that depicted a Celtic handfasting. Then Dan said how much he enjoyed staying in The Canny Man as Kenny's breakfasts were so generous, but he'd arranged to look at several houses just outside Inverness, and if they'd like to accompany him, he'd be glad of a second opinion.

Zoe dozed for a while, the chatter humming in her ears; the drone of the car engine and the thrum of tyres against the road making her feel sleepy after a restless night. When she woke, the car was hurtling down a hill, past a hydropower station. She stretched her arms with a groan and Christie called over his shoulder, 'Wakey wakey, sleepyhead. You've been out for the count.'

'You've been asleep for an hour and a half, almost. We're there.' Leah clapped her hands.

Zoe gazed at a pretty harbour, little boats with faded paintwork bobbing on glistening waves.

'Gairloch,' Dan announced, driving uphill again. 'It's a step back in time...'

'It hasn't changed,' Leah breathed as she pressed her nose to the glass. 'Look, Zo – there's the graveyard overlooking the sea. That's where Dad said they buried Uncle Duncan. Oh, and look – that beautiful church...'

'The Free Church of Scotland,' Zoe murmured, remembering, as she gazed at a building that gleamed gold in the sunshine. It was majestic, with a wide front, a high bell tower and matching orange doors.

Dan was suddenly all concern. He pulled the car to the left, stopping on a grassy verge at the side of the road. 'Would you like to visit your uncle…?'

Leah sighed. 'No, bless him. I'd rather remember him with a walk on the beach, to be honest. What do you think, Zo?'

'He'd have preferred that,' Zoe said quietly. 'I just love the beach here. I'd forgotten how much it tugs at your heartstrings.'

Dan drove on uphill as the cliffs dropped away to the left revealing the curve of a sandy beach and, beyond, waves that hurtled against craggy rocks, sending foaming spray spattering high. The car descended again and Dan parked, pulling a red woollen hat over his hair, almost covering his glasses. He wrapped the tartan scarf round his neck. 'Let's hit the beach.'

Leah found his enthusiasm contagious; she was out of the car, her arms spread wide, whirling round in the sunlight. She twisted towards Zoe. 'I'll race you to the beach.'

Zoe was amazed: she couldn't remember the last time Leah had sprinted anywhere voluntarily. She noticed her sister's flushed cheeks and sparkling eyes and grinned. 'You're on.'

The four of them dashed to the beach and Zoe accelerated over the last few metres, beating everyone easily. They stood on the golden sand, surrounded by swooping gulls, their wings lifted on the wind.

Christie grinned. 'There's no one here. Just us. It's incredible.'

'Undiscovered Scotland,' Leah announced. 'At its most beautiful.'

'You sound like a tour guide. But then, you are – an excellent one,' Dan said and as he moved closer to Leah, she wondered if he was going to take her hand in his. She took a step back, confused. He was her boss. She liked him, yes, and he seemed really fun to spend time with, but holding hands would be a step too far. She turned her attention to the view instead.

'I love this beach. Do you remember when we were kids, Zo?

Mum and Dad would sit here on huge stripy towels and we'd take buckets and go paddling...'

Dan frowned. 'There's a really strong wind today. Look at the spray. It's so high.'

Zoe felt the mist of tears in her eyes. 'Gairloch is just so lovely. I could stay here for ever.'

Leah stared at her. 'You could stay here in Scotland?' Her face was hopeful. 'And not go back to Birmingham?'

'I'd forgotten how it felt...' Zoe shook her head, pushing nostalgia away. 'It's nice to have both. But here, there's such a sense of peace and calm. It's as if time has stopped and I've stopped too, and there's nothing but the force and beauty of nature and we're standing right in the middle of it, we're part of it.'

Christie was staring at her. 'I know what you mean.'

Leah shivered. 'It's cold, though. I know, let's embrace it. Let's get ice creams, just like when we were kids.'

'Ice creams.' Dan rubbed his hands together. 'I haven't had Scottish ice cream in so long. When I was young, I used to have – what was it? A sort of honeycomb flavour, and a fudgy one.'

'Scottish tablet,' Leah enthused. 'Oh, yes please. Do you think we could get one?'

'The chemist's shop is opposite.' Zoe pointed.

'The chemist's?' Christie was puzzled.

'I remember it well – they sell everything, cushions, hot-water bottles... ice cream,' Leah yelled over the wind. 'I'll race you all there. Last one at the door buys the cones.'

Twenty minutes later, Leah, Zoe and Christie waited on the steps to the shop as Dan sidled through the door, carrying four ice cream cones precariously, handing them out. 'Here you are.' His face shone with enthusiasm. 'Do you know, I have colleagues in China who wouldn't believe this, if they saw me now...'

'Eating ice cream in a Scottish winter?' Leah stuck out a pink tongue into the frozen cone. 'Mmm, lovely.'

'I mean they wouldn't believe I was capable of enjoying myself this much...' He lifted his shoulders mischievously. 'They think I'm only capable of serious business deals. To be honest, I thought I was too – boring.'

'You're not boring at all.' Leah bumped against his shoulder, teasing. 'Don't you love it here?'

'I do...' Dan was suddenly inspired. 'Let's jump back in the car and follow the road right to the end... I bet it leads to the cliff edge where we can see the ocean – it will be like the end of the world.'

'Come on then.' Leah turned to Christie. 'We should have brought your daughter. She'd have loved it here.'

'She would,' Christie agreed. 'But she has a birthday party today that she didn't want to miss.'

Leah took her chance. 'Your wife must be a very tolerant person. Most women would grumble, being left all on their own on a Sunday.'

'There's no wife, I'm afraid.' Christie shook his head. 'My elder sister is looking after Daisy for me today. Her own kids are at the same party.'

'Oh...' Leah thought for a moment, then she peeked in Zoe's direction, checking her reaction.

Zoe glanced away, processing the new information: Christie had no wife. She wondered what had happened to her. But the daughter was his and she was called Daisy. She thought about asking her age, what hobbies she enjoyed, but Dan was in the car, starting the engine, and Christie and Leah were following.

Zoe clambered into the back of the four-by-four and stretched her legs. Her curiosity would have to wait, but the news that Christie was a single parent had intrigued her. She was looking forward to getting to know him now. The car accelerated uphill along a narrow road, the ocean now wild and choppy below to the left as the wind buffeted the side of the vehicle. They climbed higher; there were no other cars to be seen as the road narrowed and they skirted the side of a cliff.

Leah gasped. 'My goodness, this is fun.'

'It is.' Christie twisted round to smile at Zoe. 'Are you enjoying Gairloch?'

Zoe breathed out, full of new enthusiasm. 'I'm loving it. Do you know, I think I really needed this day out.'

'We should do it again, or go somewhere else for another day out,' Dan muttered, his eyes on the road. 'What do you think, Leah?'

Leah clenched an enthusiastic fist. 'Definitely.'

'Gairloch...' Zoe leaned forward. She was beginning to thaw out in the car's warmth. 'I loved coming here to see Uncle Duncan all those years ago. But now it's just great to spend time by the sea. I forgot how attached I was to the place...' She sighed. 'I haven't been sleeping well, these last few nights...'

'You've still not recovered from seeing the ghost.' Leah glanced at her sister.

'You saw a ghost?' Dan raised an eyebrow.

Zoe nodded. She wasn't sure she wanted to say more. It was Dan's castle after all, and he didn't look the type to believe in ghosts. And Christie had rebuilt most of it, so he knew the building brick by brick. They both seemed pragmatic and sensible. She wondered if they'd think her foolish, that she had an overactive imagination or that she was giddy. But she couldn't deny what she'd seen. She took a breath. 'I think I did, yes. It was – unsettling.'

'Can we help? Maybe if we can find out some more about the castle?' Christie was concerned. 'I was thinking, I'd come round tomorrow and make a start on the southwest wing, at least put some scaffolding up. Perhaps doing a few renovations will make a difference?'

'The wing certainly does need some work,' Dan agreed. 'And we definitely need to find out more about its history. I ought to speak to Mirren about what she knows – would you come with me, Leah?'

'Of course.' Leah rubbed her hands together excitedly. 'If she'll give us some background, perhaps we'll feel a bit calmer.'

'I was scared last night but now I think about it, there was an overwhelming sense of loss.' Zoe leaned back in her seat. 'I felt so sorry for the ghost. I saw her in the courtyard and... the sadness was tangible.'

'The castle does have a sense of being troubled.' Christie's eyes gleamed. 'I'm glad we managed to get away today. This is such a tonic for us all.' He paused for a moment, then he said, 'Daisy hasn't seen her mum for four years. I've spent pretty much every moment of my free time with her since.' He gave a gentle laugh. 'I expect she's glad of the break from her dad. I'm certainly feeling the difference – I keep looking around for her, to check she's all right. I'm always switched on to being a parent.'

Zoe was sympathetic. 'That must be tough.'

Christie gave a small nod, mumbling agreement. Then Dan pointed excitedly. 'This road... it's like a path to nowhere...'

They drove through a village of sparse houses, the car flanked by rolling hills on the right, a phone mast tiny at the summit. To the left, beyond the craggy cliffs, the drop to the sea was steep, the sky now a bleak white, and the battering wind thrummed against the side of the car.

Dan's enthusiasm was childlike. 'This is wonderful – we're in the wildest wilds of Scotland.'

'Oh, look,' Leah squealed.

The car was suddenly sprayed with a spattering jet from the left, and the wipers began to wave frantically.

'It's a waterfall – the wind is blowing it back up the cliff at us,' Christie pointed out.

'I've taken a photo...' Leah gasped. 'My phone won't work here, though, no signal. What's the wind speed, do you think?'

'Maybe seventy-five miles an hour, more,' Dan suggested.

The car rumbled across a rickety narrow bridge, then Zoe yelled, 'Over there – a lighthouse.'

'We're here – we've reached the end of Scotland.' Dan cheered as he brought the car to a halt.

'What do we do now?' Leah asked, listening to the wind as it howled outside, buffeting branches and gorse, flattening grass in heavy gusts.

Christie grinned. 'We'll drive back again and wash the other side of the car...'

'Let's experience windy Scotland,' Zoe exclaimed. 'Come on...'

They clambered out, racing towards a white lighthouse with a red stripe, gazing down on the jagged rocks below as curling waves slapped and crashed.

Zoe shouted over the wail of the wind. 'Oh, I love this.' She threw back her head, grabbing her hat with both hands.

'The wind is unbelievably strong. I feel totally alive,' Leah shrieked.

'It's as if there are just four people in the world and no one else...' Zoe leaned forward, feeling the push of the wind against her, heaving her backwards. 'This is so much fun.'

Christie was watching her, smiling.

Dan pulled out his camera. 'Photos, everyone. I need evidence of this – Dan Lennox at the end of the world, or at least, at the end of the west coast of Scotland, having more fun that he's had in ages.'

Dan held out his phone and they posed, grinning, their arms around each other, then they posed again in a line, arms wide, leaning into the wind's strong embrace.

Leah panted in the wind's blast, 'It's been such a wonderful day.'

'It has.' Zoe's eyes shone.

Christie's hair blew across his face beneath his beanie. 'It's not over yet, though...'

'What shall we do next?' Dan asked.

'I know,' Leah said suddenly. 'Let's go to Inverness, get a take-away and go back to the flat in the castle, get a fire roaring and open a bottle of wine.'

'Get a takeaway?' Dan gaped. 'Do you know, I haven't had a take-away for almost twenty years...'

Leah grinned. 'It's about time then...'

Christie pointed across the ocean, where a slice of silver cloud in the white sky was hurtling towards them. 'We have weather coming in.'

The first flecks fell, light as down, lodging on their hats and noses. Then it began to snow properly, thick flakes settling on the ground, swirling in the wind.

Dan yelled, 'We should get going,' and they rushed back to the Range Rover, shrieking and closing the door with a clunk against the cold as the heater chugged out warm air and Dan turned the car around, heading back to Rosemuir.

39

Snow tumbled from a bleak, crumpled sky, and the ground was heaped, thick with piles of it. Agnes slid from Sealgair and Cam was beside her, keeping her warm. She leaned against him and closed her eyes, exhausted, bitterly sad and close to tears. It had been a difficult two days. She recalled the hardest moment, when Rhona and Maidlin were huddled inside the hut washing Hendrie's body, wrapping him in a burial cloth. Agnes had stood outside with her back to the harsh wind, clutching Eaun against her, while Cam and An-Mòr dug a grave at the kirk beyond the hill. She could hear intermittent sobs coming from inside, Rhona catching her breath, Maidlin doing her best to be strong, then the women had emerged, their faces furrowed with sorrow, eyes ringed red.

They buried Hendrie deep in the ground with his sword and shield as flakes had swirled. Agnes had cried silently for Rhona and An-Mòr, for Maidlin and her son, for her unborn child. Her tears too for all the men who died in battle and for their wives and children who would not hold them in their arms again.

Now she clung to Cam more tightly. 'When will ye come to me again?'

He kissed the top of her head, wiping snowflakes and tears from her face with his thumb. 'Seven days, ten at the most. Then it will all be done.'

'The war will be won then?'

'Aye.' He kissed her again. 'Longshanks' health fails, I ken. He is an old man now, and weak. The Bruce has gathered a good army, and we will push the English back from Inverness. We will send them away from Scotia, back to their own land, and they willnae come again.'

'Then can we live together for all time?'

'Ross McNair has promised it. Ye will be safe at Ravenscraig until then, and I will come back for ye when the fighting is done.'

Their lips met and Agnes closed her eyes, searching for his soul, waiting for the meeting that always happened when they kissed, wanting to hold on. She would miss him and now she was even more afraid for his safety. 'I dinnae want ye to go...'

'Nor I...' His eyes met hers as he held her face in her hands. 'It's not for long, my love.'

Her arms tightened around his neck. 'Come back to me soon.'

'Aye, I will.'

Agnes felt Cam pull away and she tugged him back, pushing her head into his chest. 'My arms willnae let ye go.'

He kissed her again. 'I'm with ye in my soul.'

'I ken it. I feel it too.'

Cam's voice was a whisper. 'When I sleep by the campfire, or huddled alone beneath a blanket in the cold, I have ye in my arms all the time and I'm warmed.'

Agnes pulled him to her, covering his face with kisses. 'Please, be safe...'

'I promise it with all my heart.'

'I couldnae bear to lose ye.'

Cam's fingers tousled her hair. 'It willnae come to that. Ye have my word. We are one now, ye and I, and we'll always be that way.'

Agnes nodded, fighting back tears. She wanted to be strong for him, for herself. 'We'll be in each other's arms soon.'

'I swear it.' Cam kissed her once more, holding her against him for warmth, then he twisted away, leaped on Sealgair and rode into the whirling blizzard, out of sight.

Agnes stood alone, gazing towards the grey loch. The mountains were no longer visible in the distance as snow reeled and danced before her eyes. She turned back to the castle and walked across the drawbridge with a heavy heart.

The courtyard was quiet, sentries stationed at each corner, in twos against the crenelated wall overlooking the loch. Agnes thought she saw Una disappear into the castle through the heavy door. She glanced towards the forge and Bròccan emerged, a twisted smile on his face as he folded her arms and watched her. Agnes hurried forward through swirling snow. She heard him laugh, a single bitter sound.

'So ye are here now, Agnes? Then An-Mòr will be back today after burying his son.' He raised his voice. 'It's a pity – I liked being the one giving orders in the forge, making the armour, the daggers...'

Agnes ignored him, afraid of what she'd say if she stopped to challenge him.

He called after her, 'Hendrie Logan is cold in the ground. It willnae be long until Allaidh lies there too...'

Agnes almost stopped walking. Her fists clenched, but she forced herself not to respond as she scurried into the castle.

The kitchen was already bustling with activity. Effie stood alone at the huge vat, stirring hot liquid; she glanced up as Agnes came in. Agnes smiled, but Effie just looked down at the malted grains. The fire in the hearth was roaring high, logs crackling, water spitting as it heated, and Agnes paused to warm her stretched palms, watching steam rise from her damp clothes. Una nodded a curt greeting in her direction; several other servants passed and murmured her name respectfully.

An older woman who often cooked meat at the spit placed a hand on her arm and whispered, 'How is Rhona? I send kind wishes...'

Agnes lowered her head. 'She and An-Mòr are as well as can be expected, thanking ye, Mairi.'

The pressure on her arm increased and the woman muttered, 'Look to yourself, Agnes. Take care – there are mostly good people here, but others among us are traitors who would do ill to our soldiers.'

Agnes nodded and made her way to the table where she made bread. People spoke to each other in low voices; secrets hung dangerously in the air. She leaned down and opened the wooden drawer, feeling for the goblet An-Mòr had given her, the engraved handfasting cup. It was not there. She tugged the drawer open – the goblet was gone. Then she felt a light pressure on her arm and Effie was next to her, holding the metal cup.

'Is this what ye are searching for?'

Agnes took it from her fingers. 'It is...'

'Bròccan says it is a goblet made for a handfasting.' Effie frowned. 'Where have ye been these past days?'

Agnes sighed. 'Ye have heard about An-Mòr and Rhona, how they buried their son?'

'Aye...' Effie looked around the kitchen, as if remembering. 'Will Rhona be here today? It is easier work without her nagging me.'

Agnes grabbed her wrist. 'Effie...'

'I speak the truth.' Effie pushed out a lip, her expression sullen. 'I wish her no ill.' She thought for a moment. 'So, do ye have a sweetheart, a husband? I showed Bròccan the goblet and he says I should ask ye myself.'

Agnes sighed. 'I cannae talk of it, not yet.'

'But we are sisters,' Effie insisted. She was close to tears. 'Why would ye not tell me about it? Do ye not like me now?'

'Effie.' Agnes gathered her in warm arms and wondered how to explain. 'I promise ye, give me a day or two, a week, and I will speak of everything. But now I cannae...'

'Why not?'

Agnes kissed her cheek. 'Give me time.'

Effie sulked for a moment and then said, 'Very well. I'll take myself back to the brewing. The ale willnae make itself.' She wandered back towards the vat, her face creased in thought.

Agnes pulled out a large bowl for breadmaking and took a deep breath, reaching for yeast. It was a pity that she couldn't open her heart to Effie; she wanted to tell her the truth, but Agnes knew that anything she said to Effie would find its way to Bròccan and she didn't trust him with her secret. He had come between her and Effie.

* * *

An hour later, Rhona walked in, head held high, taking her place at the vat silently. She met no eyes, although the servants were staring at her. The kitchen was so hushed that the crackle of meat on the spit could be heard spattering in the hearth.

Agnes left her baking and walked over, squeezing her arm gently. 'I'm done with my work – the loaves are proving. Can I help ye, Rhona?'

Rhona nodded, her face wan and tired, and Agnes set about heating a bucket of water, bending over the fire.

Effie sidled up to her by the hearth. 'I've forgiven ye, Agnes.'

'For what?'

'For keeping secrets. Sisters shouldnae keep secrets.'

'Aye.' Agnes thought it better to say nothing more.

Effie put her mouth close to her ear. 'I've a secret for ye, though

Bròccan bade me say nothing, but ye are my sister, so I can tell ye all...' Agnes continued with her work, so Effie added, 'Bròccan and I plan to run away together.'

Agnes paused. 'Run away?'

'Aye, we'll take the daggers and the armour from the chimney and steal a horse each. We're going to Inverness and we'll live there.'

'Why can ye not just tell the master that ye wish to leave?'

Effie smiled slyly. 'Bròccan wants us to live well in Inverness. He takes things from the master sometimes – not just the dagger, but other things, coins, a brooch for me, things we can sell.'

Agnes stiffened, troubled by Effie's expression. 'Effie, it's wrong to steal...'

'Aye, but Bròccan says it is rightly ours to take – we work hard. And we're going to steal two fine horses and ride away in the dark of night. He knows someone in the stables who will let us take them while he sleeps for a pair of coins.'

'When will ye go?'

'As soon as the snow stops. We dinnae want to leave tracks, Bròccan says.'

'Effie...' Agnes sighed.

Effie's eyes were wide. 'Ye willnae tell the mistress, Agnes? It is our secret. I was going to ask ye to come with us, but Bròccan says he believes ye have a sweetheart and ye cannae leave him, but ye didnae tell me anything of him, so I'm not so sure. Will ye come?'

Agnes took Effie's hands. 'It is wrong to steal from the master, hennie...'

'Bròccan warned me you'd say that.' She pulled her hands away. 'Why de ye not want me to be happy, Agnes?'

Effie had raised her voice and Agnes glanced over her shoulder. Una was washing kale and she had stopped to listen. Other servants had turned, their eyes glowing.

'Let's go back to work, Effie – we'll talk again of it later,' Agnes muttered.

Effie's face puckered. 'I willnae tell ye anything more, Agnes Fitzgerald. If that's your name. Bròccan told me it is something else now – I forget. But he tells me ye have a husband and he's a warrior fighting for the king.'

'Aye, it's true...' Agnes turned away, moving towards Rhona, leaving Effie alone by the fireside. The work in the kitchen had stopped, and everyone was watching. Agnes said loudly, 'Let's get the grains soaked, shall we, Rhona? There is much to do and we cannae fall behind. It's bitter cold outside and everyone will be wanting a good cup of ale.'

* * *

For the next few days, snow fell heavily from a parchment sky, piling in the courtyard, on the crenelated walls. The sentries in chainmail and metal helmets stamped their feet to keep warm, their breath mist on the air. Effie made excuses several times a day to take food and water or ale to the forge, passing the soldiers furtively, her eyes cast down. Agnes stayed close to Rhona, who said little, going about her work listlessly, her eyes glazed.

Even after nine days, the snow stayed and a freezing wind blew in more flurries across the loch. Ice clung in hard spikes over door-frames and the water froze in the well. Life was all toil, servants hovering by the fire to keep warm, slower in their duties as their bones were rigid with cold. Vegetables were icy, leaves solid when they were brought in from the fields and busy fingers preparing them for the pot quickly became numb and raw. Although work went on as usual in the kitchen, voices were often lowered in conversation; several servants eyed each other suspiciously.

On one occasion, Rhona slapped out at Effie, scolding her for leaving the kitchen twice in one morning to visit Bròccan in the forge and Effie sulked, tears on her cheeks, for the next hour. Rhona whispered to Agnes that she was sorry for her temper: she slept badly most nights; sleep would not come easily and when it did, she was often woken by baby Eaun crying or Maidlin's stifled sobbing.

Food was not so plentiful now; there was less fish, and more kale and beans than ever were needed in the pot to fill hungry bellies.

That night, with Rhona and many of the other servants rushing home to Rosemuir to their smoky huts, Agnes sat at the hearthside with Effie, supping stew. Effie warmed her chapped, raw hands close to leaping flames as she whispered to Agnes, 'I wish this cold would end and the snow would go away. I long to leave here and begin a new life in Inverness.'

Agnes wrapped an arm around her shoulders. 'Keep your voice low, hennie.' Then she added, 'Do ye truly love Bròccan?'

'Aye, I do...' Effie smiled. 'I long to be made a wife and have a family of my own.' She was suddenly anxious. 'Ye dinnae think I'll die in my childbed like my own maw?'

Agnes hugged her. 'Ye are a strong woman, Effie. And if he'll look after ye...'

'He will, I'm sure of it. And yet...' Effie frowned. 'Agnes, can I ask ye something?'

'Aye,' Agnes said.

Effie's small face crumpled as she blurted her words without thinking, 'Have ye ever lain with that man, the warrior?'

'I have...' Agnes wondered if this was her chance to talk more about Cam, to bridge the chasm between her and Effie.

'D'ye like it, when he kisses ye hard and he does that thing he does to ye?'

Agnes remembered the long nights she and Cam held each other beneath a warm blanket, everything else around them melting away into darkness. 'Aye, I do.'

Effie was silent for a moment, then: 'I dinnae like it when Bròccan holds me down and pinches with his fingers, and his breath reeks... and when he pulls up my shift and does his business with me... it pains me.'

Agnes closed her eyes to hide the sadness. 'Then maybe he's not the one for ye, in truth, hennie.'

'He tells me that a lassie must bear it for the sake of a man. He thinks I am a wee bit foolish and no other man will love me, so I must do as he says...' Effie's eyes filled with tears.

'Ye can stay with me,' Agnes whispered. Her heart went out to Effie. Bròccan was a controlling, unpleasant man and she wished there was some way she could explain that to her kindly, but she knew that Effie would rush to his defence. She wrapped an arm around her. 'Pay him no mind. If he loved ye truly, he'd treat ye like a princess.'

Tears ran down Effie's nose and onto her apron. She snivelled. 'He is kind to me sometimes, and then I love him.'

'Hush – sleep now and tomorrow we'll talk of it again,' Agnes whispered. 'I'll look after ye...'

'D'ye promise?'

'Aye – and no more talk of running away, ye hear?'

'I do, Agnes.' Effie settled her head on Agnes's lap. 'And truly I'm weary from all the work today and all the fretting. I havnae told Bròccan because he makes me affrighted when he's vexed.'

Agnes pressed her hair with gentle fingers. 'Dinnae ye fret for now. Ye are safe here with me.'

She watched as Effie's lids grew heavy, her face flushed in the firelight. The kitchen was quiet, the snuffling of sleep coming from the far corner, a solitary voice whispering to another. Agnes stared into the flames and her thoughts sped to Cam, wondering if he too was staring into a campfire, thinking of her. She hoped he'd have enough food, that he'd be warm. Her mouth moved in prayer, entreating God to keep him safe in battle, to bring him back to her arms.

Her lids began to droop in the dry warmth of the blaze, and she was almost asleep. She shifted Effie from her knee onto a blanket, covering her gently, then lay beside her, breathing deeply as sleep began to tug her away.

The sudden noise of banging and shouting echoed around the kitchen and Agnes sat upright, opening her eyes. More crashing followed, the rumble of nearing thunder, the yell of men's voices, and Agnes smelled something sharp, burning wood, the choking stench of smoke, and she gripped Effie's wrist, shaking her awake. There was the sound of something breaking, a clatter from beyond the room, as the other servants stirred, voices heavy with sleep. Then one of the castle guards rushed in, waving a sword, shouting, 'Run, run for your lives. The English soldiers are here. The castle is being attacked.'

40

It had been a busy week of work, planning for a paper which was to be shared with Sharon in a video meeting the following week. Zoe was pleased to be sitting in The Canny Man opposite Christie, clutching half a pint of best Scottish beer and relaxing. Christie had been busy too; he'd put up scaffolding at the edge of the southwest wing, collected some stones in a skip, and then he'd been occupied with a barn conversion in Dingwall that was behind schedule. He sighed. 'It's been all go – I almost forgot I had a concert at Daisy's school, a nativity thing. I couldn't miss it. She played the part of a lamb.'

Zoe grinned. 'Was it a speaking part?'

'Does saying "baa" count?' Christie laughed. 'She had to sing something by herself. She has a sweet voice. She doesn't get it from me.' His eyes shone with fondness for his daughter. 'I spent the best part of three evenings trying to chop up an old Aran sweater, sew up one of the sleeves as a balaclava and draw on eyes and eyelashes with marker pen.'

'I hope you took photos.'

Christie flourished his phone proudly. 'Here – this is Daisy singing her song... and this is the bit where she sits at the shepherd's feet. She asked me if I thought it would be okay for her to mime doing a sheep poo – she said sheep were always doing it and it would make her character come to life on the stage.'

Zoe laughed, gazing at the photos, a pretty dark-haired child in a white suit with a long tail and a balaclava with huge eyes drawn on each side. 'You're a good dad.'

He shrugged. 'I try...'

'So, ah...' Zoe asked carefully. 'When did your wife leave?'

Christie took a breath. 'Daisy was two years old. Kathrin, her mother, never really recovered from the birth. She was depressed, on medication, and struggling, and I was working all the time. I didn't really help enough. She was alone for so many hours every day, and in the evening, when I came home, she was distant and tired. Then one day she told me she'd had enough and she packed her bags.'

'She left Daisy with you? Where is she now?'

'With her brother, in Southampton, I believe. That's where the divorce papers came from.'

'And she doesn't want to see her daughter?'

'I've offered to take Daisy there. I've spoken to her brother on the phone a few times. He says she's been very ill and a clean break is best for us all.'

'That's so hard for Daisy, and Kathrin,' Zoe said quietly. 'And you.'

Christie reached for his beer. 'I've done my best twenty-four seven. There hasn't been much time for anything else. My sisters are really kind, they have kids of their own and they help me out.'

'So, where's Daisy now?' Zoe asked.

'She's at my sister Jessie's. It's a girls' sleepover.'

'Oh...' Zoe's thoughts sprang to the evening that lay ahead of them and she was unsure what to say, so she said, 'Shall we have another drink?'

'I'll get them,' Christie offered. 'How's your ghost been behaving?'

'She's been quiet this week. I've been so busy with work, so I've hardly noticed.' Zoe forced a smile. 'I stay in the flat mostly, it's warmer.'

'I hope once we do some work in the wing, things might calm down...' Christie said. 'The place hasn't been touched for centuries, apart from Mirren Logan keeping the chapel in order. She seems to want to keep it locked.'

'She has family ties to the castle.' Zoe emptied her glass. 'Talking of Mirren, I wonder how Leah and Dan are doing at her house?'

'I thought they'd be here by now – she must be keeping them a long time with her stories of the Logan clan.' Christie was thoughtful. 'Another half of best?'

'Thanks.'

He laid a hand on her shoulder, a gentle gesture, then he moved to the bar, talking to Kenny. Zoe found herself examining the easy way he walked, the curl of his hair over his collar, the expanse of his broad shoulders, long legs in jeans, and she stared into the empty glass thoughtfully, at the patterns formed by the dregs of beer. She was sure that the bubbles at the bottom formed the shape of a small heart.

Leah glanced up at the thistle-shaped clock on Mirren's wall – it was half past nine – and back to the pile of heavy books in her lap. Next to her on the small sofa, Dan was wading through several huge volumes: *The History of Scotland, The Life and times of Robert de Brus, The Battle of Bannockburn, Disputed Lands, Braveheart William Wallace.* He was lifting pages, turning them over one after another and shaking his head. He muttered 'Well, well...'

Leah leaned towards him. 'What have you found?'

'Something here about Ravenscraig being captured by the English in 1307. I never knew that...'

'Does it say the castle was slighted?'

'What does that mean?' Dan peered over gold-framed glasses.

'Deliberately damaging a building like a castle to prevent an enemy from benefiting from it. Robert the Bruce slighted Scottish castles quite often after capturing them from English control, so they couldn't use them.'

'I wonder...' Dan leaned closer. 'When I bought Ravenscraig, I wanted to bring it back to its former glory for the Scots people, but I knew little about it, other than it was important in the historical period of Robert the Bruce.' He smiled. 'I'm learning so much from you, Leah.'

'But you were busy abroad, so how could you find out about it?' Leah frowned. 'Why did you choose to have caretakers to live in? Couldn't Ravenscraig just have stayed empty?'

'It was for a while. Employing caretakers was Abigail's idea. I was in China and it sounded like a good plan to have someone in situ to keep an eye on the place. Many small castles have wardens. The locals were talking about hauntings and ghosts, and Abigail thought having resident caretakers would dispel the idea.'

'But it didn't,' Leah insisted. 'It probably made it worse.'

Dan closed his book with a thud. 'The first two pairs she hired lasted less than a month. The last pair was an older couple who'd done a lot of house-sitting and we thought they'd be all right, but they handed in their resignation at the end of the three-month period. I wasn't going to advertise again, but Abigail tried and along you came...' He smiled. 'I'm glad you did.'

Mirren came in from the kitchen, carrying a tray, putting it down on the floor. 'Fresh tea and more biscuits.'

Leah reached out a hand. 'Shortbread, my favourite.' She watched

Mirren settle herself in her armchair. 'The books you've shown us are brilliant, but I really want to know about the people. What about your family, the Logans?' Leah began. 'They may be key to the castle's story.'

'The Logans have lived around here since the time of King Robert...' Mirren said.

'Tell us what you know about the southwest wing,' Leah asked eagerly. 'Is there a connection to your family?'

'Since 1307, a Logan woman has always tended the chapel. We've always put fresh flowers down.'

'Can I ask why?' Dan's face was puzzled.

'It's a memorial,' Mirren replied softly.

'For whom?'

'You've seen her.' Mirren's tone was flat. 'In the castle grounds, in the chapel?'

Leah took a breath. 'Zoe's seen her. I've felt a presence.'

'Then you know.' Mirren's voice was a whisper. 'She was wronged. What happened to her means that her spirit can't rest.'

Dan coughed. 'How can we... change that? I'd like the castle to be a proper business and a ghostly presence... probably won't help bring it into the modern day.'

'We don't want to turn her into a tourist attraction either,' Leah added. 'How can we help her find some peace?'

'I'll tell you what I know, what was handed down to me...' Mirren folded her hands in her lap. 'The war against the English was a bloody one and they slaughtered many good people, including ancestors of mine. But the woman in the castle – I've never been told her name – something terrible happened to her in the chapel, so I put flowers down for her, pray, whisper to her. Sometimes she talks back to me.'

'She talks?' Dan's eyebrows shot up.

'She moves around the chapel like a cold wind, and I hear sounds, a sob, a sigh, sometimes a word.' Mirren thought for a moment. 'I don't want her being the centre of public interest. She has suffered enough; I can sense it. She needs peace.'

'How can we give her that?' Leah asked.

'I have no idea.' Mirren shook her head. 'For over seven hundred years, she's had no rest, I'm sure of it. My father was told by his father, and by his before, that the English were responsible for it all.'

'Right, we need to resolve this poor tormented spirit,' Dan said firmly. 'I'm going to ask Christie to do some digging, literally. He can have a look in the chapel, renovate it, rebuild upstairs. What I really want to knows is what's behind the loch window? Perhaps there's an extra room, an antechamber?'

'There's no antechamber.' Mirren was alarmed.

'Christie looked in at the high window overlooking the loch when he put up the scaffolding last week. He thinks there might be another small room in there. It was pitch dark – he couldn't see anything, but there's clearly something blocking the view of the window from inside. I'm going to ask him to investigate it.'

'I didn't know there was a window.' Mirren's face clouded. 'There's just one window, the one to the courtyard...'

'There's a second,' Dan said. 'Overlooking the loch.'

'I wonder why there's another chamber...' Leah asked.

'We have to find out.' Dan's tone was firm. 'It might help us understand the castle's history and what went on.'

'I want to be there when you open it up,' Mirren said suddenly.

'Of course – you must.' Dan nodded. 'I thought we'd wait until after Christmas, after all the festivities, then we'd go for it in January, when everyone's had a decent break. Leah, you might ask your university contact in Stirling to come along too.'

'I will.' Leah's face was flushed with excitement. 'Oh, I can't wait. But we'll hang on until the decorations are down. I'm going to make the castle look spectacular this Christmas.'

Mirren was uncertain. 'I hope you won't be making matters

worse, moving things around, digging in the upstairs room...' She gave a shuddering sigh. 'The poor lamb has suffered enough, I know it.'

'We might find answers, though.' Leah brought the mug of tea to her lips. 'Dan, we should drink up. It'll be last orders in The Canny Man by the time we arrive. Zoe and Christie will be waiting. They'll have given up on us.'

* * *

In The Canny Man, two glasses were left empty on the table where Zoe and Christie had sat. Kenny wandered over, picked up the empties and chuckled to himself: he thought they made a nice couple. Zoe was a lovely young woman and Christie was one of the best. He needed a bit of happiness in his life.

Zoe and Christie had finished their drinks and driven to his cottage. They had stood in the warmth of his kitchen before staring at each other for a moment. Then their bodies had collided, kissing frantically, tugging at each other's clothes.

Now they were nestling beneath the striped duvet in his bedroom in the darkness, their limbs entwined. Christie's voice was low as he covered her face with more kisses. 'I've wanted to hold you in my arms since I met you.'

'I never knew,' Zoe replied, amazed at her own words; in her heart, she had felt the magnetism. She kissed him back. 'I'm glad though.'

Christie was quiet for a while, thinking. 'I'm a single dad. I didn't think about having anyone in my life. But you came along and I thought, wow. And I wanted to find out if you felt something for me... I thought you did, then I wasn't sure.'

Zoe snuggled closer. 'I'm a bit out of practice when it comes to relationships. I've always been rubbish at keeping them going.'

Christie examined her face in the dark, the glow of her eyes. His voice was hushed. 'Is that a brush-off? Are you telling me this is just for one time and then never again?'

'Not at all.' Zoe ruffled his hair. 'You're handsome and funny and sweet...'

'I sense a problem.'

'I live in Birmingham...' Zoe sighed. 'I'm going back there at the end of January.'

She could feel the disappointment that filled Christie's silence. Then he murmured 'Can we be... a couple for the time being, while you're here? See how it goes?'

'I'd like that.' Zoe was thoughtful. 'It's a whole month until I go. A month is a long time in romance for me.'

He held her closely. 'Tomorrow is Sunday. How would you like to have dinner with me and Daisy here? Proper Sunday dinner? I'm a dab hand at roasts. Daisy says I make the best gravy.'

'There's nothing I'd like more.' Zoe hugged him. 'Except...' She gave a muffled laugh. '...It's cold outside and I'm snug and warm here and I don't really want to go all the way home...'

'Then don't go.' Christie pulled her close to him, kissing her lips. 'Stay all night. I don't mind. Stay as long as you like.'

Zoe was pulled into his embrace and her eyes closed. The words *as long as you like* lingered in her mind and it bothered her for a moment, but then the room around them melted away and she was suddenly kissing him again, thinking how lovely it was to be kissed that way, sharing the same breath. The thought rushed through her mind: it was just like a meeting of souls.

41

The English soldiers were suddenly everywhere, rushing across the drawbridge, clattering swords against shields in the main gateway that had been blasted and broken by boulders from a trebuchet, swarming in droves into the kitchen. They waved daggers, shouting for food and ale in strange accents that Agnes thought sounded like chewing hot bread, and the servants laboured on through the night to satisfy the army's hunger. At dawn, more servants were herded into Ravenscraig from the huts beyond the castle walls. Some families, women and children were allowed to stay in the village: the English had overrun it and Rosemuir was now circled with guards. The kitchen maids stood quietly at their tables, their backs turned towards the enemy, who glared from every corner. Rhona and Agnes kept Effie close between them, their heads down, avoiding the searching English eyes.

Then, with no warning, the English soldiers hustled all the servants into the courtyard, where the cold wind blew ice in their faces. Heaped bodies of Scottish guards lay crumpled and bloodied. The main door had been burned and was now a gaping hole of smouldering wood. Agnes took her place next to Rhona and An-

Mòr; Effie was indecisive for a moment, then she moved close to Bròccan. The English soldier who appeared to be in charge shouted something in a harsh voice and the crowd was silent, then Ross and Muriel McNair were brought out by pairs of soldiers, their hands tied.

'This castle now belongs to King Edward of England.'

The servants were mostly silent, although there was a low muttering from one or two Scottish voices.

'England is your overlord and your master, and we will now show you what it means to be loyal to our king. If you do as you are bid, you will not be harmed. But we deal with traitors harshly.'

Ross McNair was dragged before the crowd and pushed roughly to his knees.

The English soldier raised his voice. 'Do you submit to the English king and give him this castle now in the name of fealty?'

Ross McNair fell forward and said something inaudible.

The soldier spoke again. 'Do you submit to the English king and freely offer him this castle in the name of fealty?'

Ross raised his head; he had a gash on one side, blood over one eye. 'I do not. I am a true Scotsman and I promise ye, King Robert will come—' He did not finish. A sword came down across his head and cleaved it open. He slumped over, blood seeping into the snow.

Then Muriel McNair was shoved forward and the soldier looked her up and down.

'The castle is ours and you belong with it, so you are the property of England.'

Muriel was held fast by the rope that bound her wrists, but she threw her head forward and spat at him.

The soldier slapped her hard across the face. 'Take her upstairs to her room, lock her in there. I have use for her before I dispatch her after this one here.' He kicked a foot out at Ross, sending his body rolling over onto his back.

Agnes took Rhona's hand in hers. She was watching the English soldier speak, but her mind was with Cam, wondering if the army had broken through the Scottish line of defence, if he was still alive.

The soldier addressed the servants, 'I repeat, you are all the property of King Edward of England. We will allow you to live, but only as servants of the king. You will be expected to carry on working as normal, but now we will be your overlords.'

Someone shouted, 'Long live The Bruce.'

The English soldier stared around keenly, and his mean eyes reminded Agnes of a hawk. He gave a mocking grunt. 'Where is your king now? I'll tell you where he is...' He puffed out his chest. 'My men met his army at Inverness. They were weak and tired and they put up a poor fight. Your king is probably lying in a ditch with ten gashes in his head. I myself dispatched at least thirty of his men yesterday, thirty more last week. I specialise in killing Scottish traitors. I claim at least three hundred of them, all ending their days at the end of my sword.'

He laughed once and there was a sudden roar, the sound of an angry bear. Agnes watched as An-Mòr hurtled forward, pushing through the crowds until he reached the English man, heaving him in the air above his head with mighty arms and dashing him against the crenelated wall. There was the dull sound of bone against stone as the soldier slumped onto the snow. Four English fighters leaped on An-Mòr, and he flung them from him easily. Agnes heard him cry out, 'For Hendrie...' then one of the soldiers pushed a dagger beneath his arm into his heart and he fell heavily. Agnes clasped Rhona in her arms, holding her tightly. An-Mòr struggled weakly as several soldiers leaped on him, raining blows upon his head and body, then he lay still.

The crowd murmured in shock and another English soldier's voice rose above the noise. 'Hear me.' He waited for the hush that followed, then he indicated An-Mòr and Ross McNair. 'The English army allows no treachery. The bodies of these men will be disposed of. They are a lesson to you all. Now go back to your work and speak to no one. You work only for us now.'

Agnes noticed Rhona's glassy eyes as she led her back to the kitchen. As they crossed the threshold into the castle where the burned door had been, she felt someone grip her arm from behind. A familiar voice hissed, 'Do not turn round, Agnes. Mark my words carefully...'

'Aye,' Agnes murmured.

It was Una, leaning against her, talking in a whisper, 'My brother was murdered here in the attack this morning. It is he I would speak to each day in the courtyard. He passed messages to The Bruce and his men and received them back, then he told them to me. My second brother fights with them, and with the one they call Allaidh, your husband. I had news before the fighting started at dawn...'

Agnes held her breath. 'What news?'

'Our men were pushed back in a struggle...' Una was breathing quickly. 'My brother is alive, the king and Allaidh too. They will be here soon, descending on this castle to save us, to send the English armies to their maker and to free Scotia.'

Agnes closed her eyes in relief. 'Thanking ye...'

'Say nought to anyone of this,' Una hissed. 'I will speak to ye if I ken more. I have others here whom I trust...' She pushed past towards the kitchen, leaving Agnes holding Rhona, her legs weak beneath her. Effie joined them, supporting Rhona's arm, and they heard shouts of soldiers behind them, urging them forward, calling out threats and insults. Agnes lowered her eyes and tugged Rhona along.

* * *

A week passed, then nine days. Agnes worked methodically, saying little to the other servants except with her eyes: a glance, a movement of the head. She was worried about Rhona, who ate very little, who returned to the village each night to see her grandson and Maidlin, coming back the next day on weak legs to brew ale in silence. The English tolerated Rhona and Effie well enough, calling them 'brewster women', urging them to work faster to satisfy their thirst. Effie was even allowed small privileges: she took food to Bròccan twice a day, and one or two of the English soldiers called her by name. One even teased her, called her Little Ale Wife, pinching her cheeks, laughing as she blushed and stumbled awkwardly.

It was hard work beneath the scrutinising gaze of the soldiers. There were casualties: the woman who worked at the spit, Mairi, handed a portion of cooked meat to one soldier and he was too eager to eat it: his burned mouth sent him into a rage and he kicked Mairi hard so that she fell into the fire and scorched one side of her face. She walked around the kitchen slowly after that, quaking beneath the taunts and jibes, afraid to raise her eyes from the ground.

Another soldier, a cruel man called Paskin, took an interest in Una and some nights he would tug her from the kitchen roughly by the hair, twisting her arm. She'd return hours later, her chin held high, an eye blackened or a bruise on her face. Agnes often heard her sob in her sleep.

Another soldier often made a point of watching Agnes work. He was a gentle-faced man with keen blue eyes; he would stand by her table and observe her baking bread. She ignored him and usually he said little, although after many days of following her with his eyes, he said, 'Peace is to the making of a poet as flour is to the making of bread.'

Agnes curled her lip and continued to pummel the dough.

The soldier repeated his words and said, 'What do you think of that?'

Agnes shrugged. 'I make bannock bread. I dinnae think.'

He scrutinised her face. 'You are very pretty. I also know you're intelligent. And I long for someone to talk to.'

Agnes made her eyes small. 'Then ye should have stayed in England with your family and spoken with them, instead of coming here and taking over our lands and killing our good men.'

The soldier shook his head. 'I am truly sorry for it. I did not want to be a soldier. I wanted to be a poet. My father caught me writing poems and he sent me away to fight for the king.' He smiled. 'My name is Elyas.'

Agnes stared down at the loaves of bread she was shaping for proving. She had nothing to say to him.

He tried again. 'I believe you are named Agnes. I have heard others call you that.'

Agnes's eyes flashed. 'My name is of no concern to ye.'

'You are right,' he said quickly. 'I did not mean to offend.'

Agnes took the loaves away to the fire, leaving them in the warmth to prove. When she returned, Elyas hadn't moved. She looked at his face framed by his metal coif; it was placid, kind even. But this wasn't the time to feel sympathy for the enemy; there was no space in her heart for the English soldier with Cam away, fighting for the king. She ignored him and reached for a pot of salt.

He coughed, a little nervous. 'So, Agnes, what do you think of my words – peace is to the making of a poet as flour is to the making of bread?'

She met his eyes, her own angry. 'It means ye are no poet, because ye cannae make peace. Ye are a killer of innocent men and women and ye come to a country that is not your own to take it away from those who it belongs to.'

Elyas sighed. 'You speak true, Agnes, although when I am in battle, I hate to use my sword in any other way than self-defence. I am better with the bow and arrow, but, in truth, I am most happy with a quill in my hand.'

'Then go home to England, back to your father and stand up to him like a man and tell him ye cannae be a soldier any more.'

'You are right.' Elyas's face was sad. 'I live in a place called Dorset. It is beautiful there, balmy and warm in spring through to the autumn. Scotland is cold and the snow is harsh.'

'Ye dinnae have to stay here.' Agnes couldn't disguise the anger in her voice. 'Scotland was free and beautiful before ye came to lay it to waste and it will be again after ye have all gone away. Our lochs and mountains may be cold, but Scotia is like its people, wild and strong, and ye are like the place you speak of, Dorset, weak and wet...'

Agnes had spoken too loudly. The other servants in the kitchen were suddenly quiet, watching, as the cruel-faced Paskin strolled over.

'Is the wench giving you trouble, Elyas?' He gripped Agnes's arm, making her wince. 'Take her outside and catch her by the *queynte*. It will quiet her mouth for a time.' He spluttered a raucous laugh and Elyas lurched forward, suddenly furious, pushing him away.

'Have more respect, Paskin.' Elyas's face was strained. 'I am not the great killer of warriors that you are, but I was always taught to defend a lady's honour.'

'Lady?' Paskin spat on the floor next to his boot. 'A Scottish wench is no more than a harlot fit for nothing other than a man's meat. Treat them as such, Elyas, and you won't be disappointed.'

Paskin leered, his face inches from Agnes, then he strode away, strutting like a cockerel.

Agnes glanced down at her hands, mixing yeast into water. She mumbled, 'I have made an enemy.' She met the soldier's eyes. 'Thanking ye for your kindness.'

'I won't stand by and hear him speak so.' Elyas clutched his sword tightly. 'I thank you for your company, Mistress Agnes.' His face, framed by the chainmail coif, was flushed with embarrassment. 'I look forward to eating the bread you have made.' He gave a brief bow. 'Until we meet again,' and walked away quickly.

Agnes frowned, reprimanding herself: in future, she would mind her tongue and do her utmost to avoid Paskin. She felt sorry for Una, for whom he'd developed a craving: Paskin was dangerous and cruel; she could see it in the tightness of his face. Then her thoughts moved to Cam. Una said he was alive; he was preparing to attack the castle, to fight the English. Her heart leaped with the anxiety and the uncertainty of it all. Where was he now?

42

It was two days until Christmas. Leah and Zoe were having a furious discussion in the living room, going forwards and backwards. It was the first row they'd had for years. Zoe thought Leah was being completely irrational.

'I want to have Christmas dinner in the great hall, Zo.'

'Let's have it in the kitchenette, up here. It's warmer.'

'It'll be warm in the great hall – we've opened the hearth. And there are five of us now Christie's bringing his daughter along. Besides, this is Dan's castle and he'll really enjoy being in the great hall with the tree and the fire blazing, just like it was centuries ago.' Leah waved a hand in protest. 'Christie's kid will love it too.'

'She's called Daisy and she's a sweet little girl.' Zoe forced herself to sound calm. 'Is this what we're really arguing about, that Christie and I are a couple?'

Leah pulled a face. 'His daughter walked in on you the next day after you slept with him, didn't she? In his house, in his bed?'

'We woke up late...' Zoe put her hands to her face, remembering. 'It was embarrassing. But I don't get why you're so upset.'

'Because I think you're being unfair to him and his child, if you're still planning on going back to Birmingham at the end of January.'

'I'm not being unfair.' Zoe raised her voice. 'He knows I'm only here for another month.' She placed her hands on her hips. She didn't want to admit how her feelings for Christie and for Daisy were growing stronger, and how guilty she'd started to feel about leaving them. She changed the subject quickly. 'And, talking of being unfair, what about you and Dan?'

'What about him? He's my boss,' Leah countered.

'He's crazy about you.'

'No, he's not – don't be silly.' Leah and Zoe were mirror images, hands on hips, leaning forward. Leah took up the gauntlet again. 'I'd never go out with my boss. Besides, he's forty, almost.'

'And?' Zoe heard the sullen tone of her voice and was reminded again of teenage squabbles. She took a breath. 'Why are we arguing?'

Leah shrugged. 'Dan offered to take me away for Christmas as a present because he appreciates what I do here. He said we could go to Edinburgh. He even talked about a helicopter flight over the mountains on Christmas Day.'

'He's mad about you, Leah. Go with him. I'll have dinner with Christie…'

Leah was astonished. 'Do you really think he has feelings for me, Zo?'

'It's obvious.'

'Then it's just as well we're all having Christmas together in the great hall.'

'I don't understand.'

'It will keep him at arm's length,' Leah said simply.

'Is that what you want?'

'I don't know. Oh no…' Leah began to laugh. 'I've just covered the castle in fifty pounds' worth of mistletoe.'

'You've done a great job...'

'Dan gave me a huge budget to decorate, and I spent it all.' Leah put her hands to her face. 'Oh, Zo, it's such a mess.'

'It looks beautiful – the courtyard is all twinkly and—'

'I mean *this*.' Leah threw out her arms, indicating Zoe and herself. 'You're leading Christie up the garden path – you'll break his heart. And I...'

'You what?'

Leah was puzzled. 'I don't know how I feel about Dan. He's great to spend time with, but I don't want to fall in love with him...'

'And are you?' Zoe wrapped her arms around Leah. 'Falling in love with him?'

'Perhaps, a little bit.' Leah's head rested on Zoe's shoulder. 'Oh, I'm not sure.'

'Oh, Leah – you can be so contrary.' Zoe hugged her close, taking a breath. 'Right, so, we'll share Christmas Day together, the five of us, and Boxing Day, and Hogmanay, and we'll just see what happens.'

Leah lifted up her face. 'Do you think that's wise, Zo?'

'We'll let time take care of it.' Zoe shrugged. 'It will all become clear soon. Besides, Mariusz and Jordan and Bex are probably coming up for Hogmanay.'

Leah breathed out slowly. 'All right, so, now we've solved that problem, swiftly moving on to the next one...'

Zoe's expression was suspicious. 'What's the next one?'

Leah forced a grin. 'When we have Christmas dinner in the great hall – who's going to cook, me or you?'

* * *

Christmas Day arrived with the perfect compromise: Zoe and Christie prepared the food in the kitchenette upstairs, helped by Daisy, who stood on a chair to stir gravy. Downstairs, Leah and Dan were transforming the great hall. A fire roared in the hearth; the tree sparkled, presents stacked beneath it, the table was laid with red and green plates and napkins, a huge centrepiece of holly and pinecones, yellow lights glowing from candelabras. Dan organised a playlist of Christmas music on his phone. Leah was putting the finishing touches together – scented candles, glasses on the table. She noticed Dan eyeing the mistletoe above his head, so she moved his attention to the tree. 'Don't the decorations look wonderful? I've never seen a tree like it.'

'Locally sourced, the best.' Dan grinned and, at that moment, he heard footsteps behind him. Zoe and Christie, in Christmas jumpers, and Daisy dressed as a princess, announced that dinner was ready, and they should help to bring the dishes down from the kitchenette.

They sat at the table, Dan holding his knife and fork in antici-pation, a red paper hat skewed on his head. Christie and Zoe served up, passing plates and dishes, as Leah said, 'This is so different from last year. I'd never have thought when we sat at our parents' table in rainy Winchester that we'd be here a year later.'

'Last Christmas was okay,' Zoe reminded her. 'We had a nice time with Mum and Dad. They'll miss out this year – they're doing their own thing this year on the Northern Lights cruise. Then they're off to Spain until February.'

Leah shook her head, the experience still vivid. 'You might've enjoyed last Christmas. I spent the whole time worrying about how I was going to find materials to support Jack and Tyler in the class-room. Then I drank too much, watched *The Holiday* and cried like a baby because I felt lonely.'

Dan leaned across the table and patted her hand.

Christie turned to Daisy. 'Can you remember last Christmas?'

Daisy giggled. 'We went to Auntie Jessie's and the potatoes were burned – they had black bits on and you said they were lovely and

Billy was just a puppy and he sat under the table and did a big jobby, and it made me laugh because the smell was so horrible.'

Christie pulled a face that suggested pure love and his inadequacy as a parent. 'We had fun.'

Daisy agreed. 'You fell asleep in front of the TV, Daddy, because you'd drunk too much whisky.'

Zoe laughed. 'You're very good at looking after your daddy, Daisy.'

'She is. There was a time a while back when I used to drink too much whisky,' Christie said sadly. 'Daisy only allows me a wee dram, but I'm all for that now...'

'Daddy says I nag him.' Daisy clapped her hands excitedly. 'But the other day when Zoe and I were making cranachan, we only put a little bit of whisky in the cream, so we both nag him now.'

'It was great making cranachan. Then we made truffles and wrapped them in cellophane as presents.' Zoe smiled fondly. 'We have fun together, don't we?'

Christie met her gaze. 'We do.'

'The best fun.' Daisy grinned.

Leah turned to Dan. 'I suppose you celebrated last Christmas in China?'

Dan noticed everyone's attention was on him, and he waved a hand as if his previous Christmas had been routine. 'I did – I was on the phone most of the day. I got a chef in to make a banquet because my parents had flown over from their place in Florida.' He pushed a hand through his hair, knocking off the paper hat, replacing it quickly. 'I hardly noticed it was Christmas.' His eyes met Leah's. 'This is the first proper Christmas I've had in years. It's incredible – thank you all so much for being here.'

'Shall we pour the wine?' Zoe asked.

'There's champagne in the big kitchen,' Dan announced.

'Daddy, can I have some?'

'You can have lemonade,' Christie countered.

'Aw...'

'I'll fetch it.' Leah was on her feet, padding out into the kitchen.

Dan gazed around the table. 'I want to propose a toast...'

Zoe indicated the steaming dishes of food, the heaped plates. 'Then we can eat...'

Leah rushed in, carrying two bottles of champagne and one of pink lemonade for Daisy. 'Here, Dan, open these – and guess what else I found?' She rushed back into the kitchen as Dan opened the lemonade, pouring pink fizz in Daisy's glass, then turning his attention to the first champagne bottle.

'Mind the chandeliers,' Christie quipped.

Leah hurried back, holding up a goblet. It was an old metal cup, engraved with the figures of a man and a woman. 'Dan, you should drink from this. I found it in the kitchen.'

'I remember that cup.' Christie nodded in recognition. 'We found it when we were digging in the courtyard, a few years ago. It's come up very nicely.'

'It must be centuries old.' Dan held the cup up to the light. 'I wonder whose hands held this...'

Zoe took a breath. 'Maybe we shouldn't use it...' She recalled touching it in the kitchen, feeling a presence behind her, peering over her shoulder.

Dan was already filling it, pouring champagne into the other glasses, lifting the cup up. 'A toast.' he grinned. They all lifted their glasses high, and Dan said, 'To a wonderful Christmas, to a happy life, to love, to joy.' He paused, thinking, then he added, 'To this wonderful castle... and to all of us who sit around this table. Lang may yer lum reek!'

'Lang may yer lum reek,' five voices chorused as the glasses clinked together just as Dan's cup was snatched from his hand as if lifted on the wind and hurled across the room. Daisy screamed; Christie hugged her and said, 'Dan just dropped it, darlin', that's all,' and Zoe froze as she felt icy breath against her neck.

* * *

Agnes held the handfasting cup in her hand and stared at it in the firelight, her vision blurred by tears. It was early morning. Most of the servants had returned to Rosemuir the night before, where the English were ever-present, but others slumbered in corners, huddled beneath blankets. Yesterday had been a sad day: news had come that the mistress, Muriel McNair, had taken her own life with a dagger the English had given her. She had chosen it, no longer wishing to be the bait of the English army, locked away in her room, kept for the humiliation and the lust of their leader.

Effie was asleep, wrapped in a rug. Una was gone again, pulled from where she slept to gratify Paskin's cruel appetite. Three English soldiers stood in the doorway, guarding the exit.

Agnes stared at the man and woman engraved on the metal cup and a tear slid down her cheek for An-Mòr. He was gone now and Agnes missed him. She cried for Muriel McNair; she and her husband had been kind people. Now Rhona was thinner, her face a mask of grief, and she rarely spoke. Bròccan had elevated himself to chief smith; she'd heard it from Effie, and he worked long hours to supply the English with more armour, daggers and swords. Agnes knew he did this to curry favour, and he was allowed time with Effie as a reward.

Agnes held the cup to her lips and thought of Cam. There had still been no word; Una had shaken her head when Agnes had raised an eyebrow in question across the kitchen yesterday morning. It had been eleven days now since she'd held him in her arms and begged him to return, eleven days since he'd promised it would soon be over. But The Bruce's army had not arrived; more snow had fallen outside and Agnes wondered if the harsh weather delayed them.

Effie sat up quietly, whispering, 'Ye are awake. Do ye think of him, the man that is your sweetheart?'

'Aye, I do.'

'Where is he now?'

Agnes sighed. 'I dinnae ken.'

Effie snuggled closely to her, wrapping an arm round her. 'Bròccan says we should escape. We have the daggers and the armour up in the chimney. We can steal horses.'

'But how can ye escape?'

'Ye can help us.'

'How can I do that?'

Effie put her mouth against Agnes's ear. 'The English soldier called Elyas. He has a liking for ye, Agnes.'

'It's no matter to me...'

'Bròccan says ye should be nice to him, lie with him. Then he'll help the three of us escape... maybe he'll come with us.'

'Nay, Effie.'

'But why not?'

'My heart is my husband's.'

'But if it helps us to escape?'

'I willnae do such a thing.'

'He is a fine man, Elyas.'

'Aye, he is,' Agnes admitted. Elyas had shown her nothing but kindness since his arrival. He'd stepped between her and a beating from the English soldiers more than once. 'And he's a poet, a man who kens his letters. I feel sorry for him, surrounded by all this hatred. He's no soldier. But dinnae ask me to betray the man I love.'

'Bròccan says ye should do it to help us all. I would do it.'

Agnes shook her head. 'Talk no more of it, Effie. It is time to sleep. Each day is long and we work hard.'

'But Bròccan says—'

'Put it from your mind. Sleep. We will escape another way.'

'How will it be?'

'The Bruce and his warriors will come, and they will free this castle and drive the English back to their own lands. I ken it.'

Effie shook her head and lay down in the hearth. Agnes held the cup towards the flames, staring at the engraved faces of the man and the woman with joined hands. Their lips were curved in a smile.

Agnes smiled too. Cam would be with her soon; she knew it in her heart.

43

The days after Christmas flew past in a flurry, like the snow that tumbled on Boxing Day. Dan drove the Range Rover high into the mountains and he, Leah, Christie, Daisy and Zoe sat on toboggans, screaming with laughter as they slid down the slopes, Christie with Daisy on his knee, Zoe behind them, Leah and Dan competitive on separate sleighs. They threw soft snowballs at each other, built a Scots snowman in a kilt with a fir cone sporran, and returned to the castle to drink hot chocolate. Zoe was keen that Daisy should not be afraid of being in the castle since the incident with the goblet; Dan had rescued the situation by telling the child that it was an old Scots tradition to hurl the drink, it would bring good luck, then the rest of the meal had passed with good cheer, although the adults had continually peered over their shoulders.

Dan took Leah on a trip to Edinburgh and they flew from Inverness airport, although Leah complained to him about the environmental implications. Dan's enthusiasm had not been deterred when they'd both set off early in the morning and had a wonderful day shopping, eating in an elegant hotel, taking in a live comedy show. Leah had decided against the Underground Ghost Tour, although

Dan had suggested it might be an interesting historical investigation.

Zoe spent most of the time with Christie and Daisy, meeting Christie's sisters Jessie and Kate, their husbands and Daisy's five cousins. She was moved by the way they welcomed her, the loyalty they shared, the strength and supportiveness, and the affection they obviously felt for each other. Each night, Zoe stayed at Christie's home, much to Daisy's delight every morning when she burst into the room, threw her arms around Zoe and cheered, 'You stayed for a sleepover again. Can we make pancakes for breakfast?'

Zoe tried to forget that she'd be going back to Birmingham at the end of January, and that Daisy seemed to be more attached to her than she could have anticipated. Christie seemed fond of her too, and she felt momentarily troubled before she pushed the thought to one side and offered her most disarming grin.

December the thirty-first brought even more snow. Mariusz and Bex arrived at Inverness airport in the late afternoon after a long delay in Birmingham. They stood in the car park clutching cases before clambering into the Range Rover behind Dan and Leah, then Mariusz groaned, 'Jordan couldn't come. He has a deadline for an upcycled three-piece suite for early next week. He sends love. He trusts me totally to check out the venue and take tons of pictures.'

'You'll love it, I promise,' Leah enthused. 'Dan spoke to Abigail and convinced her that it would be a great idea to trial a Valentine's wedding. And you'll be our first one, so the rate's very competitive.'

Bex pressed Dan's shoulder. 'And you're the owner of the castle?'

'He is,' Leah said proudly. 'And he's my boss.'

Bex raised her eyebrows, impressed. 'You must have the best boss in the world, Leah.'

'She has,' Dan agreed. He was wearing a new pair of tartan-framed glasses.

'So...' Leah explained. 'We'll go home, look round the main part of the castle, get changed and go to The Canny Man for Hogmanay. There's food, music, dancing. It'll be wonderful.'

'I've never had a proper Hogmanay in Scotland.' Bex played with her hair. 'Will you be there, Dan?'

'I wouldn't miss it.' Dan glanced at her through the driver's mirror. 'Although I'll have to be a Cinderella and leave at midnight – I have an early business meeting with some people in China and I have to take the call.'

'That's a shame,' Bex said.

'And where's Zoe?' Marius asked.

'She'll be coming later,' Leah explained. 'She's with her new man and his daughter; they've taken her and the cousins out to a forest adventure park. The kids are all staying over at his sister's tonight.'

Mariusz pulled a face. 'It's all changing. Zoe has a new man, you have a new boss – and a castle, and I'm getting married on Valentine's Day.'

'And you're completely a new woman, Leah,' Bex added. 'It's hard to think that several months ago we couldn't get you to come out with us – you'd just stay at home watching TV.'

Dan made a sound of admiration. 'I can't imagine that. Leah's just incredible – we wouldn't manage without her.'

'And do you live in China, Dan?' Bex asked, wide eyed.

'Yes, but I want to buy a house here,' Dan explained. 'That reminds me, Leah, will you come and look at a place with me next week? I have a viewing lined up.'

'I'll come with you if you need a second opinion,' Bex interrupted before Leah could answer, offering Dan her most compelling smile. 'I wouldn't need an excuse to stay on here for longer...'

The Range Rover turned a corner and they were in Rosemuir, the silhouette of the castle looming in the distance lit by twinkling lights, gold and red, the loch and mountains pale shapes beyond.

Mariusz caught his breath. 'Yes, yes, yes.' He tapped Dan's shoulder. 'I'm definitely getting married here, no matter what it takes. That's *the* place for my wedding.'

* * *

Several hours later, Leah stood in the bar of The Canny Man dressed in the new silver gown that Dan had insisted he bought for her in Edinburgh because she'd look like a princess at the ball. Dan and all the other men in the bar were wearing kilts and smart jackets, except for Mariusz, who was sporting a white evening suit. Bex had gone to so much trouble to look her best that they were late arriving: she wore a short plaid dress edged with lace, and black stockings, her hair glossy. Heads turned as soon as she entered and even Dan stared: he had never seen the Scots tartan worn in such a way.

A few minutes later, Zoe arrived wearing a black evening dress, Christie on her arm, handsome in a dark kilt, white frilled shirt and black jacket with brass buttons. Already, lively reels were being played through large speakers and Kenny, wearing a red tam-o'-shanter, was serving every guest a glass of Atholl Brose included in the ticket price, a drink Leah particularly liked as it was creamy and she couldn't taste the whisky.

Kenny had removed the furniture, placing benches around the walls for guests to sit, rest, drink and watch others dancing. To one side, there was a long table with a tartan cloth, laden with plates and bowls of food. The pub was filled with people drinking, jigging and singing, clad in their Hogmanay best.

The evening wound down like a fast-ticking alarm clock: first, the dancing and sampling of neeps and tatties and haggis, more dancing and drinking. Then the time came for the plaintive bagpipes to sound, a lone piper stepping through the main door, bringing in the new year. Then everyone in the bar joined hands, threw back their heads and bawled 'Auld Lang Syne' as loudly as they could.

The kissing began immediately. Christie and Zoe were locked in each other's arms as Dan's eyes searched for Leah. Bex grabbed him and pressed her lips hard against his. Leah stepped back, surprised: Bex had wasted no time letting Dan know her intentions. Leah was aware of a swirling feeling of something not unlike jealousy. She put her emotions down to too much Atholl Brose and looked for someone to embrace, kissing Mariusz. Then Dan found her, tugged her into his arms and her lips met his. She closed her eyes and allowed the moment to sweep her from her feet. When she opened them, she and Dan were staring at each other, breathing hard, and he blurted, 'My meeting. It's midnight. I'll be late. I'm taking it in my room upstairs.' He kissed her again awkwardly, mumbled, 'Happy New Year, Leah,' and then he was gone, leaving her blinking and stunned.

Leah said little as they walked back to the castle. She wasn't listening as Bex chatted non-stop about how attractive Dan was and how the kiss they'd shared was heaven: she was sure he liked her. Mariusz wanted to talk about the castle, about the stunning photos he'd sent to Jordan earlier, then he was on the phone, chatting to his fiancé about the gorgeousness of the great hall which would be perfect for the reception, and the incredible guest bedrooms upstairs, and how he was going to sleep in one of them tonight with a grand four-poster bed.

Leah was deep in thought; she linked arms with Zoe, Christie on the other side, and they trod carefully through the slippery snow. The castle was golden in the distance, colours shimmering on the loch. Leah had arranged so many twinkling Christmas lights as tastefully as possible, around the door, along the crenelated wall, following the shape of the castle windows. She had left the south-west wing alone: she'd thought it best to festoon the castle and leave the wing in shadow.

They approached the place where the old drawbridge had been, now a mound of grass. Mariusz stared towards the castle. 'It's all been renovated?'

Christie nodded.

'What about the chapel?' Mariusz asked. 'When can I see it?'

Leah shrugged. 'Christie has scaffolding in place. It's going to be refurbished in January. I mean, we'll keep it original, but it will look totally different when we've done it up.'

'I need photos.' Mariusz grinned. 'Jordan needs photos... We want the whole traditional thing, matching suits, a bouquet to throw, a champagne reception in the castle...'

'We can take a peek at the chapel tomorrow, when it's light,' Leah suggested.

'Why not now?' Mariusz asked. 'I'd love to see it in the dark, with the fairy lights outside...'

'There's a ghost there,' Zoe said.

'A ghost... really?' Bex laughed, incredulous; she had drunk quite a lot. 'I want to see it. Oh, let's go and see the ghost, please.'

Leah shook her head. 'She needs peace and quiet... respect.'

'Have you seen her, Leah? Zoe?' Bex was excited. 'We could open a bottle of wine and go and sit in the chapel and wait for her to come.' She became more excitable. 'We could do that thing like they do on the programme on TV, call out to the ghost and say, "If you are here, reveal yourself," and the ghost always knocks on the wall or throws something.'

'Not a good idea, Bex. Let's leave it, shall we?' Leah said firmly. She liked Bex; she'd always admired her bubbly enthusiasm, but she was still irritated by the way she'd flung herself at Dan and kissed him. Besides, Leah thought, it would be disrespectful to sit in the chapel ghost hunting. A perpetual sadness hung around the place.

'So, tell us about this ghost, Zoe... will she show up at my wedding?' Mariusz asked. 'Have you seen her, Christie?'

'We all have seen or felt something,' Christie said quietly.

Zoe added, 'Let's leave it for tonight, shall we? I'm tired. Let's just go in and go to bed...'

'I want to see a ghost, though,' Bex insisted. 'I don't believe in them, but if I saw one, I'd change my mind.'

They were in the courtyard, almost at the door. The scaffolding Christie had put up at the edge of the southwest wing hung in the shadows like a cage. Leah plunged her hand into her bag for the bunch of keys.

Mariusz started up at the castle and breathed out slowly. 'This is the perfect place for my wedding, Leah. It's just what we want, so romantic and desolate and beautiful and ancient. I love it.'

'I know what you mean.' Leah nodded. 'I love it here too.'

'It's such a pity I can't take a look inside the chapel...' Mariusz swivelled, turning towards the southwest wing and he drew in a sharp breath as a raven flew above his head.

Leah twisted round, then Bex, Zoe and Christie, gasping as they stared at the pale shape of a woman outlined in silver light, standing in the doorway to the chapel. Her hair tumbling around her shoulders, she hung on the air like a shifting mist, almost translucent, her features just distinguishable. She held out a hand towards the sweeping bird and it soared high into the darkness, plummeting down to land on the crenelated wall, uttering a sad cry.

Zoe reached for Christie's hand, squeezing his fingers. Bex turned to Leah, who wrapped an arm round her and they held their breath as one.

The woman stayed for a moment, the light around her a haze that seemed to hover, to come and go. She gazed towards the raven, and appeared to open her mouth, but no sound came. Then she merged with the chapel door, the light around her dimming, fading to darkness, and she vanished.

44

Agnes returned to the castle in the murky half-light that settled on the loch just before dawn, carrying pails of water from the well, watched by three English guards who followed her but offered no help. Bròccan stood in the courtyard, a hammer in his hand, talking to one of the English soldiers. Agnes heard them laughing together and when Bròccan called out to her, she ignored him and walked back through the courtyard with her burden.

She scanned the kitchen; several servants were cooking oats and preparing vegetables, including Mairi with her scarred face. Rhona had arrived early, tired and pale, and was pounding grain with Effie. Una was bent over her work, skinning a rabbit, and Agnes watched her fingers work deftly, believing that she was planning how she might attack and gut Paskin if the chance came. Agnes searched Una's face: it was thirteen days now since she had seen Cam, and she desperately craved a sign that The Bruce and his Scottish army might be gathering nearby, ready to attack, but Una's eyes were as dead as the rabbit she was skinning.

Agnes placed the pails over the fire to heat and brought flour to the table. Elyas was beside her almost immediately. 'Good morrow to you, sweet Agnes.' Agnes bowed her head, placing a bowl in front of her. Elyas tried again. 'I have been thinking of you...'

'The bread will be a while yet before it is baked. Go away, Elyas, busy yourself with a cup of warm ale.'

'I like our talk together,' he said simply. 'I long for it each morning.'

Agnes shook her head. 'Ye talk, I dinnae listen.'

'We could take a walk together, by the loch. The guards will allow it if I ask it...' Elyas said, his eyes misty as they came to rest on her face.

'Nay, I willnae walk with ye and well ye ken it.' Agnes felt sorry for him. He was lonely and he'd shown her nothing but gentleness. She wished he'd leave her alone; it would make her life a lot easier – he was her enemy.

'I have started to write a poem for you. It has taken me a long time to pen the first few lines.' She ignored him, so he lifted an arm and began to recite.

For though I may weep a basin of tears, Yet woe may not confound my heart, Agnesse...

'What means this?' Agnes lifted flashing eyes that met his. 'Why have ye written these words?'

He spoke quietly. 'I must protest, I love you most of all.'

'Nay.' Agnes stopped working, her hands clenched. 'Elyas, this is foolish. Ye cannot love me. Go away and leave me be.'

'But what if we could go away together? What if it is possible that two souls can love each other, across hatred and enmity?' He grasped her flour-covered hand, bringing it tenderly to his cheek. 'What if we could?'

'Ye are a good man, Elyas, but ye are my enemy.' Agnes's voice was hushed. She tugged her hand from his fingers. 'I have a husband, a man I love more than my own life. Go to, leave me now. I have no more to say to ye.'

'Where is this husband, Agnes? Why is he not here in the castle with you?'

Agnes turned her back and walked away towards the fire, picking up a bucket of steaming water, carrying it towards Rhona and Effie. She called to them, 'I have brought ye hot water for the grain. The company is more to my liking here.' She turned to Elyas, offering a glance of pity as he turned sadly and walked through the kitchen towards the corridor and out of sight. It was for the best: she wanted to release him from his suffering.

She did not see Elyas for the rest of the day. Later in the morning, Effie rushed out of the kitchen to meet Bròccan, to take him food, and she came back with the news that Elyas was now guarding the chapel, standing in the cold wind in front of the door. Agnes's refusal had broken his heart and Bròccan was annoyed that Agnes had missed an opportunity to help him and Effie escape. Effie sulked for most of the day, then, as light faded in the evening, Rhona wrapped herself in her shawl and muttered her goodbyes, leaving for her hut.

Agnes brought a cup of warm ale to the fireside and sat down, Effie creeping beside her. Agnes listened to the crackling of the fire, glancing over towards the three guards who blocked the doorway, feeling the warmth against her cheek.

Then Effie whispered, 'Is she dead, the mistress?'

Agnes nodded. 'She took her own life rather than let the English use her. I would do the same.'

Effie chewed her lip. 'I wonder if the Princess Marjorie's cloak is still in the mistress's room...'

'Think of it no more, Effie.'

Effie closed her eyes. 'And are they all gone now, An-Mòr and the master and Rhona's son?'

'Aye, they are.'

Effie brought a finger to her lips to suck. 'Bròccan says your laddie is dead too. Bròccan says he's died in battle.'

Agnes turned sharply. 'Bròccan should hold his tongue.'

'But he's abandoned ye.' A crease came between Effie's brows. 'Bròccan says he may have found another lassie, ridden north to the islands.'

'If Bròccan was here now, I'd make him stint.' Agnes showed Effie a clenched fist. 'No more of it.'

'But—'

'Nay, Effie, no more.'

Effie sighed, a long-drawn-out sound. 'Now we'll never get away. The English soldier was sweet on ye, he would have helped ye...'

Agnes stared into the flames, picturing Cam fighting in a fierce battle, clutching a shield, his sword held high above his head. Effie's words had troubled her, and she imagined in the leap of the blaze the image of Cam fighting and falling. She felt bitter tears fill her eyes, but she would not cry.

Effie's small hand slid into hers and her voice was tiny. 'I'm sorry for ye, Agnes.'

A sigh shuddered through Agnes's body, then she whispered, 'He will come, I'm sure of it. Until then, Effie, heed not what Bròccan says – he is puffed up and full of hot air.'

'I ken.'

'Let's rest awhile. It grows dark outside and cold. We are fortunate to have this fire here to sit beside.'

'We are, Agnes.' Effie's eyes glimmered. 'D'ye recall when we took the king's brother's horse and ran away from Kildrummy and how cold it was outside, even in the summer.'

'Aye.' Agnes remembered and her heart ached for Cam, in hiding, in the bitter wind and ice.

'I wonder where they are now, Morag and Biddy and all the others in the kitchen...'

'Aye.' Agnes was lost in her own thoughts.

'And the king's wife and the princess. Are they all dead, Agnes?'

'The English murdered the Earl of Atholl, just as they murdered Niall de Brus and William Wallace. The queen is in England, under close guard, and the wee princess is put in a convent there.'

'Will they live?'

'Aye – the king will defeat the English and we will all be free, and Queen Elizabeth and Princess Marjorie will come home again.'

'D'ye believe it?'

'I do, Effie, with all my heart. The one I love has promised me, and I believe it will come to pass.'

'Amen to that,' Effie whispered, placing her hands together in prayer. 'And I hope it will come soon. I hate it here.'

Agnes reached out towards the fire, warming her hands, but she was shivering inside. She wondered if she had made a mistake telling Elyas that she had a husband. At least in Elyas she'd had an ally; now she feared she had no one at all who would help her. But she had her own wits, and she was pleased that she had spoken the truth, that she had made it clear she would never love the enemy, that Cam was her life, her soul. Wherever he was now, that would never change.

Suddenly, there was shouting from beyond the door and the three guards rushed from the kitchen. Someone called, 'The Bruce – he's here.'

Agnes was on her feet, dashing into the corridor, running for the castle door. Una was next to her, then Effie, clinging to her arm, shaking. In the courtyard, snow was heaped, more of it shaken from the inky sky, whirling thick and fast. Figures leaped from nowhere in the semi-darkness, soldiers fighting furiously, the English in their full armour, the Scottish warriors raising heavy swords, bringing them crashing down, the clang of metal against metal, against bone.

Una seized Agnes's arm, Effie holding on, shivering. 'It's the king and his men...' She disappeared from Agnes's side, scurrying back to the kitchen.

Agnes pulled back, peering round the corner of the main door, then Una returned, breathless, pushing a kitchen knife into Agnes's hand, brandishing another.

'Here y'are.'

Then Una was out in the darkness, searching amid the fighting men. She ducked as if she was dancing, then she saw the one she was looking for: Paskin, his sword flailing in the air as he tried to beat down a warrior. Una hurled herself towards him, thrusting the kitchen knife in his back. Paskin turned, a snarl on his face and recognised her as the warrior brought his sword down hard on Paskin's skull and he fell heavily into the snow. Una scuttled back to Agnes, blood on the end of her knife, muttering, 'That's an end made of him, the rat. I avenged myself and my brother.'

Una sprang into action again, her eyes scanning for more English soldiers, her blade point at the ready to thrust into a leg, an arm, a neck. Agnes stared at the kitchen knife in her own hand, her arm still around a trembling Effie. A few yards away, Elyas was waving his sword. He seemed much smaller than the weapon he wielded, almost too frail to lift it as he backed away from a young warrior who held a shield in front of his face. Agnes saw the opportunity; it would be easy to attack Elyas, to plunge the knife into his shoulder, but she could not.

Her eyes scanned each warrior's face, searching for Cam; it was difficult to recognise any of the fighters, they moved so quickly. The snow was tumbling thick, blurring her vision, and the courtyard was in shadow. The noise was thunderous, battle cries, screams, the harsh thud of metal. But she would know him as soon as he was near; her soul was reaching for his even now.

Agnes saw a warrior emerge from the crowd; he wore heavy studded armour, a shining helmet, a grizzled beard, and he wielded an ornate sword. She watched as he held the shield up against his body, slicing the English as they leaped upon him. Two, three soldiers fell at his feet, and he fought on, his eyes bright, until he whirled back into the teeming snow. Agnes saw something in his bearing: leadership, strength, nobility. She was sure it was King Robert.

Then another man was hacking the air with his sword just in front of her, a Scottish warrior. An English soldier lunged, pushing his sword easily through the man's chest and he fell, his mouth open, his eyes staring straight at her. Agnes had never seen the soldier before, but he was young, like Cam. She watched as his blood seeped into the snow, spattering dark against the white.

The battle continued, voices roaring, the loud clatter of swords and clang of metal, the belligerent growl as man fought against man. There was smoke everywhere, the strong smell of burning, wood or hay or fire from the forge. Bodies fell and blood steamed as it spilled on the cold ground. Then an English voice roared, 'Get the servants back into the kitchen. Move them now.'

Una was next to her, hissing, 'Go back, Agnes. Back inside. The fighting's done for now. But our laddies will return.'

Agnes grabbed Effie's hand and they fled to the kitchen and behind her, two soldiers were dragging a third, a man no older than she was. The young man was placed on a chair, blood seeping from a wound in his chest, and one of the English voices said, 'Can you tend him, please?'

She turned to see Elyas standing beside her, opening the young man's tunic, indicating a deep gash below the shoulder. He spoke hurriedly. 'Digory is injured. Please, can you find water, bathe him, wrap the wound.'

Agnes nodded, pouring water from a bronze ewer with a hinged lid. She soaked a clean cloth and pressed it to the gaping slash, horrified by the gore that covered her hand. She tried again, stopping the flow of blood as best as she could as young Digory groaned in pain. Agnes muttered quietly, 'Peace, laddie, you'll live.'

Effie was beside her, handing her clean cloths, and Agnes was pleased that the bleeding was slowing.

The young English soldier reached for her hand. 'Thank you.'

Agnes gazed at the red water in the bowl. 'Aye, it's no more than a scratch.'

'It was a scratch from one of the best warriors in the Scottish army,' the other soldier said, pressing Digory's arm. 'You can wear that scar with pride and impress the ladies.'

'Why, is the battle done?' Agnes asked.

'It is...' Elyas said. 'And a fierce one. Many of our men fell...'

'But we were too strong for the enemy; there were twice more of us than them.' His companion smiled proudly. 'I heard The Bruce himself tell his men to pull back.'

'The Bruce...' Agnes's eyes were wide.

'He was here,' Digory muttered.

'And his army. But we fought them well, pushed them back again. The victory was ours.' The second soldier had started to brag.

Agnes turned to Elyas. 'Is this true?'

Elyas nodded. 'We outnumbered them, but they were fierce – there were casualties on both sides. The Scottish king wanted to take the castle. He'll try again, I'm sure of it.'

'Casualties?' Agnes had started to tremble.

'Prisoners, too.' The other soldier smiled. 'One we've been after for a while. That's how Digory here took the wound. It took six of us to hold him down.'

Agnes felt her legs cave beneath her: she knew before they spoke. 'Who?'

The soldier sneered. 'The one they call Allaidh, the wild one. We have him in the chapel, under guard. It's taken us a long time to catch him, but he's ours now.'

Agnes forced herself upright. Her mouth wouldn't work. It was dry; no words would come. Eventually, she managed to whisper, 'What will become of him?'

'Do not ask,' Elyas said gently. 'It is not for the ears of women.'

The other soldier added, 'He'll stay where he is, under guard until the morning. Then our sergeant will decide his fate.'

Elyas reached out an arm, steadying Agnes as she almost tumbled. He spoke quietly. 'You grow pale. Here, let me give you something to drink.' He reached for the ewer, and noticed the drawer of the table was open. He found the handfasting cup, quickly pouring water into it and handing it to Agnes. 'Here, drink deep from this. Sit yourself down, Agnes, and rest. The harsh business of soldiers is not for the ears of one as fair as you.'

Agnes took the cup and slumped down by the fire, Effie settling beside her, saying nothing. She listened to the crackling of logs, but her mind was racing: Cam was here in Ravenscraig, he was a prisoner. She would find him, she had to set him free. She stared into the flames as they spluttered, touching the engraving on the cup tenderly with her fingers. Then the image of Una came to her, the kitchen knife in her hand, how she sank the blade into Paskin's flesh. Agnes knew what she had to do, and she was filled with courage and determination. The way to Cam was clear, and the dawn could not come quickly enough.

45

It wasn't yet light, the last purple skeins of dawn blotching the sky over the loch. A low mist hung over the water, trailing chiffon. Zoe turned away from the window to gaze at Christie, still asleep in bed, his hair tousled on the pillow. Something stirred in her heart, affection, desire, love. She was filled with a sudden sense of optimism: it was the first of January, a new year, and she would make breakfast for everyone, pancakes with blueberry sauce. She pulled on her furry slippers and a dressing gown and hurried to the kitchenette. She found Leah there in pyjamas, her hair over her face, sipping coffee.

Leah looked up as Zoe came in. 'Are you off for a run?'

'Later...' Zoe pointed in the direction of her bedroom. 'Christie's still asleep. I thought I'd make breakfast for us all.'

Leah pulled a face. 'I'm not really hungry...'

'You will be when you smell the sizzle. I might take a coffee to Mariusz and Bex. I hope they slept well in the old guest bedrooms. Thank goodness for room freshener.'

Leah nodded, reaching for her coffee, pushing her hair back.

Zoe sat down opposite. 'What's up?'

'Nothing.' Leah rested her face in her hands, a pudge of cheek poking through the fingers. Zoe was reminded of the autumn, when Leah was depressed and lethargic. It was the same sadness that sat on her now.

Zoe grabbed her sister's hands. 'What is it?'

'Ah...' Leah made an effort to shake the mood off. 'I drank too much.'

'We all did. It was Hogmanay.' Zoe leaned forward. 'It's the ghost, isn't it?'

'A bit...' Leah sighed. 'I really feel sorry for her. I know how she feels. I'm the same this morning, a bit sad, a bit... like everything is hopeless.'

'Why do you feel like that?'

'I just do... I woke up like it.' Leah shook her head. 'How can we help her? If she's been going through what I am now for seven centuries, she needs some peace. When we saw her standing there, it was as if she was broken...'

'I was talking to Christie about it. I thought exactly the same – there was something about her that was so unhappy. We'll renovate the chapel. Maybe that will help. Christie has fixed a date to come round and look at the upstairs chamber in the wing, Friday, the sixth.'

'He's a builder, Zo – he just knocks things down. What if it doesn't help our ghost?' Leah met her eyes. 'Mirren might know. And I'm going to email Ally Wylie, the professor from Stirling. She'll be glad of an opportunity to find out something about the castle's history. Perhaps together we can find a way to help her rest...'

'Then that's sorted.' Zoe leaped up.

Leah nodded, but her heart wasn't in it. She picked up her mug and stared into the dregs.

'Did you enjoy last night?' Zoe asked, shaking flour into a bowl.

'Mmm.' Leah was non-committal. She was thinking about the

kiss she'd shared with Dan, how it had stirred an uneasy feeling in her stomach. She wondered why emotions were so complex, why doubt and fear mixed themselves with what might be powerful attraction and left her feeling introspective. That was the problem: she needed to trust herself. Loving someone was full of risks and pitfalls. A question tumbled from her lips. 'Do you like Dan?'

Zoe was ladling pancake mixture into a sizzling pan. 'I think he's great. He was talking to me yesterday about the best way to donate to charity, and I promised I'd give him some suggestions. He's a lovely man. You like him, don't you?'

'He's my boss.' Leah bridled, unsure how to respond to the question. 'He's fun and kind and a little bit... eccentric. Yes, I like him.'

Zoe was about to tell Leah that she thought Dan liked her too, but Bex and Mariusz were in the room in pyjamas, Mariusz's red, Bex's white.

'Are you talking about my favourite millionaire?' Bex asked.

Mariusz groaned. 'Is there any coffee? I feel dreadful. Whisky and ghosts don't mix. Oh – they are both spirits.'

Bex laughed, a high squeal, accepting the mug of coffee Zoe gave her before she returned to flipping pancakes over. 'So, I need to ask you all about Dan.'

'What about him?' Leah's tone was defensive.

'He's single, isn't he?'

Leah grunted.

Mariusz added, 'He is attractive. Do you like him, Bex?'

'Definitely.' She rolled her eyes. 'He kissed me last night at midnight and I just know I have to see him again. Do you have a number for him, Leah? Do you think I can persuade him to buy me lunch before we fly back this afternoon?'

'You're going to lure him to your lair, and reel him in?' Mariusz laughed, reaching for the coffee Zoe passed to him.

Bex spluttered. 'I'm definitely looking for an invite to come back soon. He's totally my type, Dan – enigmatic, sweet, kind – and very, very rich.'

'His money's not a good reason to make a play for him,' Leah blurted. 'I'd never want to be with a man who's so wealthy.'

'Why ever not?' Bex was perplexed. 'Surely that's the whole point?'

Leah sighed impatiently. 'Poor Dan. Women throwing themselves at him because he's rich. It's not fair.' She looked around fiercely. 'A relationship like that just wouldn't ever work. Have you never heard of equality?'

Bex stared. 'I never knew you felt so strongly, Leah? Are you a socialist?'

'No, I'm just being honest.' Leah struggled to her feet. 'I think I'll get a shower – don't worry about the pancakes for me, Zo. I'm not hungry...'

Zoe, Bex and Mariusz watched her go.

Mariusz muttered, 'Is she all right?'

'I'm not sure...' Zoe said. 'For Leah to pass on pancakes, there must be a good reason...'

* * *

On the morning of the third January, Leah sat in Dan's car as he drove towards Inverness, weaving through traffic. Snow was falling lightly, sloshing against the windscreen with every arc of the wipers. Dan was doing his best to make conversation, but Leah was unusually quiet.

'Thanks for agreeing to come with me.'

'It's no problem.'

He tried again. 'Did your friends get back to Birmingham all right?' Leah nodded and Dan said, 'Bex messaged me, left me her phone number. Apparently, she got mine from Zoe.' He frowned. 'Why would Bex do that? I hardly know her.'

Leah shrugged, gazing out of the window at the gathering crowds swarming in and out of shops. Many shoppers had braved the cold, looking for a bargain in the town centre.

Dan drove on, past Inverness Castle perched high above them, and then took the road for Beauly. He glanced at Leah. 'Christie tells me that the ghost made an appearance again.'

'Yes, she did.' Leah nodded.

'Was it scary?' Dan asked. 'The incident with the goblet took the wind out of my sails on Christmas Day.'

'You dealt with it so well,' Leah said, remembering, and Dan smiled at the compliment. She added, 'No, not scary, just so sad.'

'You seem sad too.' Dan's face held concern. 'When we've viewed this place, let me take you somewhere for lunch...'

Leah sighed again. 'I'm not sure.'

Dan concentrated his gaze on the twisting road. He had little experience of women, and he couldn't read Leah's mood at all. She was usually bubbly, friendly, affectionate even, traits he admired. But today she was distant, a little dejected. He decided to give her some space, but their silence filled the car like a chasm.

Then he slowed the Range Rover, turning the car into a gravelled drive, approaching a white stone house with four green gables. He stopped, turning off the engine, and sat back in his seat.

'We're early. The estate agent will be here in about twenty minutes.' He glanced at his expensive watch. 'Well, what do you think?'

'It's very nice...'

Dan recited: 'Speybank is a generously proportioned stone-built property offering more than 4,800 square feet of attractive accommodation arranged over three floors and located in a much-admired and sought-after location...'

Leah frowned. 'Are those the estate agent's notes?'

'From memory. Mine's photographic, pretty much.' Dan

beamed. 'There are seven bedrooms, two morning rooms and it even has a sauna.'

'It must be expensive.'

'Not really.' Dan grinned. 'I need to give this hire car back soon and buy myself a motor too, now I'm staying in Scotland. This place has a huge garage, so I thought I'd get something useful like this and maybe something sporty.'

'You see something you want and you just reach out and there it is...' Leah turned her gaze to the passenger window. Beyond, the grass was wedged with piles of snow. There was an orchard, clipped bushes and, in the distance, squares of plaid fields and high mountains. 'It's beautiful, though.'

'It is. I can't wait to go in.'

Leah frowned. 'But why do you need such a big house?'

He didn't pause for breath. 'Oh, it's not just for now, it's for the future.'

'I don't understand.'

Dan placed a hand over his mouth. He had said too much. But something propelled him to continue, foolishness, trust, something more. 'The thing is, Leah, I'm not just buying it with myself in mind...'

'Who else is there?' Leah stared at him.

Dan grabbed her hand. 'Surely you know...'

'Know what?' Leah heard the bluntness in her words and felt awkward.

'How I feel?'

'How you feel?' Leah repeated.

He lifted her hand to his lips. 'I care for you, Leah. I have since we met, pretty much. And I thought maybe you had the same feelings for me...'

Leah said, 'Oh...' She wasn't sure what else to say. Her thoughts were crashing against each other: a few months ago, she'd been jobless, her savings had dwindled and her confidence had been low.

Aaron had treated her like a spare part; she'd meant nothing to him. Now, just when she'd built herself a new life, she had a job that was going so well, she was independent and strong, Dan had rushed into her life and was declaring his feelings. He was rich, wonderful, kind – and it was all overwhelming.

'I know it's early days, but I want to buy a home where we can be together one day, and maybe we can fill it with happiness and fun and even children...' Dan stopped, amazed by his own words. He scrutinised her expression for a clue to her reaction. There was none.

Then Leah's face became closed and she said, 'Take me home, please.'

'Leah?'

'Take me back to the castle, Dan.'

'I'm... I'm sorry,' Dan blurted. 'Have I offended you?'

Leah shook her head. 'You're my boss and working in the castle is my dream job and you and I get on so well, but... Oh, I don't know.'

'I know I can be a bit eager. I'm used to making my mind up and getting things I want straight away and not waiting. But you're special... I'll wait as long as it takes.' He was still holding her hand. 'Please, let's go and look at the house?'

'Like I just said, you see something you want and you take it. A house, a car, me. We're not the same sort of people, Dan. I'm not someone who looks for a man with money and an expensive life-style. I'm just ordinary... nothing special...'

'But you are special. That's what I love so much, Leah – you're the first girl who sees me for who I am...'

'But you'd get bored with me...'

'Never.'

Leah frowned. It was too big a risk. He was complicating things. She might lose her job. She might fall in love with him and he'd grow tired of her. Both alternatives would mean that she'd end up back in Birmingham, jobless and depressed. She couldn't let that happen.

'Take me back to the castle...' Leah stared in front, her head fixed in position, not meeting his eyes. She folded her arms, and as he started the car, she glared through the passenger window, not changing position throughout the journey to Rosemuir until he drove across the old drawbridge to Ravenscraig and came to a halt in the car park beyond the well.

He turned to her, his face etched with misery. 'Can we talk?'

Leah scrambled from the car. 'I'm sorry, Dan – there's nothing to say.'

'Please, let's discuss what just happened. Leah. I'm confused...'

'It wouldn't work – it would all go wrong. I'm sorry...' Then Leah was running, through the main gate, across the snow-laden court-yard where Christmas lights winked and twinkled, to the main door, twisting a key, then she was inside, slamming the door, her face covered with tears.

Leah rushed through the castle, calling out for Zoe for a much-needed hug. The Mini had been in the car park, but Zoe was out. Leah scuttled to her room, hurling herself onto the bed, hugging the pillow, and she began to sob, just as she'd sobbed as a child when things went wrong. Zoe had Christie in her life now, and Daisy too, and although Leah wasn't sure how their relationship would develop, she knew that Zoe was happy. Leah's sobs heaved in her chest: she cared for Dan and she'd just pushed him away. What was wrong with her? The answer came immediately. She was afraid of being hurt.

Voices in her head were arguing, forward and back: Dan would not hurt her. He was kind, gentle. But she was afraid: loving someone was a commitment, it was about equality and Dan was her boss, he was rich. The voice answered immediately: equality came with love, not possessions.

Leah's mind took her back again to the evening she drank two bottles of Prosecco in the flat in Birmingham, gorging on pizza, vomiting in the basin. Her stomach had been full of bile and misery; she'd needed to empty herself of failure. Then she'd escaped; she'd found Scotland, Ravenscraig. She had been deliriously happy, then Dan came along.

She rolled over, snivelling. Dan was a wonderful man. Her feelings for him were growing, she couldn't deny it. What would Zoe tell her to do if she were here? She'd say go and grab love with both hands.

Leah's eyes closed; her lids were heavy and she was being tugged into sleep. Just as dreams dragged her away, she felt someone standing beside the bed. Leah assumed it was Zoe, as the figure touched her brow. She felt a hand stroking the top of her head, and a gentle voice whispered, 'Dinnae ye fret, hennie...'

* * *

Leah woke an hour later to the sound of constant buzzing. She pushed hair from her face, sat up and tugged the phone from her pocket. 'Hello?'

'Leah, it's Abigail Laing.'

'Hello...' Leah remembered. 'Happy New Year.'

'Is it?' Abigail sounded annoyed.

Leah frowned. 'Is something wrong?'

There was a pause, then Abigail's curt voice said, 'I've just come from a meeting with Daniel Lennox.'

'Oh?' Leah recalled the way Dan's face had creased in disappointment when she'd refused him, and she winced. Then a tidal wave of guilt and sadness took her breath away.

Abigail did not conceal her anger. 'Would you like to explain why he's just asked me to organise a one-way air ticket to China, complete with stopovers? He's told me to tell you to run the castle as you please; he trusts you completely. But now he's going back to Guangzhou – he's flying out later this afternoon.'

Leah sat up in bed and shivered. She hadn't expected him to leave.

'He's clearly very unhappy.' Abigail's voice was loud in the receiver, thick with irritation. 'I don't know what you've done, Leah, but I suggest you think about ways of putting things right, and quickly.'

46

———————

Zoe watched fondly as Daisy tore the pizza apart with her fingers and stuffed elastic cheese into her mouth. Christie caught the gleam in her eye and smiled. The café was noisy, full of parents and children doing the same thing, enjoying the last day of the holidays before school started again. Zoe stared at her own plate: she wasn't really hungry. She knew what was bothering her, what made her thoughts jumbled and her happiness tinged with anxiety. She looked from Daisy to Christie and wasn't sure how she could leave. They had become fixtures in her life.

Christie winked. 'Thanks for being here today.'

Zoe smiled and his hand covered hers. 'I wouldn't miss it. Pineapple and green pepper pizza is just about my favourite thing.' She took a bite: it was good.

Daisy continued to chew. 'I don't want to go back to school.'

Christie said, 'You won't say that when you're running round the playground, having fun with your friends.'

'But I like it here with you and Zoe.' Daisy gave Zoe the direct, open look children always give adults when they want something. 'Why are you going to Birmingham, Zoe?'

'Because that's where I live, sweetheart.' Zoe felt a familiar ache of guilt and something that felt like regret. 'It won't be for a few weeks. But I have a flat there.'

'What's a flat?'

'It's a little house,' she explained.

'A little house must be horrible.' Daisy turned to Christie, pizza in her hand, her forehead puckered. 'I don't want Zoe to go back to Birmingham.'

'It's Zoe's decision, darlin',' Christie said kindly.

'But you can live with us in our big house,' Daisy persisted. 'There's plenty of room and Daddy is happy when you're there.'

'Yes, I think he is...' Zoe sighed and closed her eyes. She felt the light squeeze of Christie's hand.

Christie took over. 'We can visit Zoe in Birmingham.'

'Can we? Every week?'

'As much as she wants us to.' Christie smiled, but his gaze was level and serious.

'Zoe...' Daisy rummaged in her pocket. 'Daddy says you work for a big charity.'

'In a manner of speaking – I work for all the charities.'

Daisy frowned, a little crease between wide eyes. 'And charities help lots of poor people, don't they?'

'They do, yes.' Zoe stared as Daisy held out a purse.

'Can you give them this?'

Zoe took the little purse. It was a sky-blue colour, designed with a unicorn standing on a rainbow. Zoe noticed that the unicorn had long eyelashes and the rainbow sparkled with sequins. 'What's in here?'

'It's money from Auntie Jessie and Auntie Kate. I got it for Christmas.' Daisy's face was sincere. 'But I want you to give it to the poor people in your charity.'

Zoe closed her eyes for a moment, thinking about pure love: Daisy brimmed with it; Christie cared for her unconditionally – he had put no pressure on her to stay – and she found herself drawn, a moth to the warmth of their flame. She opened her eyes again and saw Daisy's round stare and Christie, his expression tender. Zoe knew what she wanted to do. She'd known for some time.

'You keep it, Daisy, and you and I and your daddy can decide together which people you'd like to give it to.'

'But you'll be in Birmingham...'

'I might not go just yet...' Zoe smiled at Christie and felt the gentle pressure of his fingers.

'How long are you staying for?' Daisy clutched the purse. She had forgotten about the pizza. 'Just for the holidays?' Her face was sad. 'Can you stay longer? Can you stay forever?'

'I was going to stay until the end of January...' Zoe pressed her lips together. 'But I could stay for longer, if that's what you both want.' She took a breath. 'I might want to stay for a long time...' Zoe looked from one face to the other, '...if that's all right?'

Daisy nodded emphatically. 'It's all right with me – and it's all right with Daddy, isn't it, Daddy?'

She waited for an answer. Christie had taken Zoe in his arms; he was kissing her. Then he said, 'Yes, it's absolutely all right with me,' and Daisy clapped her hands as Zoe kissed him again.

* * *

Leah parked the Mini askew in the car park across two sets of white lines and ran towards the sliding doors of Inverness airport, her handbag bouncing up and down against her back. Her breath was warm mist in the cold air, and she almost lost her footing in the ice beneath the snow. She waved her phone in one hand – she had texted Dan six times in the last hour, but he hadn't answered.

She hurried into the airport, pausing by the car hire stand to gaze around. There was a café to the right, bustling with people eating and drinking. Leah hurried in the direction of humming voices and almost cannoned into a thick-set man wearing a red tartan kilt, carrying a glass of beer. She apologised, her face flushed. 'Sorry – I was looking for someone else.'

The man laughed, 'Aye, that's a pity, darlin',' and continued to grin as Leah stared around the café, searching for a man in glasses. She found one wearing black frames, an erudite-looking man reading a newspaper who was probably old enough to be her father, and she exhaled sadly. Then she turned abruptly, racing back into the main seating area, staring up at the departures board, whirling towards the information desk. There were a few people sitting down on benches, bulging cases at their feet. A woman was feeding a tiny baby. A young man who could have been a student, his hair in a ponytail, wearing a heavy coat, large boots on the end of long stretched legs, was reading a book called *Language and Politics*.

Over in the departures area, there was a long queue of people checking in luggage. Zoe examined everyone in the snaking line: a woman wearing a purple sari beneath a warm coat, a woman with three bags of luggage in lurid orange, a young man in a short-sleeved T-shirt who clearly didn't feel the cold. There was a family with two children, their faces bored. Then she saw him; his back was turned to her, but she knew it was him. He was wearing a dark coat, carrying a huge black case. She caught her breath and all of a sudden, she was running.

She reached the back of the queue. 'Excuse me.' Her voice was breathy with apologies as two people let her through. 'Sorry – sorry – oh, excuse me.'

One or two people eyed her with disapproval, then the woman with the lurid orange luggage turned, her face irritated. 'We are in a queue here...' She met Leah's pleading gaze and pointed furiously to the back of the line.

'Oh, I'm not here to get on the plane...'

She noticed the woman staring belligerently and Leah wondered how she could get past her and the luggage at her feet.

She tried again. 'I need to speak to that man over there, it's an emergency. Please...'

The woman thrust out her chin. She was about to say something when Dan turned round and noticed her. She was eight, ten people away from him. He frowned and his voice was filled with sudden confusion. 'Leah?'

'Dan – Dan...' She grabbed the woman's sleeve. 'Please – I have to stop that man getting on the plane.'

'Are you a police officer?' The woman was suddenly interested.

'Yes, I mean no, no...' She raised her voice and yelled: 'Dan, please don't go.'

Dan called back, 'I have a ticket... I have connections to make...'

'You can't go.' Leah had pushed her way through, further down the queue.

A large man blocked her progress, then he laughed. 'It must be life and death, lassie. That, or love.'

'It's love,' Leah breathed, her eyes full of entreaty.

'Then off ye go, and *gie it laldy*.' The man grinned as he eased her in front of him, then she was pushed forward by the person in front of her, and the next, and the next until she was gazing at Dan, filling his arms.

'You can't go to China. I won't let you,' she blurted.

'But I thought—' Dan's expression was confused.

'That house you wanted to look at, Speybank... Please, I want you to buy it.'

'But you said you didn't want—' Dan was suddenly hopeful. They were oblivious of the crowd who were watching with increasing interest.

Leah took a breath. 'It's the place where – what did you say?' She recalled the exact words. 'Where we can plan a future one day – we can fill it with happiness and fun and children...'

Dan's eyes shone behind the same round glasses he'd worn when she first met him. He was smiling. 'Really?'

'Don't go back to China, Dan. Please come back with me – come back to the castle, to Rosemuir.'

'Are you sure?'

'I'm totally sure, more than I've been sure of anything in my life.' Leah was breathless. She'd been holding herself back for far too long, but now the words tumbled out more quickly than she'd intended. She could hardly believe she'd spoken what was in her heart so eagerly.

Dan was still staring. 'Do you mean it?'

'I mean it. I do.'

'She means it.' The large man behind them called out, 'Go on, gie him a wee winch, hen.'

'He means give him a kiss,' the woman with the orange suitcases yelled.

Leah threw her arms around Dan, almost knocking him over with enthusiasm, kissing his lips. She felt his arms close around her as he kissed her back, then there was a trickle of applause from behind, and when Leah turned, flushed and breathless, everyone in the queue was smiling and clapping their hands.

* * *

Agnes wondered how she could push past the line of English guards who would be on duty in the courtyard, to reach Cam. She clasped her hands together and her lips moved in prayer. She begged for a way to get to the man she loved more than her own life, to feel him fill her arms.

She must not sleep. She would need to watch the fire. She would need to wait, to choose the exact moment just before dawn broke, before the grey light grew too strong and servants woke and began to go about their daily business. She needed to put her plan into action while Effie slept.

Agnes prayed to God for His help. Her heart hammered in her chest; she was afraid of what might come to pass, but she had to act, for Cam's sake. She pleaded that he would be well, and that she could get to him in the cell above the chapel. She would need to use her wits, and she would do whatever it took, she swore it to herself, to God. But there were risks.

Agnes took a deep breath. By this time tomorrow, it would be decided. She and Cam would be together, riding away from Ravenscraig through the snow towards the forest.

Or it would be over for them both.

47

It was before dawn and the fire was a glimmer in the grate. Effie was curled up, snuffling quietly. At the far end of the kitchen, shadows of three hovering guards loomed, immobile. Holding her breath, Agnes slithered into the protective hulk of the hearth, bunched her skirts and heaved herself inside the chimney. It took several attempts to find a foothold, then she scrabbled upwards, reaching for the thick ridge in the stones. Her fingers found the hilt of a dagger and she tugged it free. Pressing her legs and back against the chimney to support herself, Agnes felt the chainmail armour, the coif, the hauberk. She'd only need one: the other could stay where it was.

Silently, holding her breath in her throat, she slid down the dusty chimney, conscious that her clothes were now covered in soot. Piling logs onto the fire, watching them crackle and catch, she moved stealthily, wrapping the armour and the dagger in her blanket. Agnes reached the table on silent feet, opening the drawer, grasping the handfasting goblet, picking up the bronze ewer with the hinged lid that held water and a loaf of bread. She placed them in an empty pail and shuffled forward.

'Who goes there?' A gruff voice came from the darkness.

'I go to get water from the well. It is almost dawn.' Agnes bowed her head and hurried past the guards, down the corridor and into the courtyard. There were still signs of the battle in the darkness: piled bodies, bloodstained snow. Agnes caught her breath; the air was cold as she hurried along. It was not difficult to pass the guard on the gate; he knew she fetched water each morning, and he nodded as she darted past.

Looking around her, Agnes drew a bucket of water and ice from the well and shivered as she twisted to wash the back of her dress, rubbing the soot until it came away, leaving a wet grimy patch. She washed her face, shook her apron, then she tucked the blanket under her arm, the pail in one hand, the cup and ewer and the loaf of bread in the other. She scuttled back to the castle, passing the guard, who gave her a slight nod.

Her heart was in her throat. She placed the pail on the ground, where it would remain awhile. She adjusted her clothes and her cap, approaching the chapel door humbly, as if respectful to the guards. Her luck was in; Elyas was on guard with the other soldier who had watched her tend to young Digory's wounds. She gave a slight curtsey. 'I have been sent with food and water for the prisoner.'

The soldier took the loaf from her hands, ripping a crust, pushing it into his mouth and handing her the remainder. 'He won't need food...'

Agnes tried to calm her breathing: Cam *was* upstairs in the cell. She turned pleading eyes on Elyas. 'I was sent from the kitchen...'

Elyas's face was full of concern. 'Why are your clothes wet, Agnes?'

'I slipped and fell in the snow...'

'Go back to the kitchen and get on with your work,' the other soldier said gruffly.

Agnes met Elyas's eyes. 'It is no matter to ye if the poor man has a drink of water... and a blanket to warm him. It's bitterly cold.'

Elyas looked at his companion. 'It harms us not to be kind.' He indicated the door. 'Go in, Agnes. He is one of your king's warriors. It may be the last kindness he receives.'

The other soldier was unimpressed. 'Be quick about it.'

'Thanking ye.' Agnes bowed her head, ducking beneath Elyas's arm, opening the heavy door. Then she was standing in the empty chapel. It was dark except for a shaft of white light from the narrow window; she heard the fluttering of wings in the rafters. Agnes's heart thumped, but her feet were swift as she ran up the stone staircase into the chamber above. Then she saw him, his back to her, collapsed on the cold floor behind a huge metal grille. Light streamed through another vertical window, harsh sunlight brightening the gloom. She rushed to the grille and rattled it hard. A small wooden opening in the centre, a hole through which food was passed was locked, sealing the grille against the stone wall. Agnes gripped the square metal bars and whispered, 'Cam.'

He moved slowly, easing himself to his feet, and as he saw her, his face filled with a mixture of happiness and anxiety. 'Agnes – it is not safe for ye here...'

His tunic was torn and one arm hung by his side, exposed and wounded. Agnes caught her breath; there was so much blood on his shoulder. His face was bloodied too, his lip swollen.

Cam placed his hand over hers through the bars. 'My love...'

'There's no time to waste.' Tugging the blanket from beneath her arm, she unravelled the contents quickly. 'Here, look inside – a dagger, armour. Take them...'

'I dinnae understand.'

'Use the dagger to escape. Kill the guards, set yourself free. Put on the armour, steal a horse.' Agnes passed the dagger through the grille and he held it up in his strong hand, light glinting on the blade.

Cam slumped against the grille. 'I am wounded...'

Reaching for the ewer and the cup, Agnes poured water and he pressed his mouth against the bars as she held the goblet to his lips, watching him drink thirstily. His hand covered hers, dirty and crusted in blood.

He extended his fingers, brushing the skin of her cheek. 'I have thought of nothing but your face these last nights...'

'Ye must escape.' Agnes's voice was pleading. 'Take the dagger, fight.'

He nodded weakly. 'Aye.'

'When the guard comes, tell him ye need to confess in the chapel, tell him ye are dying – when he approaches, cut his throat, take the keys and the armour, leave on a horse. Ye can do it.'

'I cannae leave if ye are still here...'

'Ye can come back for me. We'll find a way.'

His face was tired, his eyes half closed in pain.

Agnes leaned against the grille, feeling his cold skin against hers, pressing her lips against his. They were warm. He kissed her back and she searched for his soul, but if it was there, it was too weak to meet hers. Something in her heart fluttered with fear and she almost lost her nerve. Then she whispered, 'Cam... ye must try harder. Hold the dagger tight. Be ready. If the soldiers should come, ye must act.'

'I will.' He seemed to gather strength from her.

Then there were footsteps on the stairs. Agnes's eyes grew wide. 'It's a chance ye must take...'

Elyas and his companion were in the chamber, holding swords aloft.

The other soldier said, 'Why do you tarry here?'

Agnes's hands flew to her mouth, her voice high with worry. 'Oh sir, the poor man is breathing his last breath and he longs to confess. Please – bring him to the chapel. Allow him this one last kindness, to pray in the house of God.'

'We don't have authority—' the soldier began, but Elyas's eyes were full of compassion.

'English or Scots, there is but one God.' He nodded towards Agnes. 'We will take him to the chapel, as ye have asked.'

The soldier was unconvinced, but he brought out the keys, twisting the lock in the small wooden door, and the grille sprang open. Then Cam was moving, the dagger clutched in his fist, grasping the guard by the throat, slicing through his flesh. Agnes watched in horror as the English soldier fell from his grip: she had never seen Cam fight and, although she knew he was feared, she was shocked by his sudden speed and strength. Then she remembered Elyas and pushed him hard against the wall, hissing, 'Stay ye there if ye dinnae want the same treatment...'

Cam had her by the arm, tugging her down the stone steps. They were in the chapel, pushing the door wide, feeling the cold winter blast of the wind against their faces, rushing out into the snow. Then Agnes reached for Cam's hand and caught her breath.

They were surrounded by a group of English soldiers, ten, twelve of them, pointing swords. Cam hesitated for a second, then there was a deep sound in his throat, the roar of a cornered animal, and he hurled himself at the soldiers, the dagger in his hand. He had taken two before they were aware of what he was doing; he had a third by the neck when he was cut down. Agnes saw a wound open in his chest, and his eyes stayed on her as the soldiers pulled him to his knees.

It was hard for Agnes to take it all in; Cam, slumped on the ground, then dragged up, blood on the snow, the twisted faces of the soldiers staring at her, their expressions full of hatred. Then she raised her chin and saw that behind them there were two figures perched high on horseback, a stallion and a palfrey. Bròccan and Effie had side bags packed: they were leaving. Effie wore a beautiful cloak trimmed with fur, clasped with a metal brooch. Her face was miserable as she said, 'I saw ye take the things from the chimney,

Agnes. They were mine, mine and Bròccan's, and ye stole them. I cannae believe you'd do that to me.'

Bròccan sneered. 'My Effie is a clever girl. She told me everything and I told the English soldiers what ye were doing and I bought our freedom. We're going to Inverness to start a new life.'

'Ye hurt me...' Effie sniffed, a tear on her cheek. Her voice was sulky as a child's. 'I thought ye loved me and that I was your true sister but ye betrayed me because ye love him more than me.' She glanced towards Cam and gave a loud sob. 'Bròccan told me about the hand joining and the cup ye hid in secret. Ye kept it all from me – ye don't care at all for me now – ye think I'm just foolish daffin' Effie, but Bròccan said we will show ye I'm no fool...'

'I always cared for ye – I was your true sister—' Agnes began.

'I thought it was so once, but ye were lying to me all the time.' Effie wiped her face with the back of her hand. 'Bròccan told me to follow ye and I did. I watched ye go to the well, then the chapel. Agnes, he showed me what ye really are – ye care only for the man who lies bleeding on the ground, never for me. And ye have broken my heart – ye kept the truth from me because ye hate me. But Bròccan will take care of me and he tells me ye have what ye deserve now, and so do I.'

'Effie, that's not true.'

'Bròccan said ye would say that. I am sorry for ye, Agnes – I thought we would stay together and you'd look after me, but I cannae trust ye now...' Effie snivelled again, her face crumpling with fresh tears as she leaned towards Bròccan for comfort. He patted her hand once, his face flushed with triumph. He looked Agnes up and down for a final time and smirked, pleased with himself, with Effie's repetition of his words. Agnes watched as Bròccan urged his horse forward across the courtyard, Effie behind him, looking sadly over her shoulder. She heard the clack of hooves as they both disappeared through the castle gate, the portcullis raised. Her face was covered in tears; she couldn't speak. Then she gazed at Cam, her expression tender.

Cam met her eyes. 'Do not fear, my love. Our souls will meet once more. I will search for ye and we will be together.' She followed his glance as he watched a raven perch on the crenelated wall. 'Just like the raven, Agnes, I will never be far. I will watch, I will wait for ye.'

'Aye, we will meet again.' She made no move to wipe away the tears. 'I will find ye, Cam, if it takes forever.'

A soldier barked an order. 'Take the woman away. Lock her upstairs. We'll show the Scots how we deal with traitors.' He pointed to Cam: 'And you know what to do with him. String him up, cut him open, let his broken body serve as an example to others in the castle. He will remain there for a week, then we will throw the corpse in the water for the fish to feed on. We will show these people no mercy.'

Something snapped in Agnes then, and she began to struggle. Two soldiers grabbed her, desperate, as they tried to tug her upstairs. She screamed Cam's name just once as she saw the men loop a rope around his neck, dragging him away through the snow, leaving a long red trail across the white. Then the chapel door was slammed shut and she was hurried upstairs, her feet hardly touching the stone steps. At the top, the soldiers pushed her into the chamber, hard fingers digging into the flesh of her shoulder, and she was hurled hard into the cell, the grille pulled closed with a clang and the key turned.

Elyas stepped forward shamefaced. 'What do you do here?'

A guard glanced down at the slumped body on the ground, the soldier Cam had killed, and he turned angrily to Elyas. 'The woman is to be locked in and a wall built around the cell. She is not to be given food or water.'

'But she will die of thirst.' Elyas was horrified.

'She is a traitor,' the guard replied. 'King Edward shows no mercy.'

Elyas held his sword limply, staring as more guards arrived, trudging up the stairs on heavy feet. He watched helplessly as they began to build the base of a wall of heavy stones, pushing one on top of another as Agnes huddled in the corner, her face in her hands, trembling with fear.

As the day passed, more stones were piled one upon another before her eyes, higher and higher until she could no longer see who heaped them there, just rough hands stacking more stones. Agnes shivered in the cold, her back against the castle wall, the high window allowing in harsh light and icy air.

That night, the wall was still not complete and Agnes crouched in darkness, the moon's frail beam a long shadow on the floor. As dawn's grey light filtered weakly in the room, she heard the harsh scraping sound as the wall rose towards the ceiling: the men had returned with more stones. Agnes cried out, 'Am I not to be given water?'

She heard a dull grunt from behind the wall and another kinder voice, Elyas's, saying, 'Will you leave a small gap? I can pass her some water in this cup.'

'She is to be denied both food and water,' a voice replied and Agnes shivered with fear.

The last stones were lifted in place and she heard Elyas plead, 'Leave a tiny gap, I beg you. I wish to put something in the wall for her.'

'She is allowed nothing.'

'It is a poem I am writing, a few words for her.'

There was no reply, just the sound of hard rasping and pounding as the final stones were set in place. Then there was silence.

Agnes screamed as loudly as she could. Then she screamed

again. No words came back to her, no sound but her own frantic breathing. She tried again, 'Have mercy – help me.' Her voice echoed in the air. Her final cry, 'Elyas?' was met with silence. The men had gone: she was alone.

Agnes rushed to the grille, pushing her hands through the holes between the metal, reaching for the stones with her fingers, scrabbling against them with her nails to loosen them, to make the tiniest opening so that she could see into the chamber. But her fingers bled and she cowered on the floor, staring up at the slice of light. Beyond the window, she knew that the loch was smooth and dark, and in several days, it would hold Cam's broken body in its depths. She recalled how she had first seen him swimming there during the summer months, his head smooth and sleek as a seal's. She had seen him rise from the loch and she couldn't breathe, she couldn't tug her eyes away.

Now he was gone and she was sealed behind cold grey stones. She was thirsty already, a thistle in need of rain, and she cried out again for help, but there was no one to hear her. She was exhausted, racked with the cold and the numbing agony of loss and sadness.

Then she remembered Cam's final promise, and hers to him: their souls would meet again. She closed her eyes, her head filled with fearful thoughts. How would they ever find each other?

Agnes wept, her body shaking with sobs. She realised that she'd been wrong: a promise was simply air, words from the soul, spoken with love, then it was gone. Like life, a promise did not last forever: it lasted only for the time that it was spoken. Agnes had lived and breathed for Cam. Soon, she would live and breathe no more. She would die here in the cell, and then her spirit would seek him, but it was too late. She had known it during their last kiss; she had searched for his soul, her mouth against his, but it had not been there. He had already gone.

She knew the truth now, cold and comfortless as the wind that funnelled through the high window from the loch and chilled her to the bone. Their love had been strong, it had been life itself, but there was nothing left of it now.

She would not see him again.

48

It was Friday morning, a cold January day, heavy clouds low over the loch and a wind that blew snow from the crenelated wall, sifting it like icing sugar. Leah and Zoe watched through the window as Christie and several men from his team wearing yellow hard hats strode through the courtyard and into the southwest wing, carrying metal poles of scaffolding and wooden planks. Dan joined them moments later, wearing a hard hat and tartan-framed spectacles, waving a hand, presumably overseeing their work. Mirren hovered in the courtyard, urging them to be careful.

Leah sighed. 'I wish she'd come in for a coffee and leave them to it. Poor Mirren. She looks so worried.'

Zoe raised an eyebrow. 'I'm worried too. It feels so strange to be sending builders into the chamber, breaking down walls and making changes.'

'It does, but we have to,' Leah said. 'Dan wants the space renovated, Mariusz and Jordan's wedding is just a month away and there's building to get done, painting, stained-glass windows to install.'

'Dan's completely behind your plans for the castle then?' Zoe asked.

'He is.' Leah's expression was dreamy. 'You know he's had the offer accepted on Speybank? He could be moved in by spring.'

'That's wonderful. What about the castle? Will you go with him? Will there be another caretaker?'

'I'm going to take my time, but maybe I'll move in with him this summer. Dan's going to ask Christie to make the main gate more secure, a solid lockable entrance as it would have been centuries ago with a portcullis, and then Mirren will be in charge of the whole place in terms of its day-to-day running. I'll just concentrate on weddings and tours...'

Zoe poured coffee from a jug. 'You'll be busy...'

'Frantic.' Leah beamed. 'I'm meeting Anne-Marie Chapman on Wednesday, the historical writer who came on my tour. She wants to use Ravenscraig as the base for a new novel set in 1300. And I have a couple coming next week to look around the castle – they need a wedding venue in May.'

'The castle is perfect for weddings,' Zoe murmured.

'It is,' Leah agreed. 'Dan was daydreaming the other day and he said we should have ours in the Caribbean on a beach. I told him not to get ahead of himself – I haven't said yes yet – but the castle definitely has a special place in my heart.'

'It's all worked out so well.' Zoe gazed through the window. Christie was carrying a sledgehammer into the chapel.

'You're staying?' Leah asked, although she knew the answer.

'I am... I'll move into Christie's and I'll keep the flat in Birmingham for a while, see what happens. It'll be nice for weekends away...' Zoe smiled as she met her sister's eyes. 'Scotland is in my heart too.'

Her gaze was tugged back to the window, watching Christie emerge from the chapel, striding towards his van in the car park beyond the main gate. She thought again how handsome he was. She found herself reliving a special moment from the previous night, locked in each other's arms beneath the warmth of the duvet, whispering plans for the future. She'd privately thought that a brother or sister for Daisy might be nice at some point, but she'd keep the idea to herself for a while.

Leah finished her coffee with a gulp. 'It's ten o'clock. We should go down. Ally Wylie will be here soon. She texted me before she left Stirling. She's so excited to see what happens when we open up the chamber.'

Zoe sat up with a jerk, suddenly nervous. 'What do you think will be in there?'

'Nothing, I suppose, but Ally has a theory. The MacDonalds raided so many castles, and she thinks the chamber might have been walled up to hide family treasures. There might be all sorts of artefacts from the period behind the wall – pottery, jewellery. Who knows?'

'Maybe,' Zoe said quietly. She felt her heart flutter. Memories of the frail ghost hovering in the chapel doorway returned to her, and again she had an enveloping sense of sadness.

Leah met her sister's eyes: she thought of the gentle hand stroking her hair as she had sobbed into the pillow in her room. Zoe remembered the intense sense of desperation and heartache that had accompanied the ghost's presence in the courtyard, and the hollow voice she'd heard on the landing. She recalled the words, singing softly.

> *O where are ye gone, my Scottish warrior?*
> *'Twixt the thistle and the mist o' the morn...*

Leah reached across the table and took Zoe's hand. 'Is it time? Should we go down now?'

Zoe nodded. She had no idea what they would find behind the

wall in the upstairs chamber, but her heart had already started to knock with anticipation.

* * *

Ally Wylie was walking briskly from the car park, silver hair tumbling below her shoulders. She held out a hand. 'Leah. This is really quite special, isn't it?'

Leah squeezed her fingers. 'I'm actually really nervous...' She indicated Zoe and Mirren, who had just joined them. 'This is my sister Zoe, and Mirren here is—'

'I'm Mirren Logan,' Mirren said firmly. She was carrying several dried flowers in her arms now. 'A Logan woman has always put flowers in the chapel, and I want to do that today.' She glanced towards Leah, her face expressionless. 'I want to say some words in prayer before we go upstairs to the chamber.'

Leah inclined her head in agreement. 'I think that would be the right thing.'

Mirren led the way inside, followed by Leah, Ally and Zoe. They were joined by Christie and Dan. Mirren placed the flowers on the hard ground, in the slice of light from the narrow high window. Leah glanced at Zoe, who clasped her hands together and Leah did the same, bowing her head.

Mirren's voice was a low monotone, the rustling of leaves in the wind.

Deep peace of the running waves to you,
Deep peace of the flowing air,
Deep peace of the quiet earth,
Deep peace of the shining stars.
May the road rise to meet you;
May the wind be always at your back;
May the sun shine warm upon your face;

May the rain fall softly on your fields.
May Nature hold you in the hollow of her hand.

Silence filled the chapel, a muffled sadness, and there was a cold gust of buffeting wind.

Zoe glanced up towards the vertical window. A raven fluttered, perching high, outlined against the white sky; its beak opened and it made a low throaty sound.

Then Dan said, 'Shall we go up?'

Christie gave everyone a hard hat to wear and he led the way up the twisting stone steps. It was dark in the chamber, except for the light from several torches. Christie and his team had placed wooden planks on the floor and a four feet square of scaffolding had been erected.

Leah caught her breath. 'I didn't expect all this...'

'We'll make a mess in here,' Christie said by way of explanation. 'The guys will come in when we've finished and take the stones away. I'm not sure whether the wall will come down easily, or whether it will be a crowbar and chisel job.'

'I want to make this space special,' Dan agreed. 'We're going to put new floors down, the walls will be white stone, and there will be beautiful windows.'

'There might be some interesting artefacts behind the wall,' Ally Wylie was visibly excited. 'I know it all belongs to you, Daniel, but the university would be in your debt if we could examine a few things forensically...'

'Let's see what we find,' Dan suggested.

Christie was already climbing up the small scaffolding, a chisel and hammer in his hand, and was chipping away at the stones. There was a clatter as crumbling rubble thundered onto the wooden planks, scattering across the floor.

'It won't be too hard to bring the wall down. It's very old, and not well built,' Christie called from above.

Leah met her sister's eyes nervously and Zoe slid her arm around her as Christie chipped away again at the stone wall. Ally leaned forward excitedly, but Mirren took a step back, her expression troubled.

Christie hammered again and stones began to fall, a shower of dust and debris tumbling, and the small group lurched away. There was the clatter and rush of falling stones as the wall disintegrated, loose gravel rattling against wooden planks.

Dan said, 'I bet it took longer to put that wall up than it's going to take to come down.'

Christie pulled a torch from his pocket, shining a beam into the large gap between the stones. 'There's a grille in here – bars.'

Ally frowned. 'Perhaps it was for safekeeping? The MacDonalds raids—'

'No...' Christie twisted to call over his shoulder. 'I don't think so.' He chipped away as the hole gaped, then he muttered, 'What's this lodged in the wall? Some sort of scroll?'

'May I see?' Ally couldn't keep the excitement from her voice.

Christie swung down from the scaffolding and handed the parchment paper to Ally. 'It looks like it has writing on it.'

Ally took it from him, her expert hands handling it gently. The chamber was silent as she took glasses from her handbag, pushed them on her face and opened the roll carefully.

'It is writing, very old, but I can make it out...' She paused, frowning. 'I think it's a poem of some sort...'

'What does it say?'

Ally began to read in an accent between English and French.

> *For thogh I wepe of teres ful a tyne*
> *Yet may that wo myn herte nat confounde*
> *Agnesse, a younge woman ther was,*
> *In fredom and curteisye, trouthe and honour.*
> *Ful worthy was she...*

'What does it mean?' Dan asked.

'Oh, what a find...' Ally puzzled over the paper for a moment. 'It's a poem from an English soldier to a Scottish woman. She was called Agnes.'

'Agnes,' Mirren repeated her name quietly.

'What else does it say?' Leah asked.

'I'll need a moment to work it out. He was clearly in love with her.' Ally moved closer to the tall window. 'Let me have a few minutes with this.'

Christie was chipping away again, a dull thud of his hammer followed by the rush of falling stones. He paused, raising his voice. 'It's a cell – a small prison.'

'Of course.' Mirren's voice was low. 'That's where she is.'

Zoe's skin was ice as she felt Leah's hand in hers.

More pebbles fell, even more, then Mirren whispered, 'She's been in there all this time.'

Dan leaned forward. 'Can you get inside yet, Christie? Can you see anything?'

'I'd have to move the grille out of the way – it's so dark in there apart from the high window. It's just an empty room, dirt floor, rubble... Hang on a moment – what's this?' Christie wriggled inside the large hole he had made. His voice came from within, a dull echo. 'I'm inside. It's a tiny cell; the floor's just dirt and there's hardly any space in here, probably enough for two, three people to stand...' He paused for a moment. There was a muffled groan, then silence.

'What is it?' Dan called.

'It's her...' Mirren said.

Christie took a while to answer. When his voice came, it was hushed. 'It's a pile of bones, a skeleton, quite intact. It's huddled in the corner in the shadows.'

'Agnes...' Mirren muttered again.

'I'm coming out,' Christie said quickly, and he emerged from the hole backwards, clambering down from the small scaffolding.

When he reached the small group, he took a deep breath, slumping against the wall, closing his eyes against what he had seen.

Zoe and Leah clutched each other's hand.

'I wonder what she did...' Dan frowned.

'I think I've worked it out.' Ally's voice was suddenly clear as she emerged from beneath the far window. 'This love poem...'

'What does it say?' Leah asked.

Ally held up the parchment. 'Our young woman Agnes was quite a character. The poem is from an English soldier who signs himself Elyas Fletcher. He was in love with Agnes, but his feelings weren't returned.'

'She wouldn't love an English soldier,' Mirren said.

'No, the poem says she loved one of The Bruce's warriors, who was captured and killed here, his body thrown in the loch,' Ally explained. 'Agnes attempted to rescue him from this cell and failed, and for her troubles she was walled in here without food or water – a practice known as immurement.'

'That's awful.' Leah breathed.

'How long would she have lasted?' Zoe asked.

Ally was thoughtful. 'It would have taken days for Agnes to die – ten, twenty – who knows? Elyas has written so beautifully about her courage and strength. There's a final stanza, tacked on at the end, explaining that he came back to place the poem in the walls in her memory after the English army had left. His last lines are so sad.

> *The teares from myne eyen let fall,*
> *Agnesse, thyne soule wente to the King of grace...*

'Can we go outside?' Zoe felt dizzy. The air in the room was thick with dust, her legs were suddenly weak and she thought she might faint.

'That's a good idea,' Dan agreed.

They walked slowly down the steps, out into the courtyard.

Zoe swallowed gulps of cold air. The wind was in her face and she began to feel better. She leaned against the wall of the chapel.

Christie put an arm around her and said, 'Are you all right? I feel shaken too.'

'I didn't expect that,' Zoe whispered. 'To find her there...'

Dan took Leah's hand. 'Are you okay?'

Leah shook her head. Her eyes shone with tears.

'You found what you needed to find.' Mirren gazed towards the loch and the wind lifted her hair, blowing it across her face. 'She was imprisoned for seven hundred years, but now we can set her free.'

'Indeed. I'd like to take the parchment away and look at it properly, under the right conditions, if that's okay,' Ally said. 'I'll have to make some calls to the appropriate people, ask them to come straight over.' She turned to Dan. 'I'd like to take the skeleton to Stirling and look at it in our lab. It might make for some really fascinating research and...' She glanced at Leah. 'We'll have to confirm that it's a young woman, our Agnes.'

'No,' Mirren said simply.

'She belongs here,' Leah added, a cold tear glistening on her cheek.

'She does.' Zoe closed her eyes tightly. The image was in her mind, a young woman huddled in the corner, weak, alone, cold and terrified.

'She'd be looked after at Stirling...' Ally tried hopefully. 'There's the legal side of it – forensics, reports. I'd take care of it. If you leave it with me, it shouldn't take long.'

'You're right, it needs to be done correctly,' Dan said. 'Thanks, Ally. You'll bring her back here soon?'

'I promise,' Ally agreed.

'Should we bury her in the castle grounds then?' Christie suggested. 'A proper funeral.'

'Not in the same place where they held her captive,' Mirren said. 'We can't do that.'

'No, I know what we'll do,' Dan said firmly. 'In the poem, it tells us that her warrior was put into the loch. Agnes will want to be with him. We should lay her to rest there.'

'You're right, Dan,' Leah agreed.

Ally nodded. 'I'll take care of the loose ends, make a few calls. Then it's over to you.'

'Whatever it takes to bring her home,' Dan said.

Zoe watched as the raven swooped down, landing on the crenelated wall. The wind ruffled its feathers as it turned a beady eye to stare blankly in her direction. Its beak opened in a throaty caw, then it flew towards the loch, skimming the surface, and was gone.

49

Dan arranged the funeral for a Sunday morning. The casket was made from willow, the lid left loose, and Agnes was inside, wrapped in a silk Scottish flag. Christie and Dan carried her to the speed-boat, followed by Leah, Zoe and Mirren, as John Aitken started the engine.

Zoe let the wind take her hair. She was shaking inside a thick coat, but it felt right to feel the breeze blow fresh against her face. There was snow on the mountains, more snow in the wind's bite and the heavy clouds promised a flurry soon. Zoe gasped as the boat tilted upwards, cutting through the inky waters of the loch. She felt Christie reach for her hand, warming it in his, and she offered him a sad smile. Then the loch filled her gaze, the still dark-ness of it, and the image of Agnes came to her again just as it had outside the chapel. She'd have been small at the end, shrunken and frail, gasping for breath, for water. Her arms would have been weak and empty. She'd have longed for her warrior to fill them, to warm her shivering body. She'd have breathed in once, closed her eyes and never breathed out again.

Leah tucked her arm through the crook of Dan's elbow, snuggling closer, resting her head against his sturdy shoulder. She'd known sadness, depression, but now she was thriving: she loved Dan and he loved her back. There could be nothing better in the world. She thought of Agnes and understood at once why her spirit had not been able to rest.

Leah gazed at Mirren, who rested a hand on the lid of the coffin, the other hand gripping the rail of the speedboat as she stared ahead, her eyes glassy. Once Agnes was at peace, Mirren would find some peace too. Leah promised herself that she would make a friend of Mirren, that she would make her feel welcome in the castle.

Overhead, several birds soared, circling. The mountains stood in the distance, hunched white giants, and Leah turned back to look at the castle, sombre and grey in the pale light. She wondered about the people who'd lived at Ravenscraig so many centuries ago, their lives each day, how they'd worked, eaten, spent their evenings, loved, mourned. The village of Rosemuir had been part of the castle then, and Leah imagined the villagers in low, smoke-filled huts. She wondered about Agnes's life, if she'd been a servant, how she'd met her warrior and fallen in love.

She sighed: life was about discovering who you were, finding love in one form or another, holding on with both hands. For her now, it was about a future, hope and happiness. It had not been that way for Agnes.

John slowed the boat down, bringing the engine to a dull rattle before switching it off, then all was quiet. The boat bobbed and lurched, the water lapping gently against the helm. Then John spoke to Dan. 'This is the middle of the loch. We're here.'

Dan looked around for help. 'Should we say something?'

'I will.' Mirren took a breath. She placed both palms on the casket and muttered, 'Agnes, it is time to let go now. *Réidh ri Dia.*'

Leah glanced at Dan. 'What does that mean?'

'It's Gaelic.' Mirren's lips moved again. 'It means, at peace with God.'

Everyone closed their eyes for a moment.

Zoe whispered, 'May she rest in peace...'

Christie and Dan took their cue from Mirren, lifting the willow casket, easing it across the side of the boat, leaning it over to lower the flag and its contents into the loch. The swirl of blue with shining white diagonals plummeted straight away, the material darkening, still visible for a moment beneath the surface of the dull water, then it was gone. Dan and Christie replaced the casket in the boat and breathed out.

Leah closed her eyes. 'I hope she will be able to find some rest.'

Zoe exhaled slowly. She stared into the water, imagining the flag unfurling and Agnes whole, swimming away, pushing strongly through the depths, her eyes open, searching, finding her lost love. She wished it with all her heart. Of course, it would never happen: Agnes's bones would lie on the bottom of the loch. But at least she was free now.

Through tears, Zoe murmured, 'I hope you find your warrior. I hope he's waiting for you.'

The boat lurched as John switched on the engine and turned to the other passengers and smiled. Then they were in motion, speeding back towards the castle, slicing through calm waters as the first flakes of snow began to tumble.

* * *

That evening, they sat in The Canny Man, staring into untouched glasses of Scotch, saying little. They were each thinking of Agnes, lying at the bottom of the loch after centuries of being hidden behind a stone wall. The sadness of it sat on their shoulders like grief. Then Dan said, 'We should probably drink a toast.'

Zoe agreed, 'We should.'

Leah held up the whisky to the light, watching the gold liquid gleam. 'To Agnes.'

Three voices chorused, 'To Agnes,' and they tipped their glasses at the same time, tasting the fire of the whisky.

They were quiet for a moment, lost in their own thoughts again.

Christie said, 'I'll start the work on rebuilding the southwest wing tomorrow.' He glanced towards Dan. 'The sooner it's started, the sooner it's done.'

Leah took a breath. 'Agnes's chapel,' she murmured. 'That's what we'll call it.'

'We will,' Zoe agreed. 'It's the place where she'll be remembered.'

'We could incorporate the design of a thistle into the walls of the chamber,' Christie suggested. 'I'm sure it wouldn't be difficult to have one or two carved from wood and placed high up.'

'I want her reflected in the stained-glass windows too,' Leah said quietly. 'Perhaps we could get someone to design one.'

Dan cradled his glass. 'I wonder what she looked like,'

Zoe sat upright. 'Remember the goblet, the one with the two figures side by side? We should have that design in stained glass, Agnes and her warrior together in the chapel.'

'It was a handfasting mug, I think.' Leah pressed her lips together. 'We should have several of them made, copies of the original for handfasting ceremonies. And our windows will be coloured glass depicting Agnes and her man, their hands joined, just as they would have been when they were married all those years ago.'

'It's right to have that image in the chapel.' Dan took Leah's hand and kissed her fingers. 'A celebration of their love, every time another couple celebrates theirs.'

Zoe's eyes filled with tears again. 'I keep thinking about her, out there in the loch. I hope she can breathe again.'

Leah agreed. 'I want to believe that.'

'We should all go back to the castle,' Christie said quietly. He touched Zoe's face with gentle fingertips. 'You're tired.'

'I am.' She drained the last mouthful of whisky in her glass. 'We all are.'

'It's been a long day.' Leah turned to Dan. 'Shall we walk back now?'

Dan was on his feet, holding out his hand. 'I think so.'

They stepped outside into the swirling flakes, white against the darkness of the night sky. In the distance, the castle walls glimmered, gold lights illuminating the courtyard. Leah and Dan walked a few paces in front, their heads down against the blizzard, silently slogging through the frozen mounds underfoot. Zoe tucked her arm through Christie's and he returned her smile. The four of them blundered into the spinning blizzard, feeling the bite of the wind through their coats.

Then they were at Ravenscraig, their feet sinking into deep drifts as they passed the old well, crossing the hump where the drawbridge would have been, beneath the arched gateway and into the courtyard where snow tumbled in the glow of the upturned lights. They stopped all at once. Zoe caught her breath.

The door to the chapel was wide open, banging in the wind, gloomy shadows shifting inside. They knew they had left it locked. In the gleam of the lights, they could make out faint footprints, indentations of light feet that seemed to stop halfway across the courtyard.

Leah frowned, puzzled. 'I don't understand. Who's been here?'

Zoe took a deep breath. 'It's Agnes.' She met her sister's eyes. 'She's gone now. The courtyard is quieter, calmer... I think she's found peace.'

EPILOGUE

Leah woke early on the morning of February the fourteenth and rushed to the window in pyjamas. There was a heavy mist over the loch, floating and shifting, a silver-grey phantom. She stared up towards the sky, a whitewash of sweeping brushstrokes, the peaks of the mountains crested with snow. She sighed. 'The haze will burn off and the sun will come out. It's a beautiful day for a wedding.'

Dan rolled over, his voice muffled with sleep. 'Come back to bed. We can talk about weddings in the warm.'

She smiled. 'I have things to do. It's a busy day. Mariusz is asleep in the Robert de Brus room and I need to change the bedding. He's been fretting about today all week. Jordan will be here at ten o'clock from Rosemuir with his brother. Bradley's the most nervous best man in the world. I've told him they can use the Elizabeth de Burgh room to get ready. I've other rooms to check, sheets to turn down in the Princess Marjorie and the Earl of Atholl... The caterers are coming later this morning and Zoe has promised to pop over to help. I have the finishing touches to do outside, flowers to arrange, and the wedding is at two.'

Dan said, 'When you move to Speybank this summer, we should do up this flat and turn it into two more guest bedrooms.'

'We will.' Leah was pulling on her dressing gown, hovering by the door on her way to the shower. 'I already have names for them – The McNair room, in honour of the original castle owners, and the Logan suite, after Mirren's family.' She paused, a smile on her face. Several months ago, she'd had no job, no direction – she'd been completely lost. She marvelled at how far she'd come in such a short time, organising weddings, naming new rooms in the castle. She gazed at Dan and her heart filled with happiness.

'Mmm.' Dan was half-asleep. 'Come back to bed when you've had a shower. It's Valentine's Day.'

Leah was almost persuaded. 'But I have a wedding to organise...'

'And another one to plan,' Dan said from beneath the pillow. 'Ours will be next year, I'm sure of it...'

Leah laughed. 'You're too used to clicking your fingers and getting things straight away, Mr Moneybags. You have to ask me properly first – and I have to say yes...' Leah winked as she disappeared towards the bathroom. 'And if I did say yes, I think I'd get married here in Ravenscraig.'

'Whatever you want,' Dan muttered before drifting back to sleep.

* * *

By one o'clock, the morning's flurry of frantic activity had slowed, now clockwork smooth. Abigail Laing, smart in a cream coat, gloves and hat took her position at the car park, greeting guests with a smile, directing them towards the main entrance. Mirren was standing outside Agnes's Chapel, wearing a wide-brimmed hat, a flower-print dress and a thistle-embroidered shawl, welcoming every new arrival with a smile. Inside the chapel, the best man, Jordan's brother Bradley, grinned apprehensively and showed people to their seats. Zoe and

Christie stood together, Daisy next to them in a pretty dress, gazing up at the newly wooden vaulted ceiling, the bright sconces from which candles shed golden light, the white flagstone floor and the cream pews. Christie had done an incredible job with the chapel; he'd maintained the authentic character and the solemnness of a place of worship. He had found reclaimed wood and it had been carved with thistles and integrated within the stonework. Leah had filled the space with pots of sweet-smelling spring flowers and tall candles in glass holders. But all eyes were on the tall window, the stained-glass light that illuminated the chapel, the figures of a dark-haired man and a woman in a white embroidered dress, their hands joined.

Upstairs, the floor was adorned with new light flagstones, the walls cleaned and painted white and the windows gleaming, filled with two stained-glass windows, one of Agnes in her pale dress, another of her warrior, standing tall. The grille and the cell had gone and, in their place stood two beautiful bronze statues, a woman and a man facing each other, their hands wrapped.

Then the congregation assembled, voices hushed, as Mariusz and Jordan stood together dressed in white suits, red velvet waistcoats and matching dickey bows. They had been in Rosemuir for a week, panicking, trying to divert themselves while Leah calmly finalised registration of the chapel and co-ordinated the wedding plans. Now, they appeared as nervous as ever, gazing over their shoulders, chewing fingernails, talking in hushed voices to the smiling registrar, who was calm and professional, dressed in a navy velvet jacket and tartan kilt.

Then a low drone came from the top of the stone steps, and a bagpipe began to play 'Flower of Scotland'. The volume increased as the piper descended, dressed in tartan, each step slow and dignified until he arrived at the chapel door where he played for another minute.

Leah stood quietly at the back of the chapel, her hand in Dan's, thinking that if it were her own wedding, she'd recruit several pipers, one on each step, playing 'Highland Wedding'. There would be choristers in the chamber that was filled with fresh flowers now. But today was Mariusz and Jordan's day.

Leah looked around at the congregation; there were so many faces she recognised, Mariusz's family, Jordan's, other friends from Birmingham. She smiled towards Bex, who was standing near the front, waving back excitedly. Then Mariusz and Jordan's voices could be heard exchanging vows. They nervously threaded rings on each other's fingers and shared a lingering kiss to a spontaneous round of applause. The piper was playing 'Mairi's Wedding' and the happy couple were smiling, walking towards the chapel entrance. Leah had arranged photographers and confetti petals were tossed into the air, falling around their faces like spring blossom.

As Mariusz and Jordan stood outside in the bright February sunlight, Leah rushed forward, pushing a posy of pretty spring flowers into their hands and called, 'You should throw the bouquet together.'

'You're bound to catch it, Leah,' Mariusz quipped. 'You'll be the next one to be married.'

'Unless Zoe beats you to it,' Jordan laughed. 'Typical twins. I bet you'll have a wedding together, all four of you.'

Dan grinned and winked towards Christie, who bent down to explain to Daisy what was happening as the grooms turned their backs and a group of some ten women crowded behind them, their hands outstretched.

Zoe took her place, hugging her sister and whispering, 'This one's yours.'

'We can catch it together, Zo...' Leah began, but the bouquet was sailing through the air in a perfect arc and a voice yelled, 'I've got it. I've got it.'

Zoe smiled, pointing towards Bex, who held the posy aloft, her face bright with excitement.

There were more photographs, spontaneous applause and cheers, then Leah announced, 'Cocktails are now available in the great hall, then the reception will begin in half an hour.' She caught Abigail's approving smile and she smiled back, then Dan took her hand.

'This is where you relax and enjoy yourself.'

'It is.' Leah called across to Mirren, 'Come on inside. Kenny from The Canny Man has set up a bar and he's serving up Flying Scotsmen and Rob Roys. A cocktail will warm us up.' She held out a hand and Mirren was next to her, smiling.

'I could do with something to take away the chill. The wind's bitter from the loch today,' Mirren said, then she lowered her voice. 'It was a beautiful service, Leah. The chapel looks quite incredible.'

'It does.' Leah smiled with satisfaction: Mirren had warmed to her; she might even call her a friend now. She looked happier nowadays, more relaxed. But of course she would, Leah thought – Agnes was at peace, and so was Mirren.

Christie took Zoe in his arms, kissing her lightly. 'Shall we go in?' He ruffled Daisy's hair. 'I've promised this one she can try a mocktail. Kenny's making her a special cranberry spritzer.'

Daisy reached for Zoe's hand, her face bright with excitement. 'You have to tell Daddy not to have too much whisky and fall asleep.'

Zoe kissed the top of her head. 'Just give me a moment, sweetheart.' She squeezed Christie's fingers in hers. 'I'm just going to pop to the car park. I've left Mariusz and Jordan's present in the boot of the car. I'll catch you up.'

Christie kissed her again. 'We'll be waiting...'

She watched him walk away towards the main door, his hand in Daisy's as she skipped along beside him. Zoe smiled: she'd never be tired of the way his muscles moved beneath his clothes, the way the wind took his hair.

Music was blaring from inside the castle, the booming of a bass, rhythmic voices: The Proclaimers' 'I'm Gonna Be (500 Miles)' was playing and Zoe remembered singing it in the Mini with Leah as they drove the long road to Scotland from Birmingham back in October. She exhaled slowly: so much had happened since then. Their lives had changed in so many ways. She'd met Christie, fallen in love with him, with Daisy too. They were a family. She'd spend weekends in Birmingham whenever she wanted, enjoy time with her friends, but her home was in the Highlands now. She had everything, the best of both worlds.

In the courtyard, two starlings were rolling in a small puddle of water, pecking at fallen flower petals of confetti. Zoe looked up towards the crenelated wall for the raven, hoping to glimpse the stretched wings, the oily feathers and gaping beak, but it was nowhere to be seen. A few people were still strolling from the chapel across the courtyard and Zoe waved at Mariusz's mother, his uncle. Bex was talking to a handsome man in an expensive dark suit; Abigail Laing had paused to speak into her phone.

Zoe turned towards the car park, clutching her keys, thinking about the package in the boot, a personalised wine carafe and two engraved glasses. The wedding gift idea had come to her easily: she had remembered the beautiful old handfasting goblet, the two faded faces.

She arrived at the old well to glance across the loch. The water was smooth, a sapphire gleaming in dazzling sunlight. The air was chilly, the wind buffeting her face, rearranging her hair. Zoe shivered. Then something caught her eye, a round shape slicing through the still waters, dark and smooth as the head of a seal. Zoe stared: a swimmer was mostly concealed beneath the surface. Then a limb was flung upwards, a man's strong arm, sunlight glinting on the sheen of his skin, and a figure rose, an expanse of tangled hair on his body. He plunged down again and, for a moment, Zoe thought she must have imagined him. There wouldn't be anyone in the loch in the bitter cold of February.

Then she saw them both, a man and a woman swimming together. The man lifted the woman high and she threw back her head, sending droplets flying from her curls. She embraced him, her arms circling his neck, her mouth against his, and they seemed to swirl once in the whirling water before sinking into the depths below.

Then they were gone.

Zoe was still staring, her face covered in tears. The loch was calm now, the surface smooth. She touched the wet trail on her cheeks and smiled. She knew what she'd do: she'd go into the castle and kiss Christie, hug Daisy, drink a cocktail laced with Scotch. She'd toast Mariusz and Jordan, join in the dancing and laugh and chatter with the others. Then later, when most of the guests had left for home, she would speak quietly to Leah and tell her what she had seen.

AUTHOR'S NOTE

In 1306, shortly after Robert de Brus was crowned King of Scotland, he was defeated in battle on the borders of Perthshire and Argyll. He sent his second wife, Elizabeth de Burgh, and her stepdaughter, twelve-year-old Marjorie, to find refuge in Kildrummy Castle in Aberdeenshire, along with his two sisters, his brother Niall de Brus and the Earl of Atholl. However, Kildrummy was betrayed and Niall de Brus was captured and executed. Elizabeth and the rest of her party managed to escape, riding further north, probably making for Orkney. They were apprehended by William, Earl of Ross. Queen Elizabeth, Marjorie and the rest of the party were taken to England and held separately.

In 1314, King Robert defeated the English at the Battle of Bannockburn. Negotiations led to the release of Queen Elizabeth and the Scottish princesses. After eight years spent in captivity in harsh conditions, they returned to Scotland.

Against this backdrop of treachery, bloodshed and battles, I created the character of Agnes Fitzgerald, a servant in the kitchen at Kildrummy. After the siege of the castle, Agnes and Effie travel north to Ravenscraig Castle in Rosemuir. While Ravenscraig comes from my imagination, I have modelled it closely on Urquhart Castle, a ruined thirteenth-century castle on Loch Ness. The staff at Urquhart were very helpful during my visits and instrumental in conveying the flavour of life in fourteenth-century Scotland. Huge thanks to them for their kindness, hospitality and support, and to the many people I met in the Highlands of Scotland who were so warm and welcoming.

MORE FROM ELENA COLLINS

We hope you enjoyed reading *The Lady of the Loch*. If you did, please leave a review.

If you'd like to gift a copy, this book is also available as an ebook, large print, hardback, digital audio download and audiobook CD.

Sign up to Elena Collins' mailing list for news, competitions and updates on future books.

https://bit.ly/ElenaCollinsnewsletter

The Witch's Tree, another heart-breaking timeslip novel from Elena Collins, is available to buy now...

ABOUT THE AUTHOR

Elena Collins is the pen name of Judy Leigh. Judy Leigh is th
bestselling author of *Five French Hens*, *A Grand Old Time* and *Th
Age of Misadventure* and the doyenne of the 'it's never too late' gen
of women's fiction. She has lived all over the UK from Liverpool t
Cornwall, but currently resides in Somerset.

Visit Judy's website: https://judyleigh.com

Follow Judy on social media:

 twitter.com/judyleighwriter

 facebook.com/judyleighuk

 instagram.com/judyrleigh

Boldw**oo**d

Boldwood Books is an award-winning fiction publishing company seeking out the best stories from around the world.

Find out more at www.boldwoodbooks.com

Join our reader community for brilliant books, competitions and offers!

Follow us
@BoldwoodBooks
@BookandTonic

Sign up to our weekly deals newsletter

https://bit.ly/BoldwoodBNewsletter

ACKNOWLEDGMENTS

Thanks always to my amazing agent, Kiran Kataria, for her wisdom, professionalism and integrity.

Thanks to the wonderful Amanda Ridout, Nia Beynon, Claire Fenby, Jenna Houston, Jade Craddock, Rachel Gilbey and the gorgeous community at Boldwood Books.

Huge thanks to Sarah Ritherdon who is the smartest, most perceptive and encouraging editor anyone could wish for.

I have so much appreciation to everyone who has worked hard to make this book happen. I'm so grateful to designers, editors, technicians, magicians, voice actors, bloggers – thanks to you all.

As always, thanks to the many beloved friends who continue to support me with kind words, hugs and wine.

Thanks to Peter and the Solitary Writers, Avril's Writing Group, all at Radio SoundArt, Radio Somerset, Lyndsay and Darren at the Plymouth Proprietary Library, Planet Rock and to the generous and supportive family of Boldwood writers.

Much thanks to the talented Ivor Abiks at Deep Studios.

Love always to my wonderful Somerset neighbours and my more distant neighbours in Liverpool, Devon, Cornwall and London.

Special thanks to our Tony and Kim, cousins Ellen from Florida and Jo from Taunton, and to Robin and Edward from Colorado.

Love to my mum, who showed me the joy of reading, and to my dad, who proudly never read anything.

Love always to Liam, Maddie, Cait and to my soul mate, Big G.

Warmest thanks to my readers, wherever you are. You make this journey incredible.

Printed in Great Britain
by Amazon